D1090010

THE

GOLDEN

HORN

Ken Tilbury

Novels by Ken Tilbury

'Mamba' Series.

BLACK MAMBA SETTLER WHITE
*Three men in a struggle for survival in war-torn
Rhodesia, a country struggling for independence,
and the subsequent horror of land invasions
in Zimbabwe after independence.*

THE GOLDEN HORN (Mpisi and the GOLDEN HORN)
*Forced to abandon their farm by land reforms in Zimbabwe
a family set off to start a deep-sea fishing business in Mozambique.
By accident they get caught up in the illegal operations of a
ruthless diamond thief and rhino poacher.*

BAREFEET & PAPERTHORNS
*Two boys, one white and the other black, grow up on a farm
in a remote part of South Africa. Times are hard in post WW2
and both boys families struggle to survive. They are intimidated
and bullied by neighbours as the political struggle for power continues.
Eventually to escape apartheid, they move to Swaziland where they grow up.*

To find out more about the author his books visit his website

http://www.kentilbury.com

AUTHOR'S NOTE

The mysterious disappearance of my family at sea, the discovery of diamonds in Zimbabwe, the plight of many deposed Zimbabwe farmers seeking a new life, and the rhino poaching problems in Southern Africa inspired me to write this book.

In August 1964 my parents and my little sister, sailed out of Durban on their 30 foot Trimiran, *Nimble Tigger,* never to be seen again. (I have changed their names in the story for obvious reasons) It was believed they had sailed south straight into a gale, and perished somewhere off the notoriously treacherous Wild Coast. At the time I was a young 20 year old policeman in the Rhodesian police and, after only learning that my family were missing two weeks after they had sailed, I was probably too quick to listen to others, and assumed that the reports were correct. In retrospect, I should have investigated more thoroughly at the time. It might have been different.

Now, many years later, while putting together material for this book, and after studying the newspaper cuttings and various other reports and sightings, I have eventually pieced it all together as I see it. Nobody in their right mind would have sailed straight into the teeth of a force 8 gale with two women on board! The first letter is a copy of the actual letter my father wrote to me when they sold the farm to Waterford School (now Waterford-Kamhlaba) and moved from Swaziland to Mozambique. The second letter is what I believe could very well have been what actually happened.

In the early 70's a friend and I did some prospecting, close to the area where alluvial diamonds have recently been discovered in Zimbabwe. We were looking for semi-precious stones, not diamonds, and might easily have cast some away thinking they were worthless pieces of granite. In the mid 90's, while travelling through the area, young boys on the side of the road held up their hands with thumbs and forefingers forming the shape of a diamond. We didn't realise they were trying to sell us diamonds. During the Rhodesian Bush War we had educated the rural people to give us the thumbs up if the area was safe and the thumbs down if there were terrorists around, and so we presumed the 'diamond' sign meant something else, and drove on by. To this day we still regret not stopping.

When the magnitude of the discovery became known in 2004, the army moved in with helicopter 'gun-ships', and took control of the whole area, massacring more than 200 men, women and children. The massive wealth generated by these diamonds is not going into the country's coffers. Instead most of it is being funnelled into the pockets of the country's leaders, people in high places and the Chinese, who are running the mining operation. The money generated could go a long way towards restoring the economy of the country; but still the hand is held out to the west for more and more aid; most of which never reaches those in need.

In 2000 Mugabe, the President of Zimbabwe, unleashed his war-vets with instructions to intimidate and force white farmers to abandon their farms in his 'Land Reform' programme. This action resulted in thousands of farmers, farm workers and their families losing their homes and their income. Needless to say these farms are no longer productive most of them have reverted to bush. The country which used to export grain and other produce to other countries now has the 'begging bowl' out as there is no food. The early part of this disastrous period, which still continues, has been covered in detail in my first book 'Black Mamba White Settler'.

The poaching and slaughter of African Rhinos by unscrupulous gangs, protected by armed guards, is a very serious problem. Rhinos are being killed almost on a daily basis. In the first six months of 2012 more than 300 rhinos were killed in South Africa alone. One horn can fetch up to US$50,000. If this continues unabated for much longer the rhino will become extinct; only be seen in museums and wild life parks in the UK and America.

Although every effort is being made by the Wild Life Conservation staff to stop this heinous practice, and to have these greedy poachers locked behind bars, they are fighting a losing battle. They need a lot more financial help to buy vehicles, equipment and employ the staff needed to hunt these monsters down.

I hope that you, the reader, will enjoy the story and by the end have a better insight into what is happening in Africa, and the difficulty and danger for those who are endeavouring to stop this horrendous practise are experiencing. In writing this novel it is my intention to generate sufficient interest and anger at the plight of the rhino and the elephant in Africa that more people help to stop this senseless killing of these magnificent animals - now facing extinction.

KT

THE

GOLDEN

HORN

A novel

Ken Tilbury

Copy right © 2011 Ken Tilbury

All rights reserved

The author retains sole copyright to this publication. No part of this
publication may be reproduced, stored in a retrieval system, or
transmitted in any form or by any means, without prior permission in
writing from the author.

ISBN - 13: 978-1475034783
ISBN - 10: 1475034784

CONTENTS

Dedication

This book dedicated to the memory of my parents, Pat and Dorothy, and my sister Felicity, who all disappeared at sea off the east coast of Africa in their yacht *Nimble Tigger* in 1964

Map showing the area and location of places mentioned in the book

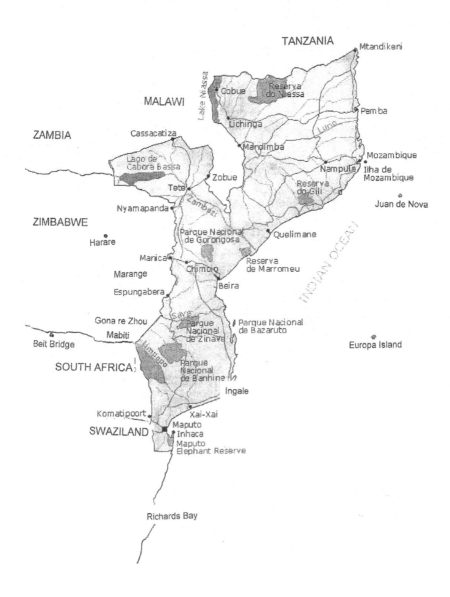

Prologue

Jan Van Zyl was born in South Africa. He was a short stocky man with flaming red hair and wore a beard trimmed to a point. His small black eyes were set close together and darted around like a ferret's eyes. He spoke English with a typical Afrikaans accent, rolling his r's and clipping some words short.

Having grown up in the poorer suburbs of Johannesburg, where his father had worked on the gold mines, he learned how to survive amongst tough people. He had a long scar on his left cheek as a result of a knife fight in his youth. He was aggressive by nature and was a bully.

At the age of sixteen after a severe beating from his drunken father, and before completing his education, he ran away from home. He moved in with some shady characters and for two years he sold *dagga* (marijuana) to make a living. He was arrested and served a short sentence in prison. After being released he moved to Rhodesia, where he went to work in the Coal mine at Wankie near Victoria Falls.

The work on the coal mine was hard and at the end of his first three year contract, Van Zyl decided to find a more lucrative but easier way of life. He left the mine, moved to Bulawayo and before long had taken to a life of crime.

With his background he quickly slipped into his new career and took to it as easily as a duck to water. However, it wasn't long before he found himself serving a sentence in Salisbury Prison for receiving and selling stolen property. In prison he became involved with hardened, more experienced criminals who had no respect for the law or society. He learned a lot of new tricks from them.

After the Rhodesian Declaration of Independence in 1965, and the government broke its ties with Britain, sanctions were applied against the Rhodesia in an attempt to bring the country to its knees. It became very difficult to obtain luxury goods and a number of everyday items.

Van Zyl saw this as an opportunity of making quick money and after his release from prison, started an import and export business. He smuggled luxury goods into the country by various means, including putting nylon stockings into the spare wheel of his vehicle, and took out emeralds obtained from illegal miners. He was eventually trapped by the police and once again sent to prison.

While serving his sentence during the Rhodesian Bush War in the 1970's, Jan Van Zyl was approached by a representative of the Government, who was looking for someone with Van Zyl's skills to assist with sanction busting. The man felt that with his contacts, and knowledge of circumventing the legal systems, Van Zyl might be useful.

After several meetings in the prison, he grabbed the opportunity and made a commitment to the government. He was sworn to secrecy and in turn given an assurance that he would not be called up for military duties. He was released from prison, before he had finished serving his sentence, and joined the undercover sanctions busting team as a freelance agent. He was pleased to be given this work as he had no desire to serve in the army, or get involved in the front line operations.

And so Van Zyl, a coward and a criminal, landed a nice plum position with very lucrative 'fringe benefits'. It was all 'hush-hush' and he was ordered not to reveal to anyone that he was involved with the government. If it became known, he would immediately be sent back to prison and would serve his sentence on border duties in the bush.

This he did not want. And so, while everyone else struggled financially, Van Zyl prospered. He spent most of his time out of the country, staying in the best hotels at the expense of the government.

Van Zyl however, soon proved his worth. He was involved in striking deals and making arrangements for Rhodesian cotton to be shipped to the world markets labelled as cotton from Israel; tobacco was sold via Thailand; sugar to South Africa; chrome to Russia; the list was endless. He visited France, Italy, Spain, the Middle-East, the Far-East and even Australia and Russia to conduct business.

During this time Van Zyl was introduced to a number of international businessmen, who were not averse to underhand ways of making money. While all other Rhodesians fought and died doing their military duty in the 'Bush War', he lived a life of luxury and developed a taste for the finer things; good clothes and fancy food, while filling his own coffers with money made while 'serving his country'. But he was 'a necessary evil' and an essential cog in the mechanism of the war effort. He was good at his job, contributing to the survival of the economy.

The end of the war brought Van Zyl's globetrotting, at the expense of the Rhodesian tax payer, to an end. But by then he was a wealthy man. Mugabe was elected President and the country re-named Zimbabwe. Van Zyl, seizing the opportunity, was quick to offer his services to the new leader.

Naturally he had to prove his worth and value, and so he made a number of good-will gestures by brokering small deals and arrangements, for a smaller than normal fee. Over the next few years Van Zyl earned the trust of Mugabe and his ministers. In return he was included in the 'inner circle' of friends by the new president, and given more and more work.

When Mugabe ventured into neighbouring African countries, to 'assist' them with his military force, it was Van Zyl who acted as his front when it came to plundering of their mineral wealth. For this purpose he used companies registered in foreign countries. One of his companies, Global Procurements Limited, he used for most of his business in Africa.

By the time diamonds were discovered in massive quantities in the Eastern Lowveld of Zimbabwe, Van Zyl was well established within the higher ranks of the ruling party. As Mugabe's recognised middle man in the Congo Diamonds, he was quick to make sure he got a piece of the action. He assisted with the illegal selling of the stones to unscrupulous buyers in the Middle-East and Far-East, bypassing international regulations and the Kimberly Process.

With international outrage and Van Zyl's involvement in the 'Congo Blood Diamonds', and now his involvement in the Zimbabwe diamonds, he became a wanted man in many parts of the world.

A number of countries issued warrants for his arrest and Van Zyl became a fugitive from the international courts, somewhat curtailing his activities and restricting him. He was forced to concentrate on his local operations and was able to travel only to some African States, the Middle-East and the Far-East.

He got his fingers into many pies; mining, land, oil and motor vehicles. Because of his relationship with Mugabe, Van Zyl became a powerful figure, who seemed to be above the law in Zimbabwe, riding rough-shod over anyone who got in his way. There were rumours that he was personally responsible for the deaths of a number of people who had dared to get in his way.

The farm invasions, taking place throughout the country, gave him the opportunity to expand his operations and again Van Zyl was quick to climb on the bandwagon. With the blessing of Mugabe and without paying for it, he took over vast tracts of land in the Lowveld.

With his passion for killing, Van Zyl managed to 'acquire' the Mabiti Safari Area where he enjoyed shooting elephant and other 'Big Five' animals. Barney Barnard, an old friend and experienced hunter who had worked with him on the coal mine and had been with him since he started his criminal activities, accompanied and guided him on all his hunting trips. During this time they accumulated a large number of elephant tusks.

When the diamond fields at Marange were taken over by the army, there was nothing for Barney to do there, and so Van Zyl gave him the job of managing Mabiti camp permanently; as well as looking after his Zimbabwe diamond operations. As soon Barnard moved there to run the small game reserve, he was to make the camp pay for itself, and do whatever was necessary to turn it into a profit making operation. He paid Barnard well and promised him a share in the profits.

After Barnard had settled into Mabiti, Van Zyl instructed him to hunt for Rhino. His connections in the East, who were buying the elephant tusks from him, were prepared to pay a fortune for rhino horn.

Van Zyl lived in a luxurious country mansion on the outskirts of Harare, where he had his headquarters. From there he controlled his empire, and was a law unto himself. He had a heli-pad at his house where he kept a helicopter, and had a twin engine Beechcraft at Mount Hamden airport.

Van Zyl had never married but had a succession of girl-friends; usually imported from the east. They never lasted long, and as soon as he became bored with them they were sent packing with a reasonable bonus. Quite by accident, one of the Eastern women had borne him a son, Joey, who was now a young man and lived with his father.

Because he was always picking on left-overs from other people's misfortunes, the locals called him *Mpisi* - the Hyena.

Chapter 1

They were still ten nautical miles from Richards Bay when the storm caught up with them. Reaching gale-force, the wind was howling from the south-west, and in no time had whipped the sea into a mad frenzy of breaking waves and flying spray.

The howling wind whistled through the taught rigging wires making them hum and vibrate, as they took the strain of the creaking mast and swinging boom. The spray blown off the wave-tops stung Bill's face, and the salty sea-water burned his eyes making it difficult for him to see, as he struggled to steer *Nimble Tigger* along in front of the storm.

When the Owens had left their Inhaca island base four months earlier, it had been with the intention of making their way to the Cape. They had been in partnership with Marjorie's cousin, Jim Walker and his wife Jean, in a fishing venture in Mozambique. After the Walkers were tragically killed in a road accident, and because of the civil war in Mozambique, their American sponsors had withdrawn, Bill and Marjorie decided it was time to shelve their fishing venture and move on.

Having used all the money, from the sale of their farm in Swaziland, to set up the fishing business, and with no prospect of clients coming to fish in an unstable African country, Bill needed to find employment.

And so, with their dreams shattered, they sailed off to Durban. It was *Nimble Tigger's* maiden voyage and the trip had not gone well. They lost their rudder on several occasions during the trip, and were de-masted during a storm as they approached Durban. Using the boom to rig a jury mast, they had limped into harbour.

The yacht was badly damaged and it took four months before finally being sea-worthy and they were ready to press on to East London on the next leg to the Cape. While they were in Durban, Bill was offered a job as the skipper of a trimiran yacht belonging to an oil exploration company, working off the south-west coast of Africa.

However on the eve of their departure for the Cape to take up the position, Pat received a telegram advising him that the company had decided, for political reasons, to abandon their exploration operations in Southern Africa.

This was a devastating blow. They were at the end of their tether, and decided that it would be best to return to their island base on Inhaca Island, where they could plan their future. And so, without notifying the port authorities - or anyone else of their change of plan - they sailed north-east instead of south-west to the Cape as had been expected.

················

When the Owens sailed out of Durban early that morning, in spite of being in the middle of the windy season, it was a clear calm August morning with only a gentle breeze blowing from the south-west. It was a perfect day for sailing. As they cleared the Harbour entrance, the wind stiffened, the sails filled and the trimiran picked up speed. To get well clear of the shipping lanes they sailed straight out to sea before turning to set a course north-east towards Mozambique.

The weather report had warned of gale-force winds moving up the coast that were expected to reach southern Natal by mid-afternoon. Bill however, was not concerned. He was confident of *Nimble Tigger's* speed and ability, and reckoned they could easily out-run any bad weather blowing up behind them. If necessary they could take shelter in Richards Bay 100 miles further up the coast.

A few hours after leaving Durban, and a lot sooner than expected, the wind started picking up. *Nimble Tigger*, a trimiran, fitted out with a new mast and rigging danced along at a good speed and with the wind behind her. By mid-afternoon as they were approaching Richards Bay the high winds caught up to them.

It was too dangerous to continue their journey, so Bill changed course to steer towards land. Marjorie and Anne helped take in the mainsail and stow it away, then they went below into the cabin, battening down the hatch behind them. They didn't want waves breaking over the yacht and flooding them with tons of water.

Now the storm had caught up to them, and they were in serious trouble. With enormous waves crashing and breaking all around; some right over the boat, the sea was a frightening place. Using only the jib to keep the trimiran on course, they ran before the gale. Making use of the waves as best he could, Bill struggled to keep *Nimble Tigger* stern-on to the wind as they surfed down into the troughs to bury the bows under the water, then after breathtaking moments wondering if they would recover, the yacht would shake free and stagger up the back of the next mountain of water.

Attaching himself to a safety line Bill cursed himself for not heeding the weather warning. He clung to the helm as he steered the yacht up and over the huge dark swells. Although *Nimble Tigger* was a trimiran and more stable than a conventional mono-hulled yacht it was still tossed about like a matchstick in the raging seas. In the cabin Marjorie and Anne clung on to whatever they could, as the boat pitched and yawed violently up and down and from side to side.

The sky got darker and the sea blacker as the intensity of the storm increased the waves grew in size until they must have been 6 or 7 meters high. The lightning came first, stabbing through the clouds in jagged flashes of light that sizzling down onto the sea, followed by loud cracks of booming thunder. Then the heavens opened up, and the rain came belting down.

With the rain and spray blasting at him from all angles Bill found it more and more difficult to keep *Nimble Tigger* on course, and prevent her from slewing sideways on to the waves; if this was to happen they would be in danger of capsizing and floundering.

Eventually, after battling for two hours to keep ahead of the following seas, with its monstrous dark green waves chasing behind their small fragile yacht, Bill saw the welcoming lights marking the entrance into Richards Bay. Swinging the yacht around across the path of the wind, to make for the harbour entrance with the waves crashing against the breakwater was a tricky manoeuvre.

When at last they sailed safely between the two breakwaters into the shelter of the bay, Bill heaved a sigh of relief and relaxed his tense muscles. Marjorie and Anne emerged from the cabin, a bit battered and shaken, to help a weary red-eyed Pat, take down the jib, start the engine and chug quietly into calm water.

They found shelter from the wind behind a high hill and dropped the anchor. Had they been any further away from the harbour when the storm hit them, they might well have floundered. It was a wise decision to take shelter, and the three of them were able to relax after their frightening experience.

·············

The storm lasted for two days while they lay at anchor. In the early hours of the morning on the third day, the wind dropped as suddenly as it had blown up. According to the weather forecast, the storm had moved further out into the Indian Ocean. And so, just as it was getting light, they weighed anchor and sailed out past the breakwater to continue their journey.

Although the wind was gentle, the sea was still rough as they sailed on with their sails trimmed. By late that afternoon the sea had calmed down, and by the following morning, after another uncomfortable night at sea, they were able to hoist the mainsail and sail along at a much better clip.

As the sun was setting, five days after leaving Durban, they rounded Elephant Point and sailed into the calm water of Delagoa Bay, to drop anchor opposite their camp on Inhaca Island. It had not been a pleasant trip and the three of them were exhausted.

Next morning, feeling refreshed after a good restful night, they went ashore to check on the camp. Tomasi, their camp attendant and boat boy was there. He had seen them arrive the evening before, and had a fire going with a kettle of water boiling ready to make tea. He was a welcome sight, and they settled down to relax for a few days, while they weighed up their options.

The Owens had been having a tough time financially, with nothing going according to plan. There was a lot to discuss and a decision to be made about what to do with their shattered lives. To start with provisions were needed to re-stock *Nimble Tigger* and the camp; their papers had to be put in order; and Sandy, their son, had to be told of their change of plan, and what their next move was going to be.

Two days after arriving back on Inhaca, the three Owens went across the bay to Lourenco Marques (Maputo) in *Escudo,* their 18 foot launch they had left in the care of Tomasi. They tied up in the small-boat harbour at the 'Clube Navale' situated below the well known and popular Polana Hotel. Bill went off to see Alfonso Garcia, their Portuguese partner in the fishing venture, while Marjorie and Anne went shopping for supplies.

After collecting his documents from Garcia, Bill put them into a large envelope marked it 'Urgent' and addressed it to his nephew Sandy Walker, who worked in Basutoland as a surveyor. He took the envelope to the British Consulate and after explaining their situation; Bill requested that the package be handed personally to Sandy via the British Consulate in Maseru, the capital of Basutoland. Sandy had gone to Rhodesia to visit his cousin Tom and Bill was unable to contact either of them by telephone.

With political changes rapidly taking place in Africa, as a back-up plan, Bill had applied to the French Government for permission to set up a base on their island of Juan de Nova (Isle of Dogs), off the coast of Madagascar. It was an island in the middle of the Mozambique Channel where the fishing would be good. At that time he felt that, if it became necessary, they might be able to continue their business from there.

There was a message from the French authorities waiting for Bill at the Consulate, advising him that he could make use of either Juan de Nova or Europa Island. This was more than he had hoped for, and the first bit of good news for some time; it gave them hope for the future.

Leaving the British Consulate, Bill took the ferry across the bay to the boat builder's yard in Catembe, where he arranged storage of the two almost completed 'Mastiff' fishing boats being built there. Before sailing to Durban they had been put 'on hold' while they re-established themselves, and could make a decision to either continue with their fishing project at a later date; or to abandon it completely.

Because of the heat, people in Mozambique took a three hour break, or a 'Siesta', at midday - then worked late into the evenings when it was much cooler. The pace of life was very relaxed and tomorrow was just another day; 'Manjané' or 'Maist Tarde'. Getting business done in Mozambique always took a lot longer than normal and it was three days before they were ready to return to their camp.

An enthusiastic fisherman, on holiday from Johannesburg, who was looking for a boat, got a bargain when he bought the *Escudo*. With business finished and all the loose ends tied up, the new owner of the launch took the Owens back to Inhaca. They spent the next week making plans; packing up camp and stowing provisions and anything else they might possibly need, aboard *Nimble Tigger*.

Their plan was to make their way up the east coast of the continent, stopping along the way to explore the islands and assess their suitability for setting up their deep-sea game-fishing business. From Inhaca they would sail to Paradise Island, Bazaruto and then on to Europa Island, Juan de Nova, the Comoros and maybe even the Seychelles.

If they were unable to find a suitable alternative to Inhaca, and if absolutely necessary, from there they would make their way to Australia via the Chagos Archipelago and the Cocos Islands. Hopefully it would not come to that, but nevertheless it would be a fascinating adventure.

Two weeks after arriving back from Durban, leaving Tomasi to look after the camp and the remainder of their belongings, the Owens once again set sail on *Nimble Tigger*. They were excited but somewhat nervous as they sailed off into the blue; completely unaware of the heartache they were leaving behind.

∎∎∎∎◇◇◇◇◇∎∎∎∎

Chapter 2

Before independence in Mozambique, Tom's father and his uncle, Jim Walker, had been involved in a deep-sea fishing business there. They had set up a base on Inhaca Island, situated at the entrance to Delagoa Bay and Maputo, or Lourenco Marques as it was known then. A year after the Walkers were killed in a car accident, Tom's parents and his sister, Anne had disappeared at sea in their yacht, the *Nimble Tigger*.

Now, years later, Tom heard that the Mozambique government was allowing people to re-claim property they had owned prior to independence; when the country was still run by the Portuguese. He had been mulling his idea over for quite a while. It was something he had been considering ever since their problems had started with the illegal invasion of their farm, and it now seemed possible.

Tom was keen to take up where his father and uncle had left off, and start a deep-sea fishing business there; but there were financial constraints. It would require a fair amount of money to get it up and running; equipment to set up camps-sites, boats, motors and fishing gear to be purchased, as well as travel expenses to promote the business overseas.

Although Tom and Maria owned their own home in Harare, and still owned their aircraft, they were not prepared to sell either of these assets to finance a fishing venture. After having lost their farm, they were not prepared to risk losing the only home they had left. They would still need the plane; Tom made a reasonable amount from hiring it out and doing private charters. It was their only income earner. The money for the new business had to be financed separately.

Tom went to visit his son Kyle in the Lowveld. Kyle had recently returned from Australia, where he had been on contract for five years, and was now the manager of a private sugar estate. Tom had a plan that he wanted to run past him, and to get his thoughts on the subject.

Kyle was most enthusiastic and thought it was a good idea. It would give his father something to do that he enjoyed, and it would give the whole family an ideal place to spend their holidays together. They would contact Stuart, Kyle's brother in England, and work out a way to finance the venture.

While he was staying with Kyle, Tom was presented with an opportunity that might well be the answer to their financial predicament. Gideon, his old senior tractor driver who now worked for Kyle, approached him with a serious expression on his usually smiling face.

"*Ishe* (sir)," he said. "I have something to tell you, but I cannot speak now. The boss will be angry with me if he sees that I am not working, and there are still spies everywhere."

"Okay Gideon. Is this good news or bad news that you have for me?"

"No *Ishe*. This is something I am sure you will be pleased to hear," he said. "Can we meet tomorrow when I am not working? It is Sunday and I can meet you at the dam. We will go fishing."

"Oh. We are going fishing are we?" Tom asked him.

"Yes Ishe. It is the only way that we can talk without people being suspicious."

"Okay Gideon. You get the worms and I will meet you at the dam tomorrow at 9 o'clock, and then we can fish together." Tom said intrigued.

Later when he told Kyle of his conversation with Gideon, and that he wanted to go fishing, Kyle decided to join them.

Next day when they arrived at the dam, near the bottom end of the farm, Gideon was already there and had started fishing. It was a small dam - only about 300 yard long by 100 yards wide at the wall. Tom joined Gideon on the earth dam wall and Kyle, having been briefed before-hand by Tom, took a handful of worms from Gideon and wandered off to the other side of the dam. He found a spot under the shade of an acacia thorn tree, and after baiting up cast his line into the water.

It was going to be another typically warm day in May. There was hardly a breath of wind, and not a cloud to be seen in the wide open blue sky above. Just turning from summer to winter, the grass was already turning brown and the trees had begun shedding their leaves. Nothing moved and only the cicada beetles had the energy to scream in the still heat of the day. A small herd of young Impala gazelle does stood quietly under the shade of the acacia trees not far from the dam - their ears flicking every now and then, listening for sounds that would alert them to possible danger from stalking predators.

Tom sat down in the dry grass, on the dam wall near Gideon, with the can of worms between them. He baited up and cast his line into the water beyond the bulrushes.

"Ishe, do you remember Tombi?" Gideon began as soon as Tom was settled. "She used to work for you as nanny looking after your children."

"Yes. I remember her very well. She worked for us for a number of years. She left because her mother died and she was needed at home."

"Good. Tombi heard that Master Kyle was working here and that I am working for him. She came here last month to visit my wife and stayed for a week."

"That is good news. How is she? Is she married?"

"No Ishe, she is not married. She is now thin because there is no food in her village. Her father has also passed away."

"I am very sorry to hear that. Is she working or does she just stay at home looking after her family?" Tombi had always been a little plump.

"Yes she is staying at home because there is no work. She needs money to buy food for her family."

"I am sure she does. Do you want me to send her some money? Is that what you want to speak about? We could have spoken about this yesterday at the house."

"No Ishe. She is not begging. She has got something to sell and asked me to speak to you. She said you will know what to do."

"Well then, come out with it. What is it she wants to sell that is so secret?"

"Ishe, in Zimbabwe these days we no not know who to trust anymore. Everyone is forced by the C.I.O. (secret police) to inform; even on members of their own family. That is why we must be very careful."

"Yes. That is true. So tell me now, what does she have that must be kept quiet?"

"Do you remember where Tombi lives?"

"Yes. She lives somewhere near Birchenough Bridge," Tom said wondering when Gideon was eventually going to get to the point of all this secrecy.

"Have you heard what has been found near that place?"

"Is that not where they have recently discovered diamonds?" Tom sat up suddenly giving Gideon his full attention. In the early days of the war he had done a bit of prospecting in the area where diamonds had been found. Without realising it he might even possibly have discarded some of them thinking that they were merely bits of quartz. He had been looking for semi-precious stones not even suspecting that there might be diamonds in the area.

"Yes Ishe. There are *hobo's* (plenty) of diamonds to be found near the place where Tombi lives," Gideon replied with a broad grin.

"I suppose you are going to tell me that she has some of these diamonds."

"Yes. She showed some to me when she was here and even left one for me to show you," he said.

Glancing around to make sure they were not being watched, Gideon pulled a piece of rag out of his pocket with a knot in the centre. Untying the knot carefully, he handed Tom a small brown stone. He took it carefully from Gideon and examined it. It looked like a small piece of broken bottle or quartz, but when Tom wet his finger and rubbed the stone then held it up to the sun, it glistened brightly.

"How does she know this is a diamond?"

"She says that she has tested it in the way they have been shown by the *ngodas* (buyers), who buy the diamonds from them."

"Why does she not sell her diamonds to the buyers then?"

"She says that they are not allowed to have stones any more. The C.I.O., the Army Brigadiers and the Chinese people want to take them all."

Tom's mind raced ahead, thinking of the possibilities this could open up.

"Is Tombi able to find other stones such as this one?"

"*Ishe*, I think that you must speak to her. She can tell you what is happening near her place."

"Yes, I think that is a very good idea. When will I see her?"

"I will send my wife with a message that you want to see her. She will go by bus tomorrow."

"Good. I will give you the money for bus fares. She must be here to see us in a couple of days," Tom said. "I will be going back to Harare at the end of the week."

"Yes *Ishe*. I will let you know when she arrives. You must keep the diamond safe until she is here," Gideon said.

They hadn't had a nibble on their bait all the time they had been talking, and so with their business concluded for the time being, they moved around the dam to join Kyle. He seemed to be having better luck and had landed a few good sized bass.

Tom easily recognised Tombi when she turned up to see him a couple of days later. He remembered her as a young woman in her early twenties. She was now just forty and in spite of the hard life she obviously lived, still looked younger than her years. She was not as thin as Gideon had led him to believe. She wore a bright yellow *doek* (cloth) wrapped around her head and, although she was neat and tidy, her clothes were a little threadbare and her shoes old and worn down. When she greeted Tom, she still had a wide cheerful smile as she respectfully held out her right hand, supported by her left, to shake hands.

"Tombi, it is good to see you. Gideon tells me I must help you with something?" Tom said after both had exchanged their news.

"Yes Sir. I am having too many problems at my home and things are not good," she replied sadly.

"Well you know that I will help you if I can. What is it you want me to do? Do you want a job?"

"No sir, you live too far from my home and I have to look after my family. Gideon gave you a diamond to look at. Have you still got it?" she said quietly, glancing around nervously.

"Yes, I have it here. Do you want me to give it to you?"

"No. I have some more. Before the soldiers came to take over the mines they were lying on the ground like sugar and were easy to find. We used to sell them to the *ngodas* who came to our villages, or met us on the side of the road. They sold to the dealers in Mutare who came from all over the world to buy."

"Why do you not sell to them any longer?"

"The helicopters and the soldiers came. They started shooting at us and chased us all away. Many people were killed. Now the *ngodas* do not come any more; they are frightened and we are not allowed to have diamonds. You must try to sell them for me. I have plenty more buried near my home. We have to be very careful. If we are caught with stones we will be beaten and killed," Tombi said handing Tom a small brown paper packet containing a number of dark brown diamonds.

"What about the police and the army? Do they not chase you away from where the diamonds are?"

"Yes they do. They have put a fence around the whole area. They force people to work and even rape women if they do not work. They shoot anyone who goes inside the fence or is caught with stones."

"Very well Tombi. I'm not going to ask you how you can get them. You must be very careful not to get into trouble, and you must not get caught. I'll make a plan to sell them to dealers, and you will get more money. This will take time because I must first go to England to see what I can do about these thieves. In the meantime you must give Kyle the diamonds to keep for you. They will be safe with him, and he will help you with money until I get back. You must not tell anyone we are doing this."

"Yes sir. I will come every month to see Kyle. When will you come back again to see us?"

"I am not sure Tombi, but it will be soon. I will give you money when I see you later this afternoon, and Kyle will give you money when you bring him the stones."

"Thank you, sir."

Later that day Tom gave Tombi sufficient money to feed her family for a couple of months. She was over the moon and Tom thought she was going to kiss him.

"Don't let anyone see how much money you have, and spend it a little at a time. You must not make people suspicious," Tom warned her. "Perhaps you should leave some of the money in safekeeping with Kyle."

"Thank you very much sir. You have helped me a lot. I will see you next time you are here. Gideon will tell me when you are coming."

"Okay Tombi. I am giving you a mobile phone with a camera - you know how to use the camera? I will show you. I want you to take photos of anything happening near the mine that is not right. As soon as you have taken pictures, send them to Kyle straight away, and do not get caught," Tom warned her. "We must get pictures of the people who are responsible for the killings and what they are doing there."

Tom had heard rumours of these killings, and the plundering of diamonds by the military, the CIO and the Chinese, but was shocked to hear first hand what was actually going on. It was also rumoured that the Chinese were supervising the labour working in the open cast pits, and getting a large share of the spoils. People were being murdered in huge numbers because of greed. He had to find out more. The world had to know what was going on, and something had to be done about it.

Tom decided to make a few discreet enquiries and find out how he could sell the diamonds to dealers. If the *ngodas* were making so much money out of other *gwejas* (diamond panners) like Tombi, then it should not be too difficult to get better money for her; and make something out of it himself. It might even help finance their fishing venture.

Chapter 3

Since Mugabe's land reforms in Zimbabwe had forced Tom and Maria to abandon their farm, 70 kilometres north of Harare, they had been living in a suburb of the city. Like most other country folk, they had always lived very active lives. Now, apart from spending a few days fishing on the Zambezi every now and then, or on the houseboat on Kariba, and the occasional game of golf or tennis, boredom was getting to them.

Politically, the situation in the country was not getting any better with land grabbing still the order of the day, and by the looks of it, was not going to improve or change for some time to come. It now seemed there was very little likelihood of them ever getting their farm back. Apart from money made from hiring out their plane, they had no other source of income. They had to find something to do that they both enjoyed, and which would also bring in some money.

Tom's idea of running a deep-sea fishing business might just be what they were looking for. With this in mind, as well as the opportunity of making money out of Tombi's diamonds, he decided it was time to do something about it. He was going to investigate the possibility of reclaiming the land on Inhaca that had belonged to his father and his uncle. If there was a chance he would contact his cousin Sandy in Swaziland, to discuss his thoughts with him. Sandy might know something; or better still, might even have the title deeds for the property.

After refuelling and clearing customs and immigration at Maputo, Tom and Maria flew on to Inhaca. The beautiful tropical island was surrounded by the crystal clear azure blue sea of the Indian Ocean with tall coconut palm trees lining the white sands along the beach. The interior of the island was covered in dense green bush and mangroves with the occasional large fig tree poking through the vegetation here and there. In the south west of the island there was a swampy area, where a couple of local fishermen poled their dug-out canoes along through the shallow water in search of mud-crabs.

A number of small boats bobbed up and down at anchor just off the pier opposite the hotel. It was mid-afternoon by the time they landed and were taken to the hotel in a gold cart. Tom was amazed at the change in the place; he remembered it as a small rustic little hotel with a few rooms and a bar. Now it was much bigger and smarter with thatched bungalows, a restaurant and reception area.

Next morning after a leisurely breakfast, Tom and Maria set off along the beach to walk the mile to where Tom remembered the camp had been. As they approached the spot they could see the big fig tree protruding above the rest of the trees and bushes on top of the ridge. A clearly defined path led from the beach up through the mangroves towards the top of the hill. Although it was twenty five years since he had been there, Tom was excited and eager to see if there was any sign of the old camp under the tree and so he hurried up the path with Maria following close behind him.

Reaching the top of the ridge, they found themselves in the cleared area under the giant fig tree. Three grass huts were under the shade of the tree and an old tarpaulin covered something off to one side. Fish nets had been hung out to dry on the branches of the bushes around the edge of the clearing, and there were two reed fish-traps lying on the ground alongside one of the huts. The cleared area under the tree was swept clean. It was just as Tom remembered it.

A thin wisp of smoke rose from the small fire burning in the middle of the clearing with two crude hand-made chairs on either side of the fire. A middle-aged man, squatting over a three legged pot on the fire, got up as soon as he saw them walk into the clearing, and stood quietly looking at them.

Memories came flooding back to him of the time he spent there with his parents and his uncle and aunt. Of working on the boats in the mornings then fishing in the afternoons; evenings spent at the hotel where, after having hot showers they drank lots of Laurentina beer while they nibbled on snacks of chicken giblets and olives; tucking into huge plates loaded with prawns and prego's; walking along the beach back to camp late at night; sleeping in grass huts on beds made of grain bags stretched over wooden frames resting on forked sticks hammered into the ground.

He remembered too, the wonders his mother had worked on the stove under the tree. Fish, periwinkles, mussels, clams and all sorts of other seafood; most of it gathered on the beach when the tide was out - was all turned into delicious meals. They were happy times and the last time Tom had spent with his family.

A year later they had been killed in a road accident in Zululand and his uncle and aunt had disappeared at sea in their yacht not long afterwards. When she saw the tears in Tom's eyes, as they stood there silently taking it all in, Maria took his hand and squeezed it.

As if coming out of a trance, Tom suddenly became aware of the man standing beside the fire staring at them. He was tall and lean with greying hair, but looked fit and well. He was wearing an old pair of khaki shorts and his shiny brown skin covered a well muscled body. He must have been in his fifties.

Tom glanced down at the man's feet. It had to be Tomasi – nobody else had feet with the toes on each foot turning inwards like fans! When Tom had been on the island with his parents, Tomasi had been their boat-boy and was much the same age as Tom. They used to fish together and Tom remembered those feet; it had to be the same man.

"Tomasi, do you know who I am?" Tom said stepping forward to greet the man. He did not respond but stood looking at Tom with a perplexed expression on his face. Maria quickly came to the rescue, greeting him in Portuguese she explained that Tom's parents had lived under the tree, and that a man called Tomasi had worked for them.

After studying Tom carefully for a few moments, his face suddenly lit up in a huge smile, then clapping his hands together in greeting, slapped his chest and said "Tomasi!" Then he took Tom's extended hand and shook it so hard that he felt as if it was going to break it off. "Yes, I remember you," he laughed delightedly. "You were a young man then, as I was. I have been waiting many years for your family to return. I have been looking after everything here for them," Tomasi explained in Portuguese. At last releasing Tom's hand he turned to greet Maria in much the same way. Walking over to the covered object he carefully folded back the tarpaulin to proudly reveal Tom's mother's old stove. Tomasi must have been cleaning and oiling it regularly - although somewhat rusted it still looked in fair condition.

"Your father and mother went away and never came back. After that the other people went away on their boat, but returned again after some months. They were here for only a short time then went away again on their sail boat. They have never returned. They left me money and said that I must stay and look after everything for them until they return. But that was a long time ago, and I am still here waiting for them."

After the collapse of Salazar's government in Portugal, there had been a mass exodus of white colonialists from Mozambique. Tom had heard stories of these loyal people staying for years on their own, looking after their previous employer's homes, farms and even abandoned hotels along the coast. To find Tomasi still here looking after a very basic camp site was truly amazing. It was strange that Sandy had not seen Tomasi, when he had been investigating a rumour that his missing family were back on Inhaca - not long after their disappearance.

"My people will not be coming back Tomasi. They have all died a long time ago. Now we want to make a plan to come back here," Tom explained. "First we must ask the new government for permission."

"I am sorry to hear the sad news of your family," Tomasi bowed his head to display his sorrow. "But if you can come back here it will be good," he said smiling again, obviously delighted with the prospect of employment.

Tom and Maria, excited by the possibility of getting the land back on Inhaca, spent the next couple of days exploring the island and spending time with Tomasi and his wife, who lived in the camp with him. They gave him money to buy food and supplies promising to return as soon as they could. They told him that he would now be working for them.

Leaving Tomasi a happy man, Tom and Maria flew to Maputo and booked in to the Hotel Girasol. It was nowhere near as smart and colonial as it had been, but was still very comfortable and the food was excellent. The hotel overlooked the harbour and Catembe with its long jetty jutting out into the harbour, only a short ferry ride across the bay.

Their next mission was a visit to the land office, to find out what could be done about the five acres of ground on Inhaca. It took hours at the office of the provincial governor before eventually getting to see someone. As Tom had no documentation to prove previous ownership of the land, he was told that unless he could produce these papers, there was nothing that could be done. A new application could be lodged, but it would take a long time, and a lot of money, before it was even considered.

Somewhat downhearted, Tom and Maria took the ferry across the bay to the small village of Catembe. Tom wanted to go to the boat builder's yard at Catembe. His father and uncle had ordered two 'Mastiff' deep-sea fishing boats to be built there. If it was still in operation and making boats, it might be possible to buy a boat for them to use when they were on Inhaca. One way or another, it looked like Tom and Maria would be going to the island quite frequently in the future, and a boat would be necessary. Tomasi would look after it when they were not there.

They walked the short distance from the jetty to the boat yard he had visited with his father. At first the boatyard seemed deserted and there did not appear to be much activity, until they found a carpenter bent over a large piece of timber shaping it with his adze; a carpenter's tool with a curved blade set at right angles to the handle. It looked as if they were still in the boat building business, making small boats for the local fishermen.

Again using Maria to interpret for him, Tom asked the man where the owner could be found. He also explained that they were looking for two boats that had been built in the yard years ago. The carpenter shrugged his shoulders, and then pointing to the shed, said there was a large boat inside that had been there for many years. It was of no use to the locals; it was too big for them.

The shed was locked up and the owner of the yard, Senhor Veloso, was away, but would be back the following day. If they returned before eleven in the morning they would be able to see him. He would know what they were talking about. This snippet of information raised a glimmer of hope in Tom.

Back at the boatyard early next morning, they found the carpenter they had spoken to the previous day, still shaping the piece of timber. He looked up when he saw Tom and Maria, raised a hand in greeting then waved them towards an elderly Portuguese man sitting on a chair in the sun, outside the double-doors of the now open shed.

A small table, half hidden under a pile of rolled up papers that were obviously boat plans and drawings, stood just inside the shed where there was some light. There didn't appear to be much boat building going on, and business was apparently slow; it didn't seem as if anything bigger than a row boat had been built there for quite some time.

"*Bom dia*. Good morning," the old man greeted them with a toothless grin. Then crushing his cigarette out under his shoe, he slowly got up from the chair.

"*Bom dia*," Maria responded in Portuguese, shaking his hand before introducing him to Tom.

"Many years ago you were building two boats for *Senhor* Owen, my husband's father. When my husband was here last with his father, one of the boats was half finished. Do you know what happened to those boats?" Maria asked explaining the purpose of their visit.

"I do not recognise your husband *Senhora*, but I do remember his father, *Senhor* Owen and his partner *Senhor* Walker. Many years have passed since they were here last. I heard that *Senhor* Walker and his family sailed away and have never returned," the old man said scratching his head thoughtfully. "*Senhor* Owen has never been back."

"Yes that is true. Both *Senhor* Owen and *Senhor* Walker died many years ago," Maria explained.

"I am very sorry to hear that. How may I help you now?" Veloso asked.

"Did you finish building those two boats?" Maria persisted.

"Yes. Both the boats were finished. They stood here for a long time waiting to be collected."

"Can you remember who took them after you finished building them?"

"After some years passed and I had not been paid, I sold one of them to cover my expenses."

"We understand. What happened to the other one?"

"It is still in there," Senhor Veloso said waving his arm towards the interior of the shed. "Like I said, I finished making it, but these days there is nobody wanting that sort of boat made from good timber. They say it's too heavy," he scoffed.

Tom was excited by what the old man had just told them, but could not be sure that they were talking about the same boats. He glanced into the dark interior of the open shed and could see very little. It appeared to be packed from floor to roof with timber and half finished boats. A thick layer of dust and sawdust covered everything. "Will you please show us the boat?"

"Yes of course. Please follow me," the prospect of getting rid of the boat obviously appealed to the old man. He turned to lead them into the dark interior of the shed, lit here and there by shafts of light where the sun shone through holes in the roof. Threading their way around all the stacks of timber and bits and pieces, he took them to the back of the shed.

There in the gloom behind all the mess, towering above all the stacks of timber was a large boat, shored up on a building dolly. It was unpainted and at first glance the hull appeared to be complete. It was a

Mastiff without any doubt. The high flying bridge almost touched the roof. It was thirty foot long with a thirteen foot beam.

True to the old boat-builders word, it was in excellent condition. A few coats of paint, an engine and all the fittings needed to be added before the boat would be sea-worthy. Over the years boat-building had moved to another level, with most boats being built with fibre-glass; but this boat was immaculate. Although heavy she was strong and would be perfect for what Tom had in mind. As a seafaring nation, the Portuguese were renowned for building good strong timber boats, which lasted a very long time.

"It has been waiting to be paid for and taken away ever since it was finished. It is in perfect condition."

"Do you remember who bought the other one?" Tom asked as he climbed up on deck and started tapping the timber all over the hull.

"It was many years ago, and I no longer have the records. I am sorry I cannot help you with the name of the buyer. He paid me cash."

"*Obrigado Senhor.* Thank you. You have been most helpful. We will need your help to get this boat finished. I will be back tomorrow with the money," Tom said after they had negotiated a price.

"*Si Senhor,* I will be here. No problem, I will help." Veloso assured them happily. It was money he had never expected to receive.

Boat fittings and engines were difficult and costly to obtain in Maputo, and so arrangements had to be made to move the boat to Richards Bay, in South Africa, to be finished off. It would have to be transported on the deck of a coaster. Two days later Tom paid old man Veloso the money he was owed, and left him to organize the shipping to Richards Bay. Tom couldn't believe their good fortune. Apart from finding the 'Mastiff' and in such pristine condition, they had picked the boat up for next to nothing.

From Maputo, Tom and Maria went to Empangeni in Zululand. Tom went to see the boat builders to arrange for the Mastiff to be collected from the docks in Richards Bay when it arrived, and to discuss what was to be done to finish her off, and make her ready to go to sea. While he was there, he looked at boat designs, and discussed the possibility of them building another fishing boat.

On their way home they stopped in Swaziland to see Sandy, Tom's cousin. If they were to reclaim the land on Inhaca, they would have to find the title deeds. Sandy might have them - besides they wanted to involve him in their plans. He was away on holiday with his daughter,

Sally, and only due back in a fortnight. Tom and Maria, both excited with the prospect of running a deep-sea fishing charter business, went home planning to visit Sandy as soon as he was back from holiday.

■■■■◊◊◊◊◊■■■■

Chapter 4

Tombi arrived home from her visit to Kyle's farm a much happier person. She stopped at the store on her way home and arrived back with bags of food, and still had enough money to provide for her family for some time. She had a small bank bag full of stones buried in the floor of her hut, and if she was very careful, there was a good chance of getting more.

She had to find a way of getting close enough to the diamond mining as she could, so that she could take the photographs of the 'diamond thieves' Tom wanted. The army was still forcing people to work like slaves, in poor conditions, only giving them a pittance for their efforts. Many people had died, and even more killed by the soldiers who guarded the area where diamonds had been discovered.

Tombi was excited and at the same time very nervous by the task Tom had set her. She was excited by the money Tom said she was going to get for her diamonds, but was nervous because of the brutality by the military controlling the fields. If it became known that she was an informer, she was sure to be beaten, raped and possibly even killed. First and foremost she and her sister must go to have a look at the area where the mining was being carried out.

Situated in the Eastern Lowveld, Marange lies at the foot of a low range of smoky blue hills heralding the beginning of the Nyanga Mountain range in the north. The high jagged Chimanimani Mountains shimmered through the haze along the Mozambique border to the east. With these two mountain ranges sheltering the area from the prevailing cool winds, it's a very hot, dry and arid part of the country. The vegetation is sparse with little grass and small patches of thorn scrub, scattered here and there with giant baobabs, knob-thorn acacia and marula trees.

From a nearby hilltop Tombi was quite taken aback to see that the whole area where, only a little while ago she and her sister had scoured the ground searching for alluvial diamonds, was now completely fenced off with soldiers and guards with dogs patrolling the perimeter. It was not a pleasant place.

Inside the fence there was a hive of activity. An area the size of four football pitches had been cleared of all vegetation and was now a huge open pit. Big yellow machines were busy digging and scraping as they burrowed down into the red soil in search of the precious stones. The soil scooped up by the machines was loaded onto huge tip trucks, with wheels twice as tall as a man, and hauled to a washing plant where the diamonds were washed out of the soil on huge sieves or trays. The muddy water was drained away into settling dams.

Around the perimeter of the pits labourers sat on the ground chipping diamonds out of lumps of rock. A huge dust cloud, created by all the activity, rose high into the air, covering everything in a thick layer of fine red soil when it settled.

Two light aircraft were parked at the end of a landing strip that had been built alongside the outside of the fenced area. Some said that millions of US$ worth of diamonds were being flown out of the country every week. Although the army controlled the whole area, the mining operations were being carried out by foreign companies, who probably had no interest in the economy of Zimbabwe, and were in cahoots with the senior government officials.

Tombi and her sister spent a day watching what was happening at Marange. A few days later she came up with a plan; she was going to sell ready cooked food to the workers. If she was allowed to, she would set up a table near the entrance gates to the mine fields, where the workers on their lunch break could buy her food. In that way she would be able to get the information Tom wanted. Only officials and registered workers were allowed in and out through the gates.

It proved to be easier than she expected. Tombi obtained permission from the security office, and was given a permit to sell food on the other side of the road; opposite the main entrance gates.

A couple of days later, after using some of her precious money to buy supplies, she prepared the food. She cooked small dough balls in boiling peanut oil, known as *vetkoek*, *mealies* (maize or corn) boiled in their sheaths, *mpotahai* (biscuits made from milled corn mixed with water and sugar), as well as cooked beans and chicken heads and feet.

Then balancing a basin on her head and carrying two baskets full of her wares, she arrived at the gates and began to sell. Because of all the dust and the flies, Tombi had to keep her food covered with cloths. Luckily her prices were good and it only took a couple of hours to sell everything to the hungry workers and security guards. By the time she finished selling for the day she was hot and covered in dust.

Over the next few weeks, Tombi earned the trust of the security guards who manned the gates, and apart from scrounging free food every now and then, they took very little notice of her. She was there every day at the same time to sell her produce. At first she dared not use the cell phone Tom had given her, but once she had settled into her role, and got over her nervousness, she began her task.

Making sure nobody saw her doing so, Tombi took photographs of anything she thought might be of interest to Tom. She had to be very careful not to be caught by the guards or the soldiers, who wandered around with AK47's slung over their shoulders. As soon as she took pictures, she sent them to Kyle then deleted them immediately from her phone. It was always a relief, physically and mentally, to pack up and head home.

A regular visitor to the workings was a white man with red hair and a small pointed beard. He was always dressed smartly and wore a large hat. He was obviously an important person and treated with respect by the guards and the soldiers. He was usually accompanied by another taller white man, who must have been his assistant, and two black guards.

Tombi heard that his name was Van Zyl and they called him *Mpisi* - the Hyena. She took pictures of him and his assistant.

Tombi had been selling at the gate for about six weeks when Van Zyl stopped at her table.

"How is your business going here?" he asked her after buying some corn on the cob. "I see many of the workers buy food from you."

"It's okay. I have to make a living to feed my family, so I am here every day selling."

"Have you ever worked in a house before?"

"Yes sir. I worked in Chiredzi as a cook and house cleaner," Tombi replied nervously wondering why he was asking.

"Well, I can see your food is good," he said turning and walking away to his car and driving off in cloud of dust.

A week later, Van Zyl was back at the diggings. Once again he stopped to speak to Tombi.

"My manager lives not far from here. He needs a woman to look after the house and to cook for him," Van Zyl told her. "Would you be interested in working there?"

"I have my own business here. I will have to first see how much you will pay me and how far from my home his house is. I will also have to speak to my family if I am to live out," Tombi replied not wanting to show her eagerness to get away from the danger she was exposing herself to with what she was doing.

"Mr Barnard will take you to the house so that you can see where it is."

"Okay sir. I am nearly finished selling my food. I will be ready to go in half an hour," she said, a little nervous at the prospect of going anywhere with these men.

"When you are ready, go to my car. My manager will take you there," Van Zyl said and without waiting for her reply, walked off to the mine offices.

Barnard was a tall thin rangy man with black hair and moustache and was usually unshaven. He had green eyes and a long hooked beak of a nose. He had a slight limp and swayed when he walked; almost like a swagger. Because he swayed like a cobra about to strike, the locals called him *Inyoka* (snake). He always wore khaki long trousers and shirt and a wide brimmed slouch hat.

The house, near Hot Springs, was not far from her home north of Nyanyadzi. It was an old, dilapidated and very basic place that obviously had not been used much in recent times and in need of a good clean. There were a few chickens wandering around the yard scratching in the dirt for bits of food and insects to eat. There was a small vegetable garden on one side of the house and a small cottage behind the house for her to use. In the front of the house there was a patch of dry lawn circled by a dusty driveway.

"Well," Van Zyl said when they returned to the mines. "Do you want the job?"

"There is plenty of work to make the place clean, and the house is old. I must discuss this with my family first. Can I let you know when you come here next time?" Tombi had already decided to accept the job offer but wanted time to think.

"Okay, I will see you here next week," Van Zyl said. "But if you do accept I will want you to start straight away."

"If its okay with the family and the money is right, I will be ready to start the following Monday. But I will have to go home every week-end."

Tombi was quite pleased with this development, and knew Tom would approve. Things at the mine were not good, and she felt very uncomfortable when she was there. Recently she had seen some of the soldiers watching her closely, and worried that they might suspect her of taking photos; or have other intentions. Van Zyl was obviously well connected and by working for him, she might be able to find out more of what was happening, and where all the stones were going. Besides, she had given as much information as she could to Tom. She would achieve nothing more by continuing at the diggings.

When she got home later that day, she called Kyle. "I have been asked by a man called Van Zyl to work in his manager's house near the mine. He knows what is going on," she told him.

"Do you think that's a good idea? You might be in danger there," Kyle warned her.

"I am afraid of taking more pictures at the diamond fields. I think some of the soldiers are watching me," Tombi explained.

"You've sent us plenty of photos. There is no need to take any more. Why don't you stop now?" Kyle said. "You don't have to go and work for this man."

"I think I must come and see you. It is difficult for me to speak on the phone."

"No Tombi, I will come to you. I will meet you on Saturday morning. We don't want to be seen together so we will have to meet somewhere along the road."

"Okay, I will meet you on the main road to Mutare just after Nyanyadzi," Tombi agreed. "I will be there at eleven."

As arranged, Kyle met up with Tombi, and they parked under a wild fig tree in a lay-by on the side of the road. She gave him a full report of everything she had seen while selling food at the mine gates. Perhaps if she worked for Van Zyl she might be able to get more information. She said that it would not raise any suspicion when she left as she was going with Van Zyl.

Before dropping her off on the side of the road, Tombi handed Kyle a small packet containing a handful of the black diamonds to look after. They arranged to meet once a month at the same place.

The following week Tombi started work in Barnard's house and her sister took over the food sales at the mine. She moved into the cottage near the house, which she shared with the Barnard's gun-bearer, Petros, and the gardener. It was only Barnard who lived there on a permanent basis - Van Zyl lived in Harare.

She soon had the house spick and span and enjoyed cooking and tried all her old recipes out on Barnard. But before long it changed. Tombi noticed that he was looking at her in a funny way and seemed to make sure he touched her whenever they passed each other in the house, and his voice became gruff when he spoke to her. And so she made sure she never got too close to him, and tried to stay out of the house as much as possible when he was there alone.

Barnard seemed annoyed at her for avoiding him, and began bringing black girls to the house at night. When she mentioned this to the gardener he told her that he liked women and asked why she did not go with Barnard; or better still sleep with him.

With this going on, Tombi was not sure how long she would continue to work there. She would have to discuss her problem with Kyle next time they met.

Barnard spent a lot of time away, and over the next few months he spent less and less time at the house. He and Petros would go away for days on end to hunt at a place Van Zyl owned near the Limpopo River.

Chapter 5

Pictures of the diamond mining operations at Marange began coming to Tom via text messages from Tombi. There were photos of soldiers sauntering about with AK47 rifles; big yellow bulldozers, front-end loaders and huge tip trucks working in the shallow pits; people dressed in rags digging with their fingers in the dirt for stones; others sitting breaking diamonds out of rocks with hammers; there were photos of important looking individuals carefully picking their way through the mud and dirt as they inspected the workings.

There were also pictures of two white men. A short dapper man with a ginger beard, dressed in a smart safari suit with the trousers tucked into ankle-boots. The other man was tall and thin with dark hair and a moustache and wore khaki clothing with a wide brimmed slouch hat. Tom didn't recognise either of these men, and so he printed the photos out and went to see Ted Hunter. Ted was an old friend and partner from earlier days and worked in the mining business; he might know them.

"Ted, do you know these two guys by any chance?" Tom asked handing the photos to his friend while seated at his bar enjoying an ice cold beer.

"Indeed I do. The smart fellow with the beard is Jan Van Zyl – he lives just over that hill," Ted said pointing through the window towards a small hill not far from his home. "He's a really nasty piece of work. The other man is his manager, Barney Barnard. He does all Van Zyl's dirty work," Ted said handing the photos back to Tom.

"What's Van Zyl's claim to fame?"

"He has his fingers in all sorts of pies - in and outside the country. He's an ex-con and was used by the old Rhodesian government to help bust sanctions during the war days. He must have learned all sorts of underhand tricks during that time. Now he's the front for Mugabe's involvement in the Congo 'Blood Diamond' fiasco. He sells the diamonds that Mugabe is helping himself to as repayment for having his troops there. Van Zyl is a completely ruthless individual."

"Well he obviously has an interest in the diamonds in Marange. What about the other fellow, Barnard?"

"I don't know too much about him, but I believe he does just about anything for Van Zyl; from flying his aircraft to looking after all his interests here in Zimbabwe; mining, ranching, hunting concessions, and so on. Rumour has it he comes from a long line of scallywags. Apparently he's a descendant of 'Bvekenya' Barnard, the renowned elephant poacher from the late 19th century, who used to hunt near Crooks Corner along the Limpopo River. Probably has a bit of mixed blood in him somewhere."

"That's interesting. I heard of that old crook when I was operating in that part of the country during the war. The Member-in-Charge of Vila Salazar told us how he used to border-hop to avoid being arrested. It is quite easy to jump from South Africa into Mozambique and Zimbabwe down there. It's where all three countries meet on the Limpopo River." Tom mused knowing the area well. "Have you had any dealings with Van Zyl?"

"I sure have. In fact I've a court case pending against him. He's moved in on one or two of my gold mining claims and won't get off."

"How did he manage that?"

"Well you know how you peg prospecting claims, then register them with the mining office. He decided to over-peg some of mine and managed to get someone at the department of mines to register his claims. I have all the necessary documents but at the moment I'm getting nowhere."

"That's bloody disgraceful, and illegal. How does he manage to get away with it?"

"From your experience of being chucked off your farm, you know there is no 'Rule of Law' here any more. Besides he's a personal friend of the 'Mad Hout' and has friends in high places." Ted said referring to Mugabe. "You don't want to get mixed up with him Tom; you'll come off second best. He's a very dangerous man and gets away with murder."

"Thanks for the warning. Is it true that all the diamond mining in the Lowveld has been taken over by the army? They've certainly tightened up the security down there."

"Yes that's true. When they found out how big the discovery of diamonds was, they moved in and took over. A lot of people were killed. I believe all the buyers from Mutare, who used to meet at Drifters, have gone to ground since the military took over. Now apparently they no longer have access to the *gwejas* who themselves have been stopped, and are no longer able to pan for gems."

"Tell me Ted, how can we sell diamonds to a dealer? I have some from Marange; collected before the army got involved and forcibly moved the locals out. I need to get rid of them.

"Don't get caught with them Tom," Ted warned sternly. "You'll be locked up. I don't even want to know where you got them. There were buyers from Belgium, Lebanon, Nigeria, Russia, China and South Africa staying in Mutare and over the border in Mozambique buying good quality diamonds from the *ngodas*. Now that the supply from the locals has dwindled down to almost nothing, they have drifted away." Ted explained. "Let me do a bit of digging with contacts of mine and I'll get back to you."

"Thanks Ted. If you can give me a name; preferably outside the country, I'll take it from there and leave your name out of it. We don't want you getting into any sort of trouble, or losing your mining interests."

....

"There's something going on," Jannie Van Zyl said to Barney Barnard when he got back to the house. He had been to see his neighbour, Ted Hunter.

"What do you mean boss?" Barnard asked.

"I went over to see Ted Hunter next door. I have a problem with him; he says I have over-pegged his claims. But that's something else. While I was with him he asked me a lot of questions; mainly about the diamond mines at Marange."

"What does he actually want to know?"

"I don't bloody well know. I think he was just trying to find out if I knew what was happening down there. He and his pal Tom Owen are up to something, and I want to find out what it is," Van Zyl said. "Owen was visiting Hunter last week and now he's asking all sorts of questions about Marange."

"How can I help? Do you want me to watch them or make life difficult for them?" Barnard was always keen to use his bully-boy tactics.

"Ja. I think you must definitely allocate a couple of our chaps to follow Owen. Make sure they do the job properly and don't get caught.

Don't worry about Hunter; he lives next door and I can keep an eye on him."

"Okay Jannie, I'll get a couple of our guys onto it straight away," Barnard said preparing to leave Van Zyl's office.

"I want them to report back to me on a daily basis. Give them mobile phones and make sure they have enough cash. I don't want them coming back here all the time with their bloody hands out asking for money."

"No problem. I'll see to it."

"I saw Owen's son, Kyle, snooping around not far from Hot Springs recently. I think he was speaking to one of the *gwejas*. See what you can find out about him as well," Van Zyl said. "He must be buying and selling diamonds on the black market; unless he's getting them for his father. We can't follow both of them and Kyle is a farmer so it will be difficult. But if you keep watching Tom we'll find out what Kyle's up to. Wherever Owen goes your men must follow him. I need to know exactly what is going on."

Chapter 6

Sandy Walker was sitting in his office in Mbabane, working on the geological survey maps of the mountainous area surrounding Bulembu asbestos mine he had been commissioned to complete. The mine had been closed for some years, but now plans were afoot to re-open the old open pits, and the investors needed the information he was working on.

The office door opened and Martha Dlamini, his secretary, walked over to his worktable and handed him a calling card.

"This gentleman is waiting in the reception area. He says he would like to speak to you as soon as possible. He wants to catch the three o'clock flight back to Johannesburg."

"Thanks Martha. Give him a cup of tea and tell him I will be with him in ten minutes."

Sandy looked at the card as Martha left the office. The name was Simon Bender – Private Investigator. Sandy was puzzled. What would a private-eye want to see him for? Ten minutes later he walked into the outer office and a middle aged, balding man with a moustache, got up from the chair in the corner and introduced himself.

"Can we speak in private? I have something which I think you will be interested in," he said.

"Certainly. Come into my office Mr Bender." Turning to Martha Sandy instructed, "Please hold all my calls."

Once seated in the office, Sandy addressed his visitor, "What is it you would like to discuss with me?"

"Before we begin, can you show me some sort of identification. I have to be sure that you are the person I am to see." After examining Sandy's drivers licence and Identification card he continued.

"Thank you. I am working for a firm of lawyers in Johannesburg. They recently received this package from their associates in London." Bender said removing a large brown manila envelope from his briefcase. "Apparently it has been held in their offices for some years - they didn't know what to do with it. It was passed on to them from lawyers who had an office in Maputo (Lourenco Marques) before they were forced to close their office, and move to Portugal after

Mozambique became independent," he explained handing Sandy the envelope with a red wax seal. "It all seems to have got a bit mixed up."

"But that was years ago. Why has it taken so long to be passed down to you?"

"Well Mr Walker, as you know things always moved slowly in Mozambique; even at the best of times. Apparently they were going through all their old files when they came across the envelope. As it was signed by the British Consulate in LM at that time, they felt it best to send it to the law firm in London. If you look at the date it was received by them, you will see that they too have sat on it for a long time."

"Is this for me to keep, or must I examine it now, and hand it back to you?"

"No. I have been instructed to hand it over to you personally. All I want from you is your signature on this receipt, and I'll be on my way."

For a long time after Simon Bender left the office, Sandy sat staring at the fat envelope lying on his desk. He had a funny feeling in the pit of his stomach; it obviously had something to do with his parents and their fishing business in Mozambique.

Eventually Sandy broke the seal and opened the manila envelope. Inside it there was a second envelope; this one older with the writing on the front a little faded. It was his Uncle Bill's writing, and was addressed to him at his old office in Lesotho. It was dated the month and the year that Tom's family had sailed from Durban; never to be seen again!

There was something wrong. How was it possible that he had written on this envelope at the same time as he had been reported missing? Across the top he had written; *URGENT - To be handed personally to my nephew, Sandy Walker*. Bender had finally tracked him down to Swaziland. It had taken twenty five years for an 'urgent' package to reach him!

Now after all the years since they had sailed out of Durban in their trimiran, *Nimble Tigger*, and disappeared, this man turns up out of the blue with a package for him; what was he going to find inside it?

Although he was excited, and keen to find out what it contained, Sandy did not want to be disturbed when he opened it. He would examine the contents when he had the time with no interruptions. For his uncle to have persuaded the British Consulate to arrange personal delivery of the package, it obviously contained important documents. But it had never been delivered to him as promised.

Now there was no hurry. What difference was another day or two going to make after all these years? If it had been that urgent Bender would have waited for him to examine the contents before leaving.

By the time Sandy finished work on the project he was busy with, it was late, and Martha was waiting to close up. He locked the brown manila envelope in the safe, and left the office.

Sandy was a widower. His wife, Coleen, had died from cancer when their daughter Sally was eleven. Sally was now at university. Although he had had a number of casual affairs since Coleen had passed away, he had never fallen in love again, nor had a really lasting relationship with another woman. Sandy lived alone, but today he felt like some company, and so he stopped at the club before going to an empty home.

"The strangest thing happened to-day," Sandy said to Richard, a friend who played golf with him most week-ends.

"Well come out with it then. What happened?" he asked.

"I had a visitor from Johannesburg. He's an investigator for a firm of lawyers. He handed me a package my uncle had addressed to me, at the time of their disappearance."

"Good God! That's a bit late in the day. The family went missing years ago."

"My thoughts exactly! The thing is I haven't looked inside the package yet. Perhaps I don't want to know what's inside."

"Have you got it with you?" Richard asked, ordering another round.

"No I left it in the office. I'll look at it on Monday when I get some spare time."

"It certainly will be interesting to see what it contains. Let me know as soon as you have had a look," Richard said, signalling to the waiter to bring a menu. "Joining me for a bite to eat?"

....

Over the week-end Sandy tried to contact Tom in Zimbabwe, but was told that he and Maria were away on holiday. On Monday Sandy opened the safe, and removed the package he had been given by Bender. He had finished his report, and there was nothing that needed his urgent attention, and so he decided to devote time to going through the contents of this long overdue package from his uncle.

Although curious, he was still reluctant to open it, and would have preferred to have had Tom with him - but as it was addressed to him, and the contents might be confidential, and for his eyes only. He also had a feeling it might well hold clues as to where and how his uncle and his family had disappeared.

Martha brought him a cup of tea, and he asked her to make sure he was not disturbed, and to hold his calls for a couple of hours. Opening the package, he found two envelopes inside; one addressed to him, and the other to Tom.

Inside his envelope were a number of documents with a note clipped to them.

Dear Sandy.

As you might be aware, we sailed from Durban a couple of weeks ago, and have returned to Inhaca. We intend sailing north in the next few days, and as I have not been able to get in touch with Tom, I would like you to get hold of him as soon as you can, and hand him the envelope I have included in this package. Perhaps you two might like to get together, and do something with the land on Inhaca and the two unfinished boats. They are part of your inheritance and I am handing it all over to you two now. You now have all the documents, and the letter I have written to Tom will explain everything.

Best of luck. Bill.

This was incredible. Sandy sat gazing out of the window deep in thought. Had the package been delivered to him as his uncle had requested, he would have received it before the search had even been mounted. Why had it been passed to lawyers in Lourenco Marques (Maputo) instead of being delivered to him via the Embassy in Lesotho? The package must have been handed back to Garcia, the lawyer in Lourenco Marques by mistake.

It was all a horrible error made by some individual on the Embassy staff, which had probably cost the lives of Tom's family. He would have to arrange to meet up with Tom as soon as her was back from his holiday.

A knock on the door brought Sandy back to the present.

"Come in." he called closing the folder and putting it away in his drawer.

"Excuse me sir, I know you said that you must not be disturbed, but there is someone from the Department of Mines who wants to see you. He says it cannot wait," Martha said. "Shall I bring him in?"

It was back to business. He would have to give his uncle's papers more attention when he had the time. He would also have to get in touch with his cousin Tom, to let him know about the documents.

....

A week later, quite out of the blue and purely by coincidence, Tom and Maria arrived to spend a few days with him. They had recently been to Inhaca and were bubbling with excitement and full of ideas.

"Before you tell me all about your visit to the island, I have something quite disturbing to tell you. This is all such an amazing coincidence, you won't believe it. A week ago a fellow pitched up at my office with a package for me. It was supposed to have been delivered to me in Maseru by the British Embassy there at the time your family disappeared," Sandy said. "It was sent to me by your father." Sandy opened his safe and took the package out and handed it to Tom. "I think you need to sit down before you read it all."

"Have you seen what is inside?" Tom was curious, and had turned a little pale.

"There are some documents with a note to me from your Dad, and a second envelope addressed to you," Sandy said handing the envelope to Tom. "His note says the letter in your envelope will explain everything."

There were two letters. The first was a copy of a letter Tom had received two years before his family had disappeared.

"My dear son.

Although you are aware of all this, I though it best to put it down on paper for the record. With all the plans for constitutional changes in Africa and with the British Government having no hesitation in selling out the Europeans in Swaziland and in spite of the wishes of the Paramount Chief to the contrary, the country has been handed over to the Swazi Nation.

For this reason we have had to make an entirely new assessment of our plans for the future. Inhaca is a delightful island almost idyllic and within twelve miles of the Mozambique Channel which is considered to be the most wonderful game fishing area in the world. There are masses of sportsmen throughout the world wanting to fish there but there are no facilities.

We are now forming a thing called the Swaziland Deep Sea Club for Game-fishing. It has to be an outside name as the Portuguese will allow anything to encourage tourism. We have a charming but very businesslike Portuguese partner called Garcia. He is an expert fisherman and knows the sea and potential near Inhaca better than anyone and never fails to make a profit when he goes fishing. One has to have a Portuguese partner in any company when applying for a concession.

We have acquired five acres on Inhaca with foreshore and beach. This is for the clubhouse and sleeping huts. We are building in Catembe two trimirans (a Nimble and a Lodestar) and three or four Mastiffs (fast inboard motor boats with cabin, fishing chairs and flying bridge). Boat-building here is very good and wonderfully cheap.

Finally, don't laugh, as a back door or escape hatch for possible future happenings in Africa, I have applied to the French Government for land on the Island of Juan de Nova (Isle of Dogs).

The second letter was dated ten days after they had sailed from Durban - only two days before the air and sea search had been put in motion to look for his missing family and their yacht *'Nimble Tigger'*. The blood drained from Tom's face and he felt quite dizzy. With trembling fingers he picked it up and began to read.

'My Dear Tom.

As you are aware, a lot has happened since I wrote to you outlining our plans when we left Swaziland and moved to Mozambique. Changes happened far more rapidly than I anticipated. Since Salazar was recently thrown out of power in Portugal, the Portuguese are becoming very nervous and getting ready to abandon this country. For this reason our investors have pulled out of our project leaving us high and dry.

After your Uncle Jim and Aunt Jean, our very dear friends and partners, were tragically killed in a car accident, we decided to pack it in and, although she was not finished, sailed to Durban in 'Nimble Tigger' taking Anne and Tula with us. This was in itself an adventure and we damn nearly floundered along the way. As you are aware, we spent four months repairing the damage she sustained on the trip and finishing her off while I looked for work.

On the eve of our departure, the job I had been offered in the Cape fell through - the company had decided to close its operations in Southern Africa. Obviously this was a major blow, and once again we have been forced to change our plans.

We sailed back here to Inhaca, where we have reassessed our situation. Due to the uncertainty of the political situation in Mozambique, and indeed in Africa, we feel it will be pointless going to the expense of setting up an operation here only to be chased away. We have now decided to make our way to Australia where we can start a new life, with no political constraints.

The French Government have agreed to allow us to set up a temporary camp on either Juan de Nova or Europa Island. We will sail north, and out of curiosity, stop to have a look at these islands - which are far too far away from the mainland to be practical for our venture. From there we will make our way around the top end of Madagascar, the Seychelles and from there to Australia.

Once we have settled, we will move the boats (which are in the final stages of completion) and our whole set-up. We will need help with this, and might very well call on you and Sandy to assist us from your end. We also hope to be able to convince our investors to continue with their financial help in our Deep Sea fishing venture, once we have found a more politically stable location.

I know this all sounds a bit vague and disorganised, but having been badly let down, our backs are against the wall. With the limited financial resources we have at our disposal, there do not seem to be any other options for us in Africa.

I have bundled all my important documents and papers together and will be handing them to the British Consulate, who have assured me that they will be delivered to Sandy personally in Lesotho, as soon as possible. At least they will be in safe hands. (Sandy is in a better position than you are to keep them as he is closer to Inhaca)

We sail within the next couple of days and assure you that we will be in touch as soon as we make landfall."

They never did. If they had ever made it to the Seychelles or Australia they would surely have been in touch with him as soon as they had been able to. This explained the mystery of their strange disappearance. Tom's head was still spinning and he felt as if he had been hit in the stomach with a sledgehammer as he handed the letters to Sandy to read.

All the time they were searching for his family, they had been searching in the wrong area; from Richards Bay to East London, when all along they had been on Inhaca preparing to sail north and on to Australia.

Nobody knew they had changed their plans at the last minute, and sailed north from Durban; not south. Had the search been conducted to the north they would have been found. 'Nimble Tigger' had sailed from Inhaca 25 years ago and nothing had ever been heard from them. They had not perished in the massive seas off the Wild Coast as believed. So where had they gone after leaving Inhaca? Desperation is what forced them to sail away into the blue.

The day of their departure from Durban a force-eight gale had blown up from the south-west that had lasted for two days. A week after their expected arrival in East London, with no reports of them having called at any port along the coast, the *Nimble Tigger* and her crew were posted as missing.

Air and sea searches had been set in motion, with Air Force Shackelton and Dakota aircraft hunting for the missing *Nimble Tigger* and her crew. Port authorities up and down the coast were alerted to keep a look-out and to question all shipping arriving in their ports. All leisure boats and small-craft that had been sailing in the area at the time were asked to report sighting they might have had of the 30 foot trimiran.

After an intensive two week air and sea search, hampered by bad weather, and with no sign or reports of the missing yacht, the search had been called off. It was feared that the Owens had sailed directly into the gale, and might have floundered and perished in the notoriously treacherous seas off the Wild Coast. There was nothing more anyone could do but wait, and hope that the yacht and its crew turned up somewhere.

"Good God Tom! That's incredible. But if they survived the storm and went somewhere north, why have you never heard from them? Do you think they might still be alive and marooned on an island somewhere, with no communications?" Sandy asked, passing the letters to Maria.

"It's all such a long time ago I don't suppose we'll ever know. With all this happening now, I feel responsible for not making a greater effort to find them. If only I had studied the winds and ocean currents I might well have questioned the port authorities, and made them search to the north. With south-westerly gale force winds forecast, my Dad would never have sailed south. Surely if they were alive, they would have found a way to get in touch with me."

"Of course, your mother would have made a plan to get a message to you. No mother just abandons her son," Maria said.

"This is now a bigger mystery than ever. They must have made it to somewhere or other. Your dad was a good sailor, and the yacht was in perfect condition. So those rumours of them being seen in LM must have been true. I wonder why the British Embassy never said anything when it was all in the news," Sandy was puzzled.

"I am certainly going to lodge a very strong complaint with them - not that it will do any good. The individual responsible will have left the service a long time ago."

"Yes, and lay it on thick Tom. You can point out that they are partly responsible for the disappearance of your folk," Maria was flabbergasted.

"Sandy have you still got that scrap-book you made up about the boat building and the fishing business?" Tom asked hopefully. Something rang a bell in the back of his mind.

Sandy pulled open a drawer in his filing cabinet and took out the scrapbook of newspaper cuttings.

"Yes, here it is. Look at this," Sandy said, opening the book and stabbing his finger at one of the newspaper cuttings.

It was an article written by the yachting correspondent for the Natal Daily News in February 1965, six months after they went missing.

"Rumours in Lourenco Marques are that the craft 'Nimble Tigger' was beached in the Inhaca area and that Mrs Owen had been seen in Lourenco Marques with her daughter. It is also rumoured that Mr Owen went on to Mombasa some months ago."

Tom had been on military duty in the bush in Rhodesia at the time, and so Sandy had gone to investigate. He had never been there before and didn't know what to expect. Apart from a deserted camp, with only signs of a local family living there, his search proved fruitless, and once again the hopes of finding the Owen family had been dashed.

Two years later, a South African yachting magazine published an article on trimirans. In the article was a report claiming that the missing yacht, *Nimble Tigger* and her crew had arrived safely in Australia. This too, was never confirmed and according to Interpol, the Australian authorities had no record of *Nimble Tigger*, or the Owen family having ever arrived in the country.

Over time interest died down and eventually, after having been missing for fifteen years, and with no sign of them being seen anywhere, Bill, Marjorie and Anne were declared 'Missing at Sea – Presumed Dead'.

The documents and papers in the envelope included partnership agreements, copies of the land concession on Inhaca, and a simple will leaving everything to Tom, with the exception of the assets of the fishing business, which were to be shared equally with his cousin Sandy.

Then like a blow to the head, a thought suddenly struck Tom. The two French islands, Juan de Nova and Europa; when it had been rumoured that his family had sailed north, why had he never thought of asking the French if *Nimble Tigger* had called at the island? The second letter now verified that they had been making their way in that direction.

The thought of his family, possibly stranded for years, on some island in the middle of the Indian Ocean; without any means of communication with the outside world, made Tom feel quite sick. All the time they were presumed to have perished, they might very well have been alive.

Tom sat for a long time staring out of the window, tears streaming down his face, as he thought that he might have been able to help them.

"I wonder what actually happened to them," Tom said. "I suppose we'll never know now. It is far too late, and a long time ago," he finished sadly. "But one way or the other I'm sure they must have died a long time ago, or I would've heard from one of them for sure. I just hope they didn't suffer," Tom said sadly.

. . . .

"Well Sandy, what do you think?" Tom asked later that evening after outlining their proposals.

"If what you say is true, then all we have to do is to apply to the Mozambique government, and we should be able to reclaim the land."

"Yes, that's what I was told. Isn't this amazing? What a stroke of fate that we should think of this at the same time as this package turns up out of the blue," agreed Tom.

"Did you say that old Tomasi is still living in the camp?" Sandy asked, incredulous.

"Yes. He says he's been there all the time." Maria said.

"Hell. What a complete cock-up. I never saw him when I went there to look for your folks after the report in the newspaper, not long after they went missing. If I had seen him things might have turned out a lot differently."

"Don't blame yourself. How were you to know about old Tomasi?"

After many hours of discussion lasting late into the night, the three of them agreed that if they could get the land back, they would take up where their parents had left off; if they could raise the necessary finance. As Sandy was only a couple of hours drive from Maputo, he would pursue the application to reclaim the land on Inhaca Island.

Tom would try to contact the companies in America and the UK, who had agreed to finance the original venture. The details were among the documents Sandy had received. Although after all this time the people Bill and Jim had dealt with would have retired and moved on - there were bound to be other people who had taken over the reins, or to whom Tom could be referred. Now that the political turmoil was over, and Mozambique had settled down, there were bound to be a lot of eager fishermen wanting to fish off the east coast of Africa.

Chapter 7

Tombi had been working in the house for two months when Barnard told her to pack up - they were moving to Mabiti Safari camp and game reserve. When she asked him where that was, he told her it was located between the Gona-re-Zhou and the Limpopo River. When she told him it was too far from her home, he insisted she help with the move. If she did not want to stay on she could leave as soon as he found a replacement. Somewhat reluctantly she agreed.

As soon as she was alone, Tombi phoned Kyle to give him the news. "Yes I know the place. We used to hunt in that area. Why is he going there?" Kyle wasn't happy with this development.

"He says the Government have chased us away from here. Perhaps they think we will steal the diamonds."

"I think this is a good time for you to stop working for Barnard. My father has gone to sell your stones, and then you will have money. When he returns he will tell us what you should do."

"I have already told Barnard I will help him move."

"Well I don't think there is a good network signal from there - it is too far away. We'll have to find a way to keep in touch."

"I will get a message to you when I know how the others do it."

"Okay Tombi that's a good idea. I'll wait to hear from you. Be careful now."

Two days later, squashed into the front of the lorry loaded with all Barnard's furniture as well as her few belongings; Tombi arrived at Mabiti Game Reserve. It had taken most of the day travelling from the sparse overgrazed region of the Eastern Lowveld to the densely wooded mopani forest area of the South-Eastern Lowveld. From Hot Springs their journey had taken them 150 kilometers to Masvingo where they turned south for 150 kilometers to Rutenga, then east onto a dusty gravel road past Chikombedzi to the Safari camp of Mabiti.

Men in brown overalls worked in the yard – some at the sheds and others at the outside abattoir. They all seemed to be busy quietly getting on with their work. A couple of brindle dogs lay in the sun near the abattoir waiting for scraps of meat. Half tame crows hopped around the yard cawing loudly at the dogs, and anything they though might get to the scraps of meat before them.

The thatched house was far better and bigger than the hot tin roofed one they had moved from, and in good condition. Every room had a family of pale transparent geckos chasing each other up and down the walls and the rafters. They lived in the thatch and left droppings all over the place. They did however serve a purpose; they kept the mosquitoes under control.

Lush green lawns with large mahogany, sausage, marula and tall knob-thorn trees gave plenty of shade and some relief from the sweltering heat. Crested brown and white hoopoes flitted from tree to tree, tapping on the tree trunks and dry branches in the hope of finding tasty morsels. Each tree seemed to have a resident snake; either a bright green boom-slang or a brown spotted grass-snake that fed off the birds eggs found in the weaver nests dangling from the branches.

Sheds and good staff quarters were located within the fenced compound about 50 metres from the house and office. Dark bottle-green, yellow-eyed glossy starlings gathered on the ground near the cook-house to pick up bits of left over meal. Overhead, lilac breasted rollers tumbled and dived out of the sky to catch grasshoppers and other insects flying around in the slowly rising smoke from the cooking fire.

A large kudu ram, shot that morning by Barnard who had arrived the previous day, was being skinned and butchered. Some of the meat was brought to the house for Tombi to use in the kitchen. The rest was cut into thin strips and hung in a wire mesh larder to dry into *biltong* (like jerky).

Once she was settled in, and had made herself comfortable in her quarters, Tombi began to take note of her surroundings and what happened there. It did not take long to learn from the workers that Mabiti was no longer a game reserve for tourists. Now it was a private hunting area used by Van Zyl and his friends for the slaughter of wild animals. Kudu and impala were killed to make *biltong* and their skins cured, salted and stacked in the sheds, ready to be sent to tanners in the East. Zebra were killed and their hides also cured but their meat was sent off to canneries in Bulawayo for dog meat.

Elephants carrying ivory were being shot for the tusks and the meat and hides left in the bush for the vultures, hyenas and jackals. As far as Tombi was aware, the shooting of elephant for their ivory tusks was forbidden. Almost every day trucks came back from hunting forays with animal carcasses piled high on them. It was a big operation.

By this time Tombi was already on good terms with the gardener who had also come with them from Hot Springs. As the days passed she heard from him that the hunting parties sometimes even crossed the Limpopo River into South Africa and Mozambique, where they killed elephant.

A short time after moving to Mabiti, Barnard went off with his van loaded with two crates filled with tusks. He was away for four days; she didn't know where he went.

Kyle knew what type of men Van Zyl and Barnard were and was suspicious of anything they were doing. Because of its remoteness and proximity to the border, Kyle suspected Van Zyl and Barnard must be smuggling diamonds out of the country from Mabiti.

Tombi felt isolated and needed support; someone to help her if she got into trouble. She had to speak to Kyle. He had warned her there might be no network at Mabiti and he was right. She had to find a way to contact him.

And so, two months after moving to Mabiti, Tombi asked Barnard if she could get a lift with the next vehicle going to Masvingo. She explained that she wanted to go home to visit her family, but assured him she would be coming back. She already knew he was going away for a week, and hoped to get a lift with him. Barnard reluctantly agreed, and dropped her off in Masvingo; he also dropped Petros, his foreman who said that he too was going home.

Before boarding the bus to Birchenough Bridge with Petros, Tombi phoned Kyle to ask him to meet her at the old hotel, near the bridge on the banks of the Sabi River. A couple of hours later Kyle met her, and they went back to his farm before taking her home.

■■■■◇◇◇◇◇■■■■

Chapter 8

Tom was relaxing in the garden with Maria after a game of tennis, when he heard the phone ring inside the house. Rushing inside he answered. It was Sandy.

"Tom. Good news. I have just returned from Maputo. We have been given back our land on Inhaca. We have to make some sort of improvements there, within the next couple of weeks, if we want to hang onto it."

"Hell that is good news Sandy. The boat is in Empangeni, and they have already started work on her; in fact they must be almost finished by now. We have the money now, so we must press on. Perhaps it's time to order the catamaran we want them to build for us," Tom was excited by Sandy's news.

"I'm going to Durban next week. I'll stop in and check the progress on the mastiff. Should I place the order for the catamaran while I am there?" Sandy offered. "Do they have all the specs?"

"That's a bloody good idea. Yes they do, but you might want to check them out while you're there. We'd better make a plan to get to Inhaca as soon as possible, and set up some sort of camp. We have old Tomasi there already. Let me know when you are back and available. We'll fly down and pick you up en-route."

"I'm only going away for a couple of days. Pick me up next week-end," Sandy said.

"Okay, we'll do that. I'll let you know our ETA before we leave Harare," Tom confirmed. "Will you be on your own?"

"Yes of course. Do you think I have a harem of girls living with me?" Sandy laughed.

"That's fine. Just checking," Tom chuckled. "Kyle will be coming with us to help with the work."

．．．．．．．．．．．．．．

Arriving at Inhaca, three months after Tom and Maria's earlier visit, they dropped their bags at the hotel and hurried off to the camp-site. Tomasi greeted them warmly, and was delighted to hear their news.

After surveying the camp-site and working out their requirements, they went back to the hotel full of enthusiasm and bubbling with excitement.

In the morning Tom and Sandy took the ferry over to Maputo. They went to the boat yard at Catembe where they hired a boat from Alfonso Da Silva, the old boat builder. From him they also bought timber, planks and poles, and from the merchant around the corner cement and other odds and ends needed for the construction of their camp. This was all loaded onto the boat and taken over to the island.

The beach in front of the camp-site was very shallow, but the tide was in and they were able to off-load their supplies opposite the camp. At low tide the water was a long way out and it was impossible to bring a boat close to the beach near to the camp. Without having their own jetty, they would have been forced to offload at the main jetty near the hotel.

Next day Sandy and Kyle returned to Maputo where they met the truck Sandy had sent down from Swaziland. It was loaded with two 500 litre water tanks, tools, a fridge, deep-freezer, a field boiler and camp stove, a small generator and most important of all; a Quad and small trailer. What they could not load on the boat they loaded onto the ferry. Everything was transported over to the island including four wooden barrels for fresh water. It was all offloaded at the jetty and moved to the camp with the quad and trailer.

With Tomasi and four of his friends recruited on the island, they set about building their camp. Two pole and daga sleeping huts and a kitchen hut were erected, and thatched with bulrushes cut near the swamp; a shower enclosure with wash stand off to one side; and a long-drop toilet was erected over a deep pit fifty meters from the camp-site. The wooden barrels were filled with fresh water from a nearby stream and rolled to the camp. The two tanks were mounted on a 10 foot high tank stand and filled from the barrels. This took a full day. The water was piped to the shower and kitchen.

A large tarpaulin was strung under one side of the tree to provide shelter from the rain and shade cloth was stretched on the ground underneath and pegged down. In the middle of the area they set up a table and chairs. Kerosene lamps were suspended from branches of the tree under the tarpaulin.

It was hard work and every evening after a shower and an early supper, the four of them collapsed exhausted in their hotel beds. At the end of a week they had a rustic but fairly adequate camp-site. Apart from stretchers, deck chairs and all the utensils, they had all they needed to start with.

Leaving Maria to supervise the finishing touches in camp, Tom, Kyle and Sandy flew off to Empangeni to take delivery of the now completed Mastiff. The Twin hulled catamaran would not be ready for another two months. The 'mastiff' was in the water and lay moored at the jetty in Richards Bay. Her name, *Tigger* painted on either side of her bows, gave Tom quite a lump in his throat. He thought how his father would have loved to see his boat completed and looking as it did now. She looked fantastic!

Tigger was 30 foot long, 13 foot wide with a draft of 18 inches when stationary in the water. Her wooden hull had been covered with a fibreglass skin and painted dark blue with the upper-deck and superstructure white. The deck was carpeted with brown weatherproof carpeting. The cabin could easily sleep four and had a galley and heads.

A back-to-back bench ran down the middle of the deck and towards the stern there was a fighting chair for big-game fishing. A diving platform had been added to the stern and bow rails around the foredeck. Rod holders were fitted along the gunwales and on a stainless steel rail above the flying bridge housing the helm and controls. A second set of controls were inside the cabin.

She was fitted with 2 Volvo Penta turbocharged engines delivering 600 hp. Satellite navigation, fish-finder instruments and ship-to-shore radio, had been fitted into the dashboard. Although an old design, she looked magnificent and very sturdy.

The boat builders had taken her out into the bay to adjust the trim and make a few minor alterations. Her sea trials proved that despite being heavy, she could perform well in the sea and moved along at a good clip easily reaching up to 30 knots on her stepped-up hull. Tom and Sandy were delighted and couldn't wait to put her to the test on her long sea trip to Inhaca.

The sun was blazing down with fair weather forecast, and so late that afternoon, the fuel tanks on *Tigger* were topped up and a couple of reserve drums stowed on deck. Fishing equipment and some of the heavy camping gear was put inside the cabin, with enough food and drink for the trip. At mid-night, after a few hours sleep in the cabin, they sailed out of Richards Bay and set off north to Inhaca.

Kyle loaded all the rest of the gear into the plane and took off at seven. An hour later and about 2 kilometers from shore he spotted the long wake and blue and white hull of *Tigger*. He flew down low over the sea to wave at Tom and Sandy as he passed by. He saw them both wave back as he waggled his wings before climbing back up to 5000 feet and flying on to Inhaca; only an hour away.

Occasionally along the way *Tigger* was escorted by pods of dolphin that frolicked around them, darting in and out in front of the bows and racing along keeping pace with her. At times they cut across in front of the bows so close that Tom felt sure he would hit one of them; but they always managed to shoot away in time. Off Sodwana Bay they passed a whale with her calf, and a few turtles and flying fish off Kosi Bay.

Eighteen hours after setting off, after a good trip in clam seas, with *Tigger* handling like a dream, Tom and Sandy entered the bay and dropped anchor opposite their camp on Inhaca. Extremely happy with the boat's performance, and very pleased with themselves, they jumped off the diving platform into waist-deep water to wade ashore. They were met on the beach by three very excited people smiling from ear to ear. Maria, Kyle and Tomasi, who had seen the boat rounding the point at Elephant Island, and now stood on the beach admiring *Tigger* rocking gently at her anchor.

"My goodness Tom, she certainly is a lovely looking boat. Looks nothing like the boat I saw in the builder's yard at Catembe a few months ago," Maria exclaimed clapping her hands in excitement.

"You can say that again. She's comfortable and fast for a heavy wooden boat. I'm very pleased with her," Tom enthused. "Dad and Uncle Pat knew what they were doing when they chose this design."

"On the way up we tested the controls topside and in the cabin. All working perfectly and the engines purr along with plenty of power to spare. We didn't even need the spare fuel," Sandy added. "We are going to have a lot of fun with her."

"When are you two going to take us out for a test run?" Maria asked looking at her husband.

"First thing tomorrow, weather permitting," Tom replied. "Come on let's go and see what you have been up to in camp while we've been braving the high seas."

"We didn't have time to catch any fish, so I hope there is something to eat in camp. I'm starved," Sandy pointed out rubbing his stomach.

"Come on let's get up the hill. I'm bloody thirsty," added Tom turning to lead the way up the path.

In the two days they had been away, the camp had been transformed into a comfortable place to stay. Maria and her helpers had worked wonders adding the little touches needed to make life easier. Kyle had arrived before noon and had been put straight to work.

"You chaps have got it all well organised. When do we start fishing?" he asked. "I want to be your first client."

"We can go out into the channel tomorrow and have a crack at catching a few for the pan," Tom suggested. "Who knows we might even land something decent."

"I'll get the rods ready while we have a few beers," Kyle volunteered always keen. "I only have to be back on the farm in three days time."

"Well if we don't get any sponsorship or fishermen, thanks to the old people, at least we have a nice camp and a good sturdy boat for us to use for our own fishing trips. Be a lovely place for all the family to use," Tom observed while sitting on a log looking around admiring their work.

"Absolutely," Sandy agreed. "We also know that in a couple of month's time we'll have another good boat. I'm sure getting our business up and running will be a lot easier now than it was for our parents when they tried. Nowadays we have the internet and email, and we can build a good website once we have pictures of the camp, the boats and some fish."

"Africa was in turmoil at that time and nobody knew what was going to happen. Now that it seems to have settled down here in Mozambique, we should have no problems; apart from the odd bribe and 'freebie' we might be obliged to hand out," Tom said.

"When are you planning on going overseas?" Sandy asked Tom. "Before you go we had better register our company. We decided on 'Santo Deep-Sea Fishing', are we still all happy with the name." They all nodded in agreement. "Good. I'll get that done this week."

"The Southampton Boat Show is at the end of the month. I'll be meeting those guys from America there. One of the Irish fishing clubs has also responded positively, so I hope that they will also be there," Tom said having been in contact with them.

"Well all we need now is to have fishermen clambering over each other to come and fish with us." Sandy laughed.

"That would be bloody marvellous." Tom agreed smiling.

They were all up at first light, had something to drink then took the rods and some refreshments down to *Tigger*. The tide was in so they waded out to the boat and clambered on board. Maria busied herself in the cabin, stowing gear and examining everything, while the men got ready to go out to sea.

"I take my hat off to you guys. Everything on this boat is just fine," Maria said popping her head out of the cabin.

"I am glad you approve," Tom bowed. "It is very basic but quite adequate for a fishing boat."

"Come on up here," Sandy called down from the flying bridge. "We're about to head out."

As soon as Maria joined them on deck, Kyle pulled up the anchor, Tom started the motors and they made for open water. Once away from the shore Tom opened the throttles and let Maria get a feel for the power of the engines as *Tigger* picked up speed and got up on the plane.

"Wow. She certainly can get a move on," Maria smiled happily with the wind blowing her hair back. "I have the feeling this is the start of something good for us all."

Chapter 9

Tom knew he was being followed the moment he stepped off the bus at Piccadilly Circus. There were two of them. As he was leaving his hotel earlier that morning, Tom recalled seeing the same two men loitering around the car park and had presumed they were fellow travellers. Now he was convinced they were following him and were not very good at it. Both of them were black men; one dressed in smart suit and the other in a blue windcheater and wore a red baseball cap.

These men had followed him from his hotel; in fact they must have followed him all the way from Johannesburg, or even from Harare. Unless they were members of the dreaded CIO (secret police) based at the Zimbabwean Embassy in London, and had been told of Tom's arrival. Tom had not seen either of them on the plane, but then who looks at all the passengers on an aircraft, especially when you were not expecting to be followed?

As he wandered along the bustling crowded sidewalk, looking at the sights and making his way towards Leicester Square, thoughts were going through Tom's mind. Somebody must have been watching the home of the diamond dealer where Tom went to sell his stones; seen him and followed him from there. Tom couldn't figure it out. There had to be a lot of other people selling diamonds in Johannesburg; why follow him? Who were they and why were they so interested in him?

He was early for his luncheon appointment and so Tom had ample time to shake off his 'tails'. Not wanting them to find out where he was going, or for them to know that he was on to them, from Leicester Square he wandered towards the Thames Embankment, where he could sit and watch the boats plying up and down the river. From there it would be easy to see what his followers were going to do; if they were following him.

When Tom stopped moving and was out in the open, there was nowhere for the two men to conceal themselves, and so they had to try and blend in with passing pedestrians and sightseers. Tom found a bench on the Thames riverbank, near the statue of Cleopatra's Needle, where he could see the giant Ferris wheel of the London Eye, turning slowly on the other side of the river to his right, its pods full of sightseers.

He sat down to think and plan his next move. He felt very uneasy knowing he was being watched. Who knew of his presence in London and where he was staying? Someone was interested enough in his movements to have him followed and to find out where he was going, or what he was doing; possibly even to make sure he never got to his destination. What worried Tom most was how anyone could have known he was coming to London?

With what Ted had told him about the man, the only person Tom could think of who would have the means and influence to have him followed, was Jan Van Zyl. He most certainly would not want any interference in his dirty but extremely lucrative operations. He was a most unsavoury character who had to be stopped. Tom had photographs to show the world; evidence that would expose dealings between certain high powered government officials and shady unscrupulous characters like Van Zyl.

But, was he going to be prevented from handing them over - why else would anyone want to follow him? Who knew that Tombi worked for him and had cottoned on to what she was doing, Tom wondered? When he had left Zimbabwe the previous week, only Maria, Kyle and Ted were aware of his travel arrangements. Had somebody got to them? Tom was worried.

With rich pickings to be had in developing Third World countries in Africa, with corrupt government officials, there was no shortage of wealthy, greedy individuals making a lot of money out of shady operations. For them it was easy to 'buy' senior officials. These parasites preyed on the poor, and would stop at nothing to prevent interference in their plundering. In Zimbabwe where there was no rule of law they felt safe from prosecution - or so they thought!

All foreign press were banned from entering Zimbabwe, and so Tom was in London to meet up with a friend he had met in the early days of the Zimbabwe farm invasions. He was an investigative reporter for a London newspaper and had agreed to get involved. If, through the media, he could stop people like Tombi from being robbed, beaten and even killed by the legalised diamond thieves, it would have been worth Tom's efforts.

While he sat there deep in thought, Tom kept an eye on his two shadows. After a while, to make sure he was not imagining things, Tom got up and sauntered off upriver for 100 yards then sat down on another bench. Sure enough the two men also moved along behind him. The one wearing a cap leant on a railing a little further along looking out over the river and the passing river traffic. The other fellow in the suit leant against a pillar, near the entrance to one of the old buildings on the other side of the road, reading a newspaper.

A boat loaded with tourists chugged towards London Bridge. Tom could hear the guide's voice as he pointed out the sights, on both sides of the river, to his charges whose heads turned in unison like spectators watching a game of tennis. As the boat moved away upstream a group of students hurried busily along the walkway, chatting and laughing as they scurried along. Tom, seizing the opportunity, quickly got up and mingled with them, doing his best to keep up with their brisk pace. At the fist cross-roads they came to, he left the group and hailed a passing cab.

As the taxi re-joined the stream of traffic Tom looked back but saw no sign of the two men following him. He had moved so suddenly and quickly that he hoped he had lost them before they had time to realize what he was doing. Tom knew he had to move fast if he was to give them the slip. They knew where he was staying, and were bound to make their way back to the hotel to try and find him there. He would have to be well away by the time they arrived. They could easily interfere with his plans, and the last thing he wanted was to worry about being followed by a pair of goons.

Back at the hotel the taxi waited while he packed his case and booked out and was then driven to the station. Tom saw no sign of either of the 'tails' at the hotel, or at the station, and felt quite relieved to have shaken them off. He caught the train to Dorking where he booked into an hotel on the outskirts of the town. Once in his room, he phoned the reporter who, after Tom explained the situation, agreed to meet him in Dorking the following morning.

Tom kept a weary eye out for the two men all afternoon but saw no sign of them. Late in the afternoon he took a stroll outside the hotel where he could see all the approaches; still his two followers were nowhere to be seen. The fact that someone had put 'tails' on him made Tom worry about Maria left behind at home in Harare; what was happening there?

He called Maria and was relieved to hear she was fine and that all was well at home. He didn't tell her about the men who had been following him; he didn't want her to worry. After speaking with her he phoned Ted.

"Ted, when I was in London this morning I was followed by two black men. I am positive they were following me but don't know why."

"Must be something to do with those items you told me about. I did warn you to take care," Ted said, careful not to use the word 'diamonds' over the phone.

"That's what I thought too. Can you check on Maria and make sure there isn't anyone watching the house? I am a bit worried about her."

"Of course I will. I'll give you a buzz if there is a problem over here. Do you want me to get Maria to come and stay with us?"

"Yes I would be a lot happier if she was with you; that is if you can persuade her. Thanks Ted."

"Good. You take care over there." Ted hung up.

Tom relaxed knowing that Maria was safe. He knew Ted would take care of her. Perhaps it was his imagination and the two men were not following him after all

Over breakfast the next morning, Tom gave the reporter a full account of what he gathered was going on at the Marange diamond fields in Zimbabwe and of Van Zyl's involvement. He handed over all the photos Tombi had taken at the mines, and Bruce assured him that he would keep Tom's name out of everything, and would not disclose his source or how he had managed to get hold of the pictures. The information Tom gave him would be very useful.

It turned out he had done some digging himself and already knew a lot about Van Zyl. He was also working with representatives of the Kimberly Process, an organisation that monitored and controlled all the diamonds sales around the world. Tom agreed to email him with any other information that came to light; apart from that he had no intention of getting further involved. He was not prepared to risk having his family exposed to any retaliation from Van Zyl or anyone in Zimbabwe as it was it seemed he was already being watched.

It was a relief to hand the whole 'dirty business' over and to be able to wash his hands of it. He would pull Tombi out of Marange as soon as he was back in Zimbabwe.

．．．．．．．．．．．．．．

Van Zyl was furious. He had just put down the phone after speaking to one of his men in the London office.

"Barney you had better get your arse up here right now," he shouted down the phone. Barnard was up from the Lowveld to deliver a handful of diamonds from Marange to Van Zyl and was staying in the cottage. He made the trip from Mabiti every month, stopping en route to collect the package from Van Zyl's supplier at Birchenough Bridge. This monthly trip also gave him the opportunity to collect supplies and meet buyers for his meat and skins from his hunting operations.

"What's the problem Jannie?" Barnard asked rushing into Van Zyl's office.

"Those incompetent bastards you have tailing Owen have gone and lost him in London. Surely he doesn't know he's being followed."

"They are the two best men for the job we have," Barnard assured his boss. "Owen won't know they are tailing him."

"Well they are just not good enough. They phoned half an hour ago to tell me that Owen had given them the slip. They have been to his hotel and he has booked out and disappeared. Now we don't even know what he was doing in London. He wasn't there for a holiday that's for sure."

"Then he must know he is being followed; or he might even have recognised them," Barnard concluded. "They have been keeping an eye on him for some months in Harare."

"No. They must have just been frigging careless. Probably walking around with their god-dam mouths wide open looking for white girls to shag instead of watching him. I didn't pay for their air tickets and fancy hotel accommodation just for them to have a holiday in London," Van Zyl ranted. "There's bugger all we can do about it now. I've told those two incompetent fools to get their arses back here ASAP. I think they had better go and work for you at Mabiti for a while. If Owen knows we are following him, he will be extra careful and we will never know what he is up to. You had better get someone to wait at the airport and see what he does when he gets back into the country. Let's hope he's not on to us."

"Okay I will see to it before I go back to Mabiti."

"Just make bloody sure they don't lose him here; at least we know where he lives. If necessary they must 'camp' outside his bloody house."

. . . .

Apart from meeting up with the reporter, the main reason for Tom's trip to England was to attend the annual Southampton Boat Show. He was meeting representatives of fishing clubs from America and Ireland there, to try and get sponsorship for their fishing venture.

With the Boat Show only due to start in a few days time, and no other appointments, Tom decided to go to Dorset to spend the time with his son Stuart and his family. They had recently moved from Canada to the UK when Stuart had been transferred by his company. He was looking forward to seeing them all. Tom wanted to put them in the picture about the fishing business, and to find out if Felicity was interested in running a booking office for them from home.

Leaving Dorking Tom travelled to Dorset where he spent a lovely couple of days with his family. The sun never came out and it rained most of the time, with a cold wind blowing from the west, and so they were restricted in their movements and spent most of the time indoors. Stuart and Felicity were excited about 'Santo Deep-Sea Fishing', and offered to be the agents in the UK.

But then it was back to business. Tom caught the train to Southampton to attend the annual boat show. He also wanted to have a good look at the latest technology in the boating world; navigation aids, fish finders and any other new innovations which might make the fishing charters efficient, and help them to satisfy the needs of their clients.

Unaccustomed to the magnitude of things in England, he was surprised at the size of the show and by the huge number of boats on display. There were yachts, ribs, luxury high-speed cruisers, open boats, fishing boats, skiing boats, jet-skis; the list was endless. They were all new with their fittings and paintwork gleaming brightly in spite of the usual dull overcast day that was part of England.

It was the first day of the show and already there was a huge crowd wandering around looking at the boats, going for boat rides, sitting in the refreshment areas and generally enjoying themselves. Tom still struggled to come to terms with the number of people crammed into the UK and had to push his way through the crowds to the stands he wanted to visit.

Tom had arranged to meet his American contacts later in the day, and so he had time to look at equipment and boats. He was taken on a short trip, in an offshore fishing boat, into deep water for a demonstration of the latest in navigation and fishing aids. He was amazed at the advancement that had been made in a few short years in the technology of on-board weather stations and fish finders. However, although only slightly behind the times, most things were available in South Africa.

After a bite to eat at one of the many food stalls, Tom set off to find the fishing equipment stand where he was to meet with the two Americans. Larry Mize from Miami and Pete Lund from Tampa Bay were already there waiting for him.

Seamus Maloney, the Irishman, never turned up but sent a message of apology with Pete; they were well acquainted. Larry was slim and of medium height, while Pete on the other hand, was a bull of a man well over six feet tall with broad shoulders. Both men were tanned and looked very healthy compared to all the pale English people in the crowds. They were both easy, cheerful, outdoor types who Tom took an instant liking to.

The three of them spent most of the afternoon discussing Tom's proposals for deep-sea fishing charters off Mozambique. He showed them the photographs he had taken and a short video clip of their set-up on Inhaca. In turn Tom listened and took notes of their suggestions and requirements.

It was obvious that American fishermen were prepared to pay top dollar, but in return demanded good service. Larry and Pete, both having been involved with fishing charters for a number of years, knew what they were talking about and Tom got the feeling that they would be very helpful.

By the end of the day both Larry and Pete had been won over, and agreed to help promote *Santo Deep-Sea Fishing* in America; providing they were happy with the fishing and the service. They both wanted to go to Mozambique for a trial charter, and were prepared to pay the full going fee. Before parting with Larry and Pete, they agreed on a date in the middle of March the following year for their charter. It was late September, and so they had nearly six months to get ready for the trial run.

This was far more than Tom had ever expected. He was ecstatic and could not wait to get back home to share the good news and celebrate with the rest of the team. Tom's share of the money from the sale of Tombi's diamonds in Johannesburg, was more than enough to kick-start their charter business; with some to spare. It was all working out very well. Two days later Tom landed in Harare and was met by a jubilant Maria. At last things were starting to look up again.

There was a message in Tom's email from Bruce Manning - the diamond problems were being taken care of by the Kimberly Process. It was pointless and would serve no purpose by snooping around the Hot Springs and Marange area any longer. It was out of their hands now. Tombi had done her job and it would be foolish to expose her any longer. Kyle had to get her away from the mines, Van Zyl and Barnard as soon as he could; she might be in grave danger.

With this in mind Tom decided that it would be wise to sell the rest of Tombi's little hoard of stones as quickly as possible; before she was caught in possession of them.

Chapter 10

Delighted with the early stages and positive response to their proposed deep-sea fishing business, Tom and Sandy decided it was time to test the fishing grounds. Both of them were experienced ski-boat fishermen having fished off the Zululand coast for a number of years, but neither of them had fished for some time and were out of practice. Now they needed to get back into it, and get to know the waters in the Mozambique Channel off Inhaca.

The only time of year they might experience problems with the weather was from November to March, when it was the cyclone season. Although cyclones along the Mozambique coast were few and far between, they could be devastating. To fill gaps at that time of year they would have to consider operating close in-shore taking divers out to explore the reefs.

Kyle and Rosa, seeing the potential, were very keen to get involved. Tom and Sandy proposed that they run a second camp further up the coast - and so they applied for second piece of land near Inhambane. It would take a while before they hoped to be busy enough to run two fishing camps, but by that time Kyle, who still had a year to complete his contract, would be ready to join them permanently; if it all went to plan. In the meantime they would all operate from Inhaca.

Both Tom and Maria, although not old by any means, were getting on in years and were keen to have Kyle and Rosa join their venture, providing it had the potential to expand. Having younger blood was a good idea.

The second boat was nearing completion and Len, an old friend and competent skipper, who managed a cane farm near Empangeni, offered to monitor the construction of the catamaran. When the boat was ready for sea trials, Tom asked him to accompany the boat builders when they tested it out in the water.

Maria chose the name *Pelé-Pelé* for their new boat. She explained that as it was going to be a good boat and the name, roughly translated from Portuguese meaning 'hot stuff', would be appropriate. *Pelé-Pelé* was a twin hulled fibreglass catamaran. She was 20 foot long with a beam of 8 foot. Twin 200 hp Yamaha outboard motors were being fitted. They

74

had chosen to have a catamaran built as opposed to a mono-hull boat because it was wider and provided a larger deck area. Catamarans were also renowned for their stability when launching off the beach and going through the surf.

"Tom, *Pelé-Pelé* is ready for you. I went out with the guys from Boat-Craft yesterday and she handles very well. They are just putting a few finishing touches to her," Len said over the phone.

"That's marvellous Len. Thanks very much for your help. How are you placed? Will you be able to take a bit of time off work in the next couple of weeks?" Tom asked.

"I was rather hoping you were going to ask me that. Yes I can take the whole of next week off. There is nothing much happening on the farm and the mill has closed for the season," Len replied eagerly. "My supervisor can easily cope."

"Good. I will fly down with Maria, Kyle and Rosa at the week-end. If you like, you and Kyle can sail *Pelé-Pelé* to Inhaca; unless of course you would prefer to fly the plane."

"No, no. I would love to go with Kyle," Len said quickly. "Has he got his Skippers Ticket?"

"Yes, he got it a few years ago. Okay Len, that's brilliant. Will you be able to pick us up at Richards Bay airport?"

"Sure thing. I'll see you there at about twelve on Friday."

· · · · · · · · · · · · · ·

After meeting them at the airport Len, who fished most week-ends, took them to the fishing tackle shop where he helped them select the latest and most suitable equipment. They did have some gear onboard *Tigger*, but would need for both boats.

They bought rods, reels, line, lures, hooks, gaffs, landing nets and one or two other bits and pieces. The smaller items they loaded into the Cessna, and the rods and bigger pieces they took down to the bay where *Pelé-Pelé* was moored.

It was the first time Tom and Maria had seen their newly completed boat and were delighted with what they saw. Unlike *Tigger*, *Pelé-Pelé* did not have a cabin and was a lot shorter, but she had just as much deck space. There were two swivel seats with back-rests mounted up front where the helm, controls and instruments were protected from the flying spray behind a windscreen. Two chrome handrails and rod-holders had been fitted on the gunwales down either side of the deck.

Bow-rails curved around the two pontoons on the bow-deck and a fighting chair had been bolted onto the re-enforced deck near the engines.

Her name, *Pelé-Pelé*, was painted on the yellow and orange sides. The bow deck was white and the main was covered with brown weatherproof carpeting. There was a diving platform between the two outboard motors at the stern. She looked magnificent.

Leaving Kyle and Len to prepare for their trip, Tom, Maria and Rosa flew to Inhaca. It was the first time Rosa had been there and so, after a cool beer, the three of them strolled down to the jetty, where *Tigger* rocked gently at her moorings. The girls clambered on board, Tom fired up the motors, untied her mooring ropes, and with the engine growling eased away from the jetty.

"What a beautiful boat. Don't tell me this is the same one you found in the shed when you came down last year?" Rosa had only seen photographs of *Tigger,* and was suitable impressed.

"Yes, it's the same boat alright. I could hardly believe it myself when Tom and Sandy arrived in her from Richards Bay," Maria said. "Isn't she just beautiful?"

Tom opened the throttles and let her run fast to the south end of the island. After about two miles he brought her about in a wide sweeping circle then stopped opposite the camp. Maria pointed out the big fig tree on top of the ridge to Rosa. One of the huts was visible though a gap in the bushes. Satisfied that everything on the boat was functioning properly, Tom took them back to the jetty.

In the morning they walked along the beach to the camp. They had been away from Inhaca for two months and were pleasantly surprised to find the camp in such good order. Tomasi had planted a small vegetable patch beyond the clearing, and there were carrots, cabbages and a few tomato bushes growing. An extra layer of thatch had been added to all the huts and a low latticed fence had been pegged in around the perimeter of the camp-site. There were even a couple of hens clucking away in an enclosure off to one side.

The area under the tree was swept clean and the tanks topped up with fresh water. Tomasi had cut away a few branches of bushes to open up the view from the camp and Maputo was just visible on the horizon 30 kilometers away.

"No wonder Kyle has been raving about this place. Maria it's fantastic," Rosa exclaimed.

"Yes isn't it just perfect. I could easily spend the rest of my days here," Maria agreed enthusiastically.

"I suppose you will have to fly most of your supplies in from Swaziland or South Africa. I hear Maputo is very expensive and has limited stocks of most things," Rosa said. "You've certainly got yourselves very well organised."

"That reminds me," Tom said. "We'll have to send old Tomasi to Maputo on the ferry to get some mealie-meal and other basics he needs - he knows what he wants and where to get it. Besides I'm sure he would like a couple of days off," he continued as he wandered around examining the huts and all the work Tomasi had done during their absence.

Tom went off on the quad with trailer to collect their gear from the plane then, to pass time while they waited for Kyle and Len to arrive, they spent the rest of the day winding line onto reels; making up steel traces and organising tackle boxes for both boats. In the afternoon, with *Pelé-Pelé* only expected much later, the three of them strolled back to the lodge.

"Tom, you've made the trip before. What time do you think the boys will arrive?" Maria asked, getting a little anxious.

"Well it really depends on what time they left Richards Bay this morning. If they got away late they might be forced to spend the night on the beach somewhere," Tom said. "It's a good eighteen hour trip and even in good weather it's not an easy trip."

"But they didn't take anything to keep warm. Knowing those two they probably only took beer and a few sandwiches," Rosa decided.

"Neither of them has made the trip before. If they left at the same time as we did, when we brought *Tigger* up, they should have arrived by now. The conditions are good and the sea is calm. *Pelé-Pelé* is every bit as fast as *Tigger*, but don't forget they are in an open boat so it won't be quite as comfortable. Anyway if it gets too late they can always beach somewhere - they have space blankets on board with the safety equipment. I don't think there is any need to panic. I'm sure they will be here sometime in the morning," Tom tried to reassure the two women; neither looked too convinced.

In the morning, after a restless night and an early breakfast, they went down to *Tigger*, slipped her mooring and headed out to sea. They were going to look for Kyle and Len. Two miles out, just as they reached the point off Elephant Island, much to the relief of Maria and

Rosa, they saw *Pelé-Pelé* come flying around the headland. Tom swung *Tigger* around to lead the other boat back to the jetty.

"What happened to you guys?" Maria demanded. "You should have been here yesterday afternoon. We were worried sick."

"Sorry Mum. We got away a bit later than we intended. The night porter at the hotel was asleep and forgot to wake us up. We only left Richards Bay at six. Eventually it got too late to carry on and so we stopped in at Ponta da Ouro for some prawns and Manica beer," Kyle grinned at his mother then turned to hug his wife.

"Did you have any problems on the way?" asked Tom, also relieved.

"None at all; apart from running out of grub and beer before we even got to Soddies," Len said. "She's as steady as a rock. Runs like a dream and rides the sea beautifully," he added patting *Pelé-Pelé* on the bows.

"Good. Now get yourselves off and have a nice hot shower and some breakfast. We'll see you in camp once you're refreshed. The walk along the beach will do your sea-legs some good," Tom smiled.

By the time Kyle and Len had finished giving a full account of their trip, and their evening at Ponta da Ouro, there wasn't much time left for fishing. When they got back to the lodge later in the day Sandy was there. He had come in on the ferry from the mainland, and was waiting for them in the bar.

By seven the next morning both boats, with their crews, were in the Mozambique Channel and they had started fishing. Over the next three days they had a certain amount of luck. The best specimens they caught were photographed before being tagged and released back into the sea.

They caught two 20 kilogram dorado, whose colours in the water were amazing, a good sized king-fish and ten shoal size barracuda, two of which they kept for their own consumption. On the third day Len landed a beautiful sailfish. It gave him a good fight, flying right out of the water three or four times displaying its magnificent sail, before giving up the battle after 20 minutes. The whole fight was recorded on camera. The sailfish weighed in at 35 kilograms - a good specimen for the brochure and website!

It was a good start. With shots of the hotel, the island and the camp, they had enough material to make a respectable brochure and a short movie on UTube. The hotel manager agreed to give them a reasonable discount on all their bookings. The cost of accommodation was to be included in the charter fees.

At the end of the week Tom took Len back to Zululand then flew on to Zimbabwe to take Kyle and Rosa home. Sandy went to Swaziland to prepare the brochure and have it printed. He emailed copies to Larry Mize and Pete Lund in Florida and a week later received replies from them confirming their arrival date and flight number. They still had three months to complete preparations.

Chapter 11

A month later Sandy, who was in Swaziland handing the bulk of his business over to his new partner, called with more news. Because the Mozambique Government were keen to promote tourism, the plot of land they had applied for near Inhambane had been granted to them. It was 10 kilometers south of the bay of Inhambane Bay and 430 kilometers north of Maputo. Sandy had been there to select a site before they applied, but Tom had not seen it. Great excitement!

And so, with time to spare, they decided to go and set up a temporary camp on their new site. Kyle and Rosa came down from Zimbabwe and Len came up from Empangeni. Leaving Maria and Rosa on Inhaca, the three men set off for Inhambane. At Clube Navale they pulled *Pelé-Pelé* out of the water and loaded her onto the trailer Len had brought with him.

It was midday by the time they left Maputo, hauling the boat behind them. The road although tarred, was in poor condition with potholes everywhere, and so it took the rest of the day to reach Inharrime, where they stopped for the night.

In the morning, after a good Portuguese style breakfast, they moved on. An hour later turned onto a dirt road leading to Ingale. Because of the heavy sand and corrugations on the road, the 20 kilometers from the turnoff to the camp site took another hour. Tom went off to report to the camp supervisor, who showed him to their site, while Kyle and Len launched the boat.

Set among tall coco-nut palms, cashew nut trees and mangroves, their plot of land was about 2 acres in size. Tom was delighted with Sandy's choice. It was perfect. Standing in the middle of their plot Tom could look onto the beach and the sea where Kyle and Len were busy launching *Pelé-Pelé*.

A natural breakwater sheltered the small bay where they could easily launch from the beach and get out to sea. As soon as the boat was pulled up on the beach on front of their site, the three of them set about pitching tents and getting organised. While they were busy, one of the local fishermen arrived to help - his name was Emanuel and he spoke a little English.

The tarred airstrip outside Inhambane was only 15 kilometers from Ingale, and there were a number of private chalets close by which they could hire. These could be used by diving clients. Overseas clients would be accommodated in the Lodge, near Inhambane, where all their needs could be better catered for. They spent a few days setting up Ingale camp, and exploring the area within easy reach.

At first light, three days after arriving, Tom, Kyle and Len pushed *Pelé-Pelé* off the beach and they set off north up the coast. They were going to test the waters further north, off the entrance to the bay at Inhambane, where it was said the fishing was excellent. The Mozambique coast bulged out into the Indian Ocean at that point, and the fish-rich Mozambique Channel was close to shore.

Half way to Inhambane they decided to investigate a small lagoon behind a narrow rocky spit of land, protected by a reef at the north end, and jagged rocks that stuck up out of the sea at the southern entrance. It was similar to the bay at their camp in that it too was protected by a rocky reef.

They slowed down to enter the lagoon from the south, where there was a gap in the rocky barrier, and the channel was quite deep. The lagoon, 300 metres long and about 100 wide, was well protected with calm water and would be a good place to catch reef fish, live bait and crayfish. They made their way to the north of the lagoon where the reef had a narrow channel leading back out to the open sea.

While they were still feeling their way carefully through the channel, with the sun just clearing the horizon, a thick blanket of fog rolled quickly and unexpectedly off the land, reducing their visibility to a few meters. Len climbed over the windshield onto the bows to help guide Tom through the channel and over the reef.

The big Yamaha outboard motors ticked over quietly, slowly pushing the boat forward. The tide was going out and they could see the reef a few inches below the keel of the catamaran; all attention was focused on the reef below as they glided over it's jagged teeth into deeper water.

Suddenly, in a loud whisper, Len told Tom to stop. Fearing they were about to hit the reef, he quickly threw the motors into neutral to stop the forward momentum of the boat. They waited, drifting in the calm waters, far too close for comfort from the small rocky island. A few moments later the instruments showed that they were over the reef and gliding into deeper water. The depth was down to 3 meters and dropping off steeply. There was no indication of another reef, only open water lay ahead; and thick fog.

"What's it Len. Is there something in the water?" Tom kept his voice down.

"No, but I think there is something up ahead. I'm sure I heard voices," Len spoke quietly. "We don't want to ram into another boat in this pea-soup."

"It's a pity about the bloody fog. The weather report last night certainly didn't predict it; must be just localised," observed Tom keeping his eyes on Len in the bows.

"Well, we're in no hurry, unless the weather turns really foul on us and we have to dash back to camp," Kyle added. "I'm sure it'll clear away soon. Surely this is just an early morning land mist."

"I certainly hope so. We're still about 4 kilometers from Miramar and the entrance to Inhambane Bay," Tom said glancing down at the SatNav.

Just then Len turned around, and with his index finger raised to his lips, signalled for them to keep quiet, indicating that he had again heard something. It was quiet and damp in the early morning light, with the sun trying to break through the mist. The only sounds were the quiet murmuring of the motors, and the soft slapping of small waves against the sides of the gently rocking catamaran. The minutes ticked by while they waited and listened.

Then they heard voices, coming faintly through the mist from somewhere ahead of them. The voices were accompanied by the occasional thump and clang of metal on metal. The sounds carried over the water were muffled by the mist and indistinct, but the voices sounded Portuguese. By the tone, there seemed to be some sort of urgency, with orders being shouted out.

"Where are those voices coming from? Surely we are too far from shore to hear people talking on land, and there are no huts or houses near here," Tom whispered.

"Well I didn't see any boats out at sea when we entered the bay. Mark you, we were all looking forward at the time, so we might not have seen a boat passing behind us," Kyle said quietly. Turning to Tom he asked. "Why are we whispering?"

"Don't know," Tom said shrugging his shoulders and cocking his head in Len's direction. "There's another bay with deep water round a small headland just ahead. It was hidden from sight by the sand dunes when we entered the lagoon. There might be something in there we would not have been able to see earlier," Tom said studying the screen on the SatNav.

Len signalled for Tom to move on and steer east, a course that would take them away from whatever it was directly in front of them. They moved forward slowly, peering through the thick mist. A few minutes later it began to clear and the shape of a large blue fishing trawler loomed up out of the gloom directly in front of them. Although visibility was still reduced, it was only about 50 meters away and quite easy to see. There was something sinister and eerie about the ship wallowing in the sea, half hidden in the mist, and close enough that is seemed to tower above them.

They were in deep water; the fish-finder now showed a depth of 10 meters, but it was still strange to find such a large trawler so close inshore, only about 200 meters from the beach. Normally a ship that size would never venture inside territorial fishing waters, and did not come much closer than a kilometre from shore; unless it had engine trouble.

It was stern-on to them, and on the port-side of the trawler they could clearly see a long open boat tied up alongside. Three men on the boat were busy transferring wooden crates onto the trawler. The crew of both boats were so pre-occupied with their task that they didn't seem to notice *Pelé-Pelé* creeping slowly past behind them. Tom, not wanting to attract their attention, kept the motors ticking along quietly and they moved further away out of sight, back into the mist.

As they sailed further out to sea and into deep water, the swell got steeper in spite of the sea being calm with no wind. As soon as they were far enough from the trawler not to be heard, Len climbed back over the windscreen, and Tom eased the throttles forward to increase their speed. He altered course to the north, and half a mile further he slowed down and stopped.

"Len, why did we have to keep so quiet back there?" Kyle was curious.

"Just a hunch I guess. It seemed strange for a ship to be so close to shore at this time of the morning," Len said defensively.

"I agree. There does seem to be something suspicious about it. I think we should just hang around here for a while until the mist clears completely. It will be interesting to know what those fellows are up to," Tom said cutting the motors.

With the sea-anchor out, and the boat drifting slowly with the current, the three of them baited up with sardines, put their lines in the water and placed their rods in the rod holders on the gunnels.

"I wonder what they were transferring from the boat onto the trawler. By the way they were handling them, it looked like those crates were full of something fairly heavy," Tom said settling back onto his seat.

"Yeah, pretty bulky stuff too judging by the size of the crates. Must be coconuts or even dried fish," Len guessed. "They were using the ship's hoist to take them on board."

"Well, why load out here at sea? Why not load in port or in a bay at one of the coastal towns. Inhambane is just around the corner from here," Kyle pointed out. "Seems a bit suspicious."

"No I don't think it was fish or coconuts; those they would have loaded from junks at the entrance to the main bay," Tom decided.

"They must have arranged to meet the trawler here. Unless of course they have portable radios," Len suggested

"Perhaps it's too shallow for the trawler to enter Inhambane Bay. There is deep water where they are right now; that might be why they have rendezvoused there. As you say Len, they must have radios, unless it is all been pre-arranged," Tom agreed. "In any case I agree with Kyle; it looks a bit fishy to me."

"If it is not a Mozambique registered trawler but a foreign one, then it should not be so close to shore. Surely they are not allowed to fish in these waters?" Kyle asked.

"I would have thought so. I'm convinced they're up to something illegal. You never know what goes on in these third world countries nowadays. It's pretty deserted around here, apart from the occasional hut. Anyway they're certainly not fishing now," Tom said stating the obvious. "I think we must just stick around here for a while and see what happens next. We can try to find out where the long boat comes from - they might even lead us to some decent fishing grounds."

"I agree with you Tom. Maybe we'll get a bite or two while we wait," Len said always keen to land a fish at the slightest chance.

"I have a nasty suspicion they were loading something far more valuable than just coconuts or dried fish. Otherwise they would not be doing so out here, out of sight of the authorities. We all know there are a lot of elephant tusks and rhino horn being smuggled out of this part of the world. Rhino horn is more valuable these days than gold," Tom pointed out.

"I'm all for seeing what they are up to. But they mustn't think we're watching them. If they are involved in the smuggling, it means that there is a lot of money involved, with some pretty powerful and ruthless people behind them," Kyle warned.

"They might even have a permit or permission to do whatever it is they are doing," Len added.

While they waited for the mist to clear, bobbing up and down in the swell. Len landed a small Bonita that he put in the live bait hatch, to be used as bait later on in the day.

They had only been fishing a few minutes, when the mist cleared away as quickly as it had rolled in, and they could see the trawler quite clearly. It looked like most other fishing trawlers; painted a dull rusty dark blue colour with a dirty cream bridge. From where they were it seemed to be about 50 meters long and was lying about half way between *Pelé-Pelé* and the white sands of the shoreline. As they watched, the dark blue long-boat pulled away from the side of the trawler, and sped off up the coast. It was moving very fast, not far off-shore and just behind the back line of the waves.

"Okay they're on the move. Kyle, pull in the sea anchor. Quick, let's get our lines in, we don't want to lose them now," Tom said, firing up the motors and moving forward as soon as the anchor was on board.

"That boat looks just like the ones used by the Somali pirates; a long-boat with a high prow and very powerful motor," Kyle said stowing the anchor.

"Don't get too close to them otherwise they'll know we're following them and things might turn nasty," Len advised, putting the rods back into the rod holders.

"No, we sure as hell don't want to spook them, or let them think we're following to see where they come from," Tom agreed.

"Look there behind us. The trawler is under way and heading out to sea in a north-easterly direction," Len said pointing to the trawler behind them. It was picking up speed, and judging by the bow wave and prop-wash behind, was in a hurry to get back to the safety of international waters.

"Surely they must have seen us by now. Let's hope they take us for what we are; deep-sea fishermen out fishing for the day," Tom said turning his attention back to the speeding boat making its way up the coast. He kept his distance further out to sea as they followed. With *Pelé-Pelé's* two big outboard motors pushing her along, keeping up was easy.

Three miles further up the coast, the long-boat rounded the headland at Miramar, and sped away into Inhambane Bay. Tom also changed course and chased after them. Without slowing down, the boat in front of them turned to starboard and made off in the direction of Morrumbene and disappeared around the first bend, where the mangrove trees hid it from sight.

"Well, there they go. There's no point in following them any further. At least we know they come from somewhere in there. Let's go back and try to get the name of that trawler, and where it's registered, then we can have it checked out," Tom said swinging *Pelé-Pelé* around and heading back out to sea. Once out of the bay he set a course south-west, which would bring them close to the approaching trawler.

"How are we going to get close enough to get the name without raising suspicion?" Kyle asked.

"We'll put our lines out and troll past them. This is where we were heading in any case, so we'll still be doing what we set out to do, without wasting any more time," Tom said. "We do also have binoculars," he added as an afterthought.

Tom slowed down well ahead of the trawler. They put lures on their lines and began to troll along slowly, heading almost directly across the path of the oncoming trawler. Their course would bring them close enough to be able to read the name and registration details of the ship, without getting near its long lines; if they had them out.

Ten minutes later as the two boats crossed, both crews waved to each other innocently, while Len made a note of the name of the ship and the registration details painted on the stern. '*Verona*'- registered in Singapore. She had long lines out as she steamed north-east away from the coast. Kyle sent a text message to Sandy. He would let the port authorities know about the trawler when he was in Maputo later in the week.

The rest of the morning was spent trolling up and down the coast north of their camp. They had a certain amount of success catching barracuda, bonito and wahoo.

"Well I don't know what you guys think, but I reckon we had a pretty good day; with a bit of excitement. The fishing seems to be good here," Tom said enthusiastically when they were back in camp.

"I think so too. The Mozambique Channel is not far out which means we can get to the fishing grounds quickly," Kyle agreed.

"We'll set up a permanent camp here like the one on Inhaca. If the fishing is not good down there, we can always fly the clients up here and you guys can handle them," Tom decided.

"Ja. That won't be a problem. We can even offer them a choice if they like," Len suggested.

"Len, I still want to know what made you so suspicious of that trawler this morning." Tom was curious.

"I don't know," Len said shrugging his shoulders. "Let's have a beer."

"Well we'll have to wait and see what the port authorities have to say about it," Kyle said turning his attention to the cold box and handing them each a bottle of ice-cold Manica beer.

Chapter 12

Since the army had taken control of the diamond mining at Marange, fencing it off and putting a cordon around the whole area to tighten up the security, Van Zyl no longer went there. Instead he used an inside man or *gweja* (diamond panner) who still managed to get diamonds for him. Because he did not want to risk losing the protection of his contacts in high places, or come under any sort of investigation by the C.I.O., he sent Barnard to collect the stones from his contact.

Every few months Barnard would meet up with the *gweja* at Birchenough Bridge. Before delivering the diamonds to Van Zyl, he always took one or two for himself which he hid away. He could sell them when he went to South Africa. He considered this his bonus; after all he was the one taking all the risk!

After collecting a consignment and needing supplies, Barnard drove to Harare. He needed salt for curing the skins, ammunition for the hunting operation, maize meal for rations and one or two other things including supplies for the camp. He stayed in the guest cottage at Van Zyl's mansion outside Harare. Apart from doing his shopping in the city, he spent most of the time in meetings.

Barnard got the distinct feeling that Van Zyl was not happy with him. Although Van Zyl, like Barnard, had never been a friendly person, this time he was unusually aggressive and rude; something was bothering him. Barnard could only put it down to the feeling he had that Van Zyl suspected him of taking advantage of their relationship in some way. This made him extremely nervous.

"Hey Barney, what the bloody hell is the matter with you? You walk around here all day with a long face like a dog that's been kicked. It there something you're not telling me? Is everything alright at Mabiti?" Van Zyl asked him. "Or is because that black bitch has not allowed you to get into her pants yet?"

"Ja Jannie. Everything is fine. I am just having a problem crossing the Limpopo into the Game Park. The river is up and we have to stay on our side," Barnard explained making a lame excuse, ignoring the reference to his taste in women.

"Since when has something like that worried you? You still have plenty of game in Zimbabwe and in Mozambique," Van Zyl said. "Don't worry about going in to South Africa for now."

"Ja, that's true. But we need to get as much rhino horn out of the South African Parks as we can before they are on to us. The longer we leave dead carcasses lying around, the more likely we are to get caught. There are very few rhino in Mozambique."

"I see what you mean. Just be bloody careful next time you go in. Get your helicopter down to Mabiti and use it to scout carefully before the rest of the team move over the river. You should be able to get across in the next couple of weeks," Van Zyl conceded. "I agree, we must get as much rhino horn as quickly as we can. The price is good and those Chinese I am dealing with are paying big bucks – more than for gold."

"I won't let you down Jannie," Barnard snivelled wiping his moustache. "I'll be heading off in the morning."

As he got up to leave the office, the radio crackled. It was Petros, the foreman at Mabiti. A messenger from Mozambique was there. Apparently after delivering the last consignment of crates to the trawler a few days ago, the crew of the longboat thought they might have been followed.

"Barney you must check this out; and bloody fast. Before we send the next load we must be absolutely sure it's safe, and that our shed is secure. Take the Beech-craft and fly down there right now," Van Zyl ordered. "We don't want the bloody Mozambique authorities getting wind of what we're up to."

Three hours later Barnard landed at Inhambane and took a water taxi across the bay to the shed. The longboat was pulled up on the bank and tucked away out of sight under the mangrove trees. Two of the men were sitting on logs outside the shed making chairs. The shed was set well back from the dirt road leading down to the beach and could not easily be seen. When Barnard arrived, Antonio, the man in charge of their operations, appeared from a hut alongside the shed.

"Bom dia," he greeted Barnard in Portuguese.

"Bom dia, Antonio," Barnard replied. "Why did you send me a message? What has been happening here? Is everything okay?" he asked in English.

"There is no problem Senhor," Antonio said. "I sent a message to warn you that someone might be watching us. We saw a boat following us after we loaded the crates onto the ship last week."

"Okay Antonio, we must be very careful. There is another load coming soon and you must not get caught with it. When you meet the ship you will have to make sure there are no other boats around."

"The last time there were no boats. But then the mist came out of the swamps and we could not see. When the mist cleared away we saw another boat not far from us. It followed us all the way to the bay. It was a fishing boat with three men in it."

"Did they see you coming here to the shed?" Barnard asked anxiously.

"No. It did not come into the bay. It turned around and went back out to sea. We waited a bit and then went back to see what it was doing. They were fishing and moving slowly south. We followed, keeping close to the shore and a long way back, to where they beached their boat. Then I walked along the beach and found where they have their camp. It is at Ingale." Antonio said pleased with himself.

"Are you sure they did not see you following them?"

"We were low in the water and moved slowly. They did not see us."

"Perhaps - but we must not take any chances. You were wise to warn me of this. Now you must take me to their camp so that I can see who those men are, and where they come from. Come, we must go now in the boat," Barnard instructed.

An hour later, Antonio ran the long-boat up on the beach, half a kilometre north of Ingale. Leaving a man with the boat, he and Barnard walked south along the beach. When they were close to the camp they approached cautiously, taking care not to be spotted. Though the mangrove trees they saw three men sitting on deck chairs outside their tent drinking beer.

One of the men was Tom Owen; the man his men had been following and lost in London! Was it just a co-incidence that he was here or was he now following them? The other two men Barnard did not recognise. Silently signalling to Antonio they crept quietly away to the boat and went back to the shed.

"I know those men," Barnard told Antonio. "You must be very careful they don't find the shed."

"Are they policemen?" asked Antonio.

"No. But they will report us if they know what we are doing here. Have you still got enough wood for furniture?" Barnard asked when they were back in the bay.

"Only the few small pieces we are using ourselves. The rest has been sold to the people in Maputo."

"I will send more with the truck next time it comes," Barnard said. "Your messenger will tell you when to expect the next truck load of crates and wood. It will be in the next few months."

They discussed a plan of action; should anyone be found prying around the shed or asking questions. There was nothing more he could do, and it was too late to fly back, and so Barnard spent the night in a dingy pensaó (boarding house) in the company of a willing local girl. In the morning he flew back to Harare to report to Van Zyl.

"We must find out why Owen and his chums are fishing right where we ship our goods. I am sure it's more than just chance that they are there," Van Zyl said thoughtfully when he heard Barnard's account of his trip.

"I saw their camp. It's just a normal fishing camp. I don't think we have anything to worry about from them," Barnard tried to re-assure his boss.

"Maybe not, but we don't want that bloody lot interfering in our business. First we see them at the diamond fields, and now they are near the place where we move goods out of Africa," Van Zyl ranted. "It's too much of a coincidence. I am going to find out exactly what they are doing."

....

Barney Barnard had a growing suspicion that Tombi was snooping. He had seen her shuffling through his papers in the office when she was supposedly tidying up. Every day in her spare time, she was at the shed chatting with the skinners. Although there was nothing wrong with it, she seemed to spend more time with them than she should. He was aware that she had no boyfriends in camp and had even made it obvious that she had no interest in him when he tried to touch her. She claimed to be married. At times he noticed that she even seemed afraid of him, and was nervous around him. He decided to keep a close eye on her to see what she was up to; if anything.

It was Van Zyl who had employed Tombi and this made him suspicious. He was concerned that she might be spying for him. And so he summoned Petros, an ex-guerrilla who had been with him since the war. He told him of his suspicions, and that he wanted her watched. Petros told Barnard that he had heard her asking a lot of questions about their hunting operations. This news made Barnard relax slightly as it was his thieving of Van Zyl's diamonds that worried him most. But he was still not sure about her.

And so when Tombi asked for time off and a lift to Masvingo, Barnard readily agreed. He also took Petros along instructing him to follow her and see what she was up to. Petros lived in the same area as Tombi, and so he would not arouse her suspicions travelling with her on the same bus.

After leaving them to catch the bus in Masvingo, Barnard drove to Harare to make his monthly delivery. A week later he drove back to Mabiti, stopping in Masvingo to collect Tombi and Petros who were waiting there for him.

....

Tom and Maria were in Harare, packing to leave for Inhaca, when Kyle called.

"Dad, Tombi was here. She says there are funny things going on down at Mabiti. She needs someone to watch her back for her." Tom felt very uneasy with Tombi working for Barnard at Mabiti. He had not been pleased when she moved there from Hot Springs.

"What type of funny things Kyle?" Tom asked reluctant to get involved in another of Van Zyl's shady operations.

"She knows a lot of wild animals are being slaughtered; including elephant."

"What sort of help does she need?" Tom's interest piqued.

"She can't use her mobile phone; apparently there is no network signal at Mabiti. She needs someone who can relay her messages to us."

"Well Chikombedzi is not too far from there," Tom said thinking aloud. "We need one of our men to base up there, and meet up with Tombi once a week to get her news and to make sure she is alright."

"That's a good idea. What about your tracker Dodi? His talents are wasted working in your yard."

"What a good idea. He is bored and doesn't really enjoy working in Maria's garden - says it's women's work."

"Tombi is on her way home to see her family. She has to be back in Masvingo next week to get her lift to Mabiti."

"Okay I'll bring Dodi down to Masvingo and meet up with you and Tombi later this week. Will you be able to pick her up from her home en route?"

"That sounds good to me. I'll organise it all from my end." Kyle agreed.

A few days later, as arranged, Tom and Dodi met up with Kyle and Tombi in Masvingo. Dodi and Tombi knew each other from the time Tom had been in the Lowveld and they had both worked for him.

"Tombi, why are you doing this? You don't need the money - you are a rich woman, you do not have to work any more."

"When I moved to Mabiti I did not know that there was money. You had not sold the stones at that time. Now that I know what is happening there I must first find out what I can. I will hand in my notice at the end of the month," Tombi assured him.

"Good. You know I am not happy with you working for those men. But now you will have Dodi to help you which makes me feel better," Tom said. "What else is going on at Mabiti?"

"Last month there was a man from Mozambique who came to see Barnard. They say he is a fisherman there and also makes chairs," Tombi said after thinking for a while.

"If he is a fisherman, what was he doing there?"

"He works for Barnard. He came to select timber for his chairs. He also sells *tamboti* (a much valued hard wood used for furniture making) to others in Maputo."

"It is a very long road to travel to get wood. I wonder how he collects it."

"*Angazi.* I don't know. Perhaps he was there to collect his wages."

They were given their instructions, and money for Dodi to live on at Chikombedzi, and then left at the market, near the bus stop where Barnard had arranged to pick her up. Dodi took the bus to Chikombedzi.

. . . .

Petros reported to Barnard that he had seen Tombi leaving Birchenough Bridge with a farmer in a Land Cruiser. He gave him the registration number and Barnard asked Van Zyl to find out who the vehicle belonged to. It turned out to be registered to Kyle Owen – the son of the man they were watching, and the man he had seen in Mozambique two days previously; Tom Owen!

As Van Zyl had said, this was more than just a co-incidence. He had to keep a very close eye on Tombi; besides he also wanted her in his bed.

Chapter 13

As soon as Tombi was back in camp, she began her mission of finding out what was happening right under her nose. Although she knew Dodi was near at hand, she was still nervous and afraid of being caught, if she asked too many questions. So she was very careful who she spoke with.

She spent a lot of time at the abattoir listening to the skinners and butchers, trying to find out where the animals were being shot. She made friends with Sipho, the tracker, and tried to find out from him where they went hunting. But it was as if a door had been closed; they avoided her questions and would tell her nothing.

One week-end Barnard went away and came back a few days later towing a trailer with a small Robinson R-22 two-man helicopter. From then on when he went out hunting for longer than a day, he sent the hunting team ahead with the truck, then followed in the helicopter. Tombi knew these machines were used by game rangers in the National Parks when they darted sick animals so that they could be treated, or when they carried out game counts, and so she wondered what he was using it for.

Every week Tombi met up with Dodi at a pre-arranged spot close to the camp, to pass on any information she had managed to gather. He camped in the open near Chikombedzi and used the phone in the trading store to phone Kyle with his reports.

Tombi had known Dodi for many years but had never taken much notice of him. When they had both worked for the Owen family, he had worked out in the bush and she had worked in the house. Now the more time she spent with him and got to know him, the more she liked him. He was a quietly spoken, tall Ndebele man with a hard well muscled body, and obviously very fit. In spite of a slight squint he had a happy smiling face. He was always clean and dressed in well worn clothing; usually khaki shirt and shorts, and wore tyre soled sandals on his feet.

Then one day, as luck would have it, things turned in her favour. Tombi heard Barnard telling his foreman to find another tracker; one was not enough for all the work. When she met with Dodi that week she told him to try for the job; he was a good tracker and knew the area well having worked there tracking for Tom on many hunting trips. He also knew Sipho, the Mabiti tracker, who recommended him to Barnard. They had worked together on a number of hunts.

"How can you be the tracker you say you are when you have cross-eyes?" Barnard asked referring to Dodi's slight squint.

"I will show you that my cross-eyes see as well as yours," Dodi responded pulling his small throwing axe from the loop on his belt. He turned quickly and threw it at a mopani tree twenty paces away. The axe spun in the air several times before lodging firmly in the trunk of the tree.

"That is very good," Barnard said admiring Dodi's skill. "Can you do the same with that throwing spear you carry?"

"Yes. But with the spear I can kill an impala at thirty paces." Dodi boasted - this impressed Barnard.

"Good you can have the job. Go and report to Petros, my head-man. He will give you a place to stay and tell you what to do."

Before starting work at Mabiti, he went back to Chikombedzi to collect his blanket roll. While he was there he called Kyle to give him the news. Kyle was delighted but warned him to be very careful, explaining that Barnard was a dangerous man.

Tombi was far more relaxed having Dodi close at hand. She was able to let her guard down a little, and take part in some of the social activities that took place over week-ends when they were not all busy. She began to attend the beer-drinks and dancing with Dodi, but never partook of the drinking. Dodi on the other hand, loved showing off. He was a good dancer and amused them all when he emulated hunting chases; leaping up and down and stamping his feet on the ground as he danced around the fire. Sometimes Tombi even got up and joined in the dancing.

When the drink took effect, and the staff slightly inebriated, some of them tried to make advances towards her. She soon shunned them off by telling them she was married with children at home. It also loosened their tongues. Gradually they were accepted into the group and some of them, to match Dodi's stories, told of their hunting forays into neighbouring countries with Barnard; but only when Petros was not in their presence.

Together Tombi and Dodi began to gather some very interesting information. She heard that when they went away for three or four days at a time, it was because they were hunting in Mozambique or in South

Africa. She was amazed to hear that they were actually crossing international borders to poach elephant. This was almost unbelievable.

In the beginning Dodi was only used for tracking when the hunters were poaching in the Gona-re-Zhou Conservation Area, close to Mabiti. When Barnard received a message from one of the game guards that a herd of elephant was in the vicinity, he flew off in the helicopter with Petros to locate them.

Once the elephant herd had been found they returned to camp. The hunting team led by Barnard and Petros in the Land Cruiser, followed by the team of skinners in the truck, headed out from Mabiti in the truck. It never took more than an hour to get close to the area where the herd of elephant had been seen, browsing amongst the mopani scrub. The vehicles were parked and the two trackers sent off into the dense scrub to find the elephant with the best tusks.

Dodi climbed on top of a large ant heap; from there he could see over the top of the scrub and thorn bushes. He saw the grey humps of a herd of elephant wandering slowly and quietly from tree to tree feeding, only a short distance away. Selecting what looked like the biggest elephant, then after checking the direction of the wind, using a little ash from his ash bag; he climbed down from the ant heap and went to have a look at it.

Dodi circled around until he had the wind blowing towards him, then began to stalk up to the animal. When he had crept close to the unsuspecting elephant, and was near enough to see it properly, he squatted down on his haunches and leaning on his assegai, watched it feeding. It was a massive bull elephant with the most magnificent long curved ivory tusks.

As Dodi watched, it ripped branches off the mopani bushes with his trunk, and then stuffed it all into his mouth. Munching contentedly the bull moved on to the next tree. Using its tusks it ripped off strips of bark that he also transferred to his gaping mouth. Mopani leaves and bark are full of protein and are excellent food for elephants.

Although the elephant had long heavy tusks; exactly what Barnard was looking for, Dodi had no intention of allowing him to kill such a magnificent specimen. It was obviously the main bull in the herd. To have such a beast destroyed would certainly have a negative effect on the gene pool.

And so after enjoying watching for a little longer, Dodi went back to where Barnard waited, to report that the elephant he had seen had one tusk missing and was not suitable. By that time Sipho, the other tracker, had identified another elephant with good tusks.

Barnard and Petros, his gun bearer, followed Sipho to where the animal was browsing. They crept up as quietly and as close to the unsuspecting elephant as possible, until Barnard was in a position to shoot. It had to be shot in the heart; with the massive skull on an elephant a brain shot was difficult, but if he missed the heart the bullet would pierce the lungs and the elephant would trumpet loudly and charge off into the forest. This was when the trackers would have to prove their worth; tracking the wounded animal so that it could be killed. Barnard was a good hunter and dropped the elephant with a clean shot.

As soon as the elephant died and fell to the ground, the rest of the team moved in to hack the tusks out of the skull, taking care not to damage them. At times they had to chop deep into the skull to prize them out. While some of them were busy with the tusks, others removed some of the skin for making whips or *sjamboks*, the softer belly skin used for making purses, belts and handbags. The testicles, believed to have aphrodisiac properties, were cut off to be eaten and the scrotum dried and used as a receptacles. The feet were cut off to be used as umbrella stands and side tables, and bits of the intestines taken for use as medicine.

When they had removed everything they needed from the elephant and loaded it all onto the truck, they all went back to Mabiti, leaving the carcass to rot in the sun, and for the scavengers to find. It was a full day's work and they never had the time to kill more than one elephant a day.

Unless it was a necessary culling operation, killing elephant was never a pleasant thing to do. Dodi wondered how his father and grandfather before him had been able to stomach being trackers for the early elephant hunters. In those early days there were many elephant and a number of hunters. There were no controls and ivory was in demand and easy to sell.

Chapter 14

Once Dodi had proved his ability and skills as a tracker, and Barnard learned to trust him, he was included in the team that crossed into neighbouring countries via Crooks Corner. This was what Tombi and Dodi had hoped for if they were to find out exactly how Barnard's poaching operations worked. And so Dodi became a member of an international poaching gang.

The day before the hunting team set out, Barnard and Petros flew off in the helicopter to find the animals they were to hunt. Three hours later they returned and the team, with Petros in charge, was dispatched to camp on the banks of the Limpopo River for the night. At first light next morning they crossed the river where a layer of sheet rock made it relatively easy to drive across the wide, shallow, sandy river into South Africa.

It was still winter and freezing cold. With no rain in the catchment area, there was only a small amount of water flowing slowly downstream. While crossing the river Dodi noticed that the weavers had built their nests high in the trees along the banks. This was a sure sign that there would be heavy rains in summer and the river level would rise.

They entered the Game Park near Pufuri just as the sun was coming up. Driving slowly, to keep the dust down, and keeping well away from the main roads, they stopped after half an hour in a thicket of flat-crowned acacia thorn trees, to wait for Barnard. It was still early and the morning air was cool; the sun had not had time to warm the earth after the cold winter night.

A small herd of young female impala, alerted of their presence by a grey lourie or 'go-away' bird, stopped grazing and pranced away nervously towards the river for their early morning drink. A large Bateleur eagle, with its black and brown plumage, short tail and red face and legs, out to find an early meal, glided past a nearby koppie, screeching its cat-like call hoping to startle *dassies* (rock-rabbits) from their hiding places in amongst the rocks. Aside from the bird calls, and an occasional baboon barking, it was quiet and peaceful.

Everyone in the team was jittery and nervous and began to perspire from fear, while they waited talking quietly amongst themselves. They were all aware of the consequences of being arrested. They were Zimbabweans illegally in a Game Park in South Africa and if caught would certainly be locked up for a long time.

When Dodi heard they were hunting *umkhombe* (white rhino) he was shocked. He hated what he had become involved in, and was extremely nervous about being caught by the game rangers in the Park. But if this poaching was going to be stopped, he had to have as much information and evidence as he could get, and this was the only way. Although there was an agreement between Zimbabwe, Mozambique and South Africa allowing animals to migrate back and forth between the three countries; especially elephant. This did not include hunting or poaching!

The early morning stillness was suddenly shattered by the high pitched whine of the engine and the clatter of the helicopter blades announcing the arrival of Barnard; only a short time after Petros reported to him over the radio that they were in position. Leaving them to wait tensely, he took Petros and they flew away to locate the rhinos they had seen the previous day. Careful not to fly too high, Barnard criss-crossed the area, keeping a wary eye out signs of wardens and game guards; or even visitors to the Park who might see what they were up to, and report them to the officials.

As soon as they found the rhinos, and Barnard was satisfied it was safe to do so, he landed where the team waited, to give them their directions and instructions. Dodi noticed that the registration number of the helicopter was covered over with brown tape. He presumed this was to prevent anyone from identifying the owner.

The team of hunters, or poachers as they had now become, after being briefed by Barnard, set off in the open Land Cruiser. As they drove through the bush, they passed a large herd of wildebeest and zebra grazing in an open patch of buffalo grass. High in the sky vultures circled an old kill.

With Barnard and Petros guiding them from the air, they drove through the bush to the place where two rhinos; one with a calf, grazed peacefully in an open area of grassland scattered with acacia thorn trees. Red-billed ox-pecker birds marched up and down their backs before pecking at insects and bits of dry skin in the rhino's ears and the corners of their eyes.

The rhinos had their peace disturbed when Barnard flew low over them while Petros, using a dart-gun, shot a tranquilizing dart into the thick hide of one of the unsuspecting victims. The poor sighted rhino, startled by the sound of the helicopter, lumbered off at a fast trot trying to escape this loud invasion of its territory. Barnard followed the darted animal until, five minutes later, the drug took effect. The rhino stopped, then slowly toppled over onto the ground and lay still.

As soon as it went down, the poachers closed in to do their work. After circling around to make sure the coast was clear, Barnard and Petros went off to dart the other animal that had trotted off in the opposite direction - away from the noise.

Although Dodi had been up close to rhinos on many occasions during his life as a tracker, he had never been involved in the hunting or killing of them and was still amazed at the size of this sleeping giant. A square-lipped white rhino is truly an amazing animal. Standing it must have been almost as tall as a man and weighed well over two tonnes. It had a long curved front horn about 20 inches long and a smaller second horn, sticking up proudly from its pre-historic nose. It was a bull and the thick slate grey hide seemed like a suit of armour.

Not wanting to be a part of what was about to take place, Dodi volunteered to keep a look-out and climbed into the top of a nearby marula tree where he had a good all round view. Sucking on the delicious thirst-quenching ripe yellow marula berries he watched aghast as the team of poachers, using a chain-saw, axes and machetes, cut deep into the rhino's nose exposing the nasal passages, as they brutally hacked off it's two horns.

Attracted by the activity, a very large white-chested Martial eagle settled nearby in the top of a tall lead-wood tree to watch the men at work below with interest. Perched upright with its chest puffed out it seemed to disapprove of what was going on.

Quickly completing their gruesome task, the team moved on to the next animal, leaving the still drugged, disfigured and bleeding rhino, to recover or die from its horrific ordeal. The whole grizzly operation had taken about half an hour.

As soon as they moved away the eagle swooped down to inspect the sleeping but now badly injured rhino. Vultures circling high above were quick to see what was happening below, and landed to inspect the mutilated rhino still lying on the ground. The birds would soon be joined by four legged scavengers - hyenas, jackals and wild dogs.

Following Barnard they moved to the next victim where the whole dreadful procedure was repeated; this time it was even more savage than the first. Again Dodi opted to climb a tree to keep a look-out for rangers, lions and other predators that might be on the prowl. The second victim was a female rhino with a calf not more than a few months old. As they approached the drugged rhino, its calf took fright and retreated about 20 paces from its mother. While the poaching gang was busy, one of the men kept it away by waving his hat at the poor confused youngster.

Dodi was completely disgusted that Barnard had selected the mother of such a young calf to rob of her horn; it was bad enough as it was, but this was awful. Although he took no part in the disfigurement of these magnificent pre-historic animals, he still felt sick by what he was witnessing. Like the Martial eagle he sat in his tree and looked on in horror while they savagely attacked the rhino cow with their chain-saw.

After the cold early morning start, it had rapidly turned into a hot, dry, windless day. The poachers, having taken off their shirts and wearing only shorts, were soon covered in sweat. The perspiration ran freely down their bare backs and chests, making their brown bodies glisten in the blazing sun.

While they were still busy chopping the horn off the second rhino, Barnard, flying around overhead, saw a trail of dust heading in their direction. It was going too fast to be someone viewing game. Suspecting that they had been seen flying around, and that it was a warden coming to investigate; Barnard radioed his men on the ground to warn them and to urge them to hurry.

The sweltering heat sapped their energy as they struggled to finish their task - but the fear of being caught by the approaching rangers spurred them on to even greater efforts; bordering on panic.

When the job was done and both horns had been removed, Barnard landed, took the prized horns from them, then flying low just above the tree-tops, he and Petros flew back to Zimbabwe. The clatter of the rotor blade soon faded into the distance, leaving the poachers far behind as they raced towards the safety of the Limpopo River and Zimbabwe.

As soon as the poachers moved off, the calf tentatively went back to its mother's side and began to nudge her desperately as it tried to revive her. Dodi knew that if they did not get help quickly both mother and calf would certainly die. The mother from the infection she would get in the open nasal passages, where her horn had been removed, and the calf from starvation.

They made it back across the Limpopo River just in time. As they drove up the river bank on the Zimbabwe side, Dodi looked back across the river-bed and saw a Games Department vehicle parked on the South African side. Two rangers were standing beside the van, with hands on hips, watching helplessly as they disappeared into the thick reeds amongst the yellow fever trees along the river bank.

He was not going to be in any other forays across the border. He felt guilty and very uncomfortable that he had been forced to take part in this dreadful poaching operation. It had taken four nerve-wracking hours.

Dodi was sickened by the whole thing and vowed to make sure something was done to stop these evil men. In the meantime he had to look after Tombi, while they gathered as much evidence as they could. He did not want them to stay at Mabiti any longer than necessary.

He decided that as soon as he had a chance, when he and Tombi were alone, he would discuss it with her. They had to get away as soon as they had a little more information.

Chapter 15

Tombi didn't trust Petros at all. When she had been home recently, he had also gone to his home, and they had travelled on the same bus. Five days later they had met up again in Masvingo where Barnard picked them up. It seemed strange that Barnard had agreed for Petros go home, and be away from the camp at the same time as he was; Petros was his supervisor. To leave the camp for five days unsupervised was unheard of; except when they were out hunting.

Whenever she was near the sheds, Petros happened to appear. He always stood close enough to hear her conversations with the skinners and other workers. She caught him looking at her in a strange way on more than one occasion. He had a reputation of being ruthless, and because he was close to Barnard, seemed to have a free hand with no feelings for any of the workers. He was just like his boss; a bully.

When he was around, Tombi took care not to ask too many questions, or appear too interested in the hunting forays. She realized that, because of her questions, she might have already attracted attention to herself and so decided to be more cautious. She would have a better chance of peeping inside the shed when both Barnard and Petros were out hunting.

There was a beer drink in the compound. As usual Tombi sat around the fire close to Dodi, listening to the men boasting about their hunting experiences and conquests of women. She liked being near Dodi; she felt safe with him. He had already established himself as the best dancer and story teller in the camp. Sometimes his stories went on late into the night. When he danced only wearing a loin cloth and *beshu* (piece of animal skin covering private parts), his sweating well muscled body glistening in the firelight excited her.

On this night Dodi was not dancing, or telling any of his stories - just sitting quietly with her.

"Aha! Dodi I see you are good friends with Tombi. You must be careful of her. She is married and does not like other men," Petros said loudly enough for the others to hear. Everyone laughed and clapped their hands together at Petros' remarks.

"I know people from her home. She does not like to play the fool. Her husband is a powerful man. Everyone is frightened of him," Dodi replied denying the allegation and supporting Tombi. Petros shrugged his shoulders and stalked off towards his quarters.

Early next morning, when it was still dark, Tombi was wakened by the sound of trucks revving up with loud excited voices and orders being shouted out. She dressed quickly and rushed outside to see what the racket was all about. She saw Dodi heading towards the truck and called out to him. He heard her and trotted over to speak to her.

"What's happening? Why is everyone in such a hurry?" she asked.

"One of the game guards came in early to report that there are two *umkhombe* (white rhino) only an hour from here. We are going to capture them," Dodi said. "I must hurry and get onto the truck. I will see you when we return."

Dodi was horrified when he realized that once again he was to be involved in a hunt for *umkhombe*. After the first venture into South Africa, he had vowed not to be included in any further poaching of rhino. It appalled him to be a member of a team killing or maiming these magnificent beasts. However the need to witness, and get as much evidence first hand as he could, made him grit his teeth and climb on the truck. After this operation, he would never go on another rhino hunt with these butchers - he would make some excuse or other to get out of it.

The truck loaded with workers and skinners, rushed out of camp and disappeared down the road in a cloud of dust. Barnard went ahead in his helicopter to search for the rhino. On the boundary of the Gona-re-Zhou conservation area, they pulled up to wait for Barnard to guide them to the two animals. Twenty minutes later he came clattering low over the tree-tops to land in a clearing. Petros, armed with an AK47 assault rifle, climbed in with him.

With the helicopter guiding them, they tracked down a large male rhino near a water hole. Barnard flew as close as he could to the unsuspecting animal then, using his AK47 rifle; Petros emptied the whole magazine of ammunition into the poor beast. The big rhino staggered and lumbered away for a few paces before dropping dead. The hunting team were quickly on the scene to cut off its horn. Barnard after failing to find the second rhino took the horn and flew back to Mabiti with the rest of them following him back to camp.

The rhino's carcass was left to be spotted by patrolling vultures, flying high in the sky. Scavengers attracted to the area by the vultures, would then use their good sense of smell to locate the carcass. The hyenas with their powerful jaws could easily rip open the softer underbelly skin of the rhino and tear off chunks of meat.

The vultures would land close by and wait in the background until the skin had been torn open. As soon as the flesh and innards were exposed, they would join the scramble for bits of meat; annoying the hyenas and jackals as they darted in and out to pull pieces off for themselves.

It was the second time Dodi had been witness to this disgusting practice, and once again vowed that this would be the last. He decided it was no longer safe for Tombi to continue working at Mabiti. He had to persuade her to find an excuse to go home. Once he knew she was safe, he too would run away and disappear.

It was three weeks before Dodi had the opportunity to go to Chikombedzi to report what *Nyoka* (Barnard) was doing at Mabiti. In the meantime the team had been in to Mozambique where they had killed another rhino. Feigning a bout of malaria, Dodi had stayed behind on that occasion. Kyle was shocked to learn what Barnard was up to, and once again warned Dodi to be very careful. He said that if there was any sign of them being suspected, he must take Tombi and get away as fast as possible.

He also knew that, if necessary, in the bush he could easily lose this bunch of half-wits.

. . . .

It was the middle of the day, and hot. The sun was beating down and there wasn't even a slight breeze to cool things down. Everyone was off for lunch and a *siesta* (rest). After giving Barnard his lunch, Tombi left the house and made her way to her quarters. She was passing the shed when she noticed that the door, normally kept locked, was slightly ajar. It was too good an opportunity to miss; she had to see what was inside. She knew Barnard usually took a nap after lunch, and so she decided to take a chance and sneak a peek inside. She reached the open door and after a quick glance around to make sure nobody was watching, she stuck her head inside. In one corner she saw a pile of elephant tusks and on the floor in the middle of the shed there were three open crates packed with tusks. Piles of dried skins filled the rest of the shed.

"What are you looking for?" Petros demanded grabbing Tombi by the arm and startling her out of her wits.

"I saw the door was open and I came to close it. It is always kept closed." Tombi said. "Now let me go." His grip on her arm was tight and painful and she could not pull away from him.

"I have been watching you for some time. Why do you want to see what is inside the shed?" Petros asked angrily, tightening his grip even more.

"I just wanted to close the door. You know boss Barnard does not want the door to be left open," Tombi replied. "Its only skins and elephant tusks kept in there."

"Come along. We are going to see the boss now."

There was no escape. Her only hope was to try and attract Dodi's attention.

"Leave me alone. What are you trying to do to me," she screamed at him at the top of her voice. "Who do you think you are?" It made no difference to Petros as he marched her back to the house.

Barnard roused from his rest by the commotion in the yard, appeared at the back door.

"What's going on here?" he demanded angrily.

"I caught Tombi looking in the shed. She says the door was left open and she went to close it," Petros reported. "I think she is lying."

"Search her then lock her in the empty store-room. I want you to search her room and bring me anything you find," Barnard instructed.

"Please sir, I have done nothing wrong. This man wants me to sleep with him, but I have rejected him. That is why he is doing this to me now. He wants me to get into trouble."

"Go! I will speak to you later," Barnard slammed the door and stormed back inside.

. . . .

Dodi heard Tombi call out and he saw her being dragged to the house by Petros. After speaking to Barnard, he led her crying to the store-room where he locked her up. This infuriated Dodi and he struggled to keep from attacking Petros; he must not lay a hand on Tombi. Then Petros went into her room emerging a few minutes later with her handbag which he took to the house and handed over to

Barnard. The only thing in the handbag, apart from usual female bits and pieces, was her mobile phone.

It was time for Dodi to get a message to Kyle; he had to know what was going on and they needed help. He had finished work for the day and so he decided to get to Chikombedzi as fast as possible. He would be back later in the night when he would make a plan to rescue Tombi.

Chapter 16

Sandy called with two pieces of disturbing news. Kyle had heard from Dodi; apparently Tombi had been caught snooping in Barnard's shed and had been locked up. Dodi was going to try and rescue her from Mabiti, and somehow get her back to Kyle's farm.

"How the hell does he plan to do that?" Tom asked. "Damn it all. I hope those blighters don't harm her in any way."

"Kyle didn't know when I spoke to him. He just said he was going to help Dodi if he could."

"Well there's bugger all we can do about that. I just hope those sods don't get hold of Dodi and Kyle as well. We'll just have to wait and see what happens," Tom said. "What's the second piece of news Sandy?"

"I've been in contact with the Maputo Port authorities. They tell me that the fishing trawler *Verona* belongs to a company operating under the name of Global Procurements Limited. I went onto the internet and found out that the managing director of the company is none other than Jan Van Zyl. What do you think about that?" Sandy said.

"Well, well. That is interesting Sandy. That means the boat we saw speeding away from Van Zyl's trawler was most certainly up to no good," Tom observed. "I would love to know what they were loading when we saw them. Must have been contraband they were smuggling out of the country; most probably something from Zimbabwe. With his camp at Mabiti right on the edge of the Gona-re-Zhou he is bound to be poaching elephant for the ivory. We all know that in spite of the international ban there are plenty of willing buyers in the east."

"Don't you think we should go and investigate? Perhaps we can find out where that boat was going when you saw it disappear inside the bay at Inhambane," Sandy suggested.

"Yes most definitely. We'll get Kyle and Len to have a look around when they go up there next week. Is Kyle flying down do you know?"

"Yes, he's picking me up then we're flying to Inhaca. What's Len's schedule?"

"Perhaps you'd better give him a call. You can go down there and pick him up before coming on here. Then we all can sit down and plan something."

"Good idea. We'll see you day after tomorrow then," Sandy said hanging up.

....

Early in the morning Kyle and Len left Ingale camp with the intention of trying to locate the longboat they had seen loading goods onto the fishing trawler. Off the point of Miramar they passed close to a large basking shark wallowing in the sea about 100 yards from shore. The dark grey patches along its back could clearly be seen as it slowly moved forward, its large mouth wide open feeding on plankton. Two dhows were outside the entrance to the bay; their crews' busy fishing and two others could be seen off-loading goods from a small coaster anchored off-shore.

Kyle slowed down as they entered the large natural bay of Inhambane. They passed a luxury lodge with bungalows built out over the water on stilts sunk into the sand; all connected to the main building with a wooden walkway. With the engines pushing the boat along slowly at 5 knots, Kyle swung the boat north to follow the same branch of the bay where they had previously seen the longboat disappearing. They followed the estuary as it swept around to the left and began to narrow. The mangrove trees along the banks closed in on them as they progressed until it was no more than 30 yards from one bank to the other.

A little further on, as they made their way towards the small village of Beula, they reached what appeared to be the end of the spur. A small jetty jutted out over the water from the village, with a few small fishing boats and one or two dhows tied up along either side. A couple of fishermen sat on the jetty repairing their nets and reed traps. But there was no sign of the long-boat, nor had they seen any similar boats on the way in.

Slightly disappointed, Kyle turned *Pelé-Pelé* around and they started to work their way back slowly. This time as they went chugging along back towards the main part of the bay, they were more thorough, peering under the mangroves and searching the banks with binoculars.

They were about 200 metres from the jetty when suddenly Len grabbed Kyle's arm. "Stop!" he hissed. "I think I saw the boat under the trees. Circle around so we can have a good look."

"What do you think you saw?" Kyle asked swinging Pelé-Pelé around in a tight circle.

"There it is! Do you see the longboat under the mangroves?" Len said pointing into the deep shade of the trees. "It's definitely the same one we saw a couple of months ago."

Peering in the direction Len was pointing; Kyle could just make out the dark blue long-boat through the densely covered branches of the mangroves. It was pulled up on the bank half out of the water. Beyond the boat, about 20 yards from the water's edge, there was a small tin shed and a grass hut. From where they were on the water, they could see no sign of activity or of anyone near the buildings or the boat.

"Well now we know where it comes from. But we still don't know what it was doing the day we followed it in here from the trawler," Len said.

"We'd better get the hell out of here, before anyone in there sees us, and thinks we are taking an interest in them," Kyle said easing the throttles forward. "If they are up to something dodgy, we don't want them forewarned." *Pelé-Pelé* picked up speed, leaving the long-boat behind under the trees.

"Maybe the next thing we should do is to investigate from land. We'll take a drive up here tomorrow and have a bit of a nose around."

"That's a good idea. It would be too obvious if we were to go snooping around among the mangroves asking them what they were up to. We might stir up a hornet's nest," Len agreed.

"Let's have a look around the rest of the bay while we're here. Except from the time we followed the long-boat, I've never been to Inhambane before." Kyle suggested. "It's a beautiful warm day and we have nothing else planned."

"Now that's a plan. We can even stop off for a couple of beers and some prawns," Len was always the practical one.

Stretching 3 or 4 kilometers inland and up to half a kilometre wide, the bay is fairly shallow. The town of Inhambane, located on the south-eastern shore with Maxixe on the west, is a busy place. Dhow sailing boats plied back and forth with their goods; bags of coconuts, fish, cashew nuts, fruit and vegetables. Others ferried people from one side of the bay to the other. A large number of small fishing boats; some propelled by small outboard motors while others were poled around the bay, as they went about their business. They tied up at the jetty adjacent to the town, paid a fisherman to keep an eye on *Pelé-Pelé* and went in search of a restaurant.

· · · · · · · · · · · · · · · ·

On the bank, near the hut, Antonio and one of the other men were squatting around the fire, eating fish and bread, when they saw the catamaran passing by slowly. By its colour, Antonio recognised it as the same boat that had followed them from the trawler. They sat quietly watching it move up the bay. There were two white men on board. Ten minutes later it came back again, going even more slowly than before and, when it was opposite them, the boat circled slowly. Antonio saw one of the men on board looking and pointing in their direction, then it picked up speed and disappeared from sight; perhaps they had seen and recognised the long-boat. Who were these men and where did they come from? What did they suspect or what did they want? Antonio wondered.

In spite of Barnard's warning, Antonio saw no problem; they were not policemen, but he had to comply with his instructions. His employer knew of these men, and so when the load arrived from Zimbabwe, they would just have to be more watchful and take extra care.

There was a load of hardwood and crates of goods due to arrive within the next few months; possibly even sooner. As soon as he knew when to expect it, and if there was any possibility of being caught with the crates of goods, he would station a man on the main road to warn the truck driver. The truck could only be allowed to come to the shed, if it was safe to offload. He would also send a man to check the bay, before they went out to meet the trawler to deliver the crates.

. . . .

After a lengthy lunch at the restaurant, Kyle and Len arrived back in camp. Next morning they drove around past Maxixe and on towards Morrumbene where they found a dirt track leading in towards the area they wanted to explore, along the edge of the bay. After driving up and down several times, through an old neglected coconut plantation, they eventually located the shed. It was set back a little way from the track, half hidden amongst the mangrove trees. Kyle drove a couple of hundred metres beyond the shed towards the sea, turned the Cruiser around then stopped about 50 yards beyond the shed facing Morrumbene; ready for a quick getaway.

Len walked back through the trees, to try and find out what was going on at the shed, while Kyle waited in the van. When he was close enough, Len stood quietly behind a tree; watching. Three black men were sitting on logs, chipping away at pieces of timber. A pile of hardwood had been stacked untidily against the side of the shed, and there were a couple of rickety chairs and tables lying around. It appeared to be a small furniture business, and looked very innocent and quite normal. After observing quietly for a few minutes, Len rejoined Kyle.

"They're making chairs and tables by the look of it. I think they are in the furniture business. I didn't see anything suspicious about the place."

"Well it certainly wasn't chairs and tables they were loading onto that trawler. This might be just a front," Kyle observed. "Unless we've got it all wrong."

After hearing what Kyle and Len had found and seen in the bay, Tom and Sandy decided it was time to get the proper authorities involved. And so they flew to the National Park in South Africa. Landing at Skukuza, they went to see the Senior Warden. He was fully aware of all the poaching in the game park and suspected that poachers were crossing the Limpopo River from Zimbabwe. His game guards had even seen a small helicopter flying around in the northern end of the park, where they had recently found two dead rhinos with their horns chopped off.

They were also having a major problem with poachers entering from Mozambique. What Tom and Sandy told him tied in with the information and evidence he and his wardens had gathered. He thanked them for the information and said he would pass it on to the man in charge of anti-poaching operations in the Limpopo district.

After offering assistance in Mozambique with their aircraft and boats, Tom and Sandy flew back to Inhaca.

■■■■◇◇◇◇◇■■■■

Chapter 17

By the time Dodi reached Chikombedzi it was late and the store was closed. In spite of running at a fast jog, it had still taken him over an hour to get there. He had to find a telephone. After trying the Mission and the school he went to the clinic. With a little persuasion the nurse on duty reluctantly allowed him to make use of their phone.

"Ishe, Barnard has locked Tombi up in the store-room. She was caught looking inside the big shed," Dodi told Kyle while a wide-eyed nurse stood listening to his call.

"Why did he lock her up? What's in the shed?" Kyle asked, concerned.

"All the elephant tusks and skins of the animals they have been killing. I think there are also some *mbejane* horns," Dodi said. "They are not allowed to be killing these animals."

"Has Barnard hurt Tombi?" Kyle asked.

"I don't know Ishe. When I saw them put her in the store-room, I came here to call you."

"Okay. You must go back to Mabiti as fast as you can. Do you think you can get her out of there?"

"Yes Ishe, I will make a plan. Where should we go when we get away?"

"There is an old airstrip near Vila Salazar. If you can get there, I will come and get you." Kyle said. "I'll be there at midday in three days time. That will be on Thursday. It is a long way; do you think you can get there?"

"If I can get Tombi out of the store-room, we will be there."

. . . .

Tombi was surprised Dodi had not tried to contact her, or even try to speak to her through the cracks in the store-room door. It felt like she had been locked up for a long time. It was pitch-black in her prison and she couldn't even see the palm of her hand in front of her. She was freezing cold and had no blankets to keep her warm. When Petros had searched her he had ripped the front of her uniform open which did not help matters.

114

She felt her way around the room and in one corner she got tangled up in a spider web. She brushed it quickly off her head, before the owner of the web found its way into her hair to make a nest. In another corner she found a dried animal skin - it was stiff and smelly but would help. The skin was fairly big so must have been either a wildebeest or zebra. She laid it on the bare concrete floor in the corner and sat huddled down on it; weeping silently at her own stupidity for being caught.

Tom had told her some time ago, to stop working for Barnard and go home. Now she was sorry she had not listened to him. She was too cold and frightened to even try to sleep. The only sound was the solitary wail-like call of a night-jar; a typical night sound in the bush of Africa.

Suddenly she was jerked out of her misery and self pity by a tapping on the door. Who was it? She wondered. Was it Dodi come to rescue her, or was it Petros coming to beat or even rape her? After all, in spite of denying it, she knew he wanted her. Then, much to her relief, she heard someone whispering at the door. It was Dodi.

"Tombi are you in there? It is me, Dodi. Are you alright?" he asked. Tombi was relieved that at last he had come; she had known all along he would not desert her.

Quickly feeling her way to the door she spoke quietly to him. "Why has it taken you so long to come to me?" she scolded. "I am frightened Dodi. You must please help me get out of here," she pleaded.

"I went to Chikombedzi to phone boss Kyle. I had to run all the way. But I am back now. Don't worry, I will get you out of there," Dodi tried to reassure her. "Did they give you food and water?"

"No. Petros locked me in here and went away. They have given me nothing and I am cold."

"I will get you water, some food and a blanket."

"The window is barred and does not open. How will you get it to me?"

"I will break the glass. Nobody will hear me," he said. "I will be back soon."

To Tombi it seemed like ages - but in fact was only minutes before Dodi was back - this time at the window. While he was away she had found a pile of dry Zebra skins leaning against the wall. Dodi covered the glass with the blanket then broke a pane. He passed her a bottle of water, some *sadza* (maize porridge) and a blanket through the broken window.

"There is nothing I can do now; there is no time. I have to go hunting for impala and kudu in the morning with *Inyoka* (Barnard). When we get back I will come to fetch you," Dodi said. "They will not do anything to you until we return."

Feeling much happier, Tombi settled down in the darkness to eat the *Sadza* which she washed down with some of the water. Then she put two zebra skins on the floor, lay down on top of them, wrapped herself in the blanket and tried to sleep. Her thoughts of escape kept her awake, but she knew she would need all the rest she could get if they were to escape - they would have a long hard journey ahead of them. Eventually fatigued, she fell asleep in the early hours of the morning.

As the morning light began to filter through the window into her prison, Tombi heard the hunting party getting ready, then the sound of the engines fading away as they left the camp. She knew there was no point in calling out for anything or anyone; only the gardener and butcher were left behind. They would be too afraid to come anywhere near the shed. She just had to wait for Dodi to come back.

As the day dragged on it got hotter and hotter in her prison. With the stench of the dried skins getting stronger in the heat, it was almost unbearable. Tombi lay near the broken window where at least there was a little cool air coming in from the outside, and at least she could breathe a bit of fresh air. It was many long hours before she heard the vehicles coming back into camp. Petros had taken her watch and so she didn't even know what the time was. Judging by the heat and the shadows, she could see outside the window, it must have been in the middle of the afternoon. She had been locked up for more than 24 hours!

Tombi knew Dodi would only be able to rescue her at night, and so she sat listening to the activity outside in the yard. Although the voices were muffled, she distinctly heard Petros' gruff voice issuing orders and shouting - he seemed to be getting closer to her prison. She moved near the door, so that she could hear what he was saying, but barely had time to move away again when the door was unlocked and flung open. Petros grabbed her by the arm and dragged her off towards the house. Coming from the dark interior of the store-room out into the bright sunshine, it took a little while for her eyes to adjust, and so she stumbled along behind Petros.

Barnard was sitting on the porch, having a cup of tea when Petros pushed her down onto the floor in front of him. Her mobile phone was on the table beside his cup.

"Well Tombi. What have you got to say for yourself? What were you doing in the shed?" Barnard demanded.

"I was doing nothing wrong sir. I promise you. There was nobody in the yard and the shed was open. I just went to close the door," Tombi said bursting into tears.

"I know there is no signal here for your phone, and I can see you have not been making any phone calls, or sending messages. Why do you have a phone?" Barnard asked ignoring her explanation.

"I use it to phone my sister when I can get a network signal." Tombi replied, breathing a sigh of relief thankful she always deleted her messages and pictures as soon as they were sent. "Can you please give it back to me?"

"Okay Tombi." Barnard said handing her phone back to her. "From now on you will stay in the house where I can keep an eye on you. At night you will be locked in the spare room. Go now with Petros and get cleaned up, then come back here with all your stuff."

She didn't like the idea of being moved into Barnard's house, but it was a lot better than being locked in the store-room, and at least she would have some freedom. She could walk around the yard but there could be no escape during the day. The gates were locked and there were game rangers and security men wandering around all the time. In the house, she would be safe from Petros.

She was busy in the kitchen, preparing supper for Barnard, when Petros came to see him. She heard them discussing the lorry going to Mozambique. All she heard was *Inyoka* (Barnard) telling Petros that it all had to go before the end of the week; as soon as everything had been crated up.

That evening when she served *Inyoka* his supper, he kicked back another chair at the table. "Get your food and come and eat here. There are things we need to speak about," he ordered, scowling at her.

"Must I come and eat with you at the table sir?" she asked. This was unheard of, and she became nervous.

"Damn it all, don't you understand me? That's what I said. Now hurry up before I change my mind."

When she was seated at the table *Inyoka* asked her who she had worked for in the Lowveld.

"I worked for many years for Mr Owen, before he left the country. He is back now, but it is too far for me to go and work for him in Harare," Tombi decided to tell the truth; it was possible he already knew.

"What about his son Kyle. Have you worked for him?"

"No sir. He was only a young boy when I used to look after him. He now works in the Lowveld."

"Have you seen him recently?"

"Yes, I saw him when I went home a few weeks ago," Tombi said. "I went to his farm to see my cousin who works for him. He gave me money to help with the children's school fees and some meat to take to my family." *Inyoka* seemed to relax and she was pleased she had told the truth. He got up from the table, poured himself a glass of brandy, and stomped off to the veranda.

Tombi finished eating, cleared away the dishes and, after cleaning up, went to her room. She was tired from her ordeal in the store-room and fell asleep almost immediately. Suddenly she was wide awake. There was an overpowering stink of smoke mixed with drink and sweat. Someone was in her room. Then in the dim light she saw *Inyoka* standing over her bed. He had been drinking, his breathing was rapid and he was obviously excited.

"What are you doing? What do you want in my room?" Tombi was nervous.

"You know what I want. Now open the blankets I am getting into bed with you," *Inyoka* growled.

"No, please Sir. You must not do this to me," she begged trying to push him away.

But there was no stopping him, he dropped his trousers, pulled the bedclothes off and climbed naked into bed with her. She knew there was nobody near who could help her if she screamed out, and was powerless against him; and so she lay rigid on the bed as he pulled her nightdress up and began to squeeze her breasts painfully. The stink of his sweaty body was almost overpowering.

Tombi knew that to try and stop him, would almost certainly anger him; then there was no saying what he might do to her. He could easily kill her then take her body out into the bush and leave it for the hyenas and vultures. And so she forced herself to lie still and let him get on with it. She gritted her teeth and wanted to cry out when he rolled on top of her, forced her legs apart with his knee then grunted as he forced

118

himself into her. The agony of this man on top of her, sweating and groaning as he pounded away, seemed to last forever.

When at last it was over, he climbed off her, picked up his clothes, and without saying a word staggered out of the room. Tombi felt sick and dirty and so she rushed to the bathroom to vomit and clean up. She got back into bed and cried herself to sleep.

She had no sooner fallen asleep when she was wakened again; this time by the dogs barking. As she lay there listening, the barking stopped, and then a few moments later she heard a tapping on the window. It was Dodi!

"Quick. Get your things. We are leaving now," he whispered quietly to her through the open window. Tombi turned away to get dressed. Picking up her handbag, her mobile phone and her toiletries she tucked them all into a bag then climbed out of the window to join Dodi, who was waiting watchfully for her outside. She couldn't get out of there fast enough.

As quietly as they could, the two of them sneaked away from the house, to where Dodi had cut a hole in the security fence behind the shed. Once through the fence, Dodi wired up the gap before they moved on, half expecting the dogs to start barking and alert someone. As soon as they were far enough away, they began to run along the road towards Chikombedzi.

They ran on and on without stopping for an hour. It was easy for Dodi; he was used to running, but Tombi was gasping for breath by the time they eventually stopped for a rest.

"How did you stop the dogs barking at the house?" Tombi gasped.

"When we were hunting this morning I cut a piece of meat from an impala and hid it in my bag. I also got some bones from the abattoir to give them." Dodi smiled breathing easily. "Come on we must move before they come after us."

"*Inyoka* was drunk last night. He will not wake early." Tombi said. She did not want him to know that she had been raped.

It was just getting light when Dodi led them off the road into the bush. After 100 paces they stopped briefly while Dodi went back to brush away any sign of them leaving the road. Then they set off at a fast walk, in the direction of Vila Salazar. It was Wednesday morning and Kyle was meeting them there the next day. They still had a fair distance to go.

■■■■◊◊◊◊◊■■■■

Chapter 18

The sun was just above the tree tops, two hours after leaving the road, when they heard the clatter of the helicopter. It was Barnard, and he probably had Petros with him. They must have found the place where Dodi and Tombi had left the road, and were searching back and forth along the direction they guessed they were going.

Taking care not to move out into open areas, and keeping under the cover of the mopani and acacia trees, the two fugitives pressed on as fast as they could; Dodi always making sure they could not be spotted from the air.

The helicopter was getting closer all the time as it searched and circled. When it seemed certain that they would be found on the next pass, Dodi pulled Tombi under cover of a mahogany tree with thick green foliage. They waited and listened as the clatter came closer and closer, and then sounded as if it had landed. A few moments later the noise grew louder again before fading away in the distance. Were they leaving?

"Perhaps they have gone back to Mabiti," Tombi suggested hopefully.

"I think they landed in a clearing to look for our tracks or to drop a tracker," Dodi said. "From here we must be very careful not to leave any sign for them to follow. *Inyoka* or Petros will come after us as soon as they find our tracks."

They moved on with Dodi always choosing the higher terrain, where the ground was firmer and they had a better view of their back-trail. They did not hear the helicopter again and presumed it must have gone back to the camp to refuel. *Inyoka* would not let them get away - they both knew too much about what went on at Mabiti.

Tombi was getting tired and needed to rest. Her feet, no longer used to going barefoot, were sore and so Dodi decided to stop for a short while. It was still and the heat was building up as the sun rose higher in the sky. He had filled the two water bottles he carried before leaving camp, and they had only used a small amount - they had plenty of water for the time being. They would have to find more water as the day got hotter.

Dodi led them to a small *koppie* (rocky hill) where there was lots of cover and they could rest. Tombi flopped down onto the ground gratefully, with her back leaning against a rock. Dodi squatted in front of her and gave her water to drink while he inspected her feet. As she handed the bottle back he put his hand over her mouth.

"Did you hear that?" he whispered.

"I heard nothing except the birds," she replied also whispering.

"It sounded like someone speaking on a radio. Hide here among the rocks. I'll go and check our back-trail," Dodi instructed before quickly disappearing down the hill. Tombi crawled under cover behind the rocks, where she could watch and wait for him to return.

Dodi got to bottom of the hill then turned to make sure Tombi was well concealed, and could not be seen. Once satisfied, he crouched low and trotted off fast in a wide circle that would bring him close to the point where he estimated he had heard the sound coming from. He was convinced he had heard voices and the crackle of a two-way radio.

When he cut back across their path he found fresh tracks. There was only one man following them; and he was close behind. It was Petros; Dodi recognised the pattern of his boot print. Dodi had now become the hunter; he had to follow him as fast as he dared, and catch up to him before he found Tombi.

. . . .

Tombi lay among the rocks waiting, watching and listening. Suddenly the birds in the trees below the *koppie* where she was hiding, took to the air shrieking. Something had disturbed them. This time she did hear the static crackle of a two-way radio, and someone speaking.

She must have disturbed a small nest of ants when she lay down on the ground; now they crawled all over her legs biting painfully, but she dare not move or try to brush them off. There was still no sign of Dodi. She was frightened and began to tremble.

Tombi knew if she was caught, *Inyoka* and Petros would not show any mercy, and something terrible would happen to her. Her eyes started watering and her ears buzzed as she strained to see through the bush or hear any sound that would give away the position of their pursuers.

As she lay there peering into the bush in the direction of the voices, her heart almost stopped with terror. Petros suddenly appeared as he stepped into the open from behind a thorn bush. He was walking slowly and stealthily along, studying the ground as he went. He held a rifle in front of him and had a radio slung over his shoulder. When he reached the foot of the hill where Tombi was hiding, he stopped and looked directly up to where she lay. She quickly ducked her head down, but feared he must have seen her.

Time seemed to stand still and the minutes ticked by slowly while she lay flat on the ground, sweating in fear. The ants were biting all over her legs but she still did not dare move a muscle.

It felt like a long time, but must have been only a few minutes, since she saw Petros at the bottom of the hill. She couldn't bear it any longer; she had to see what was happening. She raised her head to take a quick peek around the rock. Petros was not there! Where had he gone? Was he sneaking up behind her? She started to panic.

Suddenly a loud bark frightened her half out of her wits. A large male baboon had come to investigate, and was sitting on top of the rock above her. This gave her some re-assurance; the baboon would not be there if Petros was nearby. When the baboon grumbled, leaped down from his rock and disappeared, her fear returned.

Where was Dodi? What should she do? Dodi had told her to stay where she was, but she wanted to get up and run. She put her head down again and tried to think. She felt sick with fear - where was Petros?

....

"Jannie, we caught Tombi looking inside the shed. She saw all the crates packed with tusks. I think she has been spying on our operations, so I locked her up in the store-room for a day. Yesterday I took her out and locked her in a room in the house," Barnard told Van Zyl over the radio. "During the night she managed to get out the window, and has buggered off with Dodi the tracker."

"What the hell do you think you were playing at? What did you have her in the house for? I suppose you were screwing her. Couldn't you just control your fucking urges for once in your miserable life?" Van Zyl was livid. "What makes you think she's spying on us?"

"Because I know she is friendly with Kyle Owen. I was trying to get information from her, and to find out what they know about what we are doing here."

"You mean you were trying to get into her pants. How did they manage to get away?"

"The tracker must have got her out of the house. They cut a hole in the security fence and got away. I don't know how they got past the dogs."

"You better shoot your bloody dogs; they are useless. Have you found them yet?"

"Not yet. We found where they left the road, and Petros has gone after them. He is still out there tracking them down. He has a radio and will call me as soon as he catches up to them. It won't be long."

"When you catch them, you had better get rid of them. Don't take them back to Mabiti; the rest of the staff must not see them. Don't let your prick rule your head and try to screw her again."

"Ja, Jannie. I had too much to drink, and didn't know what I was doing. I'm sorry," Barney said admitting he had bedded Tombi.

"If they get away, you really will be sorry. Everything in your shed must be moved out of the country within the next few days. I will arrange for the trawler to make a pick-up next week. *Verstaan.* Do you understand?"

"Okay Jannie. I'll get the load out this week-end."

"Good. Now go and catch those two bloody spies; and you had better move your arse," Van Zyl finished.

. . . .

Dodi saw Petros stop at the bottom of the hill and look up towards Tombi's hiding place. He hesitated and seemed undecided as to what he should do; walk up the hill into an ambush or call for re-enforcements. If he called Barnard on his radio and asked for assistance they would have very little chance of escape.

Dodi knew he had to stop him before he could call in Barnard or find Tombi. Making a quick decision, he pulled his *demu* (axe) from his belt and, crouching over he closed in on Petros. He was still looking up the hill when Dodi threw the axe. It struck him in the middle of his back and he staggered forward a few paces before dropping face down on the ground.

In a flash Dodi was there to turn him over and stab him through the heart with his assegai. With a groan Petros died instantly. Retrieving his axe he wiped the blood off both weapons on his victim's shirt.

. . . .

Tombi cried out involuntarily and almost leapt out of her skin, when she felt a hand on her shoulder. Expecting it to be Petros standing over her, she turned quickly to face him. It was Dodi smiling down at her. What a relief!

"It's alright. There is no danger now. Stay here I will be back in a little while. There is something that I must do before we move on." Dodi said as he disappeared down the hill once again.

Tombi moved away from the ants and brushed them off her legs. At last the stinging stopped, but the sour smell from their poison remained. Dodi was away for some time and just as she started to worry, he re-appeared. He had a portable two-way radio and a rifle slung over his shoulder.

"Where did you get gun and the radio?" Tombi asked. "It was Petros who was following us. I saw him. Did you take them from him?"

"Yes, these were his," Dodi said, ignoring her other question and helping her to her feet. "We must move now. We have already wasted too much time here." Tombi didn't press him for an answer; he would tell her when he was ready.

There was no time to lose. They had to get away from where Petros had found them, as fast as possible. And so they set off again at a jog. *Inyoka* knew where he had dropped Petros, and roughly where he was heading, and so he might decide to start searching for him. Unless he just waited for him to return or call him on the radio. Dodi guessed he would not call Petros for an hour or two, for fear of giving away his position. This would give them time to be well away from there.

After an hour they slowed down to a fast walk, and kept going at a brisk pace for the rest of the day. With no immediate danger of being followed or tracked, Dodi led them along the well used game trails. As the day got hotter, the sun scorched the earth making Tombi's tender feet burn.

They stopped for half an hour to rest at midday. Dodi checked the back trail once again, and then they pressed on. There was still no sign of pursuit. Late in the afternoon they stopped at a small stream to fill their water bottles, and to allow Tombi to cool her burning feet.

A small duiker was grazing on the bank of the stream and Dodi, quick to seize the opportunity, killed it with his assegai - food at last! They cooked the meat on a fire made from dry sticks. Some they ate and the rest they kept for the following day. Tombi was so hungry she wolfed it down.

124

After filling their stomachs, and with night closing in, they cleared an area on the ground, making sure there were no scorpions lurking under dead branches, then huddling together to keep warm, they slept.

At fist light they were on the move again. By mid-morning, and without any further incident, or sign of pursuit, they arrived at the old airstrip where they were to meet Kyle. Flopping gratefully down in the shade of some mopani scrub, in a fairly well concealed spot, with good all around visibility, they settled down in the grass to wait for Kyle.

"How did you get the rifle and the radio?" Tombi asked. It had been worrying her and she decided it was time to find out.

"I found Petros and followed him to the bottom of the hill where you were hiding. When I saw him looking up to where I had left you, I knew he would find you. I had to do something quickly, so I killed him with my demu and the assegai," Dodi said casually removing a thorn from his foot.

"Did you just leave him lying there?" Tombi was not going to let it go.

"No. When I left you I went to find an ant-heap. I found a big one with a hole dug by an ant-bear. I carried Petros there and pushed him into the hole," Dodi explained nonchalantly watching a dung-beetle struggling to roll a ball of elephant dung along with its back legs.

"But now the police will want to arrest you for murder," she was concerned.

"Nobody will find him. *Inyoka* does not know where he is, and I covered all the tracks. Even if he does find him he will not report the matter to the police - he will not want them to find out what he is doing at Mabiti. The ants will soon clean all his bones, after the hyenas and jackals have eaten most of his flesh," Dodi was not in the least concerned.

"He hurt you and for that he had to pay. Petros and *Inyoka* would have killed you if they had caught you."

"Yes that is true. I am not sorry Petros is dead. I was very frightened of those two men. Do you think *Inyoka* will try to chase us now?" Tombi asked.

"Now that we have escaped, I think he will move the crates of elephant tusks to Mozambique as fast as he can, and hurry to cover his trail. He knows we will report his poaching operations in South Africa to someone," Dodi had it all worked out. "Nobody seems to worry about poaching in the Gona-re-Zhou any more," he finished sadly.

Two hours later, as promised, Kyle arrived to pick them up.

Chapter 19

On Inhaca they were all very excited. Their first official clients from America had booked fishing charters. Two men were coming in the first week of July, and a husband and wife were booked two weeks later. This meant that July was fully booked.

Tom, Maria and Sandy had all worked long and hard, and injected a lot of capital into '*Santo Deep-Sea Fishing*'. Now at last they were ready, and as long as they could provide good service and good fishing, their efforts would be rewarded.

Larry Mize and Pete Lund had been for a trial charter in March, and it had gone very well. Tom and Sandy took them out together and, because the two boats were so different in design, every other day they changed boats, so that Larry and Pete could experience fishing off both.

During their entire charter there were only two days the weather was bad and fishing was out of the question. On those days the two fishermen spent the mornings in camp helping make up traces and servicing reels. The sea in the Mozambique Channel was warm, and the weather good, making for ideal fishing conditions. Every day they returned with fish; some they ate themselves, some went to the camp and the Lodge took the rest.

On the second day out Larry hooked into a good size dorado, sometimes called a 'dolphin fish' and referred to by the local fishermen as the 'chicken of the sea', because it is exceptionally good to eat. As Larry brought the fish alongside, they could see its blunt bull head and long dorsal sail-fin all along the back. It was a very colourful fish and with the light shining through the water it reflected a wide range of colours; golden hues on the side; patches of metallic blue and greens on the back and sides with white and yellow on the underside. It was 5 feet long and weighed about 20 kilos.

A couple of days later they trolled for marlin and sailfish. An hour after putting out a lure, preferred in the Gulf of Mexico, and with no interest being shown by fish, they changed to a live-bait. Thirty minutes later, just after Pete had changed places with Larry, and was in the fighting-chair, they saw the sickle-shaped dorsal fin of a marlin circling the bait. After circling twice it seemed to lose interest and disappeared - then suddenly the reel screamed as the marlin took the bait and ran with it, stripping the line rapidly from the reel. The hook was set and the fight was on.

Every time Pete managed to bring the fish close to the boat, it looked at them with a beady eye, gathered its strength and swam away again - leaping high out of the water and tail-walking. The marlin came out of the water in spectacular leaps, showing off its colours, dark metallic blue along the back, with white underbelly and light blue sail-fin.

The fight lasted two hours before it tired and Pete finally managed to bring it alongside. It was a good fish weighing over 200 kilos. Larry took pictures during the fight and of the marlin before it was tagged and released to swim away.

On the last day both boats went out. Tom and Larry on board *Tigger,* with Sandy and Pete on *Pelé-Pelé,* and they held, what the Americans called, a 'small' competition between the two boats. The loser was to pay for the bar-bill and all the extras at the Lodge for the duration of their trip. At the end of the day, Larry won with the best bag but Pete caught the biggest fish, and so the competition was declared a draw.

All in all, both men were very happy with the service at the Lodge and enjoyed spending their afternoons either relaxing around the pool, wandering along the beach or in camp helping to prepare for the following days fishing.

There were a few areas where they suggested minor tweaks, but generally had thoroughly enjoyed their fishing holiday as well as the treatment and hospitality they had received. Tom, Maria and Sandy had also enjoyed their company, getting on well with them both.

At the end of their charter Larry and Pete, looking a lot more tanned than when they had arrived, flew back to America promising to do their best to fill the season with clients for *Santo Deep-Sea Fishing.* For them it was a relatively unexplored fishing arena to be enjoyed by other enthusiastic American big game fishermen.

They were true to their word, with *Santo's* first clients being booked through them.

Chapter 20

Ever since he had received the package containing his father's papers, Tom was convinced his family might still be alive somewhere; unless they had perished on an island in the Mozambique Channel. It was now obvious that when the Owens sailed away from Inhaca they had been making their way up the coast, and had planned on visiting the islands. The only way to set his mind at rest was to visit the islands, and so Tom and Sandy decided to fly off to explore Europa Island and Juan de Nova (Isle of Dogs).

As they still had two months to finish their final preparations and to be ready for their clients; it was a perfect opportunity to make the trip, and to set Tom's mind at rest. It would also be useful to know if any of the islands had the potential for a suitable third base; if their business ever warranted it.

The weather was good, and with time to spare, they decided to go and have a look at the two islands. They would be flying over a vast expanse of open-ocean, and so as a safety precaution, they took an inflatable life raft from *Tigger* with them. Refuelling stops would be needed if they went as far as Juan de Nova.

Both the islands were French possessions, with weather stations manned by the military, and each had an airstrip. Before leaving they obtained permission to land from the French consulate in Maputo.

Early morning after fuelling up, and armed with a French phrase book; the two of them took off from Inhaca and headed north. Four hours after leaving Inhaca, they dropped down to 500 feet to circle the small island, while waiting for the goats to be herded off the airstrip.

Judging by the length of the airstrip, located on the north side of the island, Europa was about 3 kilometers long and 2 wide. The whole island was encircled by a coral reef close to the shore-line with brilliant white sandy beaches. On the eastern side, a large lagoon almost cut the island in half and was surrounded by mangroves. A gap in the reef on the northern side made the lagoon accessible to small fishing boats - two could be seen floating in the middle of the lagoon.

The rest of the island had very little vegetation, with old sisal plants and dry grass along the edge of the gravel landing strip, where goats grazed. Bright red flamboyant trees and tall coconut palms provided shade around the buildings at the west end of the airstrip. Several boats were pulled up on the beach near the compound. The island was obviously not very fertile and, apart from the military base, appeared to be quite inhospitable. It looked nothing like a typical tropical island.

It was noon by the time they landed and stopped near the military garrison, where the French flag fluttered in the gentle breeze. Tom cut the engine and they climbed down from the cockpit as three soldiers in neat, tidy uniforms and wearing white pith helmets, marched up to meet them.

"*Bonjour Monsieur,*" the senior man greeted them. "We have been expecting you. I am the Sergeant in charge of this post. My name is Pierre."

"*Bonjour Pierre,*" Tom smiled responding to the warm greeting. "I am Tom Owen and this is Sandy Walker."

"And 'ow can I be of assistance? You are a long way from home, no! What brings you so far over the ocean to visit us?" Pierre asked.

"We have a fishing business in Mozambique and we believe there is good fishing in the waters around here. We have also been told of the green turtles that come here every year to lay their eggs," Sandy said only half explaining the purpose of their visit.

"With your permission of course, we would like to explore the island. If that is possible," Tom added diplomatically.

"*Oui* this is true. The turtles do lay their eggs here. The fishing is good; we live on fish. But because it is so far from the mainland the only fishing is done by trawlers. Of course we will show you around the island. But first of all we would like you to join us for lunch?" Pierre invited hospitably.

"That would be very nice; thank you. We left early this morning before breakfast, and I am starving," Sandy said, gladly accepting the invitation.

"Good. Please follow me," Pierre beamed then turned to lead the way down an avenue of blazing flamboyant trees to the garrison. It was very hot but a light breeze cooled the air making it bearable.

"How many men are stationed here?" Tom asked as they arrived in the compound. It was far bigger than he had expected.

"There are eight of us and we have ten men working for us. They come from Madagascar."

After freshening up, Tom and Sandy were ushered to the mess hall. They sat down with the eight Frenchmen and enjoyed an excellent fish stew with sweet potatoes, grown on the island.

"I must apologize. We did not know what time to expect you, and so chef has not prepared a special meal. You must share our normal food with us," Pierre said. "I am sure that he will have something better for us to eat this evening."

"The meal was excellent. Thank you," Tom said.

"We were not expecting to stay the night," Sandy explained. "But we are most grateful for your hospitality."

"How can you possibly leave today? It is a long way back to the mainland. You must explore the island and sleep here. Tomorrow you can leave." Pierre was adamant. "I am sorry, I am the only one here who speaks English, but I am sure everyone here agrees with me. Anyway I am in charge," he finished with a smile.

After lunch they clambered onto the back of a small pick-up truck, and were driven around the island on a sightseeing tour. They went to the beach, where the turtles laid their eggs in the brilliant white sands. It was the wrong time of the year, and the beach was scattered with bleached egg shells. They were shown the lagoon with big dark brown jagged lumps of lava-rock standing up out of the water like giant mushrooms. A recently wrecked ship had washed up on the beach south of the garrison, and there were pits where phosphate had been mined for export in years gone by.

Late in the afternoon, as they were coming to the end of their tour of the north side of the island, they noticed that dark blue trawler had arrived, and was lying at anchor half a kilometer off shore.

"It is a fishing trawler from Malaysia. After filling their holds with fish they anchor here to wait for their factory ship," Pierre explained. "They require permission to come ashore; but nobody has ever asked."

"How long do they usually stay?" Sandy asked. From a distance the trawler looked vaguely familiar.

"Sometimes a day, sometimes a week," Pierre said, shrugging his shoulders.

"It looks very much like the trawler we saw near Ingale a couple of months ago," Tom said turning to Sandy.

"Perhaps we can get the ship's name when we leave here. It will be very interesting if it is Van Zyl's trawler," Sandy replied. "I have a sneaking suspicion he's using that ship for more than just fishing."

The garrison had a guest room reserved for visitors to the island, where Tom and Sandy were put up for the night. Fortunately knowing they were going to be away for a few days, they had thrown toiletries and a change of clothes into a small bag. With their hosts rushing around making sure they had all they needed, they were more than comfortable.

In the evening they sat down to a feast of crayfish, caught in the lagoon, accompanied by a good French wine. Tom and Sandy thoroughly enjoyed the fine meal. During the course of the evening, the conversation turned to the Owen family and their demise.

When Tom explained to the garrison commander that his father had been granted permission to set up a camp on Ile Europa or on Juan de Nova, Pierre was fascinated and most accommodating.

"In the morning we will look at the records in the office. A log is kept of all ships and people visiting the island."

"That will be very good of you. Thank you," Tom was delighted.

"Is that the real reason for your visit? Are you trying to find out if your family came here or not?" Pierre asked.

"In a way, yes it is. We are trying to start up the fishing business where they left off when Mozambique became independent. It is some years since the troubles, and things have changed now," Sandy acknowledged.

"Will you go from here to Juan de Nova then?"

"It all depends on what your records show."

"We do keep aviation fuel here for planes bringing in supplies and equipment for us. If you need fuel, you are most welcome to have some," Pierre was magnanimous.

"That would be a great help; especially if we do go on to Juan de Nova," Tom said.

There was a separate log book for each year. Knowing the year and approximate month the Owens had sailed out of Maputo, it didn't take long to find the entries for that year. Two entries jumped out at them from the pages of the log - they were written in French and so Pierre translated.

25 September;
Yacht 'Nimble Tigger' anchors in bay near lagoon. Three people on board. Names:
– Bill Owen with his wife Marjorie and daughter Anne.

30 September;
Yacht 'Nimble Tigger' departs, believed to be sailing north to Juan de Nova. All crew on board.

Tom felt like he had been kicked in the stomach by a mule; his face went ashen, he felt quite light-headed and had to lean on the desk for support. The entries confirmed that the air and sea searches for his family had been conducted in the wrong area. Instead of searching south of Durban, they should have been searching north.

Here was the proof recorded in a log in the middle of the ocean miles from anywhere. Now they had to go on to Juan de Nova.

At ten o'clock, with the tanks full, they took off and flew low past the fishing trawler. Using the binoculars it was easy for Sandy to read the name of the vessel.

"It's Van Zyl's trawler alright; the *Verona,* registered in Singapore," Sandy said lowering the binoculars and putting them back in the pouch.

"I would be very interested to know where the factory ship comes from. We know the *Verona* meets it here to transfer its load of fish, and whatever else they have to be taken to distant ports," Tom said putting the plane into a long slow ascent, and heading north towards Juan de Nova.

"The *Verona* must be waiting to transfer fish now. Maybe we'll see the factory ship approaching from the north as we fly along," Sandy said hopefully.

The engine droned on and the hours dragged by with only deep blue sea below them. They did see a pod of whales swimming south with the current, and the occasional coaster, container ships and oil tankers, but nothing resembling a factory ship for processing fish. Three hours after leaving Ile de Europa they landed on Juan de Nova. About twice the size of Europa, Juan de Nova from the air appeared to be far more hospitable.

Once again they were met at the west end of the airstrip, adjacent to the Met station, by obliging French military personnel who treated them like royalty. Henri, the man in charge was a short fat little man with a pencil moustache. He had been forewarned of their visit over the radio by the soldiers on Europa.

After a lunch of fried fish and rice; seemed to be standard fare on the islands, they were given a tour in a small pick-up similar to the one on Ile de Europa. Like the other island Juan de Nova was completely surrounded by reefs and brilliant white sandy beaches. There were rusty remains of two wrecked ships high up on the southern shore.

Dense mangrove forests covered the central area, with patches of casuarinas and tall coco-nut palm trees. The ground below the trees was covered with dense scrub and lush grass. This island was much more fertile than Europa. There were paths and tracks leading in all directions. The staff quarters was an old French Colonial style double-story house located north of the eastern end of the runway, near where a herd of goats grazed.

The tour ended at the fairly modern Meteorological Station, where they went to check log books. Knowing the approximate dates, it didn't take long to find the entries they were looking for. This time Henri did the translation for them.

07 October – 1500 hours.
Three hulled yacht 'Nimble Tigger' anchors off north-east shore. Three people on board.
08 October – 1000 hours.
Crew of 'Nimble Tigger' report to Office. Mr Owen, his wife and their daughter. In possession of letter granting permission to camp on Juan de Nova. Allocated plot in north-east sector.

There were no other entries that year and nothing to indicate that they had sailed away. Had they left without anyone knowing? Tom asked if they could check the logs for the following year. Henri handed him the log and left them in the office to peruse the entries. Four months after they had arrived on the island, there was another entry in the log book.

05 February – 0900 hours.
Yacht 'Nimble Tigger' found wrecked on reef after Cyclone Gloria. Three crew members drowned. Bodies recovered and buried on their allocated plot. Message dispatched to Headquarters.

'Why was I never told? Why didn't I look for them?' Tom asked himself quietly. Closing the log he walked slowly outside to be alone. The message had never reached him. This was the second shock he had had in one day. Although it was many years since his family had disappeared, and he had long since accepted that they had perished, it was still a terrible blow to see it confirmed in an official log. He sat in a chair on the veranda and wept silently for his family.

A little later Henri took them to the place where Tom's family had been given their piece of ground, then left them there. The grass and scrub was tall and it took some time to find the graves. They were marked by small piles of faded whitewashed stones - each had a small cross with nothing inscribed on them.

A small square of fibreglass with the name *"Nimble Tigger"* painted on it was nailed to the cross on the middle grave; the last of the yacht!

The Owens had come ashore, made a small vegetable garden on their plot, but for comfort had lived on board *Nimble Tigger*. The cyclone must have dragged the yacht from her anchor, and thrown her onto the reef, smashing her to pieces with the Owens either trapped inside underwater, or killed on the reef. There was no wreckage left after all the years, and if there was it had most probably been buried under the sand below the water.

Standing side by side, Tom and Sandy said a prayer over the graves. It was very emotional and very personal. Tom felt like a burden had been lifted from his shoulders. At last he had closure and knew what had happened to his family and could now let them go and rest in peace.

· · · · · · · · · · · · · ·

They spent the night on Juan de Nova with the Frenchmen. In the morning after a healthy breakfast, and topping up the fuel tanks; once again courtesy of the garrison, Tom and Sandy took off. They both agreed that, due to the remoteness of the islands, both were totally unsuitable for any fishing ventures.

Tom hardly said a word during their long flight from the island; he was deep in thought as he dealt with his emotions. Twenty five years is a long time to have your family missing, not knowing what had really happened to them. They must have been in desperate straits with no money, no home and nowhere to go. They had lived out their last days almost as castaways. The thought of his sister, just entering womanhood, living on an almost deserted island was extremely sad.

Tom let Sandy fly the plane for two one hour spells, so that he could get some rest; it was a long flight. They stopped to refuel at Quelimane, on the coast of Mozambique, and to have a bite to eat and stretch their legs before pressing on to Harare. It was just getting dark when they landed at Mount Hamden. Ted picked them up and they went to his home.

"I'm shocked you were never told about your family being on the islands," Ted said addressing Tom after hearing their news. "I wonder where the lines of communication broke down."

"Yes it's disgraceful. Well there's nothing much we can do about it now," Tom shrugged his shoulders in resignation.

"When we left Europa we saw Van Zyl's trawler anchored close to the island, waiting for its factory ship," Sandy changed the subject.

"Really! It seems to be operating up and down the Mozambique coast. Be very interesting to know if it is just fish it is waiting to transfer." said Ted. "I bet you it must also be those crates you saw being loaded near Inhambane."

"Yes I think you're right. We know Van Zyl is doing a lot of poaching - elephant and rhino!" Tom agreed.

In the morning, after a good long rest, Tom called Kyle and heard the unbelievable story of Dodi and Tombi's escape from Mabiti. There was no time to waste. Van Zyl and Barnard would most certainly want to move any incriminating evidence out of the country as quickly as possible. They had to get Dodi and Tombi to a place of safety out of the country.

Chapter 21

Tom Owen was beginning to get under Van Zyl's skin, and annoy him intensely. First he was snooping around the diamond diggings at Marange, now he was trying to disrupt his hunting operations at Mabiti. Something had to be done about him - and quickly. The man had become a major thorn in his side.

Van Zyl's cook told him that Owen was staying next door with Ted Hunter. A few weeks earlier, the two men keeping an eye on Owen, had reported that he was not in the country - believed to be in Mozambique. Now that he was back, he would have to be watched. When he got the chance, Van Zyl was going to find a way to silence him, and get rid of the pest for good.

"Barney, what happened to those two bloody spies you had working in your camp? Did you find them and have you got rid of them yet?" Van Zyl asked Barnard over the radio.

"No we haven't found them. Petros is still out there hunting them down. Dodi is a clever fellow, so it's taking time. Petros is good, but hasn't reported to me over the radio either - its two days now. I think his battery must be flat."

"Do you think he's still following them?"

"Ja, I think so. If he had lost them he would have been back already."

"Well, Owen is here in Harare. You must get that lorry loaded and move it out to Mozambique as soon as you can. You will have to go along with the truck to make sure it does not run into trouble on the way."

"Okay Jan, we are leaving on Sunday morning. If Petros is not back by then I will leave a message for him to contact you as soon as he returns."

"This is a total balls-up. Don't forget to collect the other tusks in Mozambique, and make bloody sure you don't run into the police. You had better not use the road along the railway line; it's much too busy. Rather use a back road. It'll take longer but will be a lot safer. I'll meet you down there on Wednesday. Make sure you are there by then. *Verstaan?*"

....

Tom and Sandy spent the day resting after their long flight from Europa to Juan de Nova. They both needed the rest and Tom had emotions to deal with. Next morning they flew to the Lowveld where they stopped to pick up Kyle and Dodi before flying on south. The plane only had four seats, so Rosa and Tombi had to wait for Tom to come back and pick them up.

As they flew south over Mabiti, directly in the flight path between the Lowveld and the Kruger Park in South Africa, they saw what looked like Barnard's truck and pick-up driving south from Mabiti towards the Limpopo River.

Dodi seemed to think they would leave the country at Crooks Corner, where there was no border control, and it was easy to drive into Mozambique. From there they could take the road to Mapai or Malvernia, and then follow the rail to the coast. This confirmed Dodi's suspicions. They were just in time!

They landed at the Punda Maria Camp in the National Park. As soon as Kyle had told Ted that Tombi had heard Barnard mention a load of goods going to Mozambique, he had contacted the man in charge of anti-poaching in Limpopo area of South Africa.

One of the senior game rangers was waiting for them when they touched down. Kyle and Dodi, who was familiar with Barnard and his men and vehicles, stayed behind to assist the rangers. Tom was given one of the ranger's hand-held two-way radios so they could communicate with each other.

Collecting Rosa and Tombi, they headed for Inhaca. After crossing the border at Vila Salazar, they saw a trail of dust rising into the air way below them. It was Barnard's little convoy travelling along the road from Mapai towards the railway line to Maputo. It had to be the same two vehicles they had seen leaving Mabiti.

As they flew overhead they were flying low enough for Tombi to recognise them. They crossed the railway line and headed north-east on a smaller dirt road.

"I wonder why Barnard has turned away from the main road to Maputo." Sandy said studying the map on his lap.

"I suppose he doesn't want to attract any attention, and is taking a back route," Tom replied. "They have entered Mozambique illegally and will want to avoid the police. Where does the road go?"

"It leads to the Bahine National Park and Machaila. From there the road winds its way to the coast near Inhambane." Sandy said tracing the route with his finger.

"That's a hell of a long way around. I reckon those roads are in pretty poor condition; all gravel, corrugations and mud. It'll take them a couple of days to get to the coast."

Sandy called the rangers on the radio to let them know which road Barnard had taken. They would have to hurry if they were to catch up and to have a reception committee waiting at Inhambane.

. . . .

In the Kruger Park things happened quickly. Thanks to having been forewarned by Ted, a team consisting of eight men and two open Land Cruisers, had already been put together and were waiting to go. They moved off to the gate on the Mozambique border at Pafuri, with Kyle in one van and Dodi in the other. It had rained early that morning but the sun was out and it was already warming up. It was going to be a hot humid day.

No sooner had they arrived at the border when they heard the news they were waiting for. Sandy called on the radio to let them know that Barnard and his convoy had crossed into Mozambique, were on the road to Machaila. They set off immediately in pursuit. The Mozambique Parque Department had been kept in the loop, and would be waiting to meet them at the coast.

Crossing the Limpopo River, lined with reeds, yellow fever trees and one or two olive green wild figs, took time. After driving over the low-level log causeway, half buried in the sand, they had to wait for the hand operated ferry to take them across the open water.

A family of hippos wallowed in a pool, with only their pink nostrils, ears and eyes sticking up out of the water. Occasionally grunting and bellowing, and one of the bulls yawned widely to display his huge incisors and lower canines. On a large flat rock in the middle of the river, a pair of very fat, lazy crocodiles sunned themselves; their mouths wide open absorbing vitamin D from the sun.

Perched on a dead branch of a tree in the river-bed a little further downstream, a fish eagle with white head, brown chest and black plumage, called to its mate every now and then - its shrill 'weee-ah, hyo-hyo', the call evocative of the essence of Africa.

By the time they had crossed the river and passed Mapai, it was midday and the sun was blazing down. Barnard must have been about 50 kilometers ahead of them when they reached the cross-roads on the railway line at Jorge de Limpopo. Two Mozambique game guards who were to accompany them were waiting there for them.

Following Sandy's directions, they took the road towards Parque Nationale de Bahine. The Mozambique game parks were also experiencing poaching problems and they too were anxious to catch the culprits.

As the sun began to set, they stopped to camp for the night. Game rangers are well trained for this sort of thing, and in next to no time they had a fire going, with food being prepared. It had rained there earlier that afternoon and the smell of the earth, just after rain, mixed with the sweet wood-smoke from the cooking fire, are the scents of survival and peace that Kyle loved.

A night-jar's wail and the distant bark of a dog, keeping wild animals at bay, were the only sounds heard above the low murmur of the rangers talking quietly beside the fire. Kyle was in his element as he sat on a log staring into the flickering flames of the fire. This was the Africa he loved.

....

Barnard was in a hurry to reach the coast. He was getting more and more irritated by the poor condition of the road. They stopped briefly to load tusks from the hunters he had recruited on one of his recent forays into Mozambique.

They had killed the elephants in the 'Parque Nationale de Bahine' which was close to where they lived. The tusks were buried in a cattle kraal and it took half an hour to dig them up. Barnard paid the hunters for the ivory, and they moved on.

They were approaching Chigubo a few hours later when the truck had a puncture. It was late in the afternoon, and so Barnard decided to camp there for the night. They made an early start in the morning, stopping in Tesenane to repair the puncture. This took a lot longer than expected because they did not have proper tools, and so it was midday before they were back on the road.

....

The rangers were up and about before dawn. After a quick cup of coffee with biscuits, they were on the road by the time the sun began to peep over the horizon. It wasn't long before the badly corrugated road began to deteriorate even more, and progress was very slow. Along the way they had to negotiate potholes, deep sand-drifts, and detours around culverts where recent rains had washed away the approaches.

There was still a lot of water standing on the sides of the road. At times, where deep muddy patches made the road impassable, they were forced to follow temporary tracks through the bush with the raised hump or *middle-mannetjie* between the tyre marks scraping along the underside of their vehicles.

As the sun climbed higher, into the cloudless electric blue sky, it changed rapidly from being a pleasant morning to a very hot, humid, uncomfortable day, with the temperature rising well into the upper 30's. There was no wind and their forward motion was too slow to ease the discomfort of the rangers in the open vehicles.

As the road dried out, dust was stirred up by the passing vans, and hung around in the still air for quite some time before settling. With little or no breeze to blow it away, and in spite of dropping back to open the distance between the vehicles, those in the second vehicle were soon covered in the dust. It was unpleasant and both the driver and Dodi - sitting in the front of the second van, were forced to wear goggles to keep the dust out of their eyes.

After travelling through countryside very similar to the Lowveld in Zimbabwe; mopani trees, mopani scrub, acacia and tall elephant grass; the vista changed to vast open areas of sparse, almost barren, savannah scrub-land, scattered with lead-wood, mopani, knob-thorn, wild olives, marula trees and the occasional giant euphorbia cactus. Dark grey-green patches of lala-palm bushes were scattered about, close to the numerous water pans filled by the recent rains.

One of the salt pans they passed appeared to be veiled by a pink blanket. As they got closer Kyle realised it was a huge flock of flamingos feeding in the shallows. He was surprised to see these magnificent birds so far from the sea and in such a small pan so far inland.

There were no wild animals to be seen; most of them had long since been poached. Thin bony cattle, donkeys, goats, dogs and chickens could be seen in and around the villages they passed along the way.

Eventually arriving in Tesenane, and on enquiring, they were told by the villagers, that Barnard's trucks had passed through only three hours before. The rangers were closing the gap. Every small town or village in Mozambique has a small shop, and at least one 'banco' where they bought cool drinks and, surprisingly enough, ice cold beer. Wasting as little time as possible, they stocked up on refreshments and pressed on in pursuit of Barnard.

Late in the afternoon, after a long hard, hot, dusty day, driving mainly through open grassland and occasionally, heavily timbered forest areas, they entered an area of low lying savannah with extensive areas of wet marsh-land. Half way between Tesenane and Funhalouro the ranger team stopped for the night. A well deserved rest!

The going had been even slower than the previous day, and in spite of the early start, they had only covered about 200 kilometers. They had not sighted their quarry, but could see by the tracks in the sandy surface of the road, that they were still on the right track. Barnard and his vehicles would be moving even slower than the rangers, and so Kyle suspected Barnard would keep going right through the night.

They soon regretted stopping where they had. Surrounded by the wet marshes, it was an ideal breeding ground for the malaria-carrying mosquitoes. In spite of huddling around the fire, in the hopes that the smoke would keep the mozzies away, they were plagued all night and didn't get much sleep.

....

It was hot and dusty, and the sun beat down unmercifully as they travelled along slowly, doing their best to avoid all the potholes and ruts in the road. To stop for another puncture repair was out of the question. Because of the long delay in getting the tyre fixed, as well as the poor condition of the road, they were a long way behind Barnard's planned schedule. It was well after dark, of the second day, when the little convoy eventually crawled into Funhalouro where they rested for a few hours.

Before leaving Mabiti, Barnard had known that the journey was going to take two full days, but by the time they were on the road again in the morning they were into the third day. They crawled along at a snails pace and would be lucky to make it to Inhambane by nightfall. Barnard could not risk being on the road another day. They were on the last leg of their trip and had to keep going until they reached their destination. Besides, Jan had arranged to meet him the following day, and he would not be at all pleased if he was not there when he arrived.

. . . .

Long before sunrise on the third day, the rangers were on the move again. All the villages they passed had small cultivated patches of maize, millet and cassava around the perimeter and clumps of mango trees, guavas and tall paw-paws.

Each village also seemed to have its own yellow-billed kite or hawk, patrolling high overhead searching for baby chicks, rats and even left over bits of porridge. They would swoop down to steal or capture their prey and then fly back up into the sky to feed on their morsels. They watched as small sparrows flew up to attack the far larger raptors, in a valiant effort to keep them away from their nests.

By mid-morning, the road had improved considerably, and they were able to pick up speed. At last, as they crested a high rise over a low range of hills, Kyle spotted a ribbon of dust far in the distance that could only have been made by the passing of Barnard's vehicles; there were no other vehicles on the road. He estimated that they were only about 5 kilometers behind and closing in fast.

Excited by the sight of their quarry the rangers hardly slowed down as they passed through the small town of Funhalouro. Chickens took to the air squawking in fright and flying across the road in front of the vans; dogs barked at them; children playing in the dust looked up to see what all the commotion was about, and two teenage boys pulling rolling barrels of water along behind them, stopped to wave as they sped through the town.

. . . .

Van Zyl took off at 3 o'clock. After crossing into Mozambique he dropped down to 2000 feet to follow the road he knew Barney was using. As he flew over Funhalouro he saw a trail of dust. Just as he was about to fly down and buzz Barney, he suddenly realized they were not his vehicles.

The dust was being made by two open vehicles painted the distinctive olive green of the South African Parks Board; they were obviously following Barney. He pulled back on the stick and climbed away.

A little further on he saw a second ribbon of dust. This time it was Barney. Van Zyl didn't have radio communication with the vehicles on the ground, and so he turned and flew low past Barney's pick-up, waggling his wings trying to warn him of the danger behind him. Barney waved his arm out of the window of his pick-up acknowledging him. Van Zyl could only hope he realized he was being warned, and that the wing waggling was not just in greeting.

Van Zyl had to get to the base in Inhambane fast, to warn Antonio and make sure he was ready to receive the crates. If Barney and his truck could turn onto the track leading to the shed; before anyone saw where they were going - then there might just be enough time to move the crates out to sea and onto *Verona*, before the men from the Parks arrived in Inhambane.

It was imperative that nobody discovered what was inside the crates, or they would all be arrested and he would lose a fortune. The two vehicles following Barney were not far behind - probably only half an hour.

....

Further back along the road Kyle watched the twin-engine plane fly low overhead, and then climb away only to drop down again, where Kyle guessed Barnard's convoy was. It circled twice then dived and waggled its wings before flying away. It was obviously trying to attract the attention of someone on the ground; probably Barnard. They were still too far from Inhambane to contact Tom on the portable radio, to tell him about the plane.

Chapter 22

Approaching Morrumbene from the west, Van Zyl flew in low so as to buzz Antonio letting him know that he was landing. As he passed over the intersection where the road from Morrumbene joined the main Maputo to Beira road, he saw a number of police vehicles with policemen and soldiers everywhere. A road block had been set up.

Was this a trap or was it a routine traffic check? Were they expecting Barney and his convoy? If so then someone must have tipped them off. Although the lorry was registered in Mozambique, they had entered the country illegally, and of course had a load of contraband.

Van Zyl cursed out loud. Somehow he had to stop Barney and the truck, before they reached the intersection, and divert him onto another road – but how? He circled around, climbed to 2000 feet and flew back to intercept Barney.

Pulling a notebook from the cubbyhole, he scribbled a note. *'Road block up ahead. Parks vehicles are following you. Take road via Panda and go to Zavora. Off load onto beach. I will arrange for pick-up there'*. He put the note inside a plastic 'sick-bag' with an empty coke bottle to give the packet weight.

As soon as he found Barney's convoy, still labouring along slowly, he flew down low and after making two passes to attract his attention; Van Zyl opened the cockpit window and dropped the message on the road in front of him. He climbed back to 1000 feet and circled around to see if he had found the message.

Barney stopped, got out of his van and picked up the packet. A few moments later he looked up and waved to acknowledge that he understood.

· · · · · · · · · · · · · ·

The day after arriving back on Inhaca, Tom and Sandy flew to Inhambane and spent the night in their camp at Ingale. In the morning they launched *Pelé-Pelé* and Tom went off to Inhambane bay while Sandy drove there in the van to meet him.

They went to the airport and flew off to find Barnard and his convoy, and to make sure the rangers were still on his trail. As soon as he felt they might be within range of their radio, Tom tried to raise his son.

"Go ahead Dad. I am receiving you," Kyle's voice crackled in response.

"I am at 2000 feet following the road from Inhambane. Have you got me visual yet?" Tom asked.

"Yes I have you in sight. What do you see from up there?"

"I can see your dust - you are on the right road. Barnard is about 4 k's ahead of you. He is still on the road to Inhambane."

"Roger that. Can you keep watch on him and make sure he stays on this road. We are stepping up our pace and hope to catch up in two hours."

"Okay will do. As soon as I know where he is heading, I will land at Inhambane to liaise with the police."

Half an hour later they passed through Funhalouro and, according to Tom still circling high overhead, they had closed the gap. Barnard was moving very slowly.

"At this rate we should be right on his tail before we get to the coast," Kyle said. "Is the reception committee organised?"

"Yes I think so. I'm heading back to Inhambane now. Good hunting." Tom turned the plane and flew away to make sure everything was in place and ready for Barnard.

"Roger. See you there," Kyle signed off.

It was past midday and there was enough time for them to be there long before the convoy arrived. They landed, hurried back to where *Pelé-Pelé* was tied up, and went across the bay. They slowed down as they passed the place where they had previously seen the long-boat - it was still there. They tied up at Morrumbene jetty where they were in a position to quickly pursue the long-boat if it left the bay.

The two of them went to a small pavement café at the end of the rickety wooden jetty to wait for the officials. Apparently the South African Parks Board had arranged for the Mozambique Wardens to meet them there.

While they waited, they took the opportunity to nibble on bowls of chicken giblets and olives washed down with ice-cold Laurentina beer. They had only been there a few minutes when a twin-engine plane flew low overhead.

....

146

Somewhat relieved he had managed to warn Barney of the trap, and knowing he would change direction as ordered, Van Zyl flew back to Inhambane.

He buzzed the shed, and Antonio came across the bay to meet him at the airstrip. Van Zyl told Antonio of the police road block, and gave him instructions for the change of plan. He and his men were to leave immediately in the long-boat, and sail down the coast to Zavora where he would find Barnard waiting for them on the beach.

They were to load the crates and take them out to the *Verona;* it would be waiting for him some distance off-shore. He stressed the urgency of the situation, and threatened Antonio with his life should anything else go wrong.

Van Zyl watched Antonio hurry off to pick up his crew, and to carry out his instructions, then climbed back on board his plane. He took off and flew to Bazaruto, half an hour up the coast. He had decided to spend the night in the hotel on the island, where he was well away from any danger. If necessary from there he would be able to escape at a moments notice. His plan was to leave first thing in the morning.

Before landing he called the *Verona* on the radio, and gave the captain the new pick-up location. There was nothing more he could do. He would just have to sit tight and hope it all went according to plan and that Barney had managed to get his load away safely. He would hear from the ship's captain in the morning, hopefully after making the pick-up.

Having been forewarned, Van Zyl was confident Barney was smart enough to avoid the police and escape arrest; but the lorry might not get away. It was now all in Barney's hands, and he could only hope his load of ivory and rhino horn was delivered safely to the trawler. This was not the first time he had been in this sort of situation. Nevertheless he was very worried; there was a lot of money at stake.

Thinking about the whole mess over dinner, he was convinced it was Tom Owen who had found out what they were up to, and had alerted the authorities.

• • • • • • • • • • • • • •

The rangers were so close behind Barnard's convoy that, for the past half hour, they had been driving through their dust. The road surface had improved, and so they were able to move along at a reasonable speed.

After leaving Funhalouro the rangers entered an area of tall coconut plantations and mango trees, where the dust stirred up by the passing of the vehicles on the sandy road ahead of them hung in the air for some time before settling.

Dusk was coming on fast when they passed an intersection where a road branched off to the south towards Pemba. Kyle, in the lead Cruiser, knew they were closing in on Barnard. He estimated they were only a few kilometers behind him when suddenly he realized there was no dust.

Calling a halt, he jumped out of the vehicle to examine the road. There were no lorry tracks visible in the sand. Barnard must have turned off onto the Panda road and in their haste to catch up, they had missed the intersection when they went flying past.

Kyle cursed - he had been so intent on catching up to Barnard, and driving him into the trap, that he had not checked when they drove past the turn off. They turned around and went back a kilometre to the intersection they had passed only minutes earlier. Again Kyle examined the tracks and confirmed that Barnard had changed direction, and was now heading towards Panda.

The rangers had lost precious time and the gap between them had opened up again. Barnard was probably now two or three kilometers ahead.

The reception committee, consisting of police and Mozambique game department officials, were waiting near Inhambane – now with their quarry having changed direction, and with night closing in, Barnard might easily slip through the net. The plane he had seen circling must have been Van Zyl - he must have seen the road block from the air and warned Barnard, making him change direction.

"Tom. Come in please Tom," Kyle called on the radio. There was no response and so the rangers sped on in pursuit. In spite of their speed, the chances of catching up to Barnard before he reached the coast were slim – unless the police moved their road block fast. Every few minutes Kyle tried to raise his father on the radio but to no avail.

. . . .

Tom and Sandy had been sitting outside the restaurant for half an hour when two policemen approached them. After introducing themselves they explained that, acting on information they had been given, a road block had been set up, and they were waiting for the trucks from Zimbabwe.

"Do you know when we can expect them to arrive, *senhor*?" the senior man asked.

"I am not sure. If you will come with us to our boat we can try to contact my son on the radio," Tom suggested.

"Do you think Kyle will be within range by now?" Sandy asked as they all stood up.

"I am sure they must be. We saw them about two hours ago." Tom said as the four of them walked quickly down the jetty to *Pelé-Pelé*.

"Kyle, come in please," Tom tried to raise Kyle on the Parks radio as soon as they were back at the boat.

"Receiving you Dad. Go ahead," Kyle responded immediately.

"Where are you guys? The road block is set and ready."

"Barnard's lot have changed direction. They are now heading towards Panda. We saw an aircraft circling above them about an hour ago," Kyle said. "You must get a message to the police as quickly as you can."

"There are two policemen standing beside me. I will pass the info to them."

The policemen trotted off quickly to arrange a road block at Inharrime. It was the only other place where the road Barnard was driving along could take him to the sea; unless he was making for a smaller village along the coast. If the road block was set quickly, and with the rangers close behind, there was still time to corner the smugglers.

With the action likely further south, there was no point in Tom and Sandy hanging around at the jetty, and so they untied *Pelé-Pelé* and started back towards Inhambane. It was getting late. The sun was low in the sky and night would soon be closing in. There was no time to waste if they were to be there when the net closed in and Barnard was arrested.

As they rounded the bend in the bay, the long-boat backed out from under the mangroves, turned and went speeding off towards the open sea. Tom eased the throttles forward and followed at a reasonable distance, making sure they kept it in sight. Once out of the bay the long-boat turned south. Further out to sea a trawler was also steaming south. It looked like the *Verona,* and if so was probably making its way to rendezvous with the long-boat and Barnard.

"Kyle, come in please," Sandy called on the radio as they turned around and headed back to the town.

"Go ahead Sandy," Kyle responded.

"The long-boat and the *Verona* are heading south at full speed. We will tie *Pelé-Pelé* up in Inhambane and follow on to Inharrime by road."

"Roger that. See you there."

Chapter 23

An hour after turning onto the Panda road, in spite of the deep sand on the road, the rangers had made up most of the lost ground. Once again they were close behind Barnard's vehicles. By the time they reached Chakane it was dusk and every now and then, through the dust and dim evening light, they saw red tail-lights on the road ahead.

Although there were one or two other vehicles on the road, Kyle was sure none were between them and Barnard. At times the dust was so thick their headlights hardly penetrated through it, and they were forced to slow right down until it cleared.

"Barnard is only a kilometre ahead of us now. What must we do?" Kyle asked Tom over the radio.

"Just keep your distance and watch where they go. I have two policemen in front of me; we will meet you at the intersection on the main road north of Inharrime," Tom instructed his son.

"Roger. We'll see you there in about half an hour," Kyle said.

....

It was after eight, and quite dark, when Barnard and his truck turned north onto the main north road, then after a kilometer, took the road to Zavora. Before reaching the coast Barnard stopped at a wayside restaurant to buy food and refreshments for his men. They had been on the road since early that morning without stopping, and were thirsty, hungry and disgruntled.

Stressing the urgency, and the danger of being caught, Barnard sent the truck on ahead. The driver was instructed to find somewhere close to the beach, where it would be easy to manhandle the crates onto Antonio's long-boat, the moment he arrived.

Thanks to Van Zyl's warning, Barnard was fairly confident they had managed to avoid the police. He had seen no sign of them, or the parks men following them, when they turned onto the Zavora road - nobody would suspect where they were going.

Barnard had no intention of stopping any longer than necessary, and so they had to off load as fast as possible, and the truck could get on its way back to Zimbabwe. They could find a place to stop and rest, once they were well away from the main roads.

If the police had been alerted, it would not be long before they started looking for them. It was night and so there would be no danger until morning; by then they would be long gone. Barnard would wait to see the consignment safely transported out to the trawler. Antonio was on his way and should be there in a few hours.

Parking his van around the corner from the restaurant, Barnard placed his order, bought a beer, and then sat down at one of the tables on the pavement to wait for the food.

. . . .

The rangers met up with Tom, Sandy, and the two policemen, where the road from Panda joined the main north road. The two vehicles they had been following for three days had disappeared. The police got on the radio to check with the men manning the road block at Inharrime - they had seen no sign of Barnard or his lorry.

Studying the map, they worked out that the only place with access to the beach was Zavora. All the other towns and villages nearby were cut off from the sea by lakes and lagoons. And so they turned around and made for Zavora as fast as they could.

As they passed through a small settlement along the way, they spotted Barnard's pick-up parked near a small restaurant. There was no sign of the lorry. Stopping a little way further on they let Dodi off, to keep watch on Barnard. Before moving on they saw him hide under a tarpaulin covering the bin on the back the pick-up.

With the long-boat on its way, it was obvious Barnard would want to off load his goods onto the beach, where it would be easy to transfer. The police took the lead and they continued to Zavora. When they crested the high sand dunes, approaching the small holiday village, they saw the headlights of a vehicle right in front of them. As they got closer they realised it was Barnard's truck, parked near the mangrove trees on the one side of the main car-park near the beach front.

Men were busy off-loading large wooden crates, but as soon as they saw the police, they panicked and tried to hide. The rangers, catching them by surprise, quickly surrounded them, cutting off any attempt to escape along the beach. Barnard's team were quickly rounded up and the police moved in to arrest them and put them all in handcuffs. The arrested men from Zimbabwe were not at all happy.

There were six large crates and a number of hardwood logs on the lorry. Two rangers using a tyre lever opened one of the crates - it was packed full of elephant tusks.

....

Barnard was just enjoying the first gulp of his beer, when a police van, followed by two green open Land Cruisers packed with rangers, drove slowly through the village heading in the direction of Zavora. He slammed his glass down on the table, and shot out of his chair so fast that it went flying over backwards.

They had caught up a lot faster than he had expected. Giving them a few moments to move further away out of sight, he told the waiter he would be back to collect his order, then ran around the corner, jumped into his van and hurried after them.

Hoping and praying his driver had found a secluded spot to off load, and that the police had not yet found them, he approached Zavora with caution. A few hundred yards from the beach, he switched his lights off. Topping the rise he was dismayed and alarmed by what he saw below him.

The lorry, parked on one side of the parking area, was hemmed in by the police vehicle and the ranger's cruisers. All with their headlights on lighting up the whole car park. His men had all been rounded up and were sitting on the ground. They had been trapped, and there was nothing he could do about it.

There was no time to lose. Barnard had no intention of putting himself at risk, or of being arrested. To try and rescue his men was not an option. If he was arrested he would certainly be put in prison and the keys thrown away. He had to get out of there fast. Reversing away and making sure he didn't attract attention to himself, Barnard turned around and drove quietly away like a thief in the night.

Once well away from the sea-front, Barnard left Zavora as fast as he could - stopping only to pick up his order from the restaurant - he was going to need it. He realized he had no option but to make his way back to Zimbabwe fast - before road blocks were set to stop him.

As he rounded a bend in the road on the outskirts of Inharrime he saw the flashing lights of a police vehicle parked on the side of the road. It was too late to stop or try to turn away, and so he had to keep going. As he got closer, much to his relief, he realised they were checking all vehicles travelling north. He was going south, and so they didn't bother with him.

At the first fuel station he stopped to fill the tank, and then left the main road at the first intersection where a road turned inland. From there he followed a secondary dirt road that he hoped would eventually lead him to the railway line, and back to Zimbabwe.

The faster he got well away from Zavora, the better his chances were of avoiding the police. Once he was well away from Inharrime, he would have to find somewhere to stop and rest for a while. He had a long drive ahead of him and was already tired from the long day on the road. On the other hand, he had to keep going as long as he was able to stay awake.

Barnard knew the lorry, with its precious cargo of tusks and horns, had been lost; but at least he still had some of the rhino horns on the back of his pick-up. It had been a last minute decision to pack them in a separate crate and put it in his van. It was his insurance.

. . . .

Dodi had no sooner hidden under the tarpaulin in the back of Barnard's pick-up, when the door slammed, the engine fired up and they moved off. It drove along slowly for a while then stopped, reversed, turned and moved off then stopped again briefly.

Half an hour later the pick-up stopped and Dodi could hear voices and smell fuel. Barnard was filling up. It had been a long chase and Dodi was tired.

He made himself as comfortable as he could; he had a feeling it was going to be some time before he could get off the van. The drone of the engine and the hum of the tyres on the road soon lulled him to sleep.

. . . .

The crates were loaded back onto the lorry, while Sandy and one of the policemen went in search of Barnard. They drove around the village searching for him, but he was nowhere to be found and there was no sign of his vehicle. They drove back to the restaurant where they had seen his van and left Dodi, but the waiter told them that he had taken his food and left. He was not sure which way he had gone.

"Well Barnard seems to have managed to slip out of the net, and it looks like he has buggered off with Dodi. Does anyone know what

154

happened to our friend Van Zyl?" Sandy asked once they were convinced Barnard was nowhere in Zavora. "If it was Van Zyl we saw in that plane," he added as an afterthought.

"According to the police, after circling Inhambane twice the plane landed. Before they could get anyone to the airport to speak to him, he took off again and flew north," Tom said. "They have put out an alert to all the airports for any information regarding Van Zyl's plane, and for him to be detained for questioning."

"He must have seen us following Barnard, and somehow managed to warn him," Kyle surmised. "Now he's flown away, and it looks like Barnard has gone off with Dodi hiding in the back of his van. I wonder if he knows his truck has been impounded and his men arrested. He has certainly taken off in a bloody hurry, without bringing food for his men."

"You can be sure old Dodi will stick to him like glue. We'll hear from him sooner or later; when he can get away," Tom said confidently. "It would help if we knew where Barnard is heading. That long-boat we were following was going down the coast. It must be on its way here. It was going hell for leather when we turned back to Inhambane. We also saw what we think is Van Zyl's trawler steaming this way."

"What's our plan of action?" Kyle asked.

"I think we should set a trap to catch the long-boat and its crew. The police will get the trawler and Barnard," Tom said after a short discussion with the policemen.

"What about Van Zyl? Do you think Barnard has gone off to warn him?" Kyle asked.

"Perhaps. The police are setting up road blocks on all the roads; they might have seen him somewhere, or even arrested him by now. We must just make sure they don't lock Dodi up when they do catch Barnard."

The truck was left where it could be seen from the sea, so that the long-boat crew could home in on it. The other vehicles were all hidden out of sight. Four crates were taken from the lorry, the tusks removed, and the empty crates lugged down to the beach. Four rangers; two from Mozambique and two from South Africa, sat down alongside the crates to await the arrival of the long-boat.

A driver was sent to get them all food and drink. It was after ten by the time they had eaten and the trap was ready. Unless the long-boat crew knew the exact location of the pick-up, it would not be there until first light, when they could see where to go. It was a nice warm night with hardly a breath of air. They were all tired. It had been a long day, and so they took turns to sleep while they waited.

It was just beginning to get light, when they saw the white phosphorous glow from the bow wave and high prow of a boat heading straight for the beach where they waited. It was the long-boat. The rangers were awake and ready to spring the moment the boat beached. Kyle, who had joined the rangers on the beach, was hiding behind the crates; his pale skin was sure to alert the crew of the approaching boat, frightening them away. Tom, Sandy and the two policemen waited behind the trees 50 paces away.

As the boat slid up the sand onto the beach with the engine cut, the four rangers leaped up and ran to meet it. Something must have alerted the boat's crew; the rangers were almost on them, when one of them shouted a warning. They tried desperately to push the boat off the beach back into deeper water, but were too late. The rangers pounced quickly on them, before they had a chance to make a getaway.

As the rangers reached the boat, Kyle who was only a few paces behind, saw one of the boat crew tossing something away into the sea. The four boatmen, realising they were outnumbered and overpowered, gave up without a struggle and were dragged up the beach away from their boat. By then one of the policemen had arrived on the scene to arrest the captured boat men.

With the help of the rangers, they dragged the boat along the beach to where Tom and Sandy waited with the other policeman and the captured Zimbabweans. The empty crates were lugged back to the truck, and re-packed with tusks.

A quick inspection of the remaining crates revealed that one of them contained 12 rhino horns. All the rest were full of tusks. The value of the confiscated goods must have been in excess of US$4 million. Dodi had only known of six rhino horns!

When questioned about the object he had tossed into the sea, Antonio, the skipper of the long-boat, quickly admitted to the police that it was the two-way radio he used to contact the fishing trawler *Verona*. There was no point in trying to recover the radio; it would be useless.

They were still busy tidying up loose ends, and giving statements to the police when an aircraft flew past. It was a twin engine plane, similar to the one Kyle had seen the previous day, flying low out over the sea. It flew on down the coast and was soon out of sight. Once they had all made statements, and after being warned that they would be required to give evidence in court, the police thanked them for their assistance and allowed them to go.

It was mid-morning before the police were ready to move off. The long-boat was loaded onto the back of the truck, on top of the crates and the timber. The men from Zimbabwe, and the four boat-men from Mozambique, climbed up onto the back and with Barnard's driver, escorted by one of the policemen, they drove off to the police station in Inharrime.

The navy was called on to assist with the apprehension of the trawler, but not having a patrol boat in the vicinity, were unable to help. The *Verona* was nowhere to be seen; it had probably been alerted and had moved away over the horizon into the safety of international waters, where it could not be touched. With no evidence or reason to stop or search it, Van Zyl's trawler had managed to escape the net and sailed away to continue long-line fishing.

But where was Barnard? He had just disappeared along with Dodi. This was worrying as the last they had seen of Dodi was when he jumped onto the back of the van. Although Tom was concerned, he knew Dodi was very resourceful and would pitch up at some stage - no doubt, in the meantime, he would stay close to Barnard somewhere, keeping a watchful eye on him.

With the excitement of the chase, and capture of the poachers over, it was time to get back to work. The rangers, after a day's rest relaxing on the beach, went back to South Africa, well pleased with the result. Kyle flew to Inhaca leaving Tom and Sandy to pack up Ingale camp and haul *Pelé-Pelé* back to Maputo. A few days later Tom took Kyle and Rosa home to the Lowveld.

Chapter 24

The sun was just peeping over the horizon of a calm Indian Ocean when Van Zyl left the hotel. Anxious to find out if the skipper of *Verona* had made the pick-up, he called him on the radio as soon as he was airborne. The trawler was still waiting off-shore for Antonio to arrive or call on the radio. Van Zyl was worried. They should have loaded before light, and been well away from the coast by this time. What had gone wrong? Had they been caught?

Knowing there was a very strong possibility Barney and his lorry might have been trapped outside Inharrime, he had to find out - there was a lot of money at stake. He flew south and 30 minutes later, as he approached Zavora, he saw the *Verona* lying about 2 miles out to sea.

Flying half way between the coast and the trawler, he spotted Barney's truck. It was surrounded by two police and the two Parks vehicles that had been following Barney. The long-boat and the crates were lying on the ground near the lorry.

It was now quite clear that he had lost his valuable load of ivory and rhino horn. He cursed himself for not turning Barney away altogether, and sending him back to Zimbabwe; but there had been rangers close behind him, and there would have been no escape. Barney had been driven into a trap.

Not wanting to attract attention to his plane, Van Zyl stayed on his course, and kept flying south. Once he was well out of sight he climbed to 5000 feet and turned for Harare. He called the *Verona* and told the skipper to abort the mission, turn around and to get out of Mozambique territorial waters as fast as possible. He was to put long lines out and continue fishing as he made his way north back to Europa Island, and wait for his instructions.

But where was Barney? He had not seen his pick-up among the vehicles on the beach. He must have escaped the net. The only option he would have had was to head back to Zimbabwe using the fastest route. Van Zyl flew on until he found the railway line from Maputo to Zimbabwe then turned to follow it north.

An hour later, from the vehicles on the road, he picked out the long trail of dust made by Barney's van, speeding along the gravel road alongside the rail line. He was obviously making his way back to Mabiti and the safety of Zimbabwe. Van Zyl, pleased to see that Barney had managed to escape, flew on above the road and railway line to make sure it was safe for him.

With no sign of road blocks, or of anything else that might prevent Barney from getting home, he flew on to Mabiti to wait for him there. He crossed the border then buzzed the camp at Mabiti for the driver to come and pick him up.

There was no sign of Petros in camp, and nobody had seen or heard from him. He had been away for ten days, and according to the workers, Barnard had taken him to Chikombedzi. He had not returned and they suspected that he must have gone home on long leave, or even decided to leave work for good and gone home to retire.

Perhaps Barnard knew of his whereabouts, they suggested. They knew nothing of him having been out searching for Tombi and Dodi. Another worry for Van Zyl!

....

Dodi woke up when the sound changed. They had left the tarred road and were travelling on a bumpy dirt road. Dust was choking him, and so he lifted a corner of the tarpaulin to peep out. It was day and the sun was just rising. He must have been asleep for about six hours.

After a while the van slowed down and stopped in the shade of some trees, off the road so as not to be seen. The engine was switched off, and for what seemed like an hour nothing happened.

Dodi guessed Barnard was having a rest; he had been driving for nearly 24 hours and must need it, unless he had stopped earlier while Dodi had been sleeping. He was about to lift his head to see where they were when Barnard coughed, spat out of the window, then started the van and they moved on again.

The day dragged on with Barnard stopping every couple of hours, to rest briefly and to relieve himself. Dodi, who only had his small water bottle to sip sparingly from every now and again, had no need to pass water - the little he did drink was taken up by his body as he sweated under the tarpaulin. Fortunately he always carried his water bottle, along with his *demu* and his *assegai*.

He was stiff and his body ached from lying in one position for so long. Taking care not to rock the van around, he slowly stretched his limbs one at a time to ease the discomfort and stiffness.

It was very dusty in his confined hiding place and, with the sun beating down on the tarpaulin, it was unbearably hot, but there was nothing Dodi could do about it. The van stopped and again Dodi smelt diesel. Once again Barnard had stopped to re-fuel. Many hours later, as the day wore on it began to cool down, and when Dodi did manage to peep out he saw that the sun was setting.

As night closed in the temperature dropped rapidly. From being hot all day, it suddenly turned cold on the back of the van and Dodi was thankful for the tarpaulin. His bladder was full and he was feeling really uncomfortable, but still he dare not move - he was sure Barnard would have to stop soon.

Dodi lost track of time, but it must have been a few hours after night had fallen, when the van eventually stopped. Dodi peeped out and watched Barnard climb out to open a gate. He used the opportunity to ease out from his cramped position under the tarpaulin, and lie between the crate and the tailgate at the rear of the vehicle. He recognised the wire concertina gate by a small sign on the fence - they were at Crooks Corner.

Half an hour later the pick-up stopped once more, and before Barnard could open the door to get out of the drivers' seat, Dodi slipped over the tail-gate and disappeared into the darkness. He hid behind a marula tree to watch and see why Barnard had stopped.

Barnard took a spade from behind the seat and then, with the headlights still shining, he dug a hole under a fig tree on the banks of a small stream near the road. Then with some difficulty, he lifted a large hessian bag out of the crate on the back of the van. He hefted it over to the hole and buried it, patting the soil down firmly after closing it up. Then he cut a small notch on the tree and after carefully brushing away all signs of his buried treasure, got back in his van and drove away.

Dodi knew exactly where he was; he was not far from Mabiti camp. He was tired, thirsty and his bladder was full. There was a trickle of water running in the stream and so, after relieving himself, he washed the dust off his face, quenched his thirst and filled his water bottle. Feeling a lot better, although still stiff and sore from the long hours on the back of the van, he settled down under the tree to sleep. In the morning he would go to Mabiti to see what was going on there.

Chapter 25

In the early hours of the morning, when it was still dark, Van Zyl was wakened by the sound of a hooter. There was a vehicle at the gates; it was Barney and he was exhausted, hungry and thirsty. After a quick bite to eat and something to drink, he collapsed on his bed and slept for six hours. Impatient to know what had gone wrong, Van Zyl woke him up at noon.

"What the hell happened? All our bloody elephant tusks and rhino horns have been confiscated, and your men arrested. I hope like hell none of them give away too much information about us." He had been building up a rage for a day, but seeing how Barney had made the long trip on his own - and managed to avoid the being caught by authorities, made him calm down a little.

"Shit Jannie, I don't know. Someone must have tipped them off. I stopped to buy food for the men and sent them on to start off loading on the beach. Next thing there were game rangers and cops all over the place. There was nothing I could do, so I decided to make a break for it and come back here," Barnard explained. "I came all the way back without stopping."

"I know. I saw you on the road. Those bastards were waiting for you. Lucky you managed to get away. We have lost a shit load of money over this," Van Zyl pointed out. "Did they get all the rhino horns as well as all the tusks?"

"Yes. They got everything. The horns were in one of the crates with the tusks," Barnard lied. "What do you want me to do now? Have you seen Petros?"

"Hell we've lost the whole bloody lot. No, he never came back. The boys reckon he has buggered off for good."

"That means he never caught those two bastards. They have probably reported us to the police by now," Barnard lamented.

"The police I can handle. Do you think they might have gone to Owens's farm?"

"Yes I think so," Barnard agreed. "I'm bloody sure they would have told Owen what we're doing here - that's probably why the bloody game rangers came after us. They must have followed me all the way from the border."

"Yes they did. I saw them from the air. We will have to do something about Owen. I'll be in touch when I know what's happening, and what we are going to do about him. In the meantime lie low. No more elephant or rhino poaching until I say so. You must get rid of all evidence of our illegal operations here. You do realize that this whole mess is your fault. If you had left that black woman alone, and kept your bloody dick in your pants, we would not have lost all our stuff. We can never use that base in Mozambique again - do you understand?"

. . . .

Dodi was awake early. His stomach grumbled with hunger pains. He had only eaten a small portion of *biltong* (dried meat) in the last 24 hours and needed to find food. First though he had work to do.

After washing and drinking water from the stream, he used a stout stick to dig up the bag Barnard had buried, then covered the hole and left it looking as he had found it. He opened the hessian bag to see what was inside. It was full of rhino horns.

About 300 paces from where Barnard had buried his 'treasure' Dodi found a perfect place to hide the bag of horns. He went to work stripping a couple of lengths off the inner bark of a nearby mopani tree, known for its strength and used for tying roof timbers together. From a nearby a giant euphorbia he bled some of the sticky milk from one the branches onto a piece of bark which he wrapped up carefully with elephant grass.

Dodi, although by no means small in stature, struggled to pull the hessian bag high up into a large mahogany tree. Using the strips of bark he tied the bundle securely in the fork of one of the branches; well hidden from view by the dense green foliage. Then he smeared the cactus milk all over the bundle. Monkeys and baboons knowing it was sticky and bitter, and that if it got into their eyes would burn or even blind - would not touch it.

Satisfied that no inquisitive primates, or other tree climbers, would be able to get at his prize, he climbed down. Before moving on he swept away all traces of his having been near the tree.

It was still early by the time he finished his task, and knowing impala and other small gazelle would still be near water, he went off in search of food. Following the stream, as it wandered through the mopani forest, it wasn't long before he found a small duiker having a drink of water - its ears twitched back and forth as it searched for sounds of danger. Dodi crept slowly and quietly up behind the unsuspecting animal and, when he was 15 paces away, threw his assegai. It flew straight and true striking the small animal in the neck, dropping it in its tracks before it had a chance to move.

Dodi slit the duiker's belly open, removed the entrails, skinned it and cut off all the meat. He kept the skin; it would be useful later. The carcass and the entrails he took to an open area where vultures, hyenas and jackals would find them.

So as not to make smoke, he made a fire with dried twigs and bits of fallen dead wood he found lying under the trees. Then using green sticks to skewer the meat he cooked it all over the fire; he would need a supply of food in the coming days or weeks.

The liver, the heart and the kidneys he cooked first, and then feasted hungrily on them while the rest of the meat was cooking. Mopani worms, locusts, ripe thirst quenching fruit off marula trees, orange coloured fibrous fig like fruit from mahobohobo trees and roots he could gather when he wanted. There was an abundance of food to be found in the African bush at that time of year.

Once all the meat was cooked, he salted it and tucked it all away in one of the bags he always carried. Dodi, like all good trackers and hunters, always carried a couple of plastic bags, a small cloth ash bag used to test the wind, and a packet of salt. You can't live in Africa without salt. Dodi put the fire out then covered the ashes with soil. He was finally ready to make his way to Mabiti to keep watch on Barnard and the camp.

Along the way, a honey-guide bird fluttered around near the ground in front of him, trying to attract his attention. He followed the bird and found the tree where it had located a bee-hive. Half an hour later the bird had a comb full of grubs that Dodi left for it as a reward, and he had a bag of honey comb. It was a good addition to his larder.

Close to Mabiti, Dodi found a tall mahogany tree where, from the upper branches, he could see right into the camp, while at the same time being well concealed by the dense green leaves. Stripping more inner bark from a mopani he twisted it into a rope and made a loop over an upper branch in the tree.

Then he tied his bag of meat and the bag of honey on a long piece of twine he kept in his pouch; normally used to trap birds, and suspended them from the rope loop. Again he smeared the rope and twine with cactus milk. It would be safe there until he returned.

Keeping well away from the road, Dodi set off for Chikombedzi. He needed more salt, meal, a small pot and a blanket. He had a feeling he might be watching the camp for quite some time. His boss didn't even know where he was, and it might take time for him to catch up with Barnard.

....

Leaving Barney to sort out the mess, and get rid of all traces of their elephant and rhino hunting, Van Zyl flew back to Harare. He summoned the two men who had been watching Owen. They reported that he and his wife had gone to Mozambique. They had been away for a month, and there were other people staying in their house while they were away.

As Owen was out of the country, Van Zyl sent them to the Lowveld to watch the farm where Kyle Owen worked. He wanted to know the whereabouts of Tombi and Dodi. If they saw either of them they were to capture them and contact Van Zyl immediately. He would meet them wherever they were holding their captives. He stressed the urgency of their mission, and the need for secrecy.

Next Van Zyl paid a call on Ted Hunter to discuss the issue of his claims, and to try and settle the matter before it went to the courts. He had no intention of backing off, but it gave him a good reason to try and find out what Owen was up to, and his whereabouts. He was not going to rest until he had dealt with Mr Owen and his accomplices; they had cost him a lot of money.

On the markets in the East, the load of elephant tusks and rhino horn would probably have been worth in excess of US$4 million. With the high demand for rhino horn powder, used as an aphrodisiac, it was more valuable per ounce than gold. Besides, he had made promises to his agents in Malaysia, and was now in the embarrassing position of not being able to supply them.

As it was, the Wild Life Conservation people in South Africa, Mozambique and even in Zimbabwe were tightening up, and watching their animals very carefully. He had even heard that radio tracking devices were being fitted into some of the rhino's horns. His diamond trading had been somewhat curtailed by the army, and now this very lucrative sideline was also in trouble, and had to be put on hold until the dust had settled.

"Well I am sorry we can't resolve our problems. We'll just have to go to court and let them decide," Van Zyl said after making Ted a ridiculous offer of compensation for his 'supposed' claims.

"Yes I think that is best. I am not going to sit back and let you bulldoze me off my claims; like you seem to do all around the country," Ted replied struggling to keep his temper.

"Okay, I'll see you in court then," Van Zyl said turning to leave. Then as an after-thought he turned back and asked. "I need to speak with Tom Owen. Do you know how I can get hold of him?"

"He isn't in the country. He has started a fishing business in Mozambique and spends most of his time there," Ted told him before he had time to stop himself. "Why do you want to speak to him? I can pass a message on if you like."

"No thanks, its okay. Nothing too serious. Do you know when he'll be back in Harare?"

"Not until next year. It's fishing season in Mozambique so he might be busy until then," Ted responded, angry with himself for being trapped so easily into giving away Tom's whereabouts.

Van Zyl was worried about the Mozambique authorities checking up on him, or getting the Zimbabwe Conservation officials to investigate him, and so he phoned his contact at the Ministry of Lands. He agreed to try and find out if there was any communication with neighbouring wild life departments, and would let Van Zyl know if he heard anything.

It wasn't long - two days later he received an urgent call from the Ministry. Van Zyl's operations in the Lowveld were about to come under investigation. He did not want anyone going down to Mabiti to snoop around without being there himself, and so he invited the senior Minister of Lands for a week-end hunt.

They flew down to Mabiti and after two days hunting kudu, zebra and wildebeest, the minister was quite happy to squash any investigation into the Mabiti hunting operations. Bribery was the name of the game!

Van Zyl got his secretary to search the internet for companies advertising fishing charters in Mozambique. He jotted down the contact details for each of them – he would check them later to find which one belonged to Owen. As he didn't want him to suspect anything, he was not going to email or phone personally. A pal of his Andre Swanepoel was a keen fisherman and so Van Zyl invited him for a *braai* (barbecue).

"Andre, do you fancy a deep-sea fishing trip to Mozambique? I'll sponsor the whole trip, including booze," Van Zyl asked his pal as they chomped on juicy steaks and *wors* (spicy sausage).

"I never say no to fishing, especially if it's paid for by you. But you aren't a keen fisherman, why do you want to go fishing?" Andre asked.

"There's a fellow running a charter business there, and I want to see what he is up to. I don't want him to know I am coming to have a look-see; we are not on very good terms, and he owes me," Van Zyl said. "I want you to make the booking in your name. I'll give you the money."

"Sure. When do you want to go?"

"We'll book a week in September or October. As soon as I have the details we can get together to make the booking. Are you free at that time?"

"Ja. It's our off-season, and the sales floors will be closed, so it'll be fine."

Van Zyl got his secretary to email every fishing charter business in Mozambique she could find on the internet, until she found the one run by Tom Owen. A week later they had booked a week-long charter for three of them; Andre, Van Zyl and his son Joey.

The two men in the Lowveld reported that they had seen no sign of either Dodi or Tombi. They were not on the farm where Kyle Owen worked.

Chapter 26

Dodi had been watching the camp at Mabiti for a month. Barnard was still hunting impala, kudu, zebra and wildebeest, but from what he saw, there was no killing of either elephant or rhino. The only time there was a change in the daily routine was when Van Zyl brought an important looking man to hunt for a week-end.

Dodi decided it was time to report to Kyle. He was not achieving anything, and it was time his boss knew where he was.

Before leaving, Dodi took the bag of rhino horns down from its hiding place in the tree, and took it to where he had been camping close to the airstrip. He dug a hole about three feet deep then buried the bag in a hole, stamping the ground down firmly. He rolled a couple of heavy rocks on top of his hiding place, and then marked his 'territory' by urinating all around it.

This would keep inquisitive scavengers away until the next rains settled the ground, and washed away all scent of the buried horns. Satisfied that nobody would find his cache, he walked to Chikombedzi and caught the bus to Chiredzi.

. . . .

"Dad, you'll never guess who had just turned up out of the blue! It's Dodi - he stayed on Barnard's van, hiding under the tarpaulin, all the way from Inharrime to Mabiti. He's been there all this time, keeping an eye on Barnard.

"Hell I'm pleased to hear that. I knew he would turn up sooner or later," Tom was delighted to hear that his old friend Dodi had at last turned up safe and sound. "Has he anything to report?"

"No. He says nothing is happening there except the normal hunting for meat and skins."

"We know Van Zyl won't take our interference lightly. By now he will have worked out that Dodi and Tombi told us about their poaching. I think it'll be a good idea to send Dodi down to Mabiti once a month just to check on them. Ted is keeping tabs on Van Zyl from his side in Harare," Tom said. "We don't want to be caught with our pants down."

"Yes, I agree. I'll get him and Gideon to keep an eye out for any strangers hanging around near the farm, just in case he decides to have a go at us," Kyle concurred.

"Are you sure Kyle and Rosa are safe in Zimbabwe with Van Zyl looking for revenge?" Maria asked, expressing her concern, after Tom told her of his conversation with Kyle.

"I'm sure they will be. Van Zyl might know of my involvement but he can't possibly know about Kyle's; except that he's our son."

"We know he was having you followed; or we think it was Van Zyl. But don't you think he might also be watching Kyle?"

"Kyle lives out on a farm; it is isolated and if someone is watching him, he will know about it pretty dam quickly," Tom re-assured Maria. "He'll get Gideon to keep an eye out for villains hanging around near the farm. Thanks to our man Dodi, at least we know Barnard has gone to ground at Mabiti," he finished changing the subject.

••••••••••••••••

Two weeks later their first clients arrived from America. Tom picked them up at the Maputo airport and flew them to Inhaca where they were booked into the Lodge. The thatched cottages were a little rustic, but well appointed and very comfortable; all they needed.

After their long flight, the two men from Miami were tired, and so they were left alone to relax. In the evening Tom, Sandy and Maria joined them for dinner, and to discuss their fishing schedule. Tom arranged to pick them up in the morning at the jetty. Before leaving the Lodge Tom made sure that a packed breakfast would be ready for the two Americans.

Chuck and Matt were two of the most enthusiastic fishermen either Tom or Sandy had ever met. They were both happy cheerful fellows, who knew exactly what they were doing and what they wanted. It was real pleasure fishing with them. After the first day, fishing in the bay, they went out into the deep water of the Mozambique Channel to try for the bigger game-fish. The first couple of days they fished for barracuda, dorado, tunny, wahoo and kingfish.

The weather was kind. It was mild with gentle breezes and full sunshine. Every day they returned from fishing with good catches, but nothing spectacular. Tom began to worry; the first season had to be good. The second week they decided to concentrate their efforts on catching sailfish and marlin.

168

Using 'Rapala' lures they trolled from Inhaca to catch live-bait. Before long they had three or four nice bonita swimming in the live-bait hatch. Chuck and Matt baited up the marlin rods, and then after making sure their Bonita's were 'swimming' nicely, they let their out lines until the bait was just behind the bubbles in the wake of the boat. They trolled slowly out into the channel hoping to hook a bill-fish. The wind had moved around and the sea temperature had risen by a couple of degrees; it was looking good!

Both fishermen watched the water keenly, waiting for a 'take'. Again that day they didn't even have a knock, or see any sign of the 'big ones'. There were a lot of dolphins about; maybe they were chasing the fish away. Chuck and Matt, although disappointed, remained positive. Tom and Sandy wanted their clients to go home satisfied. The last thing they needed was for them to go home and spread the word that fishing in Mozambique was not good. They were starting to run out of time.

Then next day it changed for the better. Within minutes they had caught half a dozen bait fish and, with only one rod in the water, they began to troll; this time at a slightly faster speed to keep the bait 'swimming' just below the surface of the sea. Matt and Chuck took spells of half an hour each in the fighting chair.

No sooner was Chuck strapped into the chair for his second spell, with the harness tightened, when he leant forward eagerly. He was excited.

"I felt a knock! I think we have a hungry marlin taking an interest and tapping the bait with its bill," he said quietly as if the sound of his voice would scare the fish away.

"Yes, it's a marlin alright! Look there's the sickle following your bait," Sandy pointed excitedly at the curved shape of the tail fin sticking out of the water just behind the bait.

"Don't do anything. Just keep your line steady," Tom said from his position at the helm, anxiously watching the surface of the water above the bait – they didn't want to lose this one.

Chuck was a picture of concentration as he watched the spot where his line disappeared into the sea; willing the marlin to take the bait.

The marlin seemed to lose interest and disappear. Chuck's face showing his disappointment was turning to look at Tom, when suddenly his attention was jerked back to his line. Quickly he leaned back in the fighting chair; his legs braced and his hands tightening their grip on the rod clipped onto his harness.

"Yes, it's taken. I'm in!" he yelled when his reel started to scream as the marlin took the bait and swam away fast, stripping the line quickly from the reel. The hook was set.

"Let him run for a bit then start bringing him in slowly but don't give him any slack," Sandy advised. It was a blue marlin, the second fastest fish in the ocean, and in next to no time had stripped most of the line from the reel as it swam away fast with the hook in its mouth.

When the fish showed itself, it came out of the sea leaping right out of the water flying its fin and 'tail-walking' before splashing back on its side. The fight was on!

"It's a beauty Chuck, you lucky devil. Just don't lose it now," Matt although green with envy, was almost as excited as his friend.

The marlin didn't give up easily. Whenever Chuck brought his fish close to the boat, it gathered its strength and swam away again, its shiny black and grey body glistening in the sun, as it leapt high out of the water each time it felt the pull of the line. Sandy poured water on Chuck and his reel to cool them down while Tom concentrated on manoeuvring the boat around as Chuck fought his fish.

Three hours later, after a long hard fight, and numerous spectacular leaps out of the water, the marlin finally gave in and Chuck was able to reel it in. Man and fish were both exhausted. Tom, Sandy and Matt wrestled the marlin on board, pulling it in through the gate at the stern by the bill and using the two gaffs. It was a good fish and by the time they had it on board it was late and the wind had got up. It was time to head back to land.

Chuck was exhausted but elated; it was his first bill-fish. Back on the jetty the marlin was hauled up on the gantry, weighed and photographed with a proud Chuck standing beside his catch. It weighed 455 pounds; a very good size, especially for a first. The head, tail and dorsal fin were sent to Maputo to be packed and shipped to the States to be stuffed and mounted for Chuck.

The next day it was Matt's turn. He hooked into a large sailfish that gave a magnificent display, flying its sail fin each time it came out of the water. The sailfish known to be the fastest fish in the sea was amazing and the colours quite startling. It was quite beautiful; vibrant purple along the back, changing to lighter shades of blue down the sides, with a silver belly. Blue stripes and silver dots covered the whole body. The sail was indigo blue.

Forty minutes after hooking the fish, after numerous incredible leaps out of the sea, the 7 foot long sailfish was brought on board. Both fishermen decided to call it a day. They were both happy with their catches and decided to take a break.

After a day's rest, wandering around the island, they went out again for their last fishing day and had a good time. Between them they caught a Dorado, a pike, two decent kingfish and four shoal sized barracuda, and much to his delight, Matt landed a marlin. Although not nearly as big as Chuck's, it gave him a good fight and took nearly two hours to land. Everyone was happy.

That evening they all got together at the Lodge for a farewell dinner which went on well into the night. Next morning Tom flew Matt and Chuck back to Maputo. After cheerful farewells, and promises of return trips, they flew home with photographic memories of their fishing trip.

Their next clients were a middle aged man and his wife from Orlando in Florida. John was tall, tanned and a fit looking man with a mop of greying hair and an easy smile and his wife, June, a very good looking woman; tall and slim with an athletic build and green eyes set wide apart under a crown of short brunette hair. She obviously played a lot of outdoor sport.

June made an immediate impression on Sandy, who could hardly keep his eyes off her. This charter was going to be far more fun for Maria, who got on well with June right from the start.

John and June decided not to go out fishing the first day. They just wanted to relax and explore the island. The first stop on their wanderings was the '*Santo*' fishing camp where they spent most of the day. After a light lunch they all sat around preparing lures and traces for next days fishing. At sunset they all gathered in the bar at the Lodge for a few drinks and supper.

At first light, Tom & Sandy took their clients out in *Tigger* for their first day's fishing. From the outset it was clear that there was more than a bit of tension between John and June; they spent most of the day bickering and sniping at each other, and didn't seem to enjoy being together in the close confines of the boat. Tom attended to John's needs and Sandy looked after June.

The first day was a settling-in day and so they fished in the bay catching bonita, tunny and pike. The weather was good, the sea a deep dark blue and the fish were biting. At the end of the day it was mutually agreed, that for the duration of the charter, John and June, for a small additional fee would fish off separate boats. They obviously had marital problems and were using the fishing trip to try and mend their crumbling marriage.

To prevent any accusations, Maria went out every day with Sandy and June on their boat. Everyone was happy with this arrangement and it soon became a competition between the two boats. June was the first to catch a sailfish, which annoyed John immensely, and spurred him to greater efforts as he tried hard to catch a Marlin.

After a couple of days June confided in Maria, telling her the reason why she and John were having problems. He was having an affair with his secretary, and so she had booked the fishing trip to get right away from home, where they might be able to patch things up before it was too late. They had been married for twenty years and had a son who was in the last year of his college education. The affair had been going on for some time, but June decided to stay with John until Tony, their son, had graduated.

"June you two will never sort out your problems if you avoid each other the whole time," Maria pointed out.

"Yes I know. But by the time we arrived on this beautiful island, I realized that I felt nothing for John any more. I've made up my mind. When we get home I'm going to divorce him."

"Are you quite sure? Is there nothing left you can build on?" Maria asked.

"No. I feel nothing but contempt for him. I loved him for such a long time, but now I actually loathe him," June was sad.

"I am so sorry it has come to this. Have you made other plans?"

"Not really. I've been thinking about it for a long time now. I'll see what happens in the next few weeks."

When they were not out fishing, Tom, Maria and Sandy did their best to keep out of the way, and leave John and June to themselves. There were things they had to discuss and decisions to make. But June always seemed to make an excuse to be with them in the camp as often as she could, leaving John behind at the Lodge.

As far as the fishing went, the trip was not the success it should have been. Apart from the sailfish caught by June, there was nothing spectacular.

Towards the end of the charter June asked Sandy to take her out in the afternoon to fish in the bay – she needed the time away from everyone. When Maria suggested she go along, June insisted that she and Sandy went alone. They went out but stayed fairly close to shore, within sight of the camp. About quarter of a mile out there was a reef where they dropped anchor, and went over the side to explore it. When they climbed back on board, the two of them lay down on deck in the sun to dry off.

"Well, we leave tomorrow, and I have to go home and sort my life out. Have you ever been to the States?" June asked.

"Yes, once, while I was still studying geology at university. I was only there for a couple of weeks."

"Why don't you come over in your off-season? I'll show you around, and help you promote your business," June suggested.

"That sounds like an excellent idea. I'll discuss it with Tom. Come on we had better get back to the Lodge, before they all think that there is something happening between the two of us," Sandy joked.

. . . .

After the departure of John and June, Sandy spoke to Tom and Maria about going to the USA to promote their business.

"Are you sure you want to go to promote the business, or do you want to go and see June. We saw how the two of you looked at each other," Maria teased. "You think we don't know what is going on between the two of you?"

"It's nothing like that," Sandy denied the accusation. "But June has offered to help show me around. I honestly think it'll be good to get over there and put the word out. Larry and Pete are doing a brilliant job for us, but I think it will be a good idea to help them promote our business. We need plenty of bookings for next season. We have some of the best big-game fishing in the world here, and we must be ahead of the competition," Sandy said on a more serious note.

"Well it certainly sounds like a good idea. We have no bookings for next season as yet, and we do need to make sure we get clients. Maria and I can handle the last month of this season; we only have one group booked at the end of September. Maybe you can go then," Tom agreed.

"Yes, there are three Zimbabweans and only two are fishermen. The third is their pilot or something I believe. Yes, we'll be fine on our own. We can always call on Len or Kyle to give us a hand if necessary," Maria agreed quickly.

"I forgot about Len. Good, I'll get everything ready; DVDs', pamphlets, brochures and then book a flight at the end of August," Sandy said.

The next couple of months went well with only minor problems and one or two clients proving a little difficult. One of them even expected Sandy to catch a marlin for him and then give him the credit for catching it. All their clients that season came from the USA; thanks to the efforts of Larry and Pete. By and large the business had started off very well, and reports back from most of the clients were very positive.

It looked as if they had made the right decision in starting *'Santo Deep-Sea Fishing'*. They enjoyed the work, they enjoyed the lifestyle; they had a good team; and most important of all, they were happy.

Chapter 27

Kyle's management contract was coming up for renewal in December, and it was time to make a decision. He must either take an extension to his contract, or do something else. As he had leave due to him, he and Rosa decided to go to Mozambique, to have a good look at 'Ingale' with the prospect of making a living there.

They drove to Mutare where they crossed into Mozambique and stopped off in Manica for lunch with an old friend from Harare. From there they followed the road south across the Save River and after a long hot trip spent the night at Inhassoro.

Next day they arrived at Inhambane in time for a quick lunch, and to buy a few provisions, before moving on to the Ingale camp 30 kilometers away. The camp-site extended from the edge of a forest of cashew nut trees and coconut palms, right down to the white sandy beach and clear Blue Ocean. After their long hot journey, they couldn't wait to unpack and get down to the sea for a swim.

It was the first time Rosa had been to Ingale and she was suitably impressed. Standing waist-deep in the sea and looking towards the camp she remarked. "Kyle, this place is like a picture out of a travel brochure. It is almost too good to be true."

"The camp is still very much a temporary affair, but once it's established properly, like the one in Inhaca, it will be rather splendid," Kyle agreed.

"It's a bit out of the way and in the middle of nowhere. Do you think people will come here to fish?"

"I don't see why not. The area is world renowned for its fishing and is fast becoming a holiday Mecca for South Africans," Kyle explained. "There are a number of hotels around Inhambane and overseas tourists are starting to flock back into Mozambique."

The camp-site, under the palm trees, was clean and tidy. Their camp supervisor was very meticulous and kept things immaculate. Although it was some months since any of them had stayed there - everything was in place and ready for them to stay in relative comfort.

They engaged the services of a local fisherman with his dhow, to help them explore the coastal waters within easy reach of the camp.

Kyle and Rosa were looking for suitable diving spots, and so he took them to a reef at Torfu; about three kilometres down the coast south of Ingale, where he said the fishing was good and crayfish were in abundance. Both Kyle and Rosa had their diving gear with them, and so they jumped into the water to explore the reef.

"Wow. Isn't it just wonderful down there," Rosa said excitedly when they surfaced.

"Did you see that moray eel watching us from his hole?" Kyle asked her.

"No, I didn't see him. But there are heaps of beautiful reef fish with brilliant colours - colours I just didn't even know existed."

"I saw a number of holes where I think we'll find plenty of crayfish. Rosa I'm sure people will pay to dive off this reef," Kyle was excited.

"Well they say the fishing is good around here; we are close to the Mozambique Channel and now we've found a good reef. What more do we want?" Rosa said agreeing with Kyle.

"Clients! Come on let's go down and see if we can pull a couple of decent crayfish for our supper," Kyle said jumping back into the water.

The two of them spent the next three days exploring, diving and fishing before, rather reluctantly, driving on to Maputo. Arriving at the Clube Navale they found Tom and Maria waiting in *Tigger*, to take them to Inhaca. They had timed their visit perfectly; there were no clients staying at the lodge, and so Tom and Maria had a few days free to discuss their plans with them.

When they heard that Kyle and Rosa wanted to run the camp at Ingale Tom and Maria were delighted. It was far too much for them to operate two camps 400 kilometers apart without help. They planned to move to South Africa; close to the Mozambique border.

Although Kyle had accumulated a fair amount of capital from his contracts in Australia and in Zimbabwe, as they were going to be operating under the umbrella of *'Santo Deep-Sea Fishing'*, Tom offered help with finance. He also suggested that Kyle go overseas to the UK to promote the business in Europe and Ireland. Seamus Maloney had heard good reports from Chuck and Matt and was keen to get involved.

"Excellent. We'll get Sandy to include Ingale, and what it has to offer, on the website and all the brochures. He can also promote both camps when he goes to the States next week," Tom was ecstatic at the prospect of his son joining them. "You will need another couple to help when you get busy."

"Well what about Len? He's always shown an interest and has loads of experience."

"Good idea. Speak to him."

"That's settled then. Let's have a party to celebrate. You men can discuss the finer details tomorrow," Maria beamed.

Before returning to Zimbabwe, Kyle and Rosa went to Empangeni to order their boat.

....

During a two week gap in August with mo bookings, Ted and his wife Elsie came from Harare for a week. They had a marvellous time together, fishing, water-skiing, diving, feasting on prawns and prego's (steak rolls) flying up the coast to explore places of interest and other holiday resorts.

They used the opportunity to advertise their business at hotels and lodges up and down the coast, where plenty of potential clients were to be found.

"Tom, I must tell you that our friend Van Zyl was asking after you a couple of months ago. He was trying to find out where you were, and how he could get in touch with you. Have you heard from him at all?" Ted said at the bar one day.

"No I haven't. Do you think it has something to do with the rhino horns and ivory we helped to have confiscated? We know he was involved. It must have really hurt to lose that amount of money," Tom said.

"Yes, and we know he doesn't like to be opposed in any way. He has become very accustomed to having his own way all these years. He came to see me and offered me a pittance for my claims. I told him to shove it where the monkey puts its nuts. Now he has an axe to grind with both of us."

"Do you think he knows we were involved in messing up his very lucrative poaching operations? Has anything been done about it?" Tom asked.

"I haven't heard a word. If there was to be an investigation, you can bet your bottom dollar he will have used his influence to get his involvement swept under the carpet."

"Well Dodi has been keeping watch on the Mabiti set-up - he hasn't seen anything happening down there. Do you think Van Zyl might have learned his lesson, or is he waiting for his chance to have a go at us?" Tom wondered.

"I don't know. As far as I'm aware, Barnard hasn't even been to Harare to see Van Zyl for quite a while," Ted said.

"Perhaps we must get Kyle and Dodi to try and find out a bit more for us," Tom suggested.

"That's a good idea. We know what Van Zyl is capable of and forewarned is forearmed. I'll try and find out from my end and Kyle can do a bit of digging in the Lowveld," Ted agreed.

. . . .

It all happened a lot faster than Kyle and Rosa expected. When he discussed his resignation with his boss he was most accommodating. His employer, who knew nothing about farming, offered Kyle a long term consultancy contract, and agreed for Kyle to hand over the reins of the farm to a new manager, before the end of the harvesting season. He also agreed to pay Kyle up to the end of his contract period, providing a replacement was found.

By the beginning of September the new manager had taken over, and they were ready to move. Kyle and Rosa bought a lovely thatched house on the banks of the Crocodile River, near Malelane in South Africa, and within weeks had moved there. It was close enough to Mozambique to use as their base.

Dodi moved with them - he had been with the family all his life and had no intention of being left behind in Zimbabwe. He would return every couple of months to check on Mabiti when Kyle went to visit the farm.

The boat was ready for collection, and so just after settling into their new home, they went to Empangeni to collect her. She was christened the *Day Dreamer;* they felt the name was appropriate to their hopes and aspirations. The plan was to go to Ingale once the fishing season was over. Len was going to join them permanently as a partner at the start of the next season.

It was all coming together better than Tom had even dared to dream. The only thing niggling in the back of his mind was Van Zyl. Ted had told him that Van Zyl was trying to find out Tom's whereabouts and this worried him.

At the beginning of September Sandy left for the States, while Tom and Maria got ready for the last charter of the season; the three Zimbabweans.

■■■■◊◊◊◊◊■■■■

Chapter 28

June was waiting for Sandy when he arrived at Pensacola airport in the early morning. They both felt a little awkward and didn't seem to know what to expect from each other. They drove to June's apartment on the outskirts of the city. It was on the 5th floor of an upmarket building at Shoreline Park, right on the point of the spit of land guarding the entrance to Pensacola Bay. Views of the bay, and the sea beyond Santa Rosa Island were magnificent.

After unpacking and taking a welcome shower, Sandy joined June in her kitchen.

"What's our programme? I managed to sleep on the flight so I am ready for whatever you throw at me," Sandy announced cheerfully, putting his hand casually on her shoulder.

"Well I didn't think you would want to do much today, so I have nothing planned. Perhaps we can just catch up and take a tour of the city," June said without moving away from his hand.

"Sounds like a good idea. Tell me your news."

"John and I are divorced now. As soon as we got back from Africa we called it a day. We divided everything down the middle; it was all finalized in a week."

"I'm sorry it came to that, but you hadn't been happy for years. What does your son have to say about the divorce?"

"He's quite relaxed about it and says he knew for some time there were problems between us. He's independent now, and so there are no custody issues," June said. "Anyway that is all a closed chapter in my life, so no more said about it."

"That's fair enough. What have you got planned for my visit? Will I be staying with you all the time I'm here?"

"Well not necessarily here, but you will be with me the whole time - if that's okay with you."

"Perfect. I am not putting you out at all am I?" Sandy asked sitting down to devour a large helping of ham and eggs.

"Don't be ridiculous Sandy. I invited you over and I can't wait to show you around. As soon as you're ready we'll get going."

It was a pleasant day; the clouds were high and there was a gentle breeze blowing off the Gulf of Mexico. Crossing over the mile long bridge back into Pensacola, they began a tour of the city and its outskirts. It was a fascinating place with a number of open parks and nature reserves. They had a long, lazy, excellent lunch at Jaco's Bar and Grille near the 'Plaza de Luna' at the small boat harbour. Altogether it was a lovely relaxed day with both of them enjoying each other's company.

Late in the afternoon they made their way back to June's apartment. June took a couple of beers from the fridge, and sat down on the settee with Sandy, to discuss their schedule for the coming three weeks. She had already contacted a number of fishing clubs and organisations who were expecting them; including Larry Mize and Pete Lund. They decided to devote the next day to making reservations and appointments.

In the morning after a long late lie-in Sandy and June sat down together, and planned their trip around parts of America. Once they had worked out a schedule, June made all the bookings. In the afternoon, when their work was done, they took a leisurely stroll along the beach walking hand-in-hand. As soon as they had had enough fresh air they turned and hurried back to the apartment.

Much later, after a couple more drinks and a light snack, they called it a day and made their way off to bed. Sandy was just dropping off to sleep when there was a knock on his door.

"Sandy. Are you awake?" June asked opening the door and walking in. "Can I come in? I need to talk to you."

"Come in," he called out.

She was wearing a short silky night-dress that did little to hide her beautiful full body.

"Of course you can," Sandy said moving over to make room for her to sit on the bed.

"I have been so excited waiting for you to arrive. I didn't realize how lonely I have been on my own," June said lifting the covers to climb in and snuggle up to Sandy, exciting him immediately.

"Well I have to admit these past three months, since you left Inhaca, have seemed like three years," Sandy put his arm around her and pulled her close.

"I knew how much I felt for you when I saw you at the airport this morning. I've really missed you Sandy."

"I think you know I fell for you the first time I saw you on Inhaca," responded Sandy seriously. "You bewitched me!"

"I did get that impression," she teased.

"Now that you're free, what are we going to do about it," Sandy smiled mischievously.

"I have a few things in mind," June turned in his arms to kiss him long and passionately, thrusting her tongue deep into his mouth.

Without even being aware of doing so, they quickly shed their clothing and were entwined like a pair of serpents; exploring, tickling, teasing and caressing each other. It had been a long time for both of them and in next to no time it was over.

"Oh God it has been too long. Sandy I love you so much," June gasped as they fell apart breathlessly.

"I love you too," Sandy responded feeling great tenderness for this woman he had fallen in love with. "I've been waiting for this since that day on the boat."

It was the first time since he had lost Coleen, all those years ago, that he had felt such emotions for anyone. With June, somehow he knew he had at last found happiness. For a while they lay happily in each others arms recovering their breath and enjoying the moment.

"Were you never married?" June asked breaking into their thoughts.

"Yes. I was married for twelve years. She died nine years ago from cancer She was a wonderful woman and we had a daughter, Sally."

"I am so sorry. It must have been very hard bringing up your daughter by yourself."

"She's wonderful. I had to send her to boarding school and she turned out okay. She's at Cape Town University, studying to be a vet. "

"Have there been any other women in your life since your wife died?"

"Not really. I concentrated all my time and efforts raising Sally, and on my work."

"But you have had no affairs of the heart since then?"

"Yes there was one. She drank heavily and was man hungry. I caught her with other men on more than one occasion. I was the laughing stock of the village. I don't know why I put up with it, but I did," Sandy still felt anger.

"Did you leave her after all that?" June asked.

"Yes. I left her and went back to Swaziland where I started my own consultancy business. I have been very wary since then."

"Why did you put up with her for so long?"

"I don't know. I think I hoped she would come to her senses and get over her man hungry ways," Sandy said feeling very comfortable with June in his arms. It was a long time since he held a woman close, and the first time he had told anyone about his unfortunate affair.

"I'm not surprised you've stayed on your own after that experience - I am so sorry."

"Its okay - I got over her a long time ago. But I learned a tough lesson along the way." Sandy said closing the door on the matter.

Suddenly June jumped out of bed. "This bed is far too small. Come on lets go to my room; there's a big double bed there," she said pulling him along behind her. Both naked, they ran through to her room and jumped into bed, like a couple of eager students about to have their first sexual encounter. They didn't get much sleep that night.

Over the next three weeks they flew west to New Orleans, Houston, Los Angeles and San Francisco then back east to Atlanta, Jacksonville, Charlestown, Miami and Tampa Bay before finally getting back to June's apartment. Everyone they met was friendly and most interested in their presentation of *'Santo Deep-Sea Fishing'*. Sandy found Americans to be very efficient and accommodating. All the people Sandy met were very friendly and polite.

Sandy was amazed how easily June got on with everyone, and with her quiet efficiency. Wherever they went everything had been organised in advance, and went like clock-work. It was thanks to June that so much interest was taken in the deep-sea fishing charters.

When they met up with Larry and Pete, in their home towns, Sandy was delighted with the positive response they had had from their members, and sport fishermen were lined up to book charters.

Combining business and a holiday, with the person you are in love with, was a most rewarding experience for them both and they had a wonderful time together. They took time to see as much of the country and its attractions, as they had time for.

Their days were filled with meetings and sightseeing, and their nights with dining, dancing and mad, passionate love-making. They arrived back in Pensacola exhausted, but very much in love with each other.

June's shower was a double and there was plenty of room for both of them. After soaping each other from head to toe they made love under the warm water. Afterwards they lounged about in their dressing gowns. Sandy poured the drinks while June made them a light supper.

Later they made their way back to June's bed - this time there was no urgency in their lovemaking and they explored each other and spoke gently for hours, making plans for the future, eventually falling into an exhausted sleep.

A few days after arriving back at June's apartment, her son Tony came to visit, and to meet Sandy. He was a well balanced intelligent young man who, when introduced, had a firm handshake and looked Sandy straight in the eye. He was a man of medium height, with fair hair and had his mother's green eyes. He lived in lodgings in Tampa where he was studying law. He bore no animosity about his parents divorce or against Sandy. The two of them got along very well.

After spending a wonderful month with June in the USA, Sandy flew home to Swaziland. Before leaving, he proposed to June. She happily accepted his proposal and had no problems with moving to Africa - they planned to get married on Inhaca in March. It was going to be a long six months for Sandy.

Chapter 29

Tom almost stopped dead in his tracks when he arrived at the Lodge to meet the last clients of the season. There sitting at the bar was Van Zyl with two other men Tom had never seen before; a younger Oriental looking man and a rather large man.

Although he had never met or seen Van Zyl in person, Tom recognised him easily from the photographs Tombi had sent him. They would never have accepted the booking had they known Van Zyl was in the party; the booking had been made in the name of Swanepoel. However they were clients, and had paid for their charter, and so Tom went over to meet them.

"Are you gentlemen the Swanepoel group?" he asked approaching the three men at the bar.

"We sure are," the big man said turning to shake Tom's hand. "I am Andre Swanepoel. This is Jan Van Zyl and his son Joey."

"Welcome to Inhaca. I trust you guys have all settled into your rooms," Tom didn't want to let it be known that he knew exactly who Van Zyl was. "Have you had something to eat?"

"Everything is fine so far," Van Zyl said raising his glass and tossing his drink down his throat. "When do we start fishing?"

"We'll make a start tomorrow morning. According to your booking, only two of you will be fishing, is that correct? Have any of you been deep-sea fishing before?" Tom enquired.

"That's right, only Jan and I are fishing. I have fished in Kariba and on the Zambezi for years, and off the beach; but never deep-sea," Swanepoel said.

"What about you Jan?" Tom asked, turning to Van Zyl.

"No, I'm not a fisherman. This is my first fishing trip," Van Zyl said looking pointedly at his empty glass.

"And you Joey? Why aren't you fishing?" Tom asked ignoring Van Zyl's hint and turning to the surly young man.

"I get bloody sea-sick and I'm shit scared of the sea. There are big things under the water out there," Joey admitted with an expressionless face. "I might go out in the bay one day, but I'll be quite happy just hanging around here relaxing,"

"Well I'm sure we can arrange something to keep you busy if you like. Okay then, I'll get everything ready for tomorrow and pick you up on the jetty at six in the morning," Tom said. "In the meantime I will leave you to amuse yourselves."

"Hell that's bloody early. What about breakfast?" Van Zyl was obviously not an early riser.

"The Lodge will have a packed breakfast ready to take with you. Pick it up at reception on your way out. See you tomorrow," Tom turned and walked away.

Knowing Van Zyl's reputation, he felt very uncomfortable and wondered about his son Joey. In all likelihood he was much the same as his father; an apple never fell far from the tree. What was Van Zyl doing here? Was he really here to fish? He had admitted he was no fisherman, and showed no enthusiasm - so what was the purpose of his coming deep-sea fishing? How had Swanepoel, the only fisherman among them, managed to persuade Van Zyl and his son to come on a fishing trip with him?

Tom had a nasty suspicion this charter was not going to be a very pleasant one. These three men were going to be difficult. All these unanswered questions made Tom feel very uneasy; he had to find the answers fast, and so he called Ted.

"Ted you will never guess who has arrived to fish with us?" Tom said.

"I haven't a clue. Who is it?" Ted was curious.

"Van Zyl is here with his son Joey, and a fellow by the name of Andre Swanepoel. Do you know them?"

"I have seen his son a few times. He looks a bit Chinese; not a very nice character I believe!" Ted commented. "But I have never heard of Andre Swanepoel."

"I wonder why they've come here to fish. Only Swanepoel is a fisherman. I somehow don't believe Van Zyl is here to have fun."

"I wonder if he knows of your involvement in the confiscation of his ivory and rhino horn. You had better be very careful Tom."

"You bet. Thanks Ted," Tom hung up.

Not wanting to upset Maria or Tombi; who had stayed on with them since her escape from Mabiti, Tom didn't reveal to either of them the identity of their latest clients. When Maria asked about them, Tom merely said they were not a very pleasant bunch, who wanted to be left to their own devices when not out fishing.

186

Next morning Tom and Tomasi loaded the rods, tackle and refreshments on *Pelé-Pelé* and then waited for Van Zyl and Swanepoel. Both men were a little bleary-eyed and grumpy when they sauntered down the jetty half an hour late. With the two of them in their condition, Tom decided not to venture too far out to sea. They were obviously hung-over and he expected them to be more than a little sea-sick. They had clearly had a late night with far too much to drink.

"It will be a bit rough out at sea to-day, so I'm taking you guys out into the bay to get the feel of deep-sea fishing, and I can see how you manage. We can try to catch one or two king-fish, rock-cod and reds. Once you've got the hang of it, we'll go further out into the Mozambique Channel to try for something bigger," Tom told his clients.

"Will we try to catch marlin tomorrow then?" Swanepoel was keen.

"That's the general idea. Let's see how you get on today; we'll decide at the end of the day." Tom said.

"We are paying to catch big game-fish, not bloody tiddlers," Van Zyl said belligerently.

"I'm sorry, but you can't just head out to sea half-cocked and expect to catch monsters," Tom said impatiently. "I am responsible for your safety, so you will just have to accept my decision or cancel your charter," he finished, half hoping they would cancel.

Van Zyl glared at Tom briefly, obviously not used to taking orders, and then shrugged his shoulders and turned away; no longer confrontational.

It was a frustrating morning, trying to teach Van Zyl the basics of using trolled baits and lures; he expected everything to be done for him. Swanepoel had used spinners and lures before, and only needed help rigging traces and attaching live bait correctly. At noon they called it a day and returned to the jetty.

Van Zyl couldn't wait to clamber off the boat and head for the lodge, leaving Swanepoel behind to help pack the gear away.

"What was Joey doing today?" Tom asked as soon as Van Zyl was out of earshot.

"He said he was going for a walk around the island," Swanepoel replied. "He's a strange young man."

The first day had not gone well. With their hang-overs, and Van Zyl surly and reluctant to do anything for himself, they only caught a couple of reds and a potato bass. In the evening Tom didn't bother to join his clients for a drink at the lodge, as he usually did with their clients. They were not pleasant company and most probably preferred being left to their own devices.

Tom resolved to make sure none of them went anywhere near the camp. If Van Zyl saw Tombi, he would put two and two together, and realize that Tom had been involved in his rhino horn and ivory fiasco, then there would be no saying what he might do. Besides, Tom didn't want Van Zyl anywhere near Maria and Tombi or for them to be exposed to any sort of retaliation by him.

Things improved slightly over the next couple of days, with both men catching a few barracuda, pike and tunny. At times Van Zyl actually seemed to be enjoying himself, making Tom relax slightly. Unlike the keen sport fishermen from the USA, who were always eager to help prepare for the next day, these two were quite happy to get back to the lodge by early afternoon, join Joey and spend most of the time propping up the bar. This suited Tom perfectly; the less time he spent with them the better.

There was no love lost between Tom and Van Zyl, and on several occasions, he even caught Van Zyl glaring at him with obvious hatred. Tom knew he had to watch his back. All the more he wondered why Van Zyl had come on this fishing trip and suspected he was planning something unpleasant. There was nothing he could do but be on guard. At least Tom knew he had the advantage; as long as Van Zyl was not aware Tom knew who he was.

Now knowing what his clients were like, Tom went to check with the manager on their behaviour. He was told that the three of them drank heavily every day, and stayed in the bar until closing time. They were loud and disruptive, and at times had to be asked to stop disturbing other patrons. Of the three Swanepoel was the quietest although he looked like a paid thug.

•••••••••••••

"To-morrow is our last day here. I'm not going out fishing. You'll have to go on your own," Van Zyl said to Swanepoel.

"Why not?" Swanepoel asked.

"Every day we have been out, Joey has been exploring the island. There is something we must do, and I don't want to raise any suspicion," Van Zyl explained.

"What do you have to do?" Swanepoel was confused.

"It's of no concern to you. The less you know the better. I'll tell you as soon as you get back from fishing to-morrow. Just make sure Owen stays out with you until 12. We'll fly out as soon as you get back."

"Is this the reason the booking was made in my name. You are not going to get me into trouble are you?"

"Something like that, but you won't get into any shit. Just tell Owen I have to get back urgently for business," Van Zyl finished.

....

On the fifth day only Swanepoel turned up on the jetty. Van Zyl was a little under the weather and had opted to spend the last day relaxing at the lodge with Joey. Tom heaved a sigh of relief; it would be far more pleasant without him.

"Something has cropped up with Van Zyl's business and he wants to leave before three this afternoon - and so he needs to rest this morning. Can we get back before one?" Swanepoel asked.

"Of course we can. This is your last day in any case, so we will be back by about midday," Tom agreed pleased he would not have to put up with Van Zyl's moods and outbursts that day.

He would be happy to see the back of them, and made a mental note to make sure they checked all the clients carefully in the future. Tom still had an uneasy feeling; to leave both those men on the island with Maria and Tombi worried him. At least they did have Tomasi to guard them.

Chapter 30

After breakfast Van Zyl and Joey packed their bags and settled their bill with the lodge. Leaving their luggage at reception, they hired two quads and drove along the beach to the Owen camp. Since arriving on the island, it had been Joey's mission to find the camp, and he had found it one morning, when he was walking along the path on the crest of the ridge, on his way to the southern part of the island to buy crabs.

Ten minutes later they parked the quads under a tree at the foot of the hill, and walked up the path into the camp. The first person they saw was Tombi. She was sweeping the camp-site with a grass broom. When she saw them approaching she dropped the broom, her hand shot up to cover her mouth in horror, and her eyes went as wide as saucers.

"Madam!" was all she managed to blurt out.

"What is it Tombi?" Maria Owen asked emerging from one of the grass huts. "Oh, I am sorry. I didn't see you there. Good morning, how may I help you gentlemen?" she greeted the two men standing in the camp.

"Are you Mrs Owen?" Van Zyl asked.

"Yes I am. What can I do for you? If you are looking for my husband, he has gone out fishing. He will be back early this afternoon."

"No, it's you I want. My name is Jan Van Zyl and this is my son Joey," Van Zyl introduced himself and his son. "You and Tombi must come with us."

"How do you know her name?" Maria turned pale when she recognised the man's name.

"Because she worked for me - before she decided to run away."

"What do you want Mr Van Zyl. I have no intention of going anywhere with you," Maria said getting angry.

"You will do as I bloody well say," Van Zyl nodded at Joey who took a pistol out of his pocket and pointed it at her threateningly. "Now get the boat keys and you and your bloody maid will follow me back to the jetty. Don't try to be clever. Joey will be right behind you."

"Where are we going? I must be here when my husband gets back."

"You will see. Come along let's go," Van Zyl turned to lead them off down the path.

"Come along Tombi," Maria linked arms with Tombi, took the keys off the hook on the tree, and they followed Van Zyl down the path towards the beach. Joey, bringing up the rear, prodded Tombi in the back with his pistol as she followed Maria down the hill. "Where is Tomasi?" Maria whispered over her shoulder.

"He went for fresh water. He will only be back in an hour. I'm scared of these men madam," Tombi whispered. "I worked for them."

"It will be alright. Don't worry," Maria tried to reassure her. "Mr Owen will sort this out as soon as he gets back."

"Stop whispering and get a move on," Joey ordered, pushing Tombi from behind so hard that she stumbled and almost fell. .

At the bottom of the hill Maria and Tombi were made to ride on one of the quads, with Van Zyl and his son following them on the other. Joey sat behind his father pointing his pistol at them as they rode along. The jetty was almost deserted when the small group arrived, and so there was nobody who might see what was happening and help them. Van Zyl led them down to the end of the wooden jetty to where *Tigger* was tied up.

"You two, get on board with Joey. You are taking him to Maputo."

"Why didn't you just ask? I would have been quite happy to take you," Maria said. "You don't need to threaten us with a gun."

"Just do as you are told. You'll find out soon enough." Van Zyl growled. Then turning to his son he said, "Joey, go to the Clube Naval and do as we planned. I'll meet up with you later."

Van Zyl untied the mooring rope, pushed the boat away from the jetty, turned on his heel and strutted off towards the lodge.

Maria started the engines and eased away from the jetty. Once clear of the other boats, she pushed the throttles forward and they picked up speed then set off towards Maputo, 20 miles across the bay. Joey, with his pistol drawn, sat down on the seat behind them.

Maria scanned the horizon hoping to see Tom and *Pelé-Pelé* somewhere close by. It was eleven o'clock when they left the jetty on Inhaca and, if she kept the speed down, it would take two hours to get to Maputo. The longer it took the more likely Tom might be able to catch up with them.

Although she tried not to worry, Maria was very nervous and about what was happening to them. Her mind raced. With Van Zyl finding

Tombi with them, he would now know of their involvement in the capture of his load of illegal goods and would want revenge. But what did he plan to do with them? Maria reached across in front of Tombi, who stood up front with her, to turn on the radio.

"Don't turn that radio on, or I will be forced to smash it," Joey warned. "How long will it take to get to Maputo?"

"About two hours. We'll be there at about one," Maria replied.

"I'm bloody sure this boat can go faster than this. Speed up," Joey ordered moving up to stand close behind Tombi. "I have heard about you; I think you and I have things to do," he whispered into her ear and squeezed her buttocks with his left hand.

Spinning around, Tombi slapped his hand away from her. "I want nothing to do with you. Don't touch me again or I will kill you," she hissed, and spat into his face.

Quick as a snake his hand shot out, grabbed her by the arm, and twisting it, forced her down onto the deck. "We will see about that; just wait," he yelled at her. "You'd better remember who the boss is now."

Maria swung the helm over hard making the boat tilt so violently that Joey lost his balance and let go of Tombi. "Leave her alone. She has got nothing to do with you," Maria warned.

Joey flopped back onto the seat and glared angrily at the two women. He didn't move or say another word for the rest of the trip. He was a little green and obviously felt sea-sick from the motion of the boat.

At half past twelve Maria slowed down to enter the small boat harbour at the 'Clube Naval'. She tried not to show Tombi how frightened she was. How was she going to get a message to Tom? She had an idea. It was not good, but the best she could think of, and gave her a glimmer of hope.

Maria found a vacant mooring and asked Joey to jump out and tie the boat to a mooring ring.

"Don't forget I have a gun in my pocket and will use it if I have to. I know you can speak Portuguese, so had better not try and speak to anyone. Do you understand?" Joey addressed Maria who nodded her head innocently leaning around the windscreen to secure the mooring rope.

· · · · · · · · · · · · · · ·

Tigger was not at her moorings when Tom arrived back at the jetty with Swanepoel. He presumed Maria had taken her and gone fishing in the bay - as she did every now and then, when Tom was busy with clients.

After saying farewell to Swanepoel and Van Zyl at the lodge Tom went back to the boat. Joey had not been with them and he wondered where he was; probably still in his room. He spent some time refuelling and cleaning *Pelé-Pelé* half expecting Maria to arrive back in *Tigger*. He tried to raise her on the radio, but there was no response, and so Tom suspected that she had forgotten to switch it on. This annoyed him - it was important to always have the radio on when out at sea.

While he was still busy with the boat, Tom saw Van Zyl's plane fly away and head for Maputo. He was a little surprised that they were leaving so soon after Swanepoel got back from fishing, but as Swanepoel had said earlier, Van Zyl was in a hurry to get back to his business, and so he put it out of his mind.

. . . .

From Inhaca Van Zyl flew to Maputo Airport, where he left Swanepoel to catch the direct flight to Harare. Then, without even switching off the engines, he took off again. A few minutes later he landed the plane on a small dirt airstrip normally used by farmers when they were crop dusting, near Matola 30 kilometers from Maputo.

Joey was waiting there beside the hired car with the two kidnapped women sitting in the back seat. As soon as the plane came to a standstill, Joey hustled the women over to the aircraft, pushed them up onto the wing and bundled them both into the back seat. After tying their hands together with cable ties, he gagged them with strips of tape and climbed into the front seat next to his father. The car was left with the keys in.

An hour and a half later they landed at Mabiti. It was just getting dark when they drove through the gates into the camp.

Chapter 31

After cleaning *Pelé-Pelé*, and stowing everything in its place, Tom wandered over to the lodge to make sure all was in order. He didn't trust Van Zyl and his cronies, and hoped they had paid their bar bill in full before leaving. The accommodation was included in the charter fees. He was relieved to hear that everything was paid.

When he got back to camp there was no sign of Tombi, and so Tom presumed that Maria must have taken Tombi with her and gone fishing in *Tigger*. Although this was not unusual, Tom had an uneasy feeling. He tried calling her from the base radio but still got no response. He was about to have a cup of tea, when Tomasi came rushing into camp in a sweat and out of breath.

"Madam and Tombi have gone," he panted looking most concerned.

"Yes I can see that. Where have they gone?"

"My wife says they went with two white men."

"These men, did they want my wife to take them fishing?" Tom suddenly had a nasty feeling in the pit of his stomach.

"No sir. They did not want to go with them, but the white men shouted at them. They had a gun and took them away on motor-bikes."

"Where were you Tomasi? I left you here to look after the women."

"I was sent by the medem to get the water drum filled. The fresh water for drinking was finished. When I came back with the water I went to search for them. I can't find them anywhere and the big boat is not there. I think they have gone to Maputo."

"At what time did they go away with these men?" Tom felt sick.

"When the sun was half way up," Tomasi indicated with his arm – about two hours ago!

"Tomasi I want you to wait here for the madam and Tombi, in case they return while I am away. I am going to look for them. If they come back, tell madam to call me on the radio." How could this be happening; the gall of the man!

Tom jumped on the quad and raced back to the jetty. There was still no sign of *Tigger*. He started to panic, and then forced himself to think. Where had Joey been when he went to say farewell? Tomasi had said two men, so Van Zyl and Joey had taken Maria and Tombi from the camp. Joey must have gone off with the women while Van Zyl waited at the lodge for Swanepoel to return from fishing. They had flown out shortly afterwards; Tom saw the plane.

Where had Joey gone with Maria and Tombi? Tom knew something bad was happening. He had felt very uneasy the whole time Van Zyl was on the island. Now his suspicions were confirmed; why had he not taken more care? Van Zyl had planned this abduction in advance; when he booked the fishing charter in Swanepoel's name!

There was no time to lose. *Pelé-Pelé* was fuelled and ready to go, and so Tom untied her and headed for Maputo. With Van Zyl flying out leaving Joey with the two women, it was the only place they could have gone. An hour later he arrived at the Clube Naval. As he entered the harbour he spotted *Tigger* immediately; but there was nobody on board.

He tied up alongside then climbed over onto the other boat to see if there were any signs of a struggle. The keys were still in the ignition and everything appeared to be in order. He was about to jump down onto the jetty when something caught his eye. There was a word scrawled upside down in the dried salt on the outside of the wind-shield. "KIDNAP" it read!

His worst fears were confirmed. Joey had forcibly taken them somewhere; but where? How was it possible to kidnap two women in broad daylight without being seen? Tom hurried into the clubhouse to speak to the old barman who spoke English.

"Did you see a man and two women come ashore from that boat a couple of hours ago?" Tom asked pointing at *Tigger*.

"Yes señor. There was a white man and woman and there was also a black woman with them. They drove away in a small car that was in the parking place over there under the trees," the barman said pointing to the car park. "The car has been there for a week."

"Thank you. You don't know where they went do you?"

"No señor, I only saw them drive away. Nobody spoke to me."

"*Obrigado.* Thank you."

It was too late in the day for Tom to do anything more, and so he locked *Tigger* up and went back to Inhaca. If he heard nothing by the morning, he would fly out and start searching for his wife and Tombi, and bring them home.

He was going to need help. As soon as he got back to Inhaca he sent an urgent message to Kyle from the Lodge. He knew Kyle had just collected his new boat from Empangeni and was at home in Malelane. Kyle's call came within an hour.

"Dad, you sound pissed off, what's happened? Why the urgency?"

"Van Zyl was here on a fishing charter. He and his son Joey have kidnapped Maria and Tombi. I don't know where they've taken them."

"Good God. You must be joking. How the hell did they manage that?"

"It's no joke. They took them from the camp at gun-point while I was out fishing. Maria was forced to take them over to Clube Naval. I found *Tigger* tied up there."

"When did this all happen?"

"At midday today. I'll be going across to Maputo airport in the morning to see what I can find out. I'm going to need your help," Tom said to his son.

"Okay Dad. I'll be waiting to hear from you. I lay you a bet they have taken them back to their lair in Zimbabwe; probably to Mabiti. It would be far too risky for them to go to Harare where they would have to clear Customs and Immigration," Kyle reasoned, thinking logically.

"Yes I think you're right. But how would he get them out of Mozambique without passports?"

"It's easy enough to nip over the border and land at Mabiti without anyone knowing or clearing immigration," Kyle pointed out. "It's in the middle of nowhere."

"I'm sure Van Zyl is using them to get at me. He'd better not harm them at all. I wonder what he wants from me."

"To get his own back, and to recover the money he lost when his ivory was confiscated, I suppose," Kyle concluded.

"I think you've hit the nail on the head. Anyway it's too late to do anything today. I'll be taking off at first light and will be in touch as soon as I have been to the airport," Tom said hanging up the phone.

Early next morning, after a sleepless night worrying about his wife, Tom flew to Maputo Airport. Yes, the control tower had a record of Van Zyl landing and dropping off a passenger. Then he flew on to Zimbabwe on his own leaving Swanepoel to catch the late afternoon flight to Harare.

Why had Swanepoel been left at the airport? Van Zyl's plane was a four seater and he must have needed the extra seats for Maria and Tombi. Van Zyl, unbeknown to the air traffic control authorities must have landed somewhere to pick them up before flying to Zimbabwe. It looked like Kyle was right - they must have gone to Mabiti.

. . . .

Dodi was on leave in Zimbabwe. After helping Kyle move to South Africa, he had returned to take money to Tombi's family. Kyle looked after Tombi's finances and they needed it for schooling and to live on. While he was there, he decided to spend a week at Chikombedzi checking up on the activities at Mabiti. His boss had instructed him to go there every few months.

They were all determined to put an end to Barnard's poaching operations and needed to get as much evidence as they could. And so after visiting Tombi's family, and before returning to South Africa, Dodi went back to his place in the bush near Mabiti.

He had only been there two days when, from his hiding place, Dodi saw the plane land. He watched from behind some acacia thorn bushes and was shocked to see Mrs Owen and Tombi climb out of the plane. Their hands were tied and they had gags over their mouths. What was happening? To see the wife of his boss, and the woman he loved, being treated like prisoners made his blood boil.

Barnard arrived to meet the plane, took the two women away to Mabiti and then the plane flew off. He had to get word to Tom as quickly as possible; he was quite sure he was not aware of what was going on, or where the women were. Dodi hurried off to phone Ted Hunter from Chikombedzi. He would get the message to Tom.

. . . .

Less than an hour after leaving Maputo, Tom landed on the air-strip at Malelane. As soon as he touched down, he called Kyle who arrived twenty minutes later.

"Sorry I took so long Dad, but Ted phoned just after I spoke to you. Dodi is at Chikombedzi. Apparently late yesterday afternoon, just as it was getting dark, he saw a plane land at Mabiti. Maria and Tombi were on the plane - they had their hands tied and were gagged. Barnard met them at the air-strip and took the women to Mabiti, and then Van Zyl and Joey took off again."

"So that crafty devil went back to watch the camp just at the right time. Seeing as he only goes to check every three or four months, thank God he chose to be there now." Tom was relieved to know where the two women were being held. "He has an uncanny ability to be at the right place at the right time."

"What's your plan? You must have something in mind Dad."

"I don't know Kyle. We can't go charging in to Mabiti with guns blazing. Let's go to Chiredzi and plan something from there. At least now we know where they are, and Dodi knows the place well. Apart from being gagged and tied, I hope they aren't being ill-treated by that bastard Barnard. Do you think we can borrow Gideon from the farm for a couple of days?"

"Yes, I'm sure we can - after all I am still the consultant there. We'll need some transport, so I'll have to borrow a Land Cruiser," Kyle said. "Maybe I can persuade a few friends to join us. We will need arms of some sort."

"Okay. Let's go. We'll fly to the Lowveld and get organised there. We can try to work out a plan of action on the way," Tom said. "Before we take off maybe we'd better get hold of Ted, to let him know what's happening," he added as an after-thought.

It took two and a half hours to fly from Malelane to Buffalo Range in the Lowveld. After clearing immigration they got a lift to the Chiredzi hotel where Kyle phoned his replacement on the farm. An hour later Kyle was picked up and he went off to the farm to organise men and a vehicle.

Tom called Ted to find out if he had heard any more news from Dodi.

"Tom, I'm on my way down to the Lowveld as we speak. I'll meet you at the Chiredzi Hotel in an hour," Ted said. "I'll tell you what I know when I get there."

"What are you coming all the way down from Harare for?"

"What the hell do think? I'm coming to give you a hand," Ted replied.

"I appreciate your help Ted, but you really don't have to do this," Tom said when his friend arrived an hour later.

"Oh yes I do. I have my right hand man Godfrey with me. We are here to help get Maria back."

"Okay Ted. Thanks for coming. Kyle has gone out to the farm to recruit a few helpers, and to borrow a Land Cruiser. He's spending the night there and will be here at five in the morning," Tom was pleased to have Ted there. "What have you heard in Harare?"

"Well apart from his fishing trip with you guys, Van Zyl has been keeping a very low profile of late," Ted reported. "When I left Harare he was at home, but you never know his movements. He moves fast when he wants to, so he could be anywhere by now. Let's hope he hasn't flown to Mabiti while I was driving down."

"He can't possibly know we're on to them. Anyway it won't matter too much; we'll go in and see how the land lies as soon as we meet up with Dodi. What did you tell him to do?"

"I told him to carry on watching the camp, and to keep a look out for us. I said that we would be there tomorrow morning."

"Good. We'll head off as soon as Kyle gets here first thing in the morning."

Chapter 32

Maria and Tombi had been locked in camp for two days. Although they were treated roughly by Barnard, they were allowed to move around the house and garden freely, and were fed regularly by Barnard's new cook. But there was no way of getting a message out to Tom.

At Maria's insistence, the morning after their arrival, Barnard sent his driver to Chikombedzi to buy them basic toiletries. They were reasonably comfortable, but not having a change of clothes, they were both starting to feel grubby.

"We've been here for two days now. What's going to happen to us madam?" Tombi asked as they wandered around the yard.

"Tombi, I don't know. But I'm sure Mr Owen and Kyle will come for us soon. They might take a few days to find out where we are – but they will come as soon as they can. We must just be patient and wait. Already I'm beginning to smell like a dirty tramp." Although Maria was nervous and worried, she did her best to try and reassure Tombi.

"*Hau* madam! I am also stinking." Tombi replied agreeing with Maria. "Do you know this man Barnard raped me when I was a prisoner here before?" she added hanging her head in shame.

"Oh Tombi, how terrible! No wonder you are so frightened of him. Did he hurt you in any other way?"

"No. He was drunk and there was nothing I could do. I hate him. He must be castrated. He likes only black women. I know he has been with many *mahooris* (whores)."

While they were talking, a plane roared over the camp just above the trees-tops. It had two engines and so Maria knew it wasn't Tom coming to get them.

"You two!" Barnard shouted from the veranda. "Get back inside the house. Now!"

"But it's not time for us to go in yet," Maria protested. "You said we could stay out till sunset."

"That was Van Zyl flying past. I must go and pick him up. He won't be very pleased if he finds you wandering around the yard. You must stay locked in your room while he is here."

Half an hour later the door was flung open and Van Zyl stood there. "Owen, you're coming with me. You can say good-by to your maid," he sneered.

"Where are you taking me now? Why is Tombi staying here?" Maria demanded.

"Because I say so dammit! Now get out," Van Zyl shouted. "I'll deal with Tombi later."

"Please don't take Mrs Owen away. I want to be with her. I can't stay here alone," Tombi pleaded starting to cry.

Ignoring her, Van Zyl spun around. "Joey, get in here. Tie this woman's hands together and gag her. She talks too bloody much."

"Please let Tombi come with me?" Maria begged.

Van Zyl strode away ignoring her request. Joey came into the room, quickly bound Maria's wrists together and gagged her with a bandana. Tombi looked on helplessly with tears streaming down her brown cheeks. She knew what would happen to her if she was left alone with Barnard.

Joey pushed Maria roughly out of the room and locked the door behind him. Tombi, feeling deserted, helpless and frightened, lay down on the bed and cried. This time Dodi was not there to rescue her.

Before taking off from Mabiti, Joey removed Maria's gag then climbed in beside her in the rear seat. When they landed at Mount Hamden he untied her wrists, and they drove to Van Zyl's home where she was locked up in the guest suite.

She had a bathroom and there were clean clothes in the cupboard - probably belonging to one of Van Zyl's 'bought' women. Although the clothes didn't fit too well, they were clean and would have to do.

After taking a shower and putting on fresh clothes, Maria felt a lot better and sat down near the window to think. How was she going to get a message to Ted, who she knew lived just down the road? Perhaps she could persuade one of the servants to tell him she was here. She also worried about poor Tombi, left on her own with Barnard; the man who had raped her. It was very likely he would do so again!

While she sat staring out of the window onto the well manicured lawn outside, the key rattled in the door. Joey came in carrying a tray of food, put it down on a small table, and left the room without saying a word. Although she was not hungry, and not knowing what Van Zyl had in store for her, Maria forced herself to eat. She had to keep up her strength.

Next day she was up early hoping to attract the attention of a gardener, and spent most of the day sitting at the window. The day dragged past without her seeing any of the servants working in or around the house. Only Joey brought her food at meal times. It seemed he was her jailer.

Maria paged through the magazines she found lying about, but could not concentrate. Her mind was too preoccupied trying to work out how she could get a message to Ted. That night again, she hardly slept as the reality of her situation started to sink in.

Chapter 33

By eight the next morning, the rescuers were on the edge of the Mabiti airstrip. From his hiding place Dodi saw them arriving and emerged to greet them as they pulled up. He was very pleased to see his boss; he had last him when he had jumped onto the back of Barnard's van in Mozambique.

"Dodi you old rascal, I have not seen you since you ran away from us in Mozambique last year. What would I do without you?" Tom asked greeting his long-time employee with affection.

"I know we must watch these men. They are bad people Ishe," was Dodi's simple response. "I come here every three or four months to see what is happening."

"I am very pleased you were here at this time. If you had not been here watching, we would never have known where our women were," Tom said affectionately putting arm around Dodi's shoulders. Dodi smiled happily looking down at his sandaled feet.

"You know the camp; how are we going to get in to rescue my wife and your girl-friend?"

"*Hau Ishe*, how do you know Tombi is my girl-friend?" Dodi feigned indignation.

"I have seen the way you two make cow-eyes at each other on the farm. Now let's get on with it. How are we going to do this?" Tom asked on a more serious note.

"No hunting parties have left the camp this morning. Barnard is there with eight men," Dodi reported. "The gates are usually opened at seven in the morning, and left unlocked during the day. But now, since the women arrived, there is a guard. The gates are locked at 4 o'clock in the afternoon."

"Where is Barnard keeping the women?"

"They are kept locked in the house. But from my tree I have seen them walking in the garden. They do not know that I am here, and they cannot escape on their own out here in the bush. There are too many wild animals; they would not survive."

"This is true. It is an ideal place to keep the two women hostages," Ted nodded in agreement.

"Okay, so what's the plan?" Kyle asked.

"There are six of us with Dodi, Gideon and Godfrey. I think the longer we delay the harder it'll be. We should go straight in the front gate and just take them," Tom suggested. "What do you guys think?"

"Perhaps if I go in first and take Gideon with me. Barnard doesn't know me. I will make some pretence for being there. Once I have distracted him you can follow straight away," Kyle suggested.

"I'm happy with that. Ted, what do you think?" Tom asked.

"No. Barnard might know you from the Lowveld and will immediately be on his guard. I think I must go in first with my man Godfrey. He has never met me," Ted was adamant.

"Yes, that makes more sense. We'll follow on behind you, but see if you can get him away from the house so that we can get to the women - before he has time to react," Tom agreed. "What weapons do we have?"

"Yes it sounds good to me. We have three shotguns, Dodi's assegai and a couple of *knob-kerries* (wooden clubs) and machetes."

"That'll do. Just use the shotguns to threaten them and for protection - we don't want any shooting or killing. Okay let's brief the others, and get the show on the road. Ted we'll follow you in as soon as you've done your thing. We mustn't give him time to react and harm the girls, or use them to get away again," Tom said turning to brief the rest of the team and to get their input.

"If they close the gates after you go in, we'll just have to smash our way in." Kyle added.

"Dodi will come with me. He knows his way around and can jump off the back of the Land Cruiser and get to the women as quickly as possible." Addressing Dodi Tom asked, "Has anyone else been to the camp since Van Zyl left the women here day before yesterday?"

"No, I don't think so. I was away at Chikombedzi late yesterday when I tried to phone boss Ted to find out what was happening. I left here at three and returned at eight," Dodi said. "I saw no vehicles on the road."

"So we can presume its only Barnard and his team in the camp," Kyle said. "I'm sure we can handle them all; most of them are skinners I believe. What about the foreman? He can offer some resistance," Tom addressed Dodi.

"He is not there Ishe," Dodi responded quickly.

204

"What about the radio? We don't need him contacting Van Zyl before we are finished with our business," Kyle pointed out.

"Good thinking. Dodi you can cut the aerial cable as soon as we get into the camp. You know where the cable is?" Tom asked. Dodi, keen to get on with the action, nodded his head. "Okay, let's move."

The two vehicles moved off down the road towards Mabiti camp. 100 yards from the entrance, Ted pulled away, rounded a bend in the road then disappeared from sight as he drove through the open gates into the compound pulling up next to the abattoir. They both climbed out of the van as Barnard came over from the house to meet his visitors.

"Good morning. Are you Barney Barnard?" Ted asked walking over to meet Barnard.

"Ja, I am Barnard. What can I do for you?"

"My name is Bill Sykes. I am the new owner of the butchery at Rutenga," Ted introduced himself. "I'm looking for Kudu, Buffalo and Impala meat to make *biltong and wors* (dried meat and sausage). I am told you sell game meat here."

Out of the corner of his eye, Ted saw Godfrey wandering over to speak to the men working on an impala carcass, hanging up in the open shed.

"Come over to the cold room. I will show you what we have. If you give me a regular order I can supply you with all you need."

Watching proceedings from behind the large Natal mahogany, he used to watch the camp, Dodi saw Ted and Barnard heading towards the shed then waved Tom in, jumping onto the van as it passed the tree. Tom accelerated and drove straight to the house stopping in a cloud of dust at the front door.

Barnard turned to see who the new arrival was, and with him distracted, Ted, with the help of Godfrey who moved quickly to assist, overpowered Barnard. They threw him to the ground and Ted pinned him down with his knee in Barnard's back while. Godfrey fetched a length of rope from the van and Barnard was trussed up securely.

"What the hell do you think you are doing," Barnard was outraged.

"We have come to fetch Mrs Owen and Tombi. Now keep your mouth closed or I will have to gag you." Ted advised.

The workers, taken completely by surprise, stood watching with wide eyes and open mouths. When Kyle and Gideon went towards them, brandishing a shotgun and a machete, they offered no resistance, and were quickly herded into the storeroom, and locked inside.

Dodi cut the aerial cable running up the side of the house, then charged into the kitchen. The cook, who had heard all the commotion in the yard, turned to face him as he burst through the door.

"Take me to the women," Dodi ordered, pointing his assegai menacingly at the cook's chest. Without uttering a word the man turned and led the way to the spare room, unlocked the door and pushed it open.

Tombi, who had also heard the vehicles and all the noise outside in the yard, was at the window trying to see what was happening. "What do you want now?" she asked without even bothering to turn around when the door was suddenly flung open.

"Tombi, it is me, Dodi. We have come to take you home. Where is Mrs Owen?"

"*Aiewe*! It really is you," Tombi said spinning around to hug Dodi. "I am so happy to see you. I have been so afraid. I thought Barnard was going kill me after they took the madam away."

At that moment Tom stormed into the room. "Where is my wife Tombi?"

"Late yesterday afternoon Mr Van Zyl was here. He took Mrs Owen away with him."

"Damn it all. Where did he take her?" Tom asked slamming his fist against the door.

"I don't know. I think he took her away in his aeroplane."

"Okay Tombi. I am glad you are safe," Tom said rushing out of the house.

The cook, totally confused by all the rushing around, had retreated to the safety of his kitchen and stood with his back to the stove, wide-eyed watching.

Meanwhile in the yard, Ted and Godfrey had dragged Barnard to the back of his van, and were tying him onto the roll bar behind the cab.

"Barnard! Where the bloody hell is my wife?" Tom demanded as he came striding from the house.

"She is not here," Barnard smirked.

"I know she isn't you bloody fool. Where has Van Zyl taken her? I know they went away in his plane. Did they go to Harare?" Tom was seething and frustrated.

"He didn't tell me where he was taking her. He just came last night and took her away."

"The bastard!" Tom fumed. "He's played me for a fool right from the start."

"When I left Harare at lunch yesterday, he was at home. I know because I made a point of checking," Ted said.

"Nobody knew we were coming; unless one of his contacts saw us in Chiredzi, put two and two together, and warned Van Zyl. He would have had plenty of time to fly here and get away again last night," Tom was thinking hard.

"What do we do now?" Kyle spoke up for the first time since arriving in the camp.

"We'll have to go to Harare to find her," Tom decided.

"What are we going to do with Barnard?" Ted asked.

"I think we must get him across the Limpopo, and hand him over to the South African police. They want him for poaching in the Park," Tom said.

"Excuse me Ishe. When I came back from Mozambique with Barnard, he stopped and buried some rhino horns. I saw him do it. I have moved them to another place. We can take them to South Africa with Barnard," Dodi said feeling guilty that he had not seen Van Zyl fly in and take Mrs Owen away.

They were all staggered by this piece of news, and Dodi's resourcefulness. Barnard's face, when he heard that Dodi had found his rhino horns, and that he was to be handed over to the South African authorities, was a picture of anger and dismay.

"That's bloody marvellous Dodi. Now we have the evidence we need. What would we do without you?" Tom patted him on the back. "Now, I think we'd better get moving. Kyle you and Dodi must take Barnard and the rhino horns across the river, and hand him over to the Rangers at Pufuri. Dodi knows the way. He'll probably have to give them a statement. You know them and spent time on the chase with them. I'll call ahead to let them know what has happened here, and when to expect you. The police can pick him up there and then you must get back here as quickly as you can."

"What about Tombi? They'll need a statement from her as well. She also knows what was going on here," Kyle pointed out.

"Yes of course. Take her with you."

"Okay Dad. Where will I meet you when I get back?"

"We'll wait for you in Chiredzi. I have to try and find out where Van Zyl has taken Maria."

"What happens if Van Zyl decides to bring Maria back here?" Ted said.

"That is a very good point," Tom agreed. "We must leave Gideon and Godfrey here with a shotgun to guard everyone. If Van Zyl does come back they will be able to handle him. You can pick them up on your way back. Dodi will have to stay here to carry on watching the camp until we find Maria. "

"I have a satellite phone and my prospecting camping gear in my van. Dodi can use it and keep in touch with us," Ted said.

"I will stay with Dodi. If the madam is brought back here she will need me to be with her," Tombi piped up.

"I will look after her," Dodi said nodding his head and agreeing it was a good idea.

"Okay that's fine. Kyle you had better let the workers out on your way back - they're not guilty of anything."

The cook, still totally confused, offered to make tea and sandwiches for them. Kyle, Dodi and Tombi headed off to South Africa to hand Barnard over. Gideon and Godfrey waited at Mabiti, and Tom and Ted returned to Chiredzi.

Chapter 34

Despite their best efforts, neither Tom nor Ted, were able to track Van Zyl down. Ted left in the afternoon to drive back home and try and find out if Van Zyl was at his headquarters.

Tom was having supper in the hotel dining room when Kyle got back from South Africa. He was hot and sweaty, and very thirsty. All had gone well. Barnard had been taken into custody at Pufuri by the police. Dodi and Tombi, who both knew of what had been going on at Mabiti, made statements.

Kyle had bought provisions for Dodi and Tombi in the shop at Pufuri. Before dropping them off near Mabiti, with Ted's camping gear, they stopped to release the workers from the storeroom. Gideon went back to the farm with the borrowed Land Cruiser and took Godfrey with him.

In the morning Tom, Kyle and Godfrey, who had been dropped off at the hotel earlier, flew to Mount Hamden airport. By the time they arrived at Ted's house it was afternoon. It was Thursday; Maria had been a prisoner for five days.

"According to my gardener, Van Zyl was at home yesterday, but he is not sure if he's still there now. He flies in and out in his helicopter. I have sent my man off to try and find out if he is there," Ted told them.

"Now what do we do? We have no idea whether or not he has Maria locked up in his house, and no way of finding out. I wonder if anyone has seen her at Van Zyl's place?" Tom was getting desperate.

"No. Apparently he is at home with his half-breed son."

"Damn, damn, damn! Poor Maria must be terrified and going out of her mind," Tom said rubbing the back of his neck in frustration. "I hope we find her soon."

There wasn't much they could do. To try and storm Van Zyl's house was out of the question. It was well protected by a high electrified security fence with surveillance cameras, and patrolled by guards with dogs. They could not expect any help from the police. Apart from Tombi, they had no proof that she was being held against her will, and they would refuse to act, classing it a 'domestic dispute'. Because they were so corrupt, if they did take any action against him Van Zyl would easily bribe them. Somehow they had to find a way to rescue Maria themselves.

Tom, Ted and Kyle sat down to try and come up with sort of plan to rescue Maria. Without knowing where she was being held, it was impossible. They just had to wait and see if Ted's staff could find out anything. Although Tom was desperate to get Maria out of Van Zyl's clutches as quickly as possible, there was no point in rushing in 'half-cocked' without a workable plan; she might get hurt.

If Maria was being held in Van Zyl's house, they would need to recruit the help of some of their friends, and try to isolate him before he could alert anyone, when they did move in. Before they could do anything, they would first have to establish whether or not Van Zyl was at home, and if Maria was even there?

Eventually, without having thought of an alternative to smashing their way into Van Zyl's fortress, they retired to bed. Tom lay awake worrying about his wife for a long time before finally dropping off.

With a start Tom was wide awake. He had an idea. Why not sabotage Van Zyl's plane? It was light outside and so he woke Kyle who shared the room with him.

"It's suddenly dawned on me. I know the registration number of Van Zyl's plane, if he has gone away in it, he will have had to file a flight plan before taking off," Tom said when his son was fully awake. "We can phone the control tower and find out if he has taken off and if so where he has gone. If the plane is still there, we can put it out of action."

"Why the hell didn't we think of that yesterday? What idiots!" Kyle agreed hitting his forehead with the heel of his hand.

A quick phone call confirmed that Van Zyl had taken off early that morning at 0600, destined for Beira. Van Zyl had two passengers with him, a man and woman. The woman had to be Maria and the man probably his son. They were too late; they had lost their opportunity. Tom cursed out loud. While they had been sitting around trying to come up with some sort of plan; and getting nowhere, Van Zyl had been getting ready to fly away with his wife.

Why was he taking her to Beira? Tom wondered. What was Van Zyl up to? He had to find out; and fast. While they were having a quick breakfast and discussing their next move, Ted's gardener handed him an envelope. It was addressed to Tom.

"*Owen,*" the note inside read. *"You have been interfering with my operations in the Lowveld. Now it is my turn. I have your wife and I am taking her to my trawler. She will be transported to the east and sold into slavery. Now you can suffer. By the way, don't bother to try and find her, the sea is far too big. This note will be delivered to Ted Hunter after I leave - I know he will pass the message on to you.*"

The note was unsigned but had been delivered by Van Zyl's cook.

"The rotten devil!" Tom swore handing the note to Kyle. "This confirms he used the fishing trip as a cover to kidnap Maria. And I allowed him to do it. Now look what he's doing!"

"That's why he wanted to know what you were doing, and where you were, when he came to see me about the court case," said Ted.

"That still doesn't explain how he knew I was involved with the confiscation of his ivory. Unless Barnard saw us at Inharrime before he managed to escape the net in Mozambique."

"We flew over him a number of times before he got to the coast; he might have made a note of the registration number on the plane. Like we have just done, it wouldn't have taken much to discover it belonged to you," Kyle pointed out to his father.

"Yes, I suppose that's true," Tom agreed nodding his head.

"I think we're all forgetting something here. Tombi used to work for Van Zyl and Barnard. He found her with Maria on Inhaca; they will know she was involved with us," Kyle said.

"Good point. Anyway he knows we were involved, and now we need to get Maria out of his clutches as quickly as we can," Tom said. "I suspected he was having me followed when I went to London. What was that all about? I thought that was because of the diamonds. At that stage we didn't even know of his poaching activities."

"Yes, you said so when you came back. All we need now is the location of this trawler of his?" Ted said.

"I've got it!" Tom exclaimed suddenly. "It's been staring us in the face all along. When Sandy and I flew to the islands in the Mozambique Channel, we saw the *Verona* anchored off Europa Island. The French garrison commander told us it often anchored there. As Van Zyl said in his note - that's where he's taken Maria. We know there is an airstrip on the island."

"With all the business over the ivory and rhino horn smuggling, do you think he would still take a chance and have his trawler operating in those waters?" Ted asked.

"Yes I do. The Island is a French possession and has nothing to do with Mozambique. Where else would he be going if he is heading for Beira – it is in a direct line from here to Europa," Tom was excited. "I'm damned sure that's where they have gone. It's the best shot we have."

They spent the morning planning their rescue mission. Tom enlisted the help of the senior anti-poaching man in South Africa who they had helped with the capture and arrest of Barnard's men. He assured Tom that he would get in touch with Mozambique authorities and fill them in, and then get back to him. It didn't take long.

"Tom, I've been in touch with the people in Mozambique. They tell me they have got their navy involved," Tom was told over the phone an hour later. "A fast naval gun ship will be sent immediately from Beira to apprehend the trawler *Verona*."

"Thanks very much for your help. We'll be leaving here shortly for Beira, and plan to arrive on Europa Island at about six tomorrow morning. Can you pass the message on to your Mozambique friends?" Tom asked.

"I'll get on to it straight away again. Good luck Tom. I hope you get your wife back safely from that bastard. He must be caught and locked up for good." He was also keen to have Van Zyl behind bars. "By the way, thanks for catching that bloody poacher Barnard for us."

"It was a pleasure. Thanks again Johan. We'll be in touch."

Chapter 35

Van Zyl was very pleased with himself when they landed at Beira to refuel. Things were working out well and he was in his element. He was back in control and now had something of Owen's that he treasured very much - he had his wife and he would never see her again. It served him bloody well right, the interfering swine. By now Ted Hunter would have received the note and passed its message on to Owen. They would never know where he had taken her.

They were not leaving the airport so they were not required to clear Customs and Immigration. While he was busy in the control tower filing his flight plan for the next leg of their trip, Joey escorted Maria to the washroom. There was no escape; the windows were barred and Joey guarded the door while she did her best to freshen up.

She splashed water on her face and then looked at herself in the cracked and tarnished mirror. What a sight she was; her face was haggard and tired, her hair was a mess, and her clothes didn't fit. She was thankful that at least she had helped herself to a change of clothes from the cupboard in the room at Van Zyl's home.

She sobbed involuntarily when she thought of Tom trying desperately to find her. How was he ever going to know where Van Zyl was taking her now? Pulling herself together, she marched bravely out of the washroom and back to the plane, followed closely by Joey. She climbed on board and settled once again onto the back seat. As soon as they were strapped in, Van Zyl started the engines, took off and flew east over the Indian Ocean.

Maria sat in her corner lost in thought, gazing vacantly down at the sea passing slowly way below. Early on the second morning of her stay in Harare, just as it was getting light, she had been woken by Joey. She hardly had time to clean up, stuff her toothbrush and toothpaste into her pocket and brush her hair, before he had shoved her outside, bundled her into a car and they drove to the airport where Van Zyl had been waiting.

Where was she going now, she wondered as the plane droned steadily on? If not home, she hoped it was back to Mabiti. Knowing now, with them flying way out to sea, there was very little hope of ever being found and rescued. She was being taken further and further away from her beloved Tom and the family.

Two hours after leaving Beira, the tone of the engines changed and they began to descend. Maria looked down and saw that they were approaching a small coral island in the middle of the ocean. Van Zyl called on the radio and was answered by a man with a French accent.

Then something Tom had said stirred in the back of her mind and gave her a glimmer of hope. He had told her that when he and Sandy flew to Europa Island, they had seen Van Zyl's ship anchored there. This had to be the same island.

When they flew low over a ship anchored north of the island, before turning to land, she knew she was being taken to Van Zyl's ship. A few moments later, after passing low over a cluster of buildings, the plane touched down, bounced along the bumpy surface and came to a stop at the eastern end of the runway.

Van Zyl opened his cockpit door and climbed down onto the ground. A man on a motor cycle, wearing a khaki uniform and a pith helmet came bouncing down the airstrip towards them. Turning to Joey he instructed. "Keep her in the plane and make sure she keeps her bloody mouth closed. We don't want these frog soldiers to know she's our prisoner."

Joey, who had also climbed out of the cockpit and was standing on the wing, leaned back inside. "You heard my dad. Don't you dare to move or even say anything until the soldier has left, and we think it's safe," he warned waving his revolver in her face.

After a short conversation with Van Zyl, the soldier looked up towards Maria sitting in the plane. He took no notice of her, in spite of her putting on a most pitiful expression and mouthing silently 'help'. Instead he turned back to Van Zyl, made him sign a book, climbed back on his motor-cycle and puttered off back to the garrison at the far end of the runway.

After the soldier had gone, Maria climbed out of the plane. Van Zyl led the way along a path through the sparse bush with Joey pushing Maria along ahead of him. After a short walk the path opened up onto a white sandy beach. A small boat was making its way from the ship towards the beach where they waited. They waded out through the shallow water to meet the boat, climbed aboard and were taken out to the trawler anchored a couple of hundred meters from shore.

Maria recognized the name *Verona* painted on the stern of the dark blue trawler. Her spirits lifted. This was the same trawler Tom had told her about. It belonged to Van Zyl and was used to transport all his illegal goods. Tom knew the trawler anchored here, and so there was a glimmer of hope after all.

As soon as the boat had tied up alongside the trawler, Maria was made to climb up a rope ladder hanging over the side onto the deck. Once on board she was led off to a small cabin behind the wheel-house. Joey pushed her inside, slammed the door closed and locked her in.

Maria took stock of her new prison. In the cabin there was a narrow bunk and a table and chair set up under the porthole window. A basin, a bar of soap, a bottle of water and a glass were on the table. There was a bucket in one corner. On the bunk there was a blanket and pillow, and although threadbare were clean.

An overpowering stench of fish and diesel oil made Maria feel quite nauseous. The small vent above the bunk did little to remove the stench, and the porthole was bolted closed.

Through the porthole, Maria could see the island. Although it was less than half a kilometre away, it looked a lot further. She presumed Van Zyl had an arrangement with the French, who obviously allowed the trawler to anchor close inshore.

The island was her only hope of escape and freedom. As soon as an opportunity presented itself, she resolved to jump overboard and swim ashore. The thought of sharks in the water made her shudder.

As long as the ship remained at anchor near the island, she felt she had a chance of escape, or possibly even of being rescued. The French official at the air-strip had seen her and what she looked like; he might even be curious.

Knowing there was no escape from the ship for the present; Maria lay down on the bunk to consider her position. The crew members Maria had seen when she came on board, appeared to be of Eastern origin; probably Malaysian or Indonesian, so there was little chance of help from any of them.

She wondered how long it would be before Van Zyl flew back to Harare, and the trawler sailed away from the island with her on board. The longer he remained on board the better for her. It would also give Tom more time to catch up with them; if he had worked out where they had gone!

She lay on the bunk for what seemed like hours. She couldn't tell what time it was because her watch had been taken by the awful little half-caste son of Van Zyl's. She had lost all track of time; she didn't even know what day it was, and so she tried to concentrate and think about her situation.

She and Tombi had been kidnapped on Sunday and taken to Mabiti the same day. In the afternoon, three days after they had been kidnapped, Van Zyl had taken her to Harare where she had spent two days locked in one of his spare bedrooms. In the morning they had flown to this place, so it had to be late on Friday afternoon.

Going on Tom's description of his visit here with Sandy, she was convinced it was Europa Island. She got up, had a sip of water, and looked through the porthole. The sun had set and it was getting dark; she could barely make out the island in the gloom. There would be no rescue by Tom to-day; if ever!

She hoped and prayed that Tom would work out where she was. Perhaps the French soldiers on the island had already sent a message to someone. She knew she was clutching at straws but she was determined not to give up hope yet.

Eventually the door clanged open, and a rather sinister looking individual with a scarf wrapped around his head, handed her a dish of oily soup with bits of fish and rice floating around in it. Before she had a chance to ask for some clean water to wash with, he backed out of the cabin and locked the door. Maria, already feeling nauseous, tossed the contents of the bowl into the bucket before it made her retch.

Maria used a little of the water to wash her face and clean her teeth. Feeling a little refreshed and cleaner, she lay back on the bunk, closed her eyes and tried to sleep. She was physically and mentally exhausted, and very worried.

Apart from the hum of the generator and an occasional clang of a door being closed, or a voice being raised, all was quiet. As she drifted off to sleep she wondered what was in store for her. She was very frightened.

Chapter 36

A 200 foot long 'Warrior Class' Fast Attack boat was operating in the waters off Beira, where it was assisting in the control of illegal long-line fishing by foreign trawlers within the Mozambique territorial waters. At 1500 hours on Friday, the Commander received orders to proceed at full speed to Europa Island, where he was to detain and search the fishing trawler *Verona*. Plotting a course to Europa he gave their estimated time of arrival as 0600 the following morning.

As the island was a French possession, the commander requested that Naval Command obtain permission from the French to enter their waters, and then asked the purpose of their mission. Although the *Verona* had been reported fishing illegally inside Mozambique waters on a number of occasions, laying off Europa it was beyond their jurisdiction, and they would need the co-operation of the French, if they were to board the vessel.

Within the hour a message was received confirming they could approach the island, and advising the Commander that it was believed a woman was being held against her will, on board the *Verona*. The woman's husband, Tom Owen, was flying directly to the island in a light aircraft, and would liaise with the Commander on his arrival there.

· · · · · · · · · · · · · ·

At three o'clock on Saturday morning, Tom and Kyle took off from Beira and set a course for Europa. They had flown from Harare the previous afternoon and stopped to refuel and sleep for a few hours. Now they were ready to continue with their pursuit. It was calm with no turbulence or headwind, and so they made good time flying east over the Indian Ocean.

The sun was just struggling to break free from the ocean, when Kyle sighted the tiny island. It was directly in front of them, and as they got closer they could see a ship anchored off the north shore. Suspecting it might be the *Verona* Kyle throttled back, took the plane down to 500 feet, and so as not to be seen by the ship's look-out, approached Europa from the south.

Tom, who had been dozing, looked down and saw a naval vessel steaming straight towards the island from the west. By the white bow wave and long wake trailing behind, he could see that it was going at full-speed, and right on time.

"That looks like the *Verona* down there. I hope we're right Kyle. If Maria is not on that ship we'll have egg all over our faces," Tom expressed his doubts. "And worse still, we'll have to start our search all over again."

"No Dad, you're right. Look! That must be Van Zyl's plane on the airstrip. I think we're about to have some fun."

"Those bastards had better not have hurt Maria! If she has been harmed in the slightest I swear I'll kill Van Zyl," Tom was itching to get his hands on the nasty little man.

"I think it might be a good idea to put his plane out of action. We don't want him escaping again. We would never catch him in our single engine aircraft; his is much faster."

Kyle landed and taxied to the western end of the airstrip. Tom recognised Pierre, the Sergeant in Charge of the garrison, when he marched over to greet them. After explaining the reason for their visit, Pierre confirmed one of his men had seen a woman arrive with two men when they had arrived in their aircraft the previous day. They said they were meeting the trawler and she was a part owner in their fishing business. He was shocked when Tom told him that the woman was his wife, and that she was a hostage.

Pierre readily agreed to send them out to the trawler in a life-boat with four of his soldiers. In the meantime, he would place an armed guard on Van Zyl's plane to apprehend him and stop him taking off.

. . . .

Van Zyl was up early. He found it difficult to sleep on the stinking trawler. The whole ship stank of fish and it rocked around all the time. He was not accustomed to the discomfort of cramped quarters and bad food. He stood in the bows of the *Verona* where the air was cool and fresh, leaning on the rails smoking a cheroot, and looking across the water to the island.

The factory ship was due later in the morning and he wanted to be there to supervise the transfer of his hostage, when it arrived. Maria Owen would be taken to the east to work; either as a servant, or a labourer for some wealthy businessman. He planned on leaving by mid-afternoon to fly back to Harare with Joey. Then he would get down to dealing with Owen and his son himself. He smiled relishing the thought.

Van Zyl flicked the butt of his cheroot over the side and watched it curve away to land in the sea below. He moved away from the rail on his way to go and wake his son; it was time to start getting ready. As he turned, he caught sight of a ship steaming straight towards them. At first he presumed it to be the factory ship, but then with a start he realized it was a naval vessel; and it was approaching fast.

With Somalian pirates operating north of Madagascar, naval patrols in the Mozambique Channel had been stepped up. With this in mind, Van Zyl decided that the boat must be on a regular patrol, checking all the shipping in the area. Apart from the Owen woman, there was no contraband on board; the holds were all full of fish.

Nevertheless it was not worth taking a risk of being caught on board the *Verona*, with a kidnapped woman. And so he made a quick change of plan, as he hurried to rouse Joey.

"Get dressed quickly, we have company. A naval patrol boat is heading this way. I want you to take the Owen woman down to the engine room and hide her there. Then we must get back to the island, before they decide to board and search the ship," Van Zyl said over his shoulder as he hurried off to alert the captain.

．．．．．．．．．．．．．．

Maria woke with a start. People were running around on deck, shouting in a language she did not know, but sounded eastern. She was surprised to find it was day and the sun was already up. She was peering out of the porthole, trying to see what all the excitement was about, when the door clanged open and Joey came in.

"You must come with me immediately. Hurry up now, you are moving," he said in his nasal monotone voice.

"Where are you taking me? I hope it's to a better cabin - this one stinks."

"You'll see. Come on lets go," he said grabbing her by the arm and pulling her roughly out of the cabin. "I haven't got time to waste."

Joey pushed her along a corridor and down two dimly lit sets of ladders. As they progressed deeper into the dark interior of the ship, and the hum of the generator got louder and louder, she had a very nasty feeling things were getting worse for her. There was no point in resisting; Joey was much stronger than she was, and so she allowed herself to be pushed along offering little resistance.

When they seemed to have reached the very bowels of the stinking vessel, she was pushed into the dimly lit engine room. Joey forced her into a small wire cage, behind the engine, where hoses were stored, and locked her inside.

"For goodness sake! Why are you putting me down here?" Maria shouted above the noise of the generator. Without a word Joey turned and disappeared from sight, slamming the steel engine room door shut behind him as he went. Why had Joey been in such a hurry to hide her down here in the dark confines of the engine-room?

It was dark; only a single globe gave off just enough light for her to examine her new surroundings. The noise of the generator was loud enough to drown out any other sounds on the ship, and so she couldn't hear what was happening up on deck. She would never be heard if she called out. From her new prison Maria looked onto the main engine and various pumps and pipes. The smell of diesel oil was overpowering.

Maria was terrified. She sat down on a coil of hose and began to weep. Her situation was now quite desperate and all hope of escape, or ever being rescued, seemed to have been dashed.

. . . .

"Have you taken the woman down to the engine room?" Van Zyl asked Joey when he joined him up on the bridge.

"Yes. She's locked in the hose cage."

"Good. We must get the hell out of here now. Climb down into the boat and wait there for me. I'll join you as soon as I have finished here." Van Zyl watched Joey climb over the rail and scramble down into the life boat, then he turned back to the captain standing beside him.

"If the sailors from that patrol boat want to board and search the ship, get two of your crew to take the woman out of the hose store and throw her into one of the fish holds and bury her under the ice. They won't look for her there," Van Zyl instructed his skipper.

"What must I do if she freezes to death in the fish hold?"

"Weight her down, and when you are well away from the island, throw her overboard," Van Zyl instructed him casually. "As soon as the navy have moved away, report to me on the radio. If they don't come on board get the woman back to the cabin. We don't want her damaged. I will give you your orders once they have gone." The captain, a Malaysian who never spoke much, nodded his head in acknowledgement of his orders.

The gun-ship was closing in fast when Van Zyl hurried from the bridge, and went over the side to join his son and a crew member in the boat. Using the *Verona* as a shield, they made their way ashore as quickly as possible. Once on shore the two of them trotted along the path back to the plane and the boat returned to the trawler

"Oh shit. There's another plane at the other end of the runway," Joey said as they emerged from the path.

"*Bliksem!* When did it get here? We'll have to move our arses and get airborne, before those bloody frogs get here and try to stop us taking off," Van Zyl cursed. "They must be having some sort of joint exercise."

"I think we are already too late. A soldier is coming towards us," Joey pointed in the direction of the barracks at the other end of the runway. A uniformed soldier was running down the air-strip.

"Quick! Get the bloody chocks out and undo the tie-downs," Van Zyl urged his son as he climbed up into the cockpit.

In next to no time the engines burst into life, and without waiting for permission from the garrison, they trundled down the air-strip lifting off to fly over the head of the soldier, who stood helplessly on the runway pointing his rifle up at them.

They were unable to see the registration number of the other plane, and so Van Zyl presumed it must have been there as part of whatever was going on between the French and the Mozambique navy. The patrol boat looked very much like one they had flown over after leaving Beira the previous day. He hoped it was just an unfortunate coincidence that the *Verona* happened to be there at the same time.

As the plane gained altitude, they looked down and saw a life-saving boat making its way from the island towards the patrol boat, that had closed in and was lying not more than a hundred yards from the *Verona*.

"That French life-boat must be going out to meet with the Navy. Let's hope they are not interested in the *Verona*," Van Zyl said. Joey nodded his head in agreement as they climbed away from the island, on a heading that would take them back to the mainland.

"Verona, Verona, come in please," Joey called on the radio fifteen minutes later. There was no response. He tried again two or three times over the next hour, but still there was no response. Van Zyl was concerned that they were unable to raise the *Verona* over the radio, and could only assume that the captain was busy; either with the French soldiers from the Garrison, or the sailors from the Patrol Boat.

What was the naval patrol boat doing at Europa? Was it just carrying out a normal patrol, or had it been alerted to Van Zyl's poaching business?

After leaving the island, and re-fuelling at Beira, Van Zyl and Joey flew to Mabiti. A decision had to be made about Tombi. What were they going to do with her? One way or another they had to silence her.

Chapter 37

Half an hour after landing, with both of them wearing khaki overalls supplied by Pierre, Tom and Kyle were chugging out to the trawler, in a lifeboat with four French soldiers. Rounding the western point of the island, the *Verona* came into view. The Navy patrol boat, they had seen from the air, was standing off one hundred yards from the trawler.

Pierre had been in radio contact with the Commander, requesting that he stand by until Tom and his party went on board to find and rescue Maria - if she was there. As soon as they were on board he was to close in on the *Verona* and detain it.

The lifeboat was still two hundred yards from the trawler, when they saw Van Zyl's plane flying away from Europa, heading west towards the Mozambique coast. Once again he had managed to escape from Tom's clutches; but had he taken Maria with him? Tom's heart sank.

They tied up to a rope ladder hanging over the side and, leaving one soldier on the boat, scrambled up onto the deck. The ship's crew were all preoccupied, leaning on the deck rail watching the patrol boat, and so none of them saw the group from the island climbing over the side.

Not wasting a moment, two soldiers went to round up the ship's crew, the other one ran up the steps onto the bridge with Kyle, while Tom waited on deck. Up on the bridge the captain and his mate were both studying the activity on the Patrol Boat through binoculars, as it closed in and then launched a life-boat packed with sailors.

When Kyle and the soldier burst through the door, they turned quickly to face them. The sight of the soldier pointing his revolver at them, made them quickly raise their arms in surrender without uttering a word. With the ships crew taken care of, and leaving the French soldier to guard the captain and his mate, Kyle went to help his father.

Tom, after signalling for the Patrol Boat to come along-side, set off with Kyle in search of Maria. Within minutes, sailors from the Patrol Boat stormed over the railing, to take control of the trawler and its crew. After handing over to the navy, the French soldiers joined the search, working their way through the ship from stem to stern.

They searched the cabins; the galley and the crews' quarters; they worked their way down to the refrigeration plant and the storage areas until finally Tom, whose heart was getting heavier by the minute, entered the engine room.

A diesel generator was running in one corner; obviously providing the power to keep the ice machines working. The exhaust leaked filling the room with fumes, adding to the stink of diesel oil. The place was filthy. The floor was littered with pipes, spare parts, drums of oil and grease and other engine room debris.

A small wire cage, filled with rubber hoses, was tucked away in a dark corner behind the engine. Although the light was dim, Tom saw something move inside the cage, and thought it must be the ship's cat. He was about to turn away and leave the engine room when he heard a sound that made him make his way around the side of the engine to investigate. What he saw in the cage almost made his heart stop beating.

Sitting on top of a pile of hoses, with her arms wrapped around her drawn up legs and her head on her knees, was Maria; sobbing her heart out. At last he had found his wife, and she was alive! What a relief.

In his haste to get to his wife, Tom tripped over some pipes lying on the floor and nearly fell he was so excited.

"Maria! Are you alright? Thank God I've found you at last." For a moment she didn't move, and then she slowly raised her head and looked at Tom in disbelief.

"Tom! What took you so long?" Maria scolded, laughing and sobbing at the same time as she climbed down from the pile of hoses.

"Well you weren't exactly easy to find, so it took us a while. You have come a hell of a long way since I saw you last. Has that bastard harmed you in any way?" Tom asked with his heart going out to his brave wife. "Let's get you out of there."

Looking around he found an iron bar lying on the floor, which he used to smash the lock open.

"Apart from being bullied and pushed around, I'm fine. The catering on this cruise ship is not very good though. I was very worried you would never be able to find me," Maria admitted wiping her tears with Tom's handkerchief.

"So was I," Tom said smiling tenderly and hugging his wife. "We had one hell of a chase to catch up with you. Luckily Van Zyl left us a clue, and Sandy and I had seen his trawler here when we came here before. I'm sure the French cuisine on the island will be much better."

"Dad, are you in here?" Kyle called from the engine room door.

"Yes, and look what I found hiding down here," Tom yelled back appearing from behind the engine with his arm protectively around Maria's shoulders, grinning from ear to ear.

"Hell's bells Maria! You had us really worried. Thank God we found you. Do you know you were on your way to being a slave or a servant somewhere in the far-east?" Kyle smiled happily and gave Maria a bear hug.

"Come on, lets get the hell off this stinking ship," said Tom leading the way up to the deck.

"My goodness Tom; how did you manage to get the navy involved?" Maria asked when she saw the Patrol Boat alongside. "I feel quite important," she added happily filling her lungs with fresh sea air as soon as they emerged into the bright sunshine.

"You are very important! Sometimes it helps to have friends in the right places. Thanks to our help with the capture of Van Zyl's rhino horns and ivory, we used his contacts in Mozambique." Tom smiled.

They were met on deck by a Navy Lieutenant who, after Tom explained the situation to him, took control of the *Verona*.

Tom, Kyle and Maria went back to the garrison with the French soldiers, where Maria was able to take a shower, and change into a clean shirt and dungarees drawn from the Garrison stores; again courtesy of Pierre. Once they were all cleaned up, they sat down to a feast of crayfish washed down with French wine. After lunch they toured the island, and watched as the Patrol Boat turned to escort the *Verona* back to Beira.

Tom and Maria, happy to be re-united after fearing they would never see each other again, behaved like young lovers and couldn't leave each other alone for a second. Kyle, almost embarrassed by their behaviour, smiled indulgently like a doting parent.

Next morning before leaving the island, Pierre handed Tom statements made by the soldiers who had been with him when they rescued Maria. They flew to Malelane, only stopping in Beira to refuel. Tom and Maria spent the night with Kyle and Rosa; they had not seen their new home, and there was a lot to tell Rosa.

After a family discussion, although Tom had no intention of letting him get away with it, they agreed that there was no point in laying kidnapping charges against Van Zyl; unless they could get him to South Africa. Finally, after a week of worry and tension, they were able to relax.

Although Maria was no longer in Van Zyl's clutches Tom decided to leave Dodi and Tombi watching the activities at Matibi for a little longer. It might be useful to know what was happening there, now that Barnard was in prison in South Africa. Ted would keep in contact with Dodi via the satellite phone.

Sandy, to everyone's surprise, was back from America and waiting at Inhaca when they arrived in camp a couple of days later. Tomasi had already told him about the kidnapping. He was shocked to hear what had happened to Maria and Tombi during his absence.

He had flown out three weeks before the Swanepoel party were booked for their charter. By the time he got back to Inhaca, Maria and Tombi had been kidnapped and rescued. While he and June had been busy in the USA, the whole team in Africa had been chasing around trying to catch up with Van Zyl and his cronies, and rescue Maria and Tombi from their clutches.

Chapter 38

When Tombi woke up it was light and she could smell the smoke from the fire. Dodi must have been up for some time - the fire was hot and a pot of water boiled on the coals. They settled easily and comfortably in their camp, and it wasn't long before Tombi was doing the daily chores of a normal African home; cleaning utensils, washing clothes, sweeping around the tent and their camp.

She was happy with the way they got on together, and secretly hoped they would be there for some time. She was in no hurry to get back to civilization. Tombi enjoyed being on her own with Dodi. While doing her chores and preparing their food, she noticed how quietly and efficiently Dodi got things just as he wanted them.

He was a good woodsman and it was a pleasure to see how he worked in the bush. He went off at intervals during the day to see what was going on at Mabiti. The workers seemed to be wandering around aimlessly; with Barnard gone they had no manager and nothing to do.

When he was in the camp, Tombi could hardly keep her eyes off Dodi. She had been watching him all day as he went about his chores. She loved the way he moved; sure footed and confident. His lithe body seemed to flow as he moved about effortlessly. She had fallen in love with him, and desperately wanted to hold him in her arms.

That evening Tombi arranged the logs they sat on so that they would sit near to each other. When they sat down around the fire to have their meal, she was close enough to Dodi to lean against him. Every time she handed him something, she brushed her bare arm against him.

She was excited, and had butterflies in her stomach; her voice low and husky when she spoke, making her feelings known. Dodi sensed the electricity between them, and so when they had finished eating, he put his arm around her shoulders and pulled her close. They sat intimately talking quietly beside the fire in the growing darkness, prolonging the moment.

After a while they got up and prepared for bed. While Dodi doused the fire and finished putting things in order, Tombi went into the tent, undressed and lay naked on top of her sleeping mat, making her desires quite clear. When he had finished outside, Dodi joined her and, in the flickering light of the lamp, saw Tombi lying naked on her sleeping mat, waiting for him. He couldn't take his eyes off her as he quickly threw off his clothes, lay down beside her and took her in his arms.

They embraced kissing passionately with tongues flicking and teasing. Dodi slowly began to caress her breasts, gently nibbling her erect nipples, before stroking her belly and squeezing her round firm buttocks. Then his hand worked its way down towards her mound to excite her with his fingers. Tombi felt his hardness against her and reached down to take him in her hand. She gasped when she felt the size of his stiff throbbing manhood, rolled over and opened her legs to receive him. Wrapping her legs around him, they joined together like serpents, as he thrust deep inside her and they made love. She had never in her life experienced such pleasure and joy.

On the fourth day, when the sun was at its highest, they heard the sound of an aircraft approaching. Dodi trotted off to investigate and returned half an hour later. Van Zyl and his son had landed and walked to the camp. He grabbed his water bottle and went off to see what was happening at Mabiti.

The sun was setting when he came back with nothing to tell her, except that they seemed to be staying the night at Mabiti. Dodi called Mr Hunter on the satellite phone to report what he had seen, and in turn heard that his boss, Mr Owen, had flown off to Mozambique to find and rescue his wife.

In the morning Dodi went back to Mabiti. A couple of hours later Tombi heard the plane taking off and a few minutes afterwards Dodi came back. Van Zyl had gone off alone and left his son behind. Again he called Ted Hunter to report to him and was delighted to hear from him that Maria Owen had been rescued and was safe. The Owens' were on their way home.

Mr Hunter said that they were to stay where they were, keep watching Mabiti and wait for instructions. Tombi was overjoyed by the news of Mrs Owens rescue, but also pleased that she and Dodi would be alone together for a little longer. She was in love and couldn't wait for their long nights of lovemaking.

. . . .

In spite of buzzing the camp, nobody came to pick them up, and so Van Zyl and Joey walked the short distance to the Mabiti Camp. The

228

cook was sitting in the sun outside the kitchen door, picking his nose. As soon as he recognised Van Zyl, he shot off his chair and scuttled quickly into the kitchen, followed by Van Zyl.

"Where is Boss Barnard?" Van Zyl asked looking around.

"Other men came here on Wednesday. They took the boss away with them," the cook reported.

"What other men. Were they white men?"

"There were two vans. Three were white men and three were black."

"Where did they go to?"

"I do not know sir. They took Tombi, the black woman who was staying here."

"Shit!" Van Zyl was absolutely furious. How had this happened? It had to be Owen and his son - he had taken his wife away just in time. It seemed he had underestimated the Owens.

Joey came into the kitchen; he had been at the sheds talking to the skinners and butchers. They had all been locked up in the store-room when Barnard was taken away, but released later. There was nothing for them to do, and so they had been cleaning out the store-rooms, the cold room and generally tidying up around the yard. They said the meat was finished and clients would be needing supplies within the week. They also said that the van did not work because the men who took Barnard away had taken parts from the engine.

"Joey, I want you to stay here and keep things running, while we wait for Barney to return from his little jaunt. I am going to Harare in the morning to find out what the hell is going on. Let me know as soon as Barney gets back." Van Zyl said to his son at supper.

"How long do you think that will be?" Joey asked with a sulky expression - he hated the bush.

"I don't know. Just go and check the van and tell me what you need to get it running. I will get the parts to you in a couple of days."

By the time Van Zyl was up and about in the morning, Joey was already busy in the yard with the hood of the Toyota up.

"Okay. What do you need for the van?" Van Zyl asked his son at breakfast.

"Nothing. I have managed to get the van started. One of the workers fixing a hole in the fence near the gate, found the missing part lying in the bush. Whoever took it out of the van must have thrown it over the fence."

Arriving back at his home, Van Zyl was greeted with an urgent message to phone Barney in South Africa. The message had been received two days earlier and his secretary said he sounded quite anxious. What in the hell was he doing in South Africa? Then he realized what must have happened; he must have been captured by the men who had been at Mabiti, and taken there.

As it was almost noon, Van Zyl decided it would be a good time to phone.

"This is the South African Police in Makhado. Can I help you?" the voice on the other end of the line answered.

"I think I must have the wrong number. I was given this number to contact an employee of mine, Barney Barnard," Van Zyl explained.

"No sir you have the right number. Barnard is locked in our cells. He was arrested for poaching."

"Will it be possible to speak to him? I am calling from Zimbabwe." Van Zyl cursed under his breath. He was furious and found it difficult to keep his voice under control.

"Hold on while I get him for you."

"Hello Jan. Is that you?" Barney said coming on the line a few minutes later.

"Yes it is. What the bloody hell were you up to? How did you get arrested? I left you looking after things at Mabiti then, as soon as I turn my back, you bugger off to South Africa to do a bit of poaching. I thought I said no more," Van Zyl blasted.

"I wasn't poaching Jan. The morning after you came for Maria Owen, her husband and son arrived with a whole bloody army. They tied me up and took me over the river to Pufuri. The police arrested me there."

"But you had nothing in the camp they could use for evidence." Van Zyl was confused.

"That bloody tracker Dodi found some of the rhino horns we had hidden away. The police have them as evidence."

"What rhino horns? You said it was all lost when the truck was impounded in Mozambique. Were you lying to me?"

"It was insurance Jan. I'm sorry. I found them on my van when I got back." Barnard tried to explain, contradicting himself. "Can you organise a lawyer for me?"

"I still think you are lying, but we will sort that out later. Okay I'll get a lawyer for you." Van Zyl conceded. "Don't drop me in it, you hear."

"Of course I won't. I have to go back to the cell now. Cheers."

Van Zyl was livid. Not only had Barney obviously tried to cheat him, but he was now in a whole heap of trouble, and he himself might be implicated. Unless he hired a very good lawyer to defend Barney, he might just implicate him in the whole mess. He knew a fellow in Polokwane not far from Makhado who would fit the bill.

Now with Barney locked up, Joey would have to run the Mabiti operation; there were meat orders to be filled. Joey was certainly no hunter and if he could not cope with the shooting, Van Zyl would have to employ someone to do the hunting for him. It was only now that he realized how much he depended on Barney to do all his dirty work and running around for him. With him domiciled in Zimbabwe and having been arrested in South Africa, there was little chance of him being released on bail.

On the other hand, seeing that his poaching and hunting operations had been compromised, perhaps he should consider selling Mabiti. He knew of a senior government official with plenty of money who might be interested. He still had mining interests all around the country, and a multitude of other business interests around the world. It was something to consider, and would depend entirely on the outcome of Barney's court case.

Once again the Owens' had managed to mess with his operations. It seemed he just could not get rid of them and their interfering. Well he had the better of them now. He had taken Maria Owen, and there was no chance of her ever getting away.

The only things nagging in the back of his mind were the patrol boat, and the plane on the runway at Europa. What had the naval patrol boat been doing at Europa? Was it just carrying out a normal patrol or had it been alerted to Van Zyl's poaching business? The boat loaded with soldiers, they had seen going from the island towards the trawler, was obviously carrying out a routine inspection. They would not have caused a problem; he was not worried about them.

He still had not heard from his trawler and was anxious to find out where it was, and whether Owen's wife had gone to Malaysia on the factory ship. He would be a lot happier once he knew she had been absorbed into the slave trading markets of the east, where she would be lost forever. Unless the sailors from the patrol boat had boarded the *Verona,* and rescued her! But if the captain had obeyed his instructions, she would probably have died in the fish-hold, and they would never have found her. Kidnapping is a very serious offence.

The plane was another story. It was a civilian Cessna and had looked very much like the Owen's plane he had seen on Inhaca. If it was his plane, how had he caught up to them so quickly? Yes, he had sent him a note admitting he had his wife, but he had given no clue as to where he was taking her. Barney had not even known, so it was impossible that he had let the cat out of the bag. It was all far too much of a coincidence, and it worried him.

He had to admit to himself, things were not running smoothly, and with Barney locked up in South Africa accused of poaching, were getting more than a little out of hand. He had lost his precious load of ivory and rhino horns worth a small fortune; his supply of diamonds had slowed right down; his Mabiti business had all but ground to a halt and, having not heard from his captain, it looked like his fishing trawler had disappeared.

Barney Barnard's application to be released on bail, pending his trial, was denied and he was sent to remand prison for two months. Although Van Zyl had not been summoned to give evidence, his lawyer advised him not to attend the trial. His presence might aggravate the situation, making it worse for Barney. Besides, as Barney's employer, he might also be arrested for his part, or for kidnapping.

Turning his attention to matters closer to home, Van Zyl summoned the two men who had been keeping Tom Owen's house in Harare under surveillance. They arrived later in the day to report that they had seen no sign of either of the Owens'.

Was it possible that after getting his note, and realizing the helplessness of the situation, Owen had given up the search for his wife, and was back on his island? He could not see this happening and would have to be very wary of him.

He had not seen or heard from Hunter in quite a while either. When he asked the two men about Kyle Owen, he was pleasantly surprised to hear that he and his wife had left the country, and moved to South Africa. Was he rid of them at last?

There was another serious problem requiring his immediate attention. Thanks to his friendship with the minister of lands, he had been able to acquire a large irrigated sugar estate in the Lowveld along the banks of the Tokwe River. It was another chunk of property the government had earmarked for re-settlement in their land reform programme. Like most other large commercial farms that had been taken over, it would be handed over to someone in a powerful position.

Van Zyl, knowing that in the wrong hands the highly profitable estate would quickly deteriorate with production coming to a halt, had made an offer to buy the sugar estate, agreeing to give the minister a large share of the profits. Ownership was transferred to his name and Van Zyl took over, but he made no changes to the management of the estate. He was pleased with this arrangement, and only visited the place every now and then.

A week after returning from Mabiti he was called to the Tokwe Estate. The manager was having problems with war veterans, who were under the impression that they were entitled to help themselves to pieces of the sugar cane fields, wanted to build their huts everywhere. It was a new experience for him. He had always been in contempt of all those farmers who were intimidated so easily, and left their farms when confronted by the war-vets. Now it was his turn and he was angry that they should dare to try it on him.

"You must pack up and leave this farm immediately," Van Zyl said firmly, addressing a crowd of about 40 scruffy individuals who were demanding plots of land on the farm. His manager stood to one side of him and one of the two assistants on the other.

"You do not own this land any longer. We are taking the farm from you. It is ours now," the aggressive spokesman informed Van Zyl, much to the delight of the fist waving mob.

"I have friends in very high places. They will make sure this farm stays in my hands. Perhaps you had better ask your leader about this."

"No! We are not leaving," the leader responded waving his machete threateningly in the air but beginning to lose the vocal support of his followers.

"What part of 'bugger off' don't you understand? Go and speak to your superiors before you come back here again." Van Zyl was getting irritated. Turning to his staff he said. "Come on let's go back to the office and leave these people to sort them-selves out. I have better things to do with my time."

The war-vets, confused and uncertain, decided to back off and by later in the day there was no sign of them. When he got home Van Zyl contacted his ministerial friend, to tell him of the war-vets trying to occupy the sugar estate. He was assured that the message would go to the right person - he would not be bothered by them again.

Although he couldn't lay the blame for the farm invader problems on Owen, he had had a hand in all his other problems. The thought of Owen's wife on the way to the slave markets in the East brought a rare smile to his face.

Chapter 39

Kyle and Rosa set off from Malelane early in the morning. They were each driving a four wheel drive; one towing a trailer loaded up with deepfreeze, fridge, tents kitchen equipment and various bits and pieces. The other towing the boat was also loaded up with a large tarpaulin, ground sheet, shade cloth, generator, tables and chairs.

When the border post at Komatipoort opened at six they were waiting to pass though into Mozambique.

It took the rest of the day to travel the 400 kilometers up the coast to the camp at Ingale. Arriving late in the afternoon, there was just enough light to pitch one of their tents, make their beds and get the gas operated fridge and freezer into the hut and lit.

Bright and early next morning their camp supervisor was there to help off-load the rest of the equipment. When the heavy work was done, Kyle and their man went off to launch *Day Dreamer*, leaving Rosa to organise the camp-site as she wanted it. Once the boat was in the water they took her for a quick spin before beaching below the camp.

"Oh I see how it works. You two go cruising around having fun on the boat while I have to stay in camp and work," Rosa said standing on the edge of the beach under a palm tree with her hands on her hips smiling cheerfully.

"Well, I had to bring her over from where we launched, so I decided to give her a bit of a test run before I take you out to sea," Kyle was quick to make an excuse. "We need to test her out."

"As soon as you've helped me get everything ship-shape here in camp, you can take me out to catch some fish for our supper," Rosa admonished.

Shade cloth was spread out on the ground and pegged down under the tarpaulin they stretched between four palm trees. Three tents were erected around the edge of the shade cloth with tables and chairs placed in the middle. Tom and Maria were joining them in a few days, and Rosa wanted them to be comfortable while they were there.

Later in the day Kyle and Rosa went out in *Day Dreamer* and managed to catch a decent rock-cod and two reds. In the evening they sat under the tarpaulin having their sundowners and eating lovely fresh fish while they discussed their plans.

The first thing that had to be done was to erect the tank stand and build a temporary wash-room with toilet. A permanent ablution block, kitchen and huts would be built when they could get all the materials to site; bricks, cement, roof timber, door-frames and roof tiles. Water would have to be hauled in drums from a nearby well until a pump and pipes were installed.

They went into Inharrime to buy supplies and explore the town to see what it had to offer. Kyle had been there before, with Len in *Pelé-Pelé*, but had not had a good look around. There were two hotels and a new thatched Lodge had been built on stilts over the water in the bay.

There was ample accommodation for clients who came to fish. Divers would probably want to stay in camp where all the equipment was to be kept, and was closer to the reefs where they would be diving.

When Tom and Maria arrived three days later, the camp was ready for them. Since Maria's rescue from Van Zyl, she and Tom had spent a week in the Kruger National Park, as guests of the Head Warden. Being guests of the 'head honcho' they were given special treatment being taken on exclusive game drives and game captures.

They were also privileged to watch them fitting radio tracking transmitters into the rhino's horns, as a preventative measure to try and stop the poaching. Although saddened by the scale of rhinos being slaughtered for their horns, they had a wonderful time, and Maria found it therapeutic after her ordeal.

Tom and Maria stayed for a week. They went fishing, dived on the reefs, explored the area, and left heaps of brochures advertising their business at the hotels and the lodge. Kyle and Rosa were both qualified divers, but if they were going to train new divers, and were to be responsible for them, it was essential that Kyle qualify as a diving instructor. He would have to go to Sodwana Bay in Zululand as soon as he could arrange for the necessary training there. Only then would they be ready for their first clients.

From Ingale Tom and Maria drove up the coast towards Beira and on to Zimbabwe. There were things they had to do in Harare and Barnard's trial to attend on the way back via South Africa. It was a long drive but they both enjoyed the trip and the scenery. Flying around was good and quick, but you missed so much. They were on holiday and had plenty of time. Three days after leaving Kyle and Rosa they arrived at Ted and Elsie's home.

Having been held prisoner by Van Zyl in his house, only a stones' throw from the Hunters, and in spite of being assured that he was out of the country, Maria felt more than a little uncomfortable for the first few days. Being with friends and enjoying their wonderful hospitality, soon put thoughts of Van Zyl out of her mind and she enjoyed herself. It was always good to be home in Zimbabwe.

Tom and Maria spent two weeks in Harare, checking their house, visiting old friends and promoting *'Santo Deep-Sea Fishing'*.

Chapter 40

Two days before Barnard's trial, the Owens left Harare and drove down to the Lowveld. They stopped for the night at the Lion and Elephant Motel, a popular stop-over for people travelling between Zimbabwe and South Africa. The motel, situated on the banks of the normally dry, sandy Bubye River, was very comfortable with thatched cottages and a swimming pool. In the heat of the Lowveld and only an hour's drive from the border, it was very convenient and a most welcome place to stop.

In the morning Dodi and Tombi arrived from Chikombedzi, where they had been camped since Barnard's capture. The four of them crossed the Limpopo River into South Africa at Beit Bridge, and climbed the winding road to the top of the high blue Soutpansberg Mountains.

They booked into the 'Mountain View Hotel' overlooking the town of Makhado way below at the foot of the mountain. Kyle and Rosa had driven up for the court case from Malelane and were there to meet them. Sandy was on his way from Swaziland.

Next day Tom, Kyle, Dodi and Tombi went down to Makhado to give evidence at Barnard's trial. Although Tom was not giving evidence, he hoped to see Van Zyl there; he had things to settle with him.

Maria and Rosa stayed behind at the hotel. The two of them wandered around the gardens, admiring the views of the surrounding area, Makhado and the wide, flat, almost treeless expanse of the plains, extending far into the blue haze, towards the Lowveld and the Kruger Park.

It was a lovely warm day and so they lazed around the swimming pool, enjoying the sun and the excellent service provided by the hotel, while they waited for the others to return from court. They were comfortable and relaxed and in no hurry. It was just a pity Tom and Kyle couldn't be with them, instead of sitting in a hot, stuffy court-room all day.

They were lying on loungers, reading books and sipping cool-drinks at the pool-side, when suddenly Maria pulled her sun-hat down over her face and turned towards Rosa.

"Rosa! There's Van Zyl. He's just come out of the hotel and is coming down here towards us. This is the last thing I need - please don't let him see me." Maria whispered urgently, turning pale and starting to tremble uncontrollably. The shock of seeing this dreadful man, who had tried so recently to destroy her, made her feel sick and frightened.

"It's all right Maria. He's just standing there smoking a cigar and looking out over the valley," Rosa said putting her hand reassuringly on Maria's arm and glancing over her book at Van Zyl.

"Let me know when he goes back inside. I must try to contact Tom," Maria was quite distraught and on the verge of panic. "I hope he doesn't come down here."

The lunch-time gong sounded and Van Zyl ground his cigar out under his shoe, turned and went inside. As soon as he had gone, Maria tried to contact Tom on his mobile phone. It was switched off and so was Kyle's; they must be in the court-room. Maria and Rosa moved to a table under an umbrella, where they were less conspicuous, but still able to see anyone coming down to the pool. The waiter came to take their order, and they had lunch in the shade near the pool.

Maria's little holiday had just been ruined; she was nervous and worried. Van Zyl was not on the witness list so why was he here? He must be expecting Barnard to be acquitted and released, and was here to take him back to Zimbabwe after the trial. For him to be parading openly in South Africa, he obviously didn't even know she had been rescued from the *Verona*.

. . . .

Jan Van Zyl booked into a hotel high in the mountains outside of the town, to await the outcome of Barney's trial. The lawyer was confident that he would be fined and released, and so he had come to take him home. He had seen the list of witnesses and knew Kyle Owen and those two traitors, Dodi and Tombi, were giving evidence. This worried him as they all knew that, as the owner of Mabiti, he must have sanctioned the poaching operations.

Van Zyl strolled outside, and stood on the terrace smoking a cheroot before lunch. There were two women lying in the sun on loungers at the pool-side, reading magazines. The lunch gong sounded and he went in to eat. After lunch he sat in the lounge, where he could keep an eye on the reception, reading the papers and drinking coffee. He was curious to see who came in and out; he always made sure he was not caught off guard.

Van Zyl was about to put the paper down and head for his room, when a familiar figure walked in the front entrance. He quickly lifted the paper to hide his face. It was Tom Owen. He had not expected them to be staying here in the mountains. There was no time to waste; he had to get out of the country and back to Zimbabwe fast. There was no protection for him in South Africa. If Owen knew he was there, he would be arrested by the police for kidnapping, and for his part in the poaching.

. . . .

Maria and Rosa were still at the pool when the others returned from their day in court. Sandy had arrived in the morning and was with them. When they heard that Van Zyl was in the hotel, Tom and Kyle dashed off to find him, only to discover that he had booked out and left a few minutes before. He must have seen them arrive back from court, and made a quick departure. Tom felt very uneasy knowing that the monster responsible for Maria's kidnapping, was somewhere close by. Had he seen Maria?

Tom wasted no time in contacting the police Sergeant who was handling the poaching case, to let him know that Van Zyl had been seen at the hotel. Half an hour later he arrived to take statements from Maria and Rosa. The whole process took far too long, and by the time he had finished, and set off to look for Van Zyl, they all knew it was too late. He would be across the border back in Zimbabwe; only an hour's drive away. Once again the man had managed to get away.

When Kyle, Dodi and Tombi went to court next day, Sandy, who had given his evidence and was no longer needed, stayed with Tom to look after the two women. Van Zyl might still be around somewhere, and knowing his capabilities, they were taking no chances.

As part of his defence, Barnard accused Tom of being the man responsible for attempting to smuggle ivory and rhino horn out of the country. He claimed he had seen Tom in the camp at Ingale, when he had been in Mozambique recently. It did not work, but did explain a lot of things, and how Van Zyl knew of their involvement in the confiscation of his 'treasure'.

At the end of the two day trial, Barnard was found guilty of being in possession of rhino horn, for poaching in the Kruger National Park and for entering the country illegally. He was given a lengthy prison sentence with the option to pay a hefty fine, and be deported back to Zimbabwe.

Chapter 41

During his trial, Barney heard that their men, who had been arrested at Inharrime, had been locked up for five years in a Mozambique prison. On completion of their sentences they were to be deported back to Zimbabwe. The truck and the crates of ivory and rhino horns were handed over to the National Parks.

Because of his dishonesty, Van Zyl was tempted to let Barney linger in jail for a while, before paying his fine, but he needed him back at work. And so after arranging for the fine to be paid, Van Zyl picked Barnard up at the Beit Bridge border post a week later; where he was taken under escort, and took him back to Mabiti.

Joey, relieved of his duties, was happy to go back to Harare and Van Zyl was pleased to have Barney back at work. In next to no time he was back making deliveries of diamonds, supplying meat to butcheries and canning factories as he had done before his arrest.

Being a thief and crook himself, Van Zyl could understand his motives, but his actions were still not acceptable. He would deal with the matter of his dishonesty at a later stage; he was going to hit him where it hurt and take some of it out of his bonus.

Now that everything was back on track and running smoothly, Van Zyl decided it was time to find out what had happened to the *Verona* and its precious human cargo. With all that had been going on in recent months, Van Zyl decided it was time to take a break, and go on holiday to Kuala Lumpur with his son. This would also enable him to check with the owners of the factory ship and find out why he had not had a payment for fish in months.

Up to now he had not been too concerned that he had not heard from the captain. Normally he only got in touch when repairs were needed. The agent in Jakarta handled all the fish sales and sent monthly reports to him. The ships crew were paid a commission for the fish they caught, and so the operation required very little attention from him.

On the eve of their departure, Van Zyl received an email from the factory ship agents. It had arrived in Jakarta to report that it had not met up with the *Verona*. The trawler had not been waiting off Europa

Island when they went to collect its load of fish. Van Zyl was under contract to supply fish and so they were not happy; even threatening to sue him for losses. This was not good news and made Van Zyl nervous. He wondered what had happened. Where was the *Verona,* and what had become of Maria Owen?

The *Verona* used Quelimane, a port north of Beira, to replenish supplies and re-fuel. Van Zyl used a shipping agent there to assist the captain with his needs. All communication between the agent and Van Zyl was done via his bank and the trawler captain. The bills for fuel, repairs and supplies were paid directly into the agents account as soon as he received the details from his captain. The agent kept a float in an account which he used for *Verona's* business, and all it needed was authorization from Van Zyl for funds to be transferred directly into that account.

It was a good place to start, and so Van Zyl and Joey flew to Mozambique. Arriving in the sprawling coastal town of Quelimane, they took a rickety taxi to the agent's office.

"I am sorry Senhor, but I have bad news for you. I got a message from your captain not long ago but we were unable to contact you. Your ship has been impounded in Beira," Veloso, the agent informed Van Zyl.

"For what reason has it been impounded?"

"The Navy escorted it into the harbour. They say it was fishing illegally inside Mozambique waters. The captain and the crew are being kept on board under armed guard. They are not even permitted on shore," Veloso said giving him the details. "The Port Authorities and Fishing Control in Beira want to see you."

"What is it that they want from me? The captain is responsible for his actions - not me."

"That is true, but you are the registered owner of the trawler."

There was no point in berating Veloso, he had nothing to do with it. And so with no other option, Van Zyl and Joey flew to Beira. After nearly two days, being pushed around from office to office, and being made to wait for hours on end, Van Zyl was eventually taken out to his ship to speak to the captain. The *Verona* was lying at anchor off-shore.

The captain and his crew, having been imprisoned on the trawler for three months, with no means of communication, were not a happy crowd.

"What the hell happened? Why has the ship been impounded?" Van Zyl demanded.

"When you left that day, leaving the white woman with me, we were boarded by the French soldiers and kept under guard while they searched the ship. They found the woman and took her away. Her husband was with them, and he was very angry."

Van Zyl was completely taken aback by this news. So it must have been Owen's plane they had seen on Europa. Why had he not reported the kidnapping to the police; surely he would have heard from them by now. Owen had proved to be a very clever adversary, and this made him feel extremely uneasy.

"Why did you not put her in the fish hold like I told you?"

"Nobody saw the soldiers coming on board. They caught us by surprise."

"That was bloody stupid. What happened after the French soldiers left the ship?"

"The Mozambique Navy put sailors on board to guard us. I was ordered to sail to Beira with the Patrol Boat escorting us all the way. We have been here ever since."

"Why did you not contact me on the radio?"

"The radio was put out of action. They used portable radios to communicate with the Patrol Boat."

"What must I do now to get them to release the ship?"

"There is a fine for fishing inside their waters, and anchorage fees to be paid."

"But they did not catch you fishing inside their territorial waters. What happened to the fish you had in the holds?"

"They say they have witnesses who saw us fishing close inshore near Inhambane. The fish was offloaded as soon as we arrived here, and all sold to merchants."

If he wanted to get his trawler released, Van Zyl had to accept the situation - he was losing money by the day. The *Verona* had to get back to fishing as soon as possible, to try and recover some of his losses. After a further two days haggling with the authorities an agreement was finally reached.

The fish had been confiscated as it was Mozambique fish; there was a fine for illegal fishing, there were anchorage fees to be settled, and escort expenses to be paid. All in all Van Zyl had to pay US$1.5 million to get his ship and crew released. This took another day to arrange, only then did the *Verona* sail away to continue fishing; this time outside Mozambique waters.

Van Zyl was not a happy man. Not only had he had to pay out a lot of money because of his own stupidity, but he had also allowed Owen's wife to be rescued. Now there was a very strong possibility that charges would be brought against him for kidnapping. He could not see Tom Owen letting it rest.

Chapter 42

It was three months since the Barnard trial, and time for the wedding. A week before the big day, June and her son, Tony, arrived in Swaziland from Pensacola. Sandy and his daughter, Sally, met them up at Matsapa Airport and took them to his home, on the slopes of the Malagwane hill, below Mbabane.

From Sandy's house, the views of the surrounding mountains and the Ezulweni Valley below were quite magnificent. On the right Execution Rock with its high cliff-face stood on it's own at the end of the range of mountains. According to Swazi legend it was where people had been thrown to their death way below.

Alongside were the two high pinnacles of Sheba's Breasts, so named by the early Cornish tin-miners. On the other side of the valley the huge granite slopes of the mountain glistened in the sunlight where water, oozing out of cracks, ran down the smooth rock-faces.

Over the next few days they toured the small Swazi Kingdom. Sandy showed them where he had grown up and lived on the top of a mountain overlooking Mbabane. An exclusive private school, Waterford-Kamhlaba College, had been built there after his parents sold the land to the school developers, and moved to Mozambique to start their fishing venture.

Travelling up to the pine forests in the highlands, Sandy showed them where he had swum in the rivers and pools around the town; he took them to the small game reserve in the valley he had helped to stock with game when he was at school, and took them to the Swazi Markets and the Ngwenya glass factory.

At the end of the day they were treated to a massage at the 'Cuddle Puddle'; a natural hot sulphur spring in the Ezulweni Valley where cheerful Swazi women with strong hands worked their magic.

Two days before the wedding, they drove the 250 kilometers to Maputo where Tom waited at the 'Clube Naval' in *Tigger* to take them over to the island. June was excited, and felt like she was coming home, when they arrived at Inhaca. She took Tony by the hand and dragged him off to show him around.

Maria and Tombi were busy helping at the Lodge with all the wedding preparations. Although it was to be a small personal affair, everything had to be perfect. Maria remembered her own wedding on the shores of Lake Malawi and wanted June's to be even better. She sent Tom, Kyle and Tomasi to catch crayfish, prawns, mussels and clams. What they couldn't find in the sea themselves; they bought from the local fishermen. All the other catering arrangements and the drinks were left in the capable hands of the Lodge manager.

On Friday morning Sandy and Sally helped Maria put the final touches and made sure everything was ready. To get her out from under Maria's feet and to take her mind off things, Tom took June and Tony out fishing in the bay. They hoped to catch a nice shoal sized barracuda, kingfish or even a Dorado for the festivities. Kyle, Rosa, Ted and Elsie arrived on the ferry with Len, who was the 'official' photographer.

With very little left to do, they all relaxed in the sun around the pool, waiting for the fishermen to return. It was time for the celebrations to begin. Tony, with his witty charm and dashing good looks, was a credit to his mother and he and Sally daughter took to each other instantly.

Next day at 1100 the priest arrived from Maputo on the morning ferry and at one o'clock the wedding got under way. The Alter was set up on the lawn alongside the pool, under the tall coconut palm trees. The azure blue sea and the bright white sands on the beach visible through the tall coco-nut palm trees, made a perfect backdrop.

Instead of the normal 'Wedding March', June opted to have Dodi perform the traditional, very energetic, high kicking Ndebele wedding dance with Tombi singing and beating on a cow skin drum. Both were dressed in tribal costume.

The weather was perfect; clear electric blue skies with a gentle breeze keeping it cool and comfortable. There were half a dozen guests staying in the Lodge who were also invited to join in the festivities. The catering was out of this world. All the shell-fish were displayed on ice around a whole 10 pound barracuda, caught that morning by Tony as the centre piece.

The celebrations went on late into the night until everyone drifted off to get some sleep. They were all booked into the lodge for the night. Sometime in the middle of next day, Kyle and Rosa took Sandy and June across the bay to Maputo, and they set off on their honeymoon.

The first week they spent in the Kruger National Park, working their way up from Crocodile Camp in the south to Skukuza then on to Satara, Olifants and finally Shingwedzi in the north. Every camp seemed to have its own pair of horn-bills that called to each other as they flew from tree to tree, in search of insects and grubs.

It was summer time; the trees were thick with foliage and the grass lush and green. It was not the best time of year for game viewing, but they still saw just about everything there was to see, including the elusive Leopard.

Then it was on to Zimbabwe to spend a day exploring the Zimbabwe Ruins. June was fascinated by the neat precise construction of the ruins of the ancient place. Sandy told her that it was believed the ruins had originally been built by gold seekers and the Arabs to house slaves in the days of the early slave traders.

According to Tom, there were other similar ruins across the country forming a chain into Mozambique and Sofala, an old historical port on the coast south of Beira.

After a long hot day on the road, they arrived in Victoria Falls and booked into the grand Victoria Falls hotel, overlooking the bridge across the Zambezi Gorge into Zambia. They spent four days riding elephants, going on booze cruises up the river at sunset, watching fools bungee jumping off the bridge, while others paddled canoes upstream or went white water rafting in the gorge.

They took the 'Flight of Angels' to view the stunning falls from the air. It was the rainy season and so the Zambezi River was flowing strongly with a massive amount of water cascading over the edge of the falls creating a heavy cloud of mist and spray rising hundreds of feet into the air. Wandering through the 'Rain Forest', they were soaked in minutes.

Leaving Victoria Falls behind, they drove to Mlibizi and boarded the car ferry to Kariba. It was a 200 kilometer, two day cruise down the vast expanse of Lake Kariba to the dam wall. After a night at the Carribea Bay hotel, they continued to Harare where they stayed with Ted and Elsie, at their magnificent home north of the city.

The last four days in Zimbabwe, Sandy and June spent at the Troutbeck Inn, high in the Nyanga Mountains, on the eastern border of the country. They were amazed to hear that the fire in the lounge had been lit just after the hotel was opened in the early 1950's and had never been put out. They fished for trout, played golf and went for drives in the mountains and up to Worlds View, to gaze in wonder over the landscape far below.

Back into Mozambique via Mutare they drove to Chimoio and on along the road going south towards Maputo. They crossed the long bridge over the Save River and arrived late in the afternoon at Inhassoro. A water taxi ferried them over to Bazaruto Island where Sandy and June spent the last two days of their honeymoon in the luxurious Indigo Bay Lodge.

Chapter 43

In the months since Van Zyl had been to Mozambique to arrange for the release of his fishing trawler, everything had gone from bad to worse. For thirty years he had been accustomed to having his own way and at times, to get what he wanted, resorting to bully-boy tactics and sometimes even violence. With connections in high places he had always been able to get away with it.

Now it was all changing. His contacts in the government were distancing themselves from him, making life more difficult. He had a growing suspicion he would not be getting the protection he had previously been afforded by the President, and some of his senior men. It was as if he had become an embarrassment. He heard a whisper that it had something to do with the fiasco in Mozambique, when his truck-load of precious contraband had been impounded and with Barney's subsequent conviction.

War-vets moved onto the farm again, and this time refused to move. The fields were pegged with each war-vet allocated a piece of land 50 metres square. His appeal for help fell on deaf ears and Van Zyl, no longer enjoying the luxury of being able to call on his government contacts to help, could do very little about it.

Within weeks his manager was forced to leave the estate, after being threated with his life. His family had moved some time before. Just after he left, the house was burnt to the ground.

And so Van Zyl, after laughing at the previous owner when he had been in a similar situation, now had his property taken from him for re-settlement. Like thousands of other commercial farmers, he lost it all with no financial compensation from the government. But unlike the others who had spent a lifetime developing their farms, he had merely bought the estate for a token amount from the government, and purely as an investment.

Van Zyl decided it might be a good time to get rid of Mabiti; before it too was invaded, and he lost it. Barney was short staffed because five of their best men were locked up in prison in Mozambique. Mabiti was very remote, and he was having difficulty replacing them. Workers were reluctant to work there because they were afraid of losing their jobs, if

Mabiti was invaded by the war-vets. The result being that their meat sales were down by half.

If he did sell Mabiti and move out of the Harare country to his house in Malaysia for a while, he could leave Barney to manage all his operations in Zimbabwe. It all depended on whether or not he could get back into favour, and restore his former status. He thought it would be a good idea to have a hunting safari to try and win back the confidence of his connections; then he would know where he stood and what to do with his life.

In any case before he made important decisions, there were things he had to do. Van Zyl blamed Tom Owen and his son Kyle for all his misfortunes and problems. They were responsible for the loss of his ivory and rhino horns; they had been responsible for his trawler being impounded, and the huge fine he had been made to pay for its release. Now because of their interfering, he was out of favour, and had lost his sugar estate. The fact that Van Zyl himself had kidnapped Owen's wife was not considered.

The more Jan Van Zyl thought about it, the more obsessed he became. He had to get revenge on the Owen family. Somehow or other he would lure one of the Owen men to Mabiti, where he could deal with him. Then he came up with a plan. To try and get back in his good books, he was going to invite the Deputy Minister of Mines on a hunting safari.

He would also invite Ted Hunter at the same time, to discuss their mining dispute with the minister. Hunter was going to be his bait to get Tom Owen. Once he had Hunter, Owen would come to his rescue.

"Barney, when are you coming up to Harare?" Van Zyl asked his man.

"I'm coming up next week," Barney replied. "I will be meeting up with your man at Birchenough Bridge on the way."

"Okay I'll see you next week then. There is something we need to discuss."

A week later, Barney arrived in Harare bearing more bad news. Security at the Marange mines and the surrounding area was so tight that the *ngoda* was finding it extremely difficult to get hold of any diamonds. People were being arrested, tortured, beaten and even killed, if it was suspected they might have some of the precious stones hidden away.

So now it looked like his diamond supply had dried up and the future of Mabiti was hanging by a thread.

· · · · · · · · · · · · · · ·

After consulting with Barney, who said there was a small herd of Buffalo moving around the lower end on the Gona-re-Zhou, Van Zyl decided it was going to be a buffalo hunt. If they could drive the herd even further south; out of the Conservation Area and away from the protection of the national game guards, it would be safe to hunt them.

In view of the recent attitude of Simba Machona, the Deputy Minister of Mines, and his main connection in government, Van Zyl decided to invite him for the hunt. He knew the man was keen to bag a 'big one'. On a previous visit, Machona had mentioned he was interested in acquiring a game ranch, and had asked Van Zyl if he was interested in selling. Perhaps he could still be persuaded to buy Mabiti.

He went over to see Ted Hunter. "I know we have our differences Ted, but I think it's time we buried the hatchet. I have invited Simba Machona down to Mabiti next month, to hunt for buffalo. I thought you might like to join us. It'll be a good opportunity for us to sort out our problems," Van Zyl was speaking to Ted at the entrance gate to his home. He had not been invited in.

"There's nothing to sort out. You know bloody well the court has made a judgement against you. I just want you to get the hell off my property," Ted was amazed at the audacity of the man.

"Yes I know. But I have a proposition I think you will be very interested in. We need to discuss it with the Minister; preferably away from his office," Van Zyl persisted.

"How will this plan of yours benefit me?" Ted asked pricking up his ears.

"As you are probably aware, I hold the papers for some of the biggest mines along the Dyke - part of the reason for our problems. I'm busy putting a package together which will consolidate my interests, while at the same time enable you to expand yours,"

"It all sounds very interesting, but how can I trust you? If I agree to this meeting at your Game Park, I will want to bring my partner as well as our financial advisor with me," Ted was curious to know what he had in mind.

"No problem. If you do decide to come, just let me know in good time so that I can arrange the accommodation and catering for the week-end," Van Zyl agreed smiling.

Then, deciding not to push Hunter any further for fear of making him suspicious, he turned and walked away leaving Ted speechless.

By inviting Hunter to join the hunt, and to meet with the Deputy Minister of Mines, he had set the wheels in motion. He knew Hunter wouldn't waste any time telling Owen about his invitation.

Ted was staggered. Why was this evil man suddenly being so friendly and obliging? It didn't fit at all. He had to get hold of Tom to discuss this latest development, and Van Zyl's proposal.

■■■■◊◊◊◊◊■■■■

Chapter 44

When Tom heard that Van Zyl had invited Ted to go hunting with him, he was flabbergasted. Van Zyl obviously had something up his sleeve - the man never did anything to benefit anyone except himself!

"Ted, the man's a monster. He's obviously planning something nasty - be very careful. I could understand him trying to have a go at me, but apart from encroaching on your mining claims, what does he want to try and diddle you out of now?" Tom asked his friend over the phone.

"I don't know Tom. He has been served with a notice to clear off my claims along the Dyke, now he suddenly wants to talk. I just don't trust the bastard at all," Ted agreed with Tom.

"Nor do I Ted, especially as he wants you to go to his safari camp in the middle of the sticks."

"He did agree for me to take a friend, and my finance man with me. Maybe he does want to make a deal of sorts."

"I don't think so Ted. Anyway we have time. I think we must send Dodi in to keep an eye on the camp. He might be able to shed some light on what's going on down there," Tom suggested. "We need some inside information."

"That sounds like a good idea. When can you get him there?"

"Most probably in about a week's time. I reckon it will take him a day to get organised, then he can go to the border by bus or rail, and walk in from there. He can meet you next Wednesday."

"Tell him I'll meet him at Boli. I'll take him as close as I can, then let him have my camping gear and the satellite phone," Ted agreed. "In the meantime I'll try to find out what Van Zyl's game is. I think I'm going to accept his invitation."

It was clear that if Van Zyl was up to something, and if they could find out what he was planning, this might present an ideal opportunity for them to turn the tables on him. It was not in Van Zyl's nature to be pleasant or forgiving.

·············

A week later Dodi was in the general dealer in Chikombedzi, buying one or two items he needed, when Sipho, one of the trackers from

Mabiti, walked into the shop. After greeting each other and completing their purchases, they went outside to sit on a log under a flamboyant tree, to swop news.

It was a year since Dodi had rescued Tombi from the camp and ran away with her, and so there was quite a lot to catch up on. They laughed about the time when, more recently, he had been back to rescue Tombi the second time, and they had taken Barnard away to South Africa. Sipho had been locked in the shed with the rest of the workers and later released by Dodi.

When he enquired about Petros, he was told that he had never returned to work. Nobody had seen him since that day he went after Dodi and Tombi.

Apparently the men working at Mabiti were not at all happy with Barnard. Since he had returned from South Africa, and without having Petros to bully the workers for him, he was treating them badly. He did not even seem to care about the men who had never come back from Mozambique, and expected the same amount of work as when they had been fully staffed.

When Dodi asked if he would be willing to help put an end to Barnard's poaching, he readily agreed. After chatting for about an hour, they walked back along the road together; Dodi going to his camp and Sipho to Mabiti. Before parting, Dodi told him that he would be near the big mahogany tree, close to the main gate, at the same time every day. If he had anything to tell him, or heard anything strange or out of the ordinary being planned, he was to meet with him there.

It didn't take long. Three days later they met at the tree. Barnard was sending his game guards out to look for herds of buffalo in the Gona-re-Zhou. There was going to be a hunt for buffalo in two weeks time. As soon as he knew where the herd was, he would let Dodi know. Next day he was told of a small herd that had been found right at the bottom end of the game conservation area.

. . . .

"Dodi has a plan. He knows we want to arrest Van Zyl, and so he suggests moving the buffalo herd across the Naunetsi River to the south." Ted told his friend over the phone after Dodi had briefed him on the situation at Mabiti.

"How is that going to help us?" Tom asked.

"He knows the area well, and seems to think it will be easier to isolate Van Zyl, if the hunt is further away from Mabiti."

"Yes that's a good point. How does he propose moving a whole herd of buffalo?" Tom was curious.

"He says he has a plan that he thinks will work."

"Well if he can do it, it will make things a lot easier for us. But buffalo won't move easily."

"Dodi says it's only a small herd and most of the workers in the camp will co-operate and help. Apparently they are totally pissed off with Barnard. He suggests we split the group up once they cross the river to hunt. Then we should be able to isolate Van Zyl."

"Well I suppose that could work. We can block off the road back to Mabiti as soon as they are all over on the other side."

"What do we do with the main guest; the deputy minister of mines?" Ted asked.

"I am guessing Van Zyl will hang back and leave Barnard to lead the hunt. Somehow we'll have to work out how we are going to separate them, and then we should be able to grab Van Zyl and take him over the border. The same as we did with Barnard."

"I don't think it's going to be as easy as that," Ted said. "Anyway I'll tell Dodi to carry on with his plan. He can let us know as soon as the buffalo have been moved. Now that he knows there is a herd near Mabiti, I'm sure Van Zyl will be heading off pretty soon to the Lowveld for his hunt."

Hanging up the phone, Ted decided it was time to call Van Zyl and let him know he was accepting the invitation. He would meet him at Mabiti to join the hunt. Then using the satellite phone, Ted called Dodi to give him the go-ahead. Dodi was enthusiastic saying they should be able to move the buffalo in a couple of days without even frightening them.

·············

Next day when Dodi met up with Sipho, he heard that the work was already being done for him. On Barnard's instructions, the game guards had been sent to start moving the buffalo slowly towards the Naunetsi River, and closer to Mabiti. Dodi was told roughly where he could find the game guards, and that they too were disgruntled with the way they were being treated by Barnard - they would help.

Having worked with most of the game guards when he was employed as a tracker, Dodi went to join the group to make sure the animals were being moved to the area he had suggested to Ted. When he met up with them, he explained to the *induna* (senior man) that he was helping the Game Conservation Department. They were investigating the poaching activities at Mabiti and if they did not help him they might also be in serious trouble. It was a small lie but the only way he thought he could get them on his side, and to co-operate with him. They all knew about Barnard's poaching in the Gona-re-Zhou and agreed to help. Dodi's friend joined them later in the day, after persuading Barnard to allow him to join the herders.

It was slow work getting the animals to move. Working upwind of the buffalo, combined with the occasional stick breaking, cough or whistle, the buffalo gradually wandered off in the opposite direction, away from the sounds and smells. Buffalo can be extremely volatile, and so they had to be slow and careful as they encouraged them to move - without sensing the presence of their herders.

Dodi and the game guards spent three days slowly moving the buffalo further and further south. Eventually they crossed the Naunetsi River, and settled in a lush grassy area scattered with mopani forests and acacia thorn scrub. With the Naunetsi River north and the Limpopo River further south, there was ample water. All they had to do now was make sure the herd did not move away or drift back into the Gona-re-Zhou.

The game guards positioned themselves in a wide circle, well away from the grazing herd, where buffalo would not get their scent or see them, and to ensure they did not cross the river when they went to water in the mornings and afternoons. His friend stayed with the game guards, and Dodi went back to his camp. He called Ted to let him know that the job was done. The hunt was planned for the following week.

. . . .

Two days after hearing from Dodi, Tom and Kyle met up with Ted at the 'Lion and Elephant' motel. They were there to discuss their strategy, and work out how they were going to capture Van Zyl, and get him to South Africa to face charges of kidnapping and poaching.

The day after arriving at the motel, Dodi called to say that the hunt was taking place the following day. Ted phoned Van Zyl to excuse himself and his companions from the hunt, promising to be at Mabiti the following day, when they could sit down with Simba Machona, to discuss their mutual problems. Van Zyl, still playing the perfect host, was quite agreeable to this arrangement and said he was sorry Ted would not be there to enjoy the hunt. Machona had already arrived and that they were going to hunt in the morning.

As dawn was breaking next morning, the three of them drove to Chikombedzi, meeting up with Dodi two hours later. Without wasting any time they made their way down the road towards Mabiti, but instead of taking the road leading to the camp, they drove on straight to the Naunetsi River.

They crossed the drift and stopped on the side of the road. A magnificent lone grey kudu bull, with long twisted horns, was nibbling on the tender new shoots of the scrub bushes near the river. When it saw them stop it snorted, then putting his head back, to prevent his horns from hooking on branches, loped off into dense thorn scrub where it was well concealed.

Dodi trotted off to make contact with Sipho and the game guards, while they parked the van out of sight in the mopani thicket. From there they would be able to see Van Zyl and his hunting party arriving. The clouds were low and heavy - rain was on the way. It was quiet with a light breeze rustling the mopani leaves and a pair of bush-shrikes could be heard fritting around in the bushes looking for grubs.

"What happens now? All we know is that the buffalo are in there somewhere, and we don't even have a plan." Kyle waved his arm to where Dodi said the herd was grazing.

"I don't really know. We'll just have to wait and play it by ear. Somehow or other we'll have to separate Van Zyl from the others, so that we can nab him." Tom wasn't comfortable with this loose arrangement either. "We'll probably have to leave it to Dodi and one of the other men to split the group up somehow," he added as an afterthought.

"Well, I think we must block off their retreat. If Dodi is right, they'll stop on the other side of the river. Once they're on foot we stand a better chance of separating them," Ted suggested.

"But how do we do that, and at the same time make sure Machona doesn't see us grabbing Van Zyl?" Kyle asked. "If he sees what we're up to, we'll be in hot water."

"We might have to leave that to Dodi and his team. Barnard is the hunter, so I'm sure he will lead the hunt. He will have Machona with him, so that he can get the first shot at a buffalo. That's when we must be in position, and ready to move in on Van Zyl. We'll have to move fast," Tom said with a plan starting to form. "Dodi is our expert. He knows what we want to do so he can work it out as we follow along behind them."

It wasn't long before Dodi was back. The buffalo had settled down in the grassy area, where he had left them with the game guards the previous week. They had worked out a plan. When Barnard moved ahead of the group with Machona, the tracker and two of the game guards were to lead Van Zyl and his gun-bearer away in the opposite direction; supposedly towards another buffalo.

Dodi would then fetch Tom and Kyle who would capture him, tie him up and take him away as quickly as they could; before Barnard cottoned on to what was happening. The plan was simple, and with the co-operation of the game guards, it might work. It was the only plan they had.

. . . .

The hunting party, after a lavish breakfast, set off from Mabiti. The buffalo herd was reported to be close to the camp; only about 5 kilometres away, so there was no rush. The game guards had been sent out early to make sure the herd had not wandered off into thick bush or dense forest, where they would be difficult to hunt, and liable to stampede if threatened or disturbed. A tracker would be waiting at the Naunetsi River.

It was an overcast day, with rains expected later in the afternoon. As predicted there had been heavy overnight rains further upcountry in the Naunetsi River catchment area. The flood waters were only expected to reach them, and raise the river level later in the day. By that time they had to be back across the river, or they would have to go back to camp the long way around via Chikombedzi. This would take hours.

. . . .

Dodi had only been back for quarter of an hour when they heard the drone of a vehicle approaching. Barnard's van came into view around the bend in the road and parked under a wild fig tree on the north bank of the river. A few minutes later Barnard, Van Zyl and Simba Machona, who was dressed smartly in a khaki safari suit and highly polished ankle boots, followed by their gun-bearers, crossed the river on foot.

The tracker was there to meet them and took the lead, with Barnard and his gun-bearer close behind. The rest of the party followed in single file, walking slowly and quietly, so as not to disturb any animals or birds that might easily spook the herd. A gentle breeze was blowing from the south, and with them approaching from the north there was little chance of the buffalo picking up their scent. The last thing the hunters needed was to have the whole herd stampede, and disappear into the thick mopani forest before they were in position for Machona to make his kill.

As soon as they disappeared from sight, Dodi set off after them. Kyle and Ted went to let down one of the tyres on Barnard's vehicle, and Tom stayed with the van, still trying to come up with a better plan. One way or the other, he was determined to take Van Zyl back to South Africa to face charges for the kidnapping of Maria and Tombi. If necessary he would confront him directly and arrest him, even if it was in front of the Minister.

Chapter 45

Half an hour after crossing the Naunetsi River, while they were walking slowly through an area of thorn scrub, the tracker stopped and signalled for the hunters to get down. He squatted behind a mopani tree and peered through the bush in front of him. After a minute watching quietly, he indicated that the buffalo were close. Barney crouched over and crept forward to join the tracker.

Standing quietly in a small open area, forty paces away, was one of the biggest, most magnificent dark brown buffalo bulls he had ever seen. It stood almost the height of a man and must have weighted well over a tonne. Its horns, fused together at the base to form a thick 'boss', bent downwards from his head then curved up and out. They were about a meter from tip to tip. The bull's ears drooped down below the horns. Three oxpecker birds were busy plucking ticks off the buffalo's back.

He was standing side-on to them, with his head raised and his glistening wet nose sniffing the air, as if sensing danger. His harem of four cows grazed nearby. It was perfect for a shot. Barnard turned and signalled to Machona, who moved up alongside him to make the kill. It was important to Van Zyl that Simba Machona bagged a good bull, and so, bent over double and as quietly as possible, he crept up behind Machona and Barnard.

Dodi, following behind the group of hunters, was hiding behind a thorn bush, and cursed when he saw what was happening. This was not what he wanted. With Van Zyl closing up behind Machona and Barnard, there was no chance of splitting them up. He signalled to the tracker, hiding behind an ant heap 20 paces away, and they waited to see what was going to happen next.

"You have to get closer to him," Barney whispered to Machona. "When you are close enough and have a clear shot, aim for the heart, just behind the elbow at the top of the front leg. When you are ready, give him both barrels as quickly as you can and be sure you make them count. If you don't drop him we will have a major problem."

Simba Machona, who had never shot a buffalo before, although excited, was nervous and sweating profusely. He nodded his head and then began to stalk closer to the bull. Van Zyl pushed past Barnard to follow just behind him. Creeping forward, putting one foot carefully in front of the other and making sure not to stand on any dry twig that might crack loudly and disturb the buffalo, they worked their way slowly towards the bull. Barnard, when he saw how nervous Machona was; he was shaking like a leaf, felt very uneasy.

Just when Machona was close enough, and about to take his shot, the bull put his head down and wandered off into a thicket of bush, where visibility was limited to about fifteen paces. With the buffalo half hidden in the bush it was far too dangerous for an inexperienced hunter to even think of shooting. It would be very difficult to make a clean kill. Barnard had to stop him before he made a mess of it.

Before Barnard had time to get close enough to warn him not to shoot, Machona raised his double-barrel .470 rifle and fired two shots in quick succession making him stumble backwards. Barnard heard the slap of the heavy 500 grain bullets striking the bull, but instead of dropping, it bellowed loudly and ran off into the thick undergrowth, followed by the cows.

The bullets must have struck it in the lungs or the belly, missing the heart completely. The wounded buffalo was now a very dangerous beast. Van Zyl, excited and desperate for Machona to claim the kill, threw caution to the wind, and brushing Barnard aside, went charging recklessly off in pursuit of the wounded buffalo, with the tracker beside him.

Machona, thinking he had fired a killing shot, left the follow-up to Van Zyl. He had no intention of being caught in the middle of a stampeding herd of buffalo. That would be fatal. He turned around and trotted off in the opposite direction, re-loading his rifle as he hurried away. He was not taking any chances. Leaving Sipho behind to watch the fiasco, Dodi followed Machona.

Barnard, realizing the danger, quickly followed Van Zyl into the thicket. He was an old hunter and knew that the wounded buffalo was extremely dangerous, and so he moved with great care. Wounded buffalo have been known to charge off, then double back and wait quietly to ambush the attacker. A number of hunters had met their fate in this manner. With this in mind, Barnard hurried after them to make sure the buffalo was killed, before it turned on Van Zyl or the tracker.

With his tracker leading the way, and Van Zyl right behind him, they followed the spoor and the blood trail left by the injured bull, as it moved away fast with his cows. Half a kilometre from where Machona had fired the shots, they found a pool of blood where the wounded bull must have stopped briefly. 200 paces further on Van Zyl and his tracker rounded a small koppie and entered a thicket of acacia thorn and mopani bush, where they lost the trail.

They were casting around, on the hard ground, searching for signs of the spoor and blood on the ground, when suddenly with a loud ear-splitting bellow, the buffalo bull burst from its hiding place behind a thick clump of acacia thorn scrub. It had doubled back and now came charging towards them from the side of the koppie.

Van Zyl's tracker seeing the danger, and fearing for his life, sprinted to the nearest mopani tree, quickly scrambling up into the safety of its branches out of reach of the angry bull. Van Zyl was slower off the mark and stood frozen with fear.

The wounded animal had started to chase the tracker but when it saw him shin up the tree, it turned its attention on Van Zyl. Shaking its head from side to side it came charging straight at him stirring up puffs of dust with its hooves.

With the enraged bull almost on him, and no time to aim carefully, Van Zyl fired quickly with his .375 Holland. The bullet bounced harmlessly off the horn-boss on the top of its head and didn't even slow it down. There was no time to re-load, and realizing he was in great danger, Van Zyl panicked and turned to run. He was far too late. As he turned he tripped over a fallen log and fell into a thorn bush, dropping his rifle.

Before he could get up or move away, the massive animal was on top of him. With a turn of its huge head the buffalo scooped Van Zyl up with its horns, and flung him high into the air. He landed in a heap on the ground; winded and gasping for breath. He tried desperately to crawl to safety, but the bull was there and again tossed him into the air. This time when he hit the ground the buffalo pinned him down briefly with its horns, before backing away to charge in and make another attack.

By this time Barnard had caught up, and seeing what was happening, with his hunters' skill, quickly shot the buffalo through the heart, dropping it in its tracks three metres from where Van Zyl lay crumpled in the dust and not moving.

He had been badly gored in the side of his chest; his left leg was broken and his head covered in blood. He was badly hurt and unconscious, but still alive. Barnard tore his shirt sleeves into strips and did his best to stem the flow of blood coming out of the gaping hole in Van Zyl's side.

The tracker climbed down from his tree, and Van Zyl's gun-bearer, who had caught up and been just behind him when the bull charged, appeared from behind the ant-heap where he had taken refuge; both with eyes wide as saucers. Barnard sent them to cut a mopani branch, which he used to make a splint for Van Zyl's leg. There was nothing more he could do; he had to get Van Zyl to hospital fast, before he died from loss of blood.

After stemming the blood as best he could, they moved Van Zyl carefully to a place under a wild olive tree, and made him as comfortable as possible. He was groaning and starting to recover consciousness when Barnard ran off to get the Land Cruiser, leaving the tracker and gun-bearer to look after him.

. . . .

While they waited for Dodi, they heard two heavy calibre rifle shots in quick succession. The shots came from quite close.

"Sounds like they've found the buffalo herd and shot one of them," Tom guessed.

"Yes it does. Why is Dodi taking so long? He should have been back by now," Kyle was concerned.

A few minutes later there was a rustling in the bush, and Machona came bursting out into the road clutching his rifle. He was on his own, had lost his hat and seemed to be in a panic. He ran past their hiding place to Barnard's Land Cruiser, and climbed up onto the back.

Machona had no sooner climbed onto the van, when Dodi appeared from the same direction he had come from. He reported that Machona had wounded a buffalo then run away, leaving Van Zyl and Barnard to go after it. A few minutes later there was another shot followed a short time later by yet another. It sounded like the wounded animal must have been killed.

"What are we going to do now?" Kyle wanted to know.

"Well it's all working in our favour. Machona is out of the way now, and we can handle Barnard, so I think we must go and get Van Zyl," Ted suggested.

"Barnard will probably come back to get his van so that they can load the buffalo. If he comes on his own we can stop him, then go and get Van Zyl," Tom said. Turning to Dodi he asked. "Do you know where they shot the *inyati* (buffalo)?"

"Yes, I can take you there. We can go with the van."

"Okay. Let's give it a few minutes to see what happens, before we move. I'm bloody sure Van Zyl won't walk all the way back to the van. He's far too bloody lazy!" Tom decided.

"He'll have to change his wheel before he goes anywhere," Ted grinned.

Just then it started raining; it came pelting down in buckets. Ted was about to start the van, and drive out of their hiding place when, as predicted, Barnard came jogging along the road with his head bowed against the rain. He crossed the river, jumped into his Cruiser with Machona, and instead of coming back for Van Zyl as they had expected, he turned the van around and made off towards Mabiti.

Something was very wrong. Why was he on his own and in such a hurry; leaving Van Zyl and the gun-bearers behind?

. . . .

It took Barnard ten minutes to cross the river and reach his van where he found Simba Machona waiting on the back, sheltering under the tree.

"Where is Jan?" Machona asked

"He has been badly gored by the buffalo you wounded," Barnard replied not mincing his words.

"Is he dead?" the deputy minister asked.

"No. But he's badly injured and losing a lot of blood. If I don't get him to a doctor fast, he will die," Barnard said. "I need a stretcher or a mattress from the camp, so that I can put him in the back of the bakkie (van). I must hurry before the river comes down." Barnard cursed under his breath at the thought of his helicopter away in Harare being serviced.

"Good. I will wait in the camp until you get back," said the man responsible for the mess.

Barnard knew there was no time to waste - Jan was losing blood fast. They jumped into the van, turned around and made off along the road. As they rounded the first bend in the road Barnard stopped - the van had a flat tyre. It took precious time to change the wheel and get going again.

Dropping Machona at Mabiti, and loading a mattress and stretcher, Barnard was back at the river half an hour later. The river was in full flood and the level had risen too high for him to drive across. He knew it would be hours, possibly days, before the level dropped and he would be able to drive over. The only way to get to Jan was to turn around, drive back past the camp,, and go via Chikombedzi where there was a bridge over the river.

On the way through town, he stopped at the hospital to pick up a nurse. They drove over the bridge which was just above the flooding river, and hurried back to get his employer.

Chapter 46

Slipping and sliding through the mud, with Dodi sitting on the front bull-bar guiding them through the bush, they went in search of Van Zyl. It was still raining and before moving off, Kyle noticed that the river behind them was flowing strongly and the level was already over the drift. The flood waters from up-country had arrived.

They stopped near the place where Dodi had seen Van Zyl and Machona disappear into the thicket of thorn scrub, before the shots were fired. Sipho was there waiting for them. The rain stopped as suddenly as it had started, and the clouds began to clear away. Ted drove on slowly with Sipho guiding him and stopped 100 yards closer to where the sound of the shots had come from.

Then, keeping a sharp look-out for Van Zyl in case he ambushed them, and with Dodi and Sipho leading the way, they went on foot to see what had happened. The muddy ground made progress slow, and so it was a few minutes before they found the huge dead buffalo bull. It was lying on its stomach with its legs splayed out and its nose buried in the wet red soil where it must have ploughed into the ground as it died.

Van Zyl's hat was hooked in a small thorn bush near the dead animal, but there was no sign of him or anyone else. Dodi, who with Sipho had been busy searching around in the bush near the dead buffalo, called from behind an ant-heap close by. They had found Van Zyl lying on the ground under a wild olive tree.

He was unconscious and in a bad way - his face was badly grazed and cut, his left leg was in a rough splint and he had a nasty wound in his side where he had been gored. There was nobody with him.

Tom, tempted to walk away and leave the monster lying there in the mud, bent over Van Zyl to check his injuries and see if he was alive. "Van Zyl, can you hear me?" he asked when he saw his eyes flutter open.

"You! I knew you would come when you heard I had Hunter. That bloody buffalo has killed me instead of you," Van Zyl croaked in a barely audible voice; still as aggressive as ever.

"So you did want to trap me as we suspected. We were waiting for you when you came across the river. Now Barnard has gone and left you here by yourself. What do you expect me to do?"

"Help me. Please," Van Zyl gasped, then with a groan of pain he sighed and slipped back into unconsciousness.

"What do we do with him Dad? We can't just leave him here." Kyle said showing compassion.

"I would love to leave him to die right here, but I think we must get him to a doctor," Tom said. "Dodi, cut some Mopani poles so that we can make a stretcher to carry him on."

"It's too late Tom," Ted said squatting down next to Van Zyl. "I think he's dead."

"Well there's no point in moving him. I'm sure Barnard will come back for him soon," Tom said confirming Ted's diagnosis.

"Are we just going to leave him lying here?" Although Van Zyl had been responsible for causing the family a lot of misery, Kyle felt uncomfortable leaving him lying in the bush for the hyenas to devour.

"Yes. Why not? Dodi reckons his gun-bearer and the tracker are around here somewhere. They never went back across the river with Barnard; they can stay here with him," Tom said. "I'm buggered if we should worry about taking his body to Mabiti. In any case we won't get across the river."

"Where is Dodi by the way?" Kyle asked looking around.

"I am here Ishe," Dodi pushed through a clump of scrub, followed by Van Zyl's gun-bearer carrying a bundle of mopani branches. "This man went to find some leaves to keep the rain off the injured man."

"Well you can tell him his boss is dead. He must wait here for Barnard to come and get him. We will phone Mabiti when we get to Chikombedzi," Ted explained to Dodi who relayed the message. The gun-bearer's face showed no emotion at this news.

"Dodi will you also tell him he must go and cut open the belly of the dead buffalo. When the hyena and jackals come, they will smell it and leave Van Zyl alone."

Even though he had hated the man for what he had done to Maria, Tom, like his son, was not comfortable leaving Van Zyl lying in the bush for the scavengers to devour.

"There's nothing more we can do here. Come on, let's get going before we get stuck between the flooding rivers," Ted stressed the need for urgency.

"Now the bastard won't stand trial. Anyway in the end he got what he deserved. Okay let's get the hell out of here." Tom stood looking down at Van Zyl and felt cheated. He had wanted Van Zyl to stand trial and go to prison. In spite of being killed, he felt that Van Zyl had still got off far too lightly.

As they walked away, leaving the gun-bearer with Van Zyl, it started raining again. Unable to cross the river, they took the road along the south bank to Chikombedzi. Just short of the town, Barnard went flying past, going in the opposite direction. He had a nurse with him.

Crossing the swollen river at Chikombedzi, they drove straight through the town and on towards Mabiti to collect Dodi's camping gear. With Van Zyl out of the picture, he would not need it any longer. It had stopped raining, and after loading up, they drove back to town. They wanted to wait and see if Barnard had Van Zyl's body with him, when he came to drop the nurse.

It was noon, and they were all hungry. There were no cafés' or restaurants in town, and so they had to make do with a loaf of bread, a couple of tins of bully beef, baked beans and cool drinks bought from the general dealer.

....

By the time Barnard and the nurse arrived where he had left Van Zyl lying under the tree, it had stopped raining. Parking as close as possible and taking the stretcher and the blanket, they hurried to fetch him.

The clouds had cleared away and the sun was beating down. With the rain having fallen for such a short time onto the hot dry earth, the sun was already drying the ground, making little wisps of steam rise from the small cracks in the soil surface as it heated up.

Van Zyl was not where he had left him under the tree, and there was no sign of either the gun-bearer or the tracker. Barnard was puzzled until he saw hyena spoor and drag marks in the mud. He presumed the two men had moved Van Zyl to a safer place, away from the wild animals. He followed the marks in the wet soil, with the nurse close behind him, and thirty paces from the tree they found him lying face down in the mud.

The scavengers from hell had arrived! It had not been the gun-bearer and tracker dragging him away, but a pack of hyenas *(Mpisis)* - their spoor was all around him.

Barnard turned Van Zyl over onto his back, and stepped back quickly in horror. Half his face had been bitten off, and his stomach ripped open with his entrails hanging out. He was dead. The sound of them arriving in the van must have disturbed the hyenas, making them slink away.

He felt quite sick seeing the man he had worked with for so many years, lying dead in the mud, with his body so badly mutilated. The nurse, looking somewhat ashen, put her hands over her face then, looking around nervously, she turned away and scurried quickly back to the safety of the van.

Barnard could hear yelping and snarling noises coming from the direction of the dead buffalo, and so with his rifle at the ready, he went to see what was happening. Only about fifty paces from where Van Zyl lay, the hyenas were having a feeding frenzy - ripping and tearing lumps of meat and entrails off the buffalo, and then running away from the others to eat. A pack of wild dogs had also arrived and were arguing noisily with them over the carcass. The vultures had started circling overhead and would soon attract other animals.

Knowing it would not be long before they returned to Van Zyl's body; a human body is far softer than that of a buffalo, Barnard hurried back and without wasting a moment, wrapped his body in the blanket, rolled him onto the stretcher, and then dragged him back to the van. The scavengers were too busy fighting over the dead buffalo to notice what he was doing, and follow him. The nurse helped load the stretcher onto the back, and they set off back to Chikombedzi.

There was still no sign of the two men he had left looking after Van Zyl. Apart from hyena and wild-dog spoor, there were no other tracks in the mud. The rain had washed all other sign away.

....

It had turned into a nice warm day. The clouds had dispersed, the sky was clear and there was a nice gentle breeze. The 'after rain' feel was always good with everything looking clean and fresh. All the trees and grass glistened in the sun after having had all the dust washed off by the rain. Tom, Ted, Kyle and Dodi were sitting on the back of the van, eating out of tins, when Barnard pulled up in front of the hospital. He and the nurse climbed out of the van and went inside.

Kyle, curious to see if Barnard had brought Van Zyl's body with him, wandered over to look in the back of his van. He lifted a corner of the blanket covering the form in the back then turned away quickly to vomit. Half Van Zyl's face was missing, and he had been disembowelled. The flies had already started to settle on the blanket covering his body.

Kyle was horrified. When they had left him with the gun-bearer, apart from the injuries sustained when the buffalo attacked him, his body had been intact. Now there was only half a man lying in the back of Barnard's van.

"He was badly wounded by a wounded buffalo, but it was the hyenas that killed him," Barnard said coming up behind Kyle, who was still feeling queasy. "Their spoor was all around him."

"Was there nobody with him?" Kyle asked.

"After he was gored by the buffalo and I shot it, then I left two men with him while I went to get my van and the stretcher to bring him here to the hospital. When I got back there they had both buggered off. They must have been scared away by the hyenas."

"We were on our way to Mabiti when we saw you. Your boss had invited me to the hunt but I couldn't make it in time. Looks like we were lucky," Ted said wandering over to join them.

"Van Zyl did say he had invited you Mr Hunter. You certainly didn't miss anything. It was a total ball's up!"

"He was a bad man, and got what he deserved," Tom said also joining them at Barnard's van. "We know he was planning something nasty for us. I feel no pity for the man, but I am sorry it ended this way."

"Ja, he was a bastard. I hated him for all the years I've worked for him. But, he paid me well and looked after me okay. I'm very sorry about what he did to your wife Mr Owen. I swear I never knew he was taking her. I just did what he told me to do. I suppose you want to have me arrested for kidnapping."

"Barney, let's just hope it's all over now. Yes, you did do some pretty bad things and Tombi can vouch for that, but most of the time I know you only did what you had to. I am not going to take the matter any further. Besides you didn't kidnap my wife, you just held her in your house and she says you treated her well. We did actually come here to arrest Van Zyl, not you."

"Thanks very much Mr Owen. If there is anything I can do for you, to make up for my part in your wife's kidnapping, please let me know." Barnard said gratefully, relieved to be let off the hook.

"What are you going to do now?"

"I'll have to take his body to his son in Harare. Then I'll see what he wants me to do."

"Barney, there is one thing you can do for me. I want you to make sure Van Zyl's false claims on Mr Hunter's pegged property are permanently removed as soon as you get to Harare."

"Of course Mr Owen, I'll see to it."

"And you'd better make bloody sure that son of his, Joey, doesn't get any ideas of taking revenge, or interfering with us in any way. Warn him that if he tries anything, we will have him arrested for his part in the kidnapping of my wife and Tombi. As you know, he was directly involved. If Joey does try to start any nonsense, Tombi might just decide to press charges against you for what you did to her," Tom finished with an unveiled threat.

"He won't be making any trouble. He will inherit all he needs and probably move to Malaysia. He hates living here."

. . . .

Barnard transferred Van Zyl's remains into the pine coffin he bought in the shop. He would have to get the body to Harare as quickly as possible - in the heat it would deteriorate rapidly. He went to Mabiti to put things in order and to pack the coffin with ice before leaving for Harare. Machona had already left and was on his way home. It seemed he was in a hurry to get away from the disaster he had been responsible for.

Barney Barnard was a happy man. Things had worked out well for him. At last he was free of the man who had bullied and treated him like a personal servant all those years. If he played his cards right he could take control of all Van Zyl's operations in Zimbabwe; Tombi was not taking action against him and he had his stash of diamonds to sell. He would have to find a buyer in Mozambique; he was not allowed back in to South Africa.

. . . .

Leaving Barnard to get on with things, the others went back to the Lion and Elephant to celebrate the end of their feud with Van Zyl. Tom was in a jovial mood. It felt like a massive weight had been lifted from his shoulders. The monster who had been responsible for causing so much suffering and misery to Maria and Tombi, had met his end.

On reflection it had turned out for the best. Maria and Tombi would not have to go through the trauma of giving evidence at a trial. He was however pleased that he had been the last person Van Zyl saw before dying.

In the morning they parted ways; Ted went home to Harare and Tom, Kyle and Dodi headed for the border to make their way back to Malelane and Inhaca.

It was fitting that the man nick-named *'Mpisi'* - the hyena, had been killed by an *Inyati*, a buffalo, which was Tom's Ndebele nick-name, and partly devoured by the animal he was named after. Justice had been done in the bush and by the wild animals.

It was as if the rain had washed everything clean and they could all get on with their lives and realise their own dreams.

One less poaching operation the game conservationists had to worry about.

KT

GONE

Our last African Rhino died today,
The press of course had much to say,
They questioned why so little was done,
To stop the merciless poachers gun.

They blamed the buyers from the East,
Huge sums were paid for one dead beast,
Shot for the trophy of its 'magical' horn,
Marked for culling from the day it was born.

Ounce for ounce, more precious than gold.
Containing no aphrodisiac power we're told,
Gone now forever in the name of greed,
No-one held accountable, all poachers freed.

The world points fingers, but it's too late,
The majestic White Rhino has met it's fate.
The Black and the White, enigmatically aloof.
Africa's rarest beast on cloven hoof.

Now we invite visitor to see the 'Big Four',
As the fifth, our beloved Rhino, is no more
It is a day of grief and unbelief we all say
Because our very last Rhino died today...

Alf Hutchison

Acknowledgements

As an aspiring writer I tend to become totally absorbed in the story I am writing and 'steam along' forgetting all those around me; especially the person closest to me, my wife Collette. She has been a fine example in patience and understanding (although at times she did get somewhat annoyed with me) and for that she deserves a medal. Without her help I don't think I would ever have started to write, or have completed this book. Her support and encouragement over the years while I have been writing has been incredible. I also thank her dearly for her assistance with the editing of the book.

Special thanks must go to my Boet, Phil, who painstakingly read the manuscript, made useful suggestions and finally edited the book. Well done indeed. I am most grateful.

A book needs a good title It is always difficult to give a book a title and one that will appeal - not only to people from Africa but to world-wide readers and so I have kept it simple. Rhino horn is more valuable than gold hence 'The Golden Horn' (I have also published it with the title 'Mpisi and The Golden Horn' (*Mpisi* being the African name for a hyena) for readers from Africa; after all story is more about the pursuit of Van Zyl (called *Mpisi*).

A book also needs an appealing cover. It takes someone with an artistic flair who has read the book and knows what it is about to help with the design. It has taken Collette and I many hours to come up with something appealing and I think we have eventually produced a presentable cover that interprets the requirements perfectly.

Finally I must thank Ant and Elise Hiscock for keeping me up to date with the rhino situation in Zimbabwe and the fitting of transmitters to their horns, and to Alf Hutchison for his poem 'Gone' which is most appropriate to this story.

Tatenda, thank you

KT

About the author

Ken, a farmer's son, was born in Port Elizabeth, South Africa in 1944, while his father served in the Western Desert during WW2. At the age of 7 he was sent to boarding school in Natal and finished his education at St. Marks in Swaziland. He grew up among the indigenous Swazi people learning to speak their language and understand their culture. Leaving school at sixteen, Ken went to work on a cattle ranch as a ranch hand and hunter for two years before leaving Swaziland to join the British South Africa Police force in Rhodesia (now Zimbabwe).

As a policeman at the time of the break-up of Federation, he was involved in the political disturbance and riots during the struggle for independence. With his love of farming and the country life, Ken left the police force to work on a tobacco and dairy farm. At this time (1965) Rhodesia wanting their independence, broke ties with Britain. The resulting conflict and struggle against terrorist incursions lasted for 15 years until independence in 1980. As a member of the crack Police Anti Terrorist Unit and leader of a 'stick' or unit, during the 'Bush War' Ken was involved in a number of skirmishes and ambushes as the country fought against terrorist incursions and attacks on innocent farmers, school children and civilians.

Towards the end of the war, realizing the futility of it, Ken left the country and returned to Swaziland where he worked on a developing sugar estate; Simunye. After 9 years he moved to Kwa-Zulu Natal where he and his wife Collette started a successful cleaning, garden and tree felling business. Drawn back to the countryside, they sold their business and moved to the South Coast to grow bananas and breed crocodiles, rabbits and chickens.

With political changes in South Africa, and plagued by theft, they sold up and returned to Zimbabwe to farm there. In 2001 their farm was invaded by war-vets and eventually in 2003 they were forced to abandon their farm and leave the country. Ken and Collette have now settled in the UK.

With Ken's love of Africa, wild-life, the bush and wide open spaces, he has drawn on his life's experiences and time spent in the 'sticks' to write books set in the country he loves. His first book 'Black Mamba White Settler' was published in 2010.